BEYOND THE

PROMISE

BARBARA BICKMORE

BEYOND THE PROMISE

KENSINGTON BOOKS

http://www.kensingtonbooks.com

KENSINGTON BOOKS are published by

Kensington Publishing Corp.
850 Third Avenue
New York, NY 10022

Library of Congress Card Catalog Number: 97-071646
ISBN 1-57566-220-5

First Kensington Hardcover Printing: November, 1997
10 9 8 7 6 5 4 3 2 1

Printed in the United States of America

Dedicated to friends who add incredibly to my life:

Nancy and Willard Bollenbach,

Patricia Rowe,

Barbara Daviss,

and to the memory of my beloved lifetime friend,
Gladys Hollwedel.

One

The jury had been out eleven hours and forty-three minutes.

"Even that is a triumph of sorts. Everyone knew this was an open and shut case. You've at least given them a run for their money."

This didn't reassure Cat, who sat on her desk wondering how much longer she could stand the tension. "Am I the only one who thinks he's innocent?"

The senior law partner smiled. "I guess not. Someone on the jury must be a holdout."

When the case had been thrown at Morton, Cavett, Benjamin, Burnham, and Sawyer, they all knew it was down the drain. Pro bono. Their turn. They hated such cases. A waste of time and money just so that it could be said democracy was still alive and well.

Bert Tandy was a known pusher.

Cat had begged for it. "Let me," she cried with enthusiasm, even though it would be her first trial. She'd been waiting for this opportunity for a year and a half, ever since she'd gotten her law degree and come to work at Morton and Cavett.

She'd been in the top 10 percent of her law class at B.U., so all the large prestigious Boston law firms had offered her a job. She'd chosen a medium-sized one whose reputation was sterling and who frankly admitted they needed women. She liked Harry Morton, the most senior partner, who had taken her under his wing and was old enough to be her grandfather.

None of them had dreamed this case would garner the publicity it had. Partly because the lawyer was a novice and was better-looking than any of the other lawyers in town. Probably in the state. Maybe in the country.

But it was a particularly gory case, and the media had seized upon it and blown it out of proportion, and Cat found herself staring at her photograph nearly every morning in the *Boston Globe*. She'd even made it into *Time* and *Newsweek*, which had said she had a natural flair for the dramatic.

Circumstantial evidence all pointed to Bert Tandy's guilt, and Cat wondered if she'd been on the jury if she'd have even half believed him when he took the stand. He looked scruffy even though she'd bought him a suit and made him change his shirt and tie every day. He did have an irresistible smile, which she hoped would play to the five women on the jury. His pale blue eyes looked straight into hers when he told her, "I'm not guilty, Miss Browning, I'm not."

Whether he was was beside the point. She'd had to defend him as though she believed him. She had come to the conclusion that though he might be a two-bit pusher, he was not a murderer, certainly couldn't have committed the gory crime of which he was accused. He wasn't too intelligent, she realized, and he couldn't have lied convincingly. Each time he told the story it was a bit different, and that reassured her. When people told a story the same way repeatedly one could be pretty sure they weren't telling the truth.

She'd put her life on hold for the past six months. Now the trial, which had lasted only four and a half days, was over. It had taken the jury a quarter as long to determine a verdict. And here Harry Morton was, trying to cheer her up and prepare her for a guilty verdict. Well, she wasn't prepared.

Harry's hand reached out for the phone as it rang. He listened, saying nothing but nodding his head. When he hung up he told Cat, "The jury's coming back in. Want me to come over to the courtroom with you?"

"I'd appreciate that," she said.

"Okay. Straighten up. Look like nothing will faze you. Don't let your face show a thing when the verdict's announced. As for your client, he doesn't think he stands a snowball's chance in hell. He's not going to be surprised."

Did he have so little faith?

They caught an air-conditioned cab to relieve them of the humidity of late June in Boston. Walking up the stairs of the courthouse Cat was surrounded by reporters. Harry ran interference and warded them off, but the noisy group followed her to the third floor, trying in vain to crowd around her. Harry opened the door to the courtroom and followed Cat in, sitting behind the defense counsel's chair.

Bert Tandy sat stone-faced, not looking at her, but studying the jury, which did not look over at him as they filed in.

Cat had heard that if the jury didn't look at the client it was because they felt dreadful to be rendering a guilty verdict. Her heart nearly stopped.

At the judge's instructions, the foreman stood and handed a sheet of paper to the bailiff. The bailiff handed the paper, folded in half, to the judge, who silently studied it and handed it back to the bailiff. He looked at the still-standing foreman and asked, "How do you find the defendant?"

The silence could be cut with a knife. Now the foreman looked at Bert. "Not guilty, Your Honor."

Cat closed her eyes. Relief swept over her in warm waves. She felt Harry's hand on her shoulder, but when she opened her eyes the first person she looked at was Bert Tandy. He was grinning.

The judge was rapping his gavel on his desk, trying to diminish the commotion in the courtroom.

"What happens now?" Bert asked.

"They'll take you back to jail and release you from there. Oh, Bert, I'm so pleased."

"It ain't nothing," he allowed, "to how I feel. Thanks, Miss Browning. I'm grateful."

She was glad. Glad justice had triumphed and he hadn't been penalized for his past convictions for petty stuff, which had nothing to do with this murder case.

"Straighten up your life now," Cat suggested as she folded papers into her briefcase. "If you need a job, I may be able to help."

"That's nice of you, Miss Browning."

Cat turned to find Harry waiting for her as the courtroom cleared of people. "My dear, that was a surprise. You can be proud you pulled it off. Sorry I didn't get to see you in action. You must have been impressive."

A glow spread across her face. She'd put her heart and soul into this case.

"I'll buy you a drink," Harry offered.

She thought it was the least he could do.

On her way home she stopped and bought a bottle of champagne. Across the hall, in the converted brownstone where she lived on Newbury Street, Annie Nicholas had an apartment. Annie designed wallpaper. At least three or four times a week they shared dinner, dining at one of the little ethnic restaurants along Newbury, or taking turns cooking. Annie always prepared something so American that Cat had to laugh. The kind of cooking her mother had done. Cat was more into nouvelle cuisine, and one of her bookshelves was devoted to cookbooks.

There was no answer when she knocked on Annie's door.

She unlocked her own door, found a pencil and a Post-it, wrote, "Come help me celebrate," and stuck it on Annie's door.

She kicked off her shoes and, holding the champagne bottle against her chest, danced around the room. She'd never felt more wonderful in her whole life. Or more exhausted.

She took a shower, ended by sluicing cold water across her body. As she toweled herself dry the doorbell rang. Holding the towel around her, Cat answered the door.

"Celebrate?" A wide smile flowed across Annie's face. "That means you won?"

"I did indeed. Champagne's in the fridge, and I thought I might splurge and take us to that Indian restaurant up the street."

It was so expensive they reserved it for celebrations like birthdays or Annie's raise in salary or seeing Dennis Quaid in a movie.

"You deserve a vacation," Annie said as she bit into the crisp spicy naan. "I'm going home for my brother's wedding in ten days. Come with me. You've never been to Oregon. No place, but no place, is more beautiful than eastern Oregon in the summer."

"I don't have the energy. I need to relax. I was thinking of the Bahamas or Aruba."

"There's nothing to do in Cougar. You can relax to your heart's content. Enjoy my mother's cooking, stare at the mountains, which will rejuvenate your soul . . ."

"If it's so wonderful, why did you leave?"

"No jobs. At least not for an artist. Not unless you're into ranching or run a small business. And I do mean small. There aren't more than sixteen or seventeen thousand people in the whole county."

Cat had visions of men in overalls and polyester dresses on women, of a tidy little town with a church steeple rising above the roofs, of people sitting on porch swings and nodding to friends who passed by. She wondered if there were streetlights.

"You mean it's boring?"

"And then some," Annie nodded. "I go back there to get away from it all, but I wouldn't want to live there."

"What's the name of it again?"

"Cougar," Annie said. "It's in Cougar Valley, and the nearest big town is Baker, which has about nine thousand people. Cougar just has nineteen hundred."

"Are there still really cougars there?"

"You better believe it. And Cougar is fighting the environmentalists who don't want us to shoot any of them though they kill our cattle and dogs and even a baby not too long ago."

"I imagine they're an endangered species."

Annie shook her head. "Not in Cougar Valley. Not in Oregon at all. There are even a few over in the Coast Range. Some have recently been sighted in Eugene, our second largest city."

"I suppose," Cat's voice was teasing, "you still have Indians."

Annie nodded. "It's true. Though generally they've been assimilated, but some of our most respected citizens are Indians."

Cat laughed. "I don't know a thing about Oregon."

"Oregon's beautiful," Annie said, "but I want what cities offer. I don't want hunting and fishing and redneck philosophy and everybody knowing my business."

"You don't make it sound appealing."

Annie shook her head from side to side. "It's not, really, except for the scenery. It's small-town America, Cat. But you could get away from the rat race and sit on the swing on the front porch, and it's not humid like this, and you could smell Mom's roses."

"You know, I've never really seen tall mountains. The Catskills and the Berkshires . . ."

"Anthills," Annie said. "The mountains here aren't mountains."

"Let me think about it."

When Cat walked into work at nine the next morning everyone stopped by her office to congratulate her.

She wished she could purr. She tried to contain her pleasure.

There'd been an article about her in the morning's *Globe* calling her Boston's "glamorous young defense lawyer." Glamorous, huh.

Harry Morton had a dozen red roses sitting on her desk, and her secretary, Lee Ann Taylor, said, "I feel like I'm working for a celebrity. Coffee?" she asked.

"In lieu of champagne?"

They both smiled.

Lee Ann indicated a list of phone numbers on Cat's desk. "A reporter is insistent. She wants to do a feature article about you in Sunday's paper, and today's the deadline. I suggest you call her first."

"Okay, would you get her for me?" Cat said, sitting behind her desk.

She spent the entire morning on the phone, then went out to lunch with the reporter, who interviewed her for nearly two hours, discovering Cat had been born in Philadelphia and her goal was to become a female F. Lee Bailey, Alan Dershowitz, even a Johnnie Cochran. Her ultimate goal, she admitted to the reporter, was Congress.

"The House or the Senate?"

"Oh, maybe start out in the House and work my way up."

"And marriage?"

"Of course. I want it all."

"Good luck," said the reporter, closing her notebook and putting the pencil in her purse. "And you know what, I have the distinct feeling that, given a bit of time, maybe you're going to be one of those women who can do it all."

Cat was inordinately pleased.

On the plane to Portland, Annie told Cat a bit about her hometown. Her parents lived in a small ranch-style house on one of the side streets. Her father ran the True Value Hardware store on the only main street.

"Mom said Mr. McCullough will fly over to meet us; otherwise, it takes about seven hours to get home by bus or five and a half by car. He'll knock your socks off."

Cat stopped listening to look in awe out the window. "My God, look at these mountains."

"There to our left, that's Mt. Hood."

"There are mountains and mountains and mountains beyond it."

"They're the Cascades."

"Look, they're covered with snow even in July."

The plane had begun its descent into Portland nearly twenty minutes before.

"You'll recognize Mr. McCullough," Annie went on. "He looks a little like John Wayne, not his face maybe because he's got red hair and a bushy mustache. He'll be the tallest and ruggedest-looking guy in the airport."

With this description, Cat immediately recognized Red McCullough, who was a good head taller than those around him. His high-heeled boots only added to his stature. He was also the only one at the Portland airport wearing a Stetson.

He looked, as Annie had warned her, like he could have ridden out of a Western. His fringed suede jacket was out of place in Portland, even though dress in the West was not as formal as in the East. As though any part of America was formal anymore. He wore a turquoise bolo around his neck, and his silver belt was studded with squares of the same stone.

Red McCullough gave Annie a bear hug and looked appreciatively at Cat. His sideburns had a few gray hairs but his twinkling blue-green eyes gave the impression of youth. Cat guessed he might be in his mid to late forties.

His voice sounded like gravel. His face was tanned, reflecting years spent outdoors.

After they'd gotten their bags at the luggage carousel, Red hailed a taxi which drove them a short distance to his little silver plane. MISS JENNY was painted in blue on its side.,

"Miss Jenny is his mother. I'll get in the backseat," Annie said, "so you can look out the front and Mr. McCullough can explain what you're seeing."

As Red taxied down the tarmac, Cat's knuckles were white as she held on to the arms of her seat. She'd never flown in such a small plane, but Red was in the air before she felt butterflies. He grinned and said, "You can relax now."

She stared out the window in awe.

Annie leaned forward, pointing. "Over there to the left, that flat-topped one is Mt. Saint Helens . . ."

"The volcano?"

"And beyond it, that's Mt. Rainier."

Cat glanced to her right and saw Mt. Hood again. "It looks like an ice-cream cone," she said.

"We're leaving them right away," Red said. "We'll follow the Columbia River, see, down there." Cat saw a ribbon of blue winding down a narrow chasm.

"We'll follow that to Pendleton, and then head south."

The little plane rocked only a little. "Pretty soon what you'll see is high desert country."

"How come this isn't famous, like Colorado?" Cat asked, in awe at the majestic scenery below her.

"Probably because it's so far off the beaten track. Oregon and Washington are America's best-kept secrets."

Annie said, "Mom wrote that Torie's come back home to teach."

Red's eyes sparkled. "That she has. Mrs. Peterson died in May, and as soon as Torie heard that she phoned Bill O'Rourke."

"He was the boys' phys-ed teacher when I was in high school," Annie said.

"He's been the principal four or five years," Red added.

Annie shook her head. "Torie was a cheerleader for his football team, I remember."

"Maybe that's what did it. He hired her over the phone."

"I imagine that makes you happy."

"Me and Joseph," Red grinned. " 'Course Sarah tried to talk her into a city, but Torie would have none of it."

"Are she and Joseph going to get married?"

"I would hope so, but they've hurdles to overcome."

"You mean his father and Mrs. McCullough?"

"You've got it."

The plane turned south, away from the river, flying over thickly forested mountains until a valley broke forth, ringed at the far east by a chain of snowcapped mountains. "They're the Wallowas," Red explained. "What we're flying over are the Blue Mountains."

The valley widened, the eastern mountains a haze in the distance and a rugged short range to their immediate right. "These are ours," Red said as if he owned them.

"Down there"—he nodded as he began his descent—"is the Big Piney. We fly about a mile beyond the big house, to the landing field. See, there's the hangar, down the valley."

Cat saw a brown, wooden two-story house, longer than any house she'd ever seen. They flew south of it, circling above the asphalted strip, where Red landed smoothly.

It might be hick town, USA, as Annie had described it, but it was certainly the most gorgeous place Cat had ever seen.

"Let me put the plane in the hangar," Red told Annie, "and I'll get the jeep and drive you into town."

He helped Cat out of the plane and turned to Annie.

"I could hardly wait to leave this place," Annie said, turning full circle, her arms outstretched. "But it's true that there's no place like home. Oh, look, there's Scott."

Cat turned to see a young man astride a tall white horse whose hindquarters were speckled with brown spots. He wore a straw cowboy hat so that his face was in shadow. But he looked as if he'd ridden out of those mountains ready to fight Indians, protect his land, expand his horizons.

He rode toward them, looking down at Annie and saying, "Nice to see you," then turning his gaze to Cat. His eyes glowed like coals, and, as he smiled, his white teeth glittered against his tanned face.

Cat felt herself go weak in the knees when he said, "I'll drive them into town, Dad," not taking his eyes from Cat's.

Two

Annie's parents' house was a small white ranch-style building on one of the town's side streets. It was as Cat had imagined. Close enough to the sidewalk to say hello to those passing by.

"Well, the McCulloughs are certainly something, aren't they?" Annie said, once they had unpacked and were sitting on the porch sipping lemonade. "And Miss Jenny is a character. I guess when you're that rich you can be anything you want. Everybody loves her. But now Mrs. McCullough, she's another thing."

"Mrs.?"

"Red's wife. She and Torie are probably the two best-looking women in the valley, Hollywood beautiful. Scott looks like his mother, so does Torie, but they don't look alike except for their black hair and eyes. They all have that. But Mrs. McCullough's strange. I think she's an alcoholic, but as long as I've been alive she's been . . . well, I don't know. She's not a popular person. She's standoffish and keeps to herself. That doesn't keep Red from attending the town functions. He and Bollie, the town's banker, and Ken Amberson just about run this county. In a benign way. If it weren't for the three of them we'd still be being bused to school in Baker, and we wouldn't have the good things we have going for us. There are a helluva lot of people on welfare in this part of the country, but our county has the lowest percentage, thanks to jobs created by that triumvirate. They do it low key, in the background, but we all know."

"Do the McCulloughs have a big ranch?"

Annie smiled, putting her lemonade glass on the arm of her chair. "We call 'em spreads. They're not measured in acres but in sections.

I'd guess the McCulloughs own about fifty-five or sixty sections, not counting land they own in other places."

"How big is a section?"

"Six hundred forty acres."

Cat multiplied silently. "Why that's over thirty thousand acres," she said.

"At the very least. We didn't drive by the big house on their land yesterday, but they own a goodly portion of the valley. Certainly all they can see from their front porch. I'll invite us out there so you can see. It's been in the family a long time, though I think my parents told me Mr. McCullough has added a lot to it. The McCulloughs are a force to be reckoned with, though a good one. If we had a popularity contest around here, it'd be between Red McCullough and the sheriff."

"The sheriff? I didn't know lawmen were popular."

"Maybe not in the East, but Jason is here. Jason Kilpatrick. He tries to solve everyone's problems and is probably the best thing that's hit us in years. He came while I was still in college, and there again, a ditzy wife. Cold as an Eskimo's igloo. It's all you can do to force a smile out of her whereas probably nearly everyone in the valley thinks of Jason as family. I bet he's dined in every house in the valley. We don't even have crime around here, and it's not 'cause people are afraid of Jason. They just don't want to let him down."

Cat thought Annie must be naive.

"But, funny isn't it, that such nice men have strange cold wives. Not fair, I'd say. Here we are, a couple of warm vivacious sociable creatures who would die for such relationships, and we don't have any."

"I haven't had time for any," Cat murmured. "My life's been on hold for months."

"Ah, I can tell from your tone of voice that you're thinking it's time to rectify that with Scott McCullough."

"Well, he sure is attractive."

"I think that's the very least that can be said of Scott."

"Did you ever go out with him?"

"I'm two years older. In a town like this, that makes a difference. But every girl in his class and for about ten years below that has wanted Scott. And probably, from what I hear, had him."

"Oh."

"Be forewarned."

"I don't think you have to want to marry everyone you go to bed with."

"I don't either, but you're likely to get your heart involved if you go that far with Scott."

"Let's hope I get to find out. I'm ready for a little relaxation and romance."

As she half suspected, she didn't have long to wait.

Cat liked Annie's family immediately. Her mother, in polyester slacks and a tailored shirt, directed their setting the long trestled picnic table in the backyard, where delphinium and lilies bloomed. A picket fence, its faded white paint peeling, surrounded the yard, where a willow tree at least thirty feet high shaded them from the late-afternoon sun.

They'd borrowed chairs from the Grange Hall and Kevin, the groom, had set them up. He was a thin young man with sparkling blue eyes who had just graduated from Oregon State and landed some sort of job with the state over in Salem. He didn't have to report for work until August, so he and his bride were going camping for ten days over at Steen's Mountain and in the Strawberry Mountains.

Camping, on a honeymoon? Cat's idea of a honeymoon was White Sulphur Springs in West Virginia, where there were pools and tennis courts and drinks were served poolside and romantic music played during dinner. Or the Royal Hawaiian on Oahu, where ocean breezes softly bathed you and the scent of tropical flowers filled the air as the music of steel guitars wound its way inside you.

The bride and her family arrived in a battered pickup and a newish Taurus. Her brothers and sisters were in their teens; everyone hugged each other and all were gracious in welcoming Cat. They had known each other for years, probably their whole lives. Cat wondered what it would be like to live in the same place and know the same people all your life.

An enormous side of roast beef and a whole ham covered large platters at the end of the picnic table. Tureens of potato salad and cole slaw, bowls of Jell-O fruit salad and pickles and olives, jars of mustard and mayonnaise and thick slabs of homemade bread were inviting. Cat hadn't seen a spread like this since she was a kid. She didn't know people still ate this way.

Pitchers of lemonade and bottles of cold beer were in coolers at the other end of the table. The men helped themselves to beer; the women and children to the lemonade. The bride and groom looked at each other with lovesick eyes, and Cat wondered if they'd slept together yet. It was a different world out here. She had an idea its values would seem old-fashioned back East.

And then the hair on the back of her neck stood up.

Loping along the side of the house, dressed all in white, including his ten-gallon hat and his jeans, was Scott McCullough. Rugged wide shoulders, narrow tapered waist, a face that would have stopped girls on the streets of LA, shaggy black hair tending to curl, an enormous grin on his face. She was perfectly aware that her heart skipped a beat.

He stopped to kiss both the mothers, shook hands with all the men, tousled the hair of the two teenage boys as he simultaneously shook their hands, grabbed the sixteen-year-old sister in a bear hug and swung her around, saw Cat, and stopped, his obsidian black eyes riveted on her.

She didn't move.

No one else seemed aware of the electricity of the moment. Annie's father called loudly, "Chow's on. Help yourselves."

It wasn't exactly a stampede, but everyone started toward the long table. Annie grabbed Cat's hand and led her toward the food. Cat wanted to toss her head and see if Scott was coming, but she refrained.

"Be careful," Annie warned.

"Is something wrong?" But she knew what her friend was implying.

"Grab a plate but save room for dessert. Mom bakes the best Black Forest cake in the whole world."

With plates piled high, the two young women sauntered over near the willow and sat in Adirondack chairs. Laughter filled the air.

Cat observed the company, looking at the way everyone so casually interacted, as though they already knew what the other might say but wanted to hear it anyhow. Would that be comfortable or threatening? Would it become dull to know the same people forever, see the same people day after day after day?

Wasn't that what she did anyhow? Saw the same lawyers or clients. Annie was really the only friend she'd had time to make since graduation. When she dated, it was other lawyers or occasionally another professional of some sort whom she'd met at a party.

She'd been ready to laugh at this quaint place and these people who seemed part of America gone by, but she was studying them now. There was a warmth about them and a lack of self-consciousness that she found attractive.

The sun's western rays cast a golden glow; the little white house with its green shutters, the willow tree, the neat rows of flowers which nevertheless appeared wanton with all their bright colors, the men in their white shirts, the bridal couple. Norman Rockwell country. A lifestyle she thought had vanished twenty years ago.

"This time of year it doesn't get dark til well after nine-thirty," Scott McCullough said, dragging a chair up opposite Cat and Annie.

"Same in Boston," Cat responded, trying not to let her eyes reflect what she felt.

"You just missed the granddaddy of all picnics," he told them. "The annual Fourth of July one."

Cat smiled at him, but again, once her eyes met his, she was caught.

"How did you two meet?" he asked.

Annie answered. "Cat lives across the hall from me. We met the night she moved in, when the hallway was littered with boxes and I couldn't even plow through them. I took pity and invited her to spaghetti dinner, and we've been friends ever since."

"What kind of work do you do?" he asked, slathering mustard on his ham.

"I'm a lawyer."

Fork poised in midair, he gazed at her. Finally, he ate the piece of ham, and after an unconscionably long time said. "A woman lawyer, you say."

"Your tone indicates disapproval."

"It's admiration. We don't see many women lawyers around here."

"There are scads in Portland and Eugene," Annie said. "You didn't even vote for ERA out here. You think *Roe versus Wade* is against God and the Constitution. In the Nixon era you thought Henry Kissinger was subversive because he has an accent. Unless your forebears came across country on the Oregon Trail, you're suspicious of anyone."

"Hey." Scott waved his hand in the air. "Don't confuse me with that stuff, just 'cause I live here. I may be fiscally conservative, but like the rest of my family I'm socially liberal. Hell, my father even voted for McCarthy and John Anderson. Oregon's one of the more progressive states."

"Yeah." There was a belligerent tone in Annie's voice. "Thanks to the west and the cities. But here, you're too close to Idaho and its neo-Nazis. Idaho's one of the most conservative states in the country."

"We're Oregon," Scott said. "Don't confuse me with them either. Hey, I even vote for gay rights even though I don't understand what the hell they've got to be that way for."

There was a lull while both Annie and Scott cooled down. He

turned to Cat and asked, "You defend criminals or what?" She liked the sound of his voice, low and intimate. It made the question sound far more personal than it was.

"I defend innocent people."

"Sure." He didn't believe it. "Let them go free to commit murder or whatever again. That's one of the things wrong today. Too much crime, too little punishment."

"I think most Americans would agree with you. And you're not going to get an argument from me."

Scott abruptly changed the topic. "You ride?"

Cat shook her head. She'd ridden once, on a family vacation in Vermont when she was twelve. She'd held on for dear life and hated every minute of it.

"What do you think, Annie, would you girls like to come out to the Big Piney for a ride up into the mountains?"

"I think that'd be an experience Cat would remember. Sounds great."

"Come on out midafternoon Monday and stay for dinner."

"That'd be real nice," Annie murmured. To Cat she said, "One of the great things you'll find here is that everyone we know will invite us to dinner or something. Hospitality is Cougar's middle name."

The groom interrupted. "Ready?" he asked Scott. "We're going to the church for rehearsal."

"Yeah, sure," Scott answered, rising to tower over almost everyone. His boots were polished so that Cat imagined she could see her reflection in them. Like his father, he wore a bolo around his neck rather than a tie. He looked as if he had walked right out of a Western movie where no one would be in doubt about who was the hero.

Annie noticed Cat's eyes following Scott as he walked across the lawn and disappeared around the side of the house.

"Something, isn't he?" she asked.

"He and his father both are," Cat said.

"Be careful. Scott's a heartbreaker. Girls around here have been trying to marry him since he was seventeen."

"Well, I'm not thinking of . . ." she paused, "marrying him."

Three

The road to Big Piney was eighteen miles from town, six of it on a dirt road off the secondary blacktop, winding back toward the base of the mountains. Cougar Valley was dotted with yellow fields of mustard, lush grass, and brown and black cattle as far as the eye could see.

"Is this what they mean by a spread?" Cat asked.

Scott had driven into town to pick her and Annie up. Cat was surprised that he drove a long black Cadillac with smooth red leather seats.

The sky was a cerulean blue against the jagged snow-covered peaks. Willows dotted the landscape. When Cat commented about that, Scott said, "Where you see willows there'll be a creek. Fortunately, water is not one of our overriding problems here. Snow never completely melts from the mountains, and back in there"—he pointed at the pine forested mountains ahead of them—"are lakes. A ski area in winter, but great for fishing and picnicking at this time of year. We hunt back there in the fall."

"Hunt? For what?"

"Cougar, of course," he answered. "Elk, bear, deer."

A vision of Bambi floated before her. She couldn't imagine killing an animal.

"Do you own all this?" she asked, spreading her arm in an arc.

"We own pretty much all that you see, even those houses in the distance. We own that mountain and land behind it, and farther across the valley, plots of land almost to the Wallowas."

Cat twisted in her seat to glance out the back window at the snowy ridges that covered the eastern horizon. "I've never seen such a beautiful place."

Scott nodded. "That's because it's without compare. We out here can't understand how anyone can live in a city, particularly those eastern prisons."

A city a prison? To Cat, it was where culture was, where excitement centered, where everything worthwhile went on. Why, here in Cougar there wasn't a movie, or a library, and only a weekly newspaper. There was one bank and no one would call it a financial center. There was one grocery store—the Safeway—and the True Value Hardware. There was Rocky's Cafe smack at the midpoint of Main Street and, at the edge of town, a Dairy Queen newly opened. There were two gas stations, the BP at the south end of town and the Texaco at the north exit, a dozen or so blocks away. There was one eleven-room motel, Shumway's Hospitality Inn, and Davis's Western Clothing Store. If you wanted to buy anything else you drove into Baker or up to La Grande or even Pendleton, which had a population of nearly fifteen thousand. In Cougar there was also the Co-op where farmers and ranchers bought their feed and sold their wool and ordered their chicks each spring. Farmers who owned small dairy herds left their big silver milk cans at the Darigold drop. If the herds were really large, the Darigold truck stopped at the ranch for the canisters.

Vlahov's Pharmacy had a soda shop and an area which sold tee shirts and locally made pottery and earrings and some Indian dreamcatchers as well as the current twenty best-selling paperbacks.

There was a doctor and a veterinarian, who sometimes tried to solve each other's problems. Each of them made visits as far as twenty or twenty-five miles away. They had cellular phones and often drove from one remote area of the county to another without getting back to town before dark.

There was a third-generation Japanese florist who grew only miniature roses and designed bonsai, shipping them all over the country. His greenhouses covered nearly three acres. He trucked the flowers up to Pendleton three times a week, where they were shipped out to Portland and then to the East. He made a bundle of money, especially in the winter.

Cat tried to imagine winter here, holed up for months on end. That would be more of a prison than any city.

"I'm in a city six hours and I get claustrophobia," Scott was saying. "No green. Just walled canyons. No birds. No wide horizons. I don't know how you stand it."

Cat turned her head and grinned at Annie, who said, "When I'm back here I do wonder if I'm nuts to opt for big-city living. But what would I do here?"

"Get married," was Scott's brief reply.

"Yeah. There's no other choice."

"Well," he glanced at her in the rearview mirror. "What have you got against marriage?"

"Nothing," she answered. "In fact, I think I'd like it, but only if I could go on doing my thing."

"Your thing," he said, "would be having kids and taking care of your family."

"Oh, gawd," Annie voiced Cat's reaction too. "And nothing more, huh?"

To change the subject, Cat said, "The air feels pure out here."

"Nearest factory is over three hundred miles, that's why. Now, you know you want to smell something good? Go in a barn. New-mown hay . . ."

"Yeah," said Annie. "And manure . . ."

He glanced in the mirror again to see if she was being sarcastic, but she wasn't. She even had a dreamy expression on her face.

"It's true," he told Cat. "The smell of hay and manure . . . no other smell like it."

Then the house at the end of the dirt road came into view.

"My heavens," she gasped, "it looks a mile long."

"Got twenty-six rooms, not counting the bathrooms," Scott said, grinning. "Home sweet home."

Not quite nestled up against the mountains, the house was just far enough removed from them so that their peaks could still be seen. Two stories high, it had a porch that ran along the first floor. Wide steps led up to the veranda, stained dark brown against the harsh weather.

She was to discover that every room had high ceilings and fireplaces and overlooked mountains. The rooms in front looked east across the wide lush Cougar Valley to the Wallowa Mountains, which were, today, like ephemeral pointed clouds floating in the sky. The back windows focused on the jagged Elkhorns.

"I've never seen such a place in my life."

"In Wyoming and Montana and Texas there are larger spreads," Scott said, turning into the circular driveway that led to the wide front porch steps. "And maybe some *as* pretty, but for sure there's not a prettier place in the world."

Cat believed it.

"We'll go meet Mother, then we can head for the barn. One of the hands will have the horses ready for us. We'll head back up the mountains so you can get a panoramic view."

As they got out of the Cadillac Annie shook her head. "You have to understand that though I love my parents to hell and gone, I could never live back here again. I don't love it here. It can kill your spirit if you're a woman with ambition. Or yearning for learning. I've discovered that the more outrageously gorgeous places are, the more redneck and narrow-minded the people tend to be, and the more difficult it is to earn a living."

"That can't be true."

"I'll be glad to have you prove me wrong."

"Well, I haven't traveled that much."

Just then one of the most beautiful women Cat had ever seen appeared, like an apparition, in the doorway. She wore a pale lavender chiffon dress that swirled against her legs as she walked. Flowing through her thick coal black hair was a narrow band of white, starting at her left temple, enhancing her dramatic appearance. She must have been in her late forties. Cat stopped to stare at her sheer beauty. Her figure was that of a woman in her twenties, and her legs, in their high-heeled patent leather shoes, were stunning.

Cat had worn slacks and Nikes today since she would have a riding lesson, but even dressed up, she could never compare with this woman, who greeted her guests with fluttery gestures and a handshake so light that Cat wondered if she'd really touched her at all.

Mrs. McCullough let Annie hug her, and said, "Oh, how I envy you. What an exciting life you must lead in Boston. It's so good to see you. You didn't come out here to see us when you were home last Christmas." It sounded like a scolding. Then the woman turned to Cat, and said, "I'm so glad you came along if that's what it takes to get Annie out here."

"We're going riding, Mother," Scott said. "Probably be gone a couple of hours."

"Miss Jenny's coming tonight."

Miss Jenny—the name painted on the little Cessna.

"My grandmother lives up at the hunting lodge," Scott explained.

"Whenever we have guests, Miss Jenny likes to come down from the mountain," Sarah McCullough said, and smiled.

Though she had never felt closer to nature, and never experienced such primitive wilderness, Cat could only concentrate on the soreness of her derriere. They had ridden for two hours, and now she felt she didn't really want to sit. Yet she didn't want to evidence any weakness. She gritted her teeth and smiled as a woman in her late sixties strode into the room. She wore black slacks and a pink cotton shirt. Her only jewelry was a diamond solitaire and a Rolex. She wore the same sort of high-heeled boots her son and grandson wore, and she'd ridden down from the hill on her horse.

"Going to be moonlight tonight," she explained. "So Boo Boo and I won't get lost. Nothing much nicer than a moonlight ride."

Cat could think of many nicer things. She had already decided never to get on a horse again.

The living room was spacious enough for a hotel lobby, its wide timbered beams larger than most tree trunks. Cat had immediately been impressed with the shining wide planked floor, covered with handwoven Indian rugs. It was a richly textured room whose colors of wine red, navy, and dark greens lent drama to a space already reeking of elegance.

"This room is just as it was when I moved here in 1944," Miss Jenny told Cat.

"Well, I've had the furniture recovered," Sarah McCullough interjected, "though in the same colors. But your mother-in-law had that prickly horsehair, and I couldn't take that for long."

Miss Jenny smiled. "I took it for longer than I liked. I redid the bedroom though."

Cat gathered keeping the house in the style that it had been originally was a sacred duty to the daughters-in-law who lived here.

"This house is on the historical register," Annie said, accepting the whiskey and branch water that Scott offered her.

"Do you have any wine?" Cat asked.

"You want it, we have it."

Red entered the room. Rather he filled it. Everyone else suddenly became pale. He had obviously changed from whatever clothes he'd been working in, for the creases in his dark brown cotton pants were razor-sharp, and he wore a richly embroidered vest.

Cat found him fascinating. Yesterday at the wedding reception he'd danced with her twice, and she was surprised at the grace of such a large man. Probably someday Scott would look like him, when he became middle-aged and lost that slimness. She wondered if the sense of power came with age or if that had always been a part of Red.

"Your usual, Dad?"

Red's eyes had quickly skipped around the room, nodding to each person. He kissed his mother, and then walked over to Scott. "Sure. Thanks," he said.

Scott poured his father a Scotch and soda, filled to the brim with ice cubes. He himself drank whiskey neat.

"You must come visit me," Miss Jenny was telling Cat. "I have an incomparable view of the valley and the Wallowas."

"She lives in what years ago used to be the hunting lodge," Scott said, sitting next to Cat. "The only way to get up there then was by horse. Though Miss Jenny often does it that way now, like tonight, even though there's a dirt road and she has a pickup."

"It's not that I'm against modern conveniences," Miss Jenny quickly added. "I just like horses. I like leisurely traveling through the woods, hearing the birdsong and seeing the quail and the rabbits and the squirrels and deer."

"Did you grow up around here?" Cat liked the woman. There was something so no-nonsense about her. She wondered how the two McCullough women got along. On the surface all seemed smooth, but they were so different.

"St. Louis," Miss Jenny responded.

"Isn't that where the Oregon Trail began?"

"I'm not *that* old. But, yes, you know your history. I came out one summer to visit my aunt and uncle, who had moved to La Grande. And at a strawberry social at the Methodist Church I met his"—she glanced at Red—"father. You think he's a sight! You should've seen Jock." She smiled fondly at her son. "But then I guess were I to meet Red today, I'd have felt the way I felt about his father in 1944. It was during the war, of course, and Jock was home on leave from Europe. He was on his way to the Far East. I took one look at him and we got married before he left for overseas. In two weeks! I knew the minute I saw him, and I never felt different in the forty-two years we spent together. Not once."

No one said anything. Cat was thinking, how can you tell in two weeks that here'd be someone you wanted to spend your life with?

"Of course, I didn't see him for a whole year after that, but once he got home from the war I felt just the same."

"And nine months to the day after he got home, I arrived." Red grinned at his mother.

"Did it take long to adjust to life here, so different from St. Louis?"

Miss Jenny nodded. "I thought I'd never get the hang of riding a horse or the informality of life here after a big city. But I wanted so much to fit in, to be a part of Jock's life, that the learning was fun. I wouldn't live anyplace else now. He's Jock, Junior." She nodded toward her son. "But once he arrived in the world he's never been called anything other than Red."

Despite his dark auburn hair, Cat could imagine him as a carrottop as a kid.

"So"—Cat turned to Scott—"you're named for the old country, I gather."

"Smart girl," Miss Jenny said.

"Doesn't take too many brains, with a father named Jock McCullough, to figure that out."

"The original immigrant, Ian McCullough, came in 1851 and wound his way west until he joined a group coming over the Oregon Trail in the late fifties. Went all the way to the Willamette Valley, which was the goal of all those not headed for California's gold fields, but he found the valley too crowded and the winters too long and gray and he remembered passing near here. Actually the Trail's tracks are still visible north of here. So, he came on back, found this land, and built a cabin, which you can still see down the road a piece. Bought some cattle, longhorns then, and started the Big Piney. He didn't marry until late, near forty. There weren't many women out here, so he headed to San Francisco to find a wife but stopped overnight in Wolf Creek and was so taken with a widow who was traveling from California to Portland on the stagecoach that he followed her up there and talked her into coming to the Big Piney for a visit and married her within the month."

"You have a history of hasty marriages," Cat commented.

"We broke the pattern." Red glanced toward his wife. "We knew each other four years. Met at a freshman dance the first week of school at the University of Oregon and married a week after graduation four years later."

Sarah McCullough gazed out the window, at the lush green meadows, at the clump of yellow mustard far out in the valley, at the distant mountains that, from here, looked like pointed clouds. She didn't say anything.

"Where's Torie?" asked Miss Jenny.

Sarah, without turning to look at anyone, shrugged her shoulders. "Victoria is probably with that Indian."

Just then a tall, thin, rawboned woman, wearing jeans and a man's blue shirt, announced, "Dinner's ready."

All through dinner, while the conversation ranged from a debate about whether or not Congress had been right to derail Clinton's health care reforms and whether or not CNN really beat the other networks at news, or whether there would be two or three hay harvests this year, Scott McCullough didn't take his eyes from across the table, staring at Cat.

She became so embarrassed she tried not to meet his eyes, glancing at everyone else. But his will was too strong, and she found herself locked in his visual embrace more often than made her comfortable. He sure knew how to get a girl's interest. Not that he had to try hard. She'd been aware of him all afternoon. Aware of his tall erect body as he rode ahead of her up the mountain trails, aware of the way he interacted with his family, of his soft voice, his wide shoulders, his jet-black eyes. More than once she'd wondered what his kisses would feel like.

When he drove her and Annie back to town, he said to Annie, "Am I allowed to steal Cat all on my own tomorrow night?"

"I don't think anything special's planned. Mom's tired from the weekend's activities."

"Well," he asked. "How about it. Just you and me for dinner?"

Cat glanced at Annie, who nodded an okay.

Cat knew, as sure as she'd known anything, that Scott McCullough would kiss her the next night.

Four

"I decided there's not a restaurant in eastern Oregon that can compete with the kinds of places where you probably dine nightly, so I'm not even going to try. Instead, I'll take you to a place like I bet you've never been to."

The Chuck Wagon. A sprawling restaurant with the longest bar in the state, on the outskirts of Pendleton. The waitresses wore short skirts, satin blouses, high-heeled boots, and bandannas around their necks. A lone fiddler played country songs.

"Weekends they have a quartet," Scott said. "And I better warn you no one orders meat well-done."

All the way up to Pendleton he'd asked her probing questions. Cat didn't think she'd ever told anyone so much about herself—at least not all at once. He'd learned that her mother had died when she was eleven, hit by a drunken driver. That her father had remarried within eighteen months and had three children, who were fourteen, fifteen, and sixteen years younger than Cat. His wife was closer to Cat's age than to his. They lived in Philadelphia and she hardly saw them—just at Christmas, when she went home, through a sense of duty rather than pleasure. Maybe she'd go to Barbados or Aruba for Christmas this year, instead of Philadelphia.

She told him she loved the theater and movies, she enjoyed symphonies but hated opera. Actually the music she really liked was from the sixties. John Denver, Peter, Paul and Mary, Mama Cass—she hated today's music where she couldn't understand the words and people just shouted. She liked a song with a melody.

She couldn't fall asleep without a book in her hands. She had to read something, even a page or two, before falling asleep. She had had trouble sleeping ever since her big case came into her life.

He told her he'd attended Oregon State for two years, but he had put in more time at parties and in sports than in studying and decided he didn't need a degree to ranch. He knew more about ranching than half the professors he had, whose knowledge came only from books. His father would have liked him to get a degree in business so that the ranch could be run with more financial know-how, but it had been zooming along without that for well over a century, and he'd missed the outdoors. Scott liked it in the spring when they rounded up the cattle and counted the calves and branded them, when they culled the ones ready for market and herded them into trucks. He liked the smell of burning flesh at branding time and the camaraderie with the other men. "Sure, now we round up by helicopter and on motorcycle, so some of the romance of ranching is gone, but it's still a magical time. I can't think of anything I like more than sleeping out under the stars with the men, sitting around a campfire at night telling tall tales, and listening to the lowing of cattle and the occasional cry of some wild animal."

He enjoyed the roundup of the sheep, too, though there weren't nearly as many of them, maybe seven or eight thousand head. There was a shearing shed which was only used once a year when the shearers came from Canada. A bunkhouse was near it, the shearers brought their own cook, and they only stayed about a week or ten days. Scott flew the helicopter to round up the sheep then, too, but he didn't get the same kick that he did with cattle. Sheep didn't evoke anything within him the way cattle did. "Why, I get a bang just out of standing on our front porch and looking out at those fields of Herefords and Angus as far as I can see. I mean I get a lump in my throat just looking at them." He brought his hand up to his chest.

Cat had never met a man who expressed emotion so freely. A pounding heart, just to see acres upon acres of cattle!

Without asking her what she wanted to drink, Scott ordered whiskey for himself and red wine for her. They sat sipping their drinks while waiting for their rare roast beef.

"You ever been to a square dance?" he asked her.

She shook her head.

"There's one Friday night at the Grange. You don't have to know how. There's line dancing Thursday, but that's over in La Grande. I like to dance."

She told him, "I may embarrass you. I haven't danced in years."

He grinned. "Well, we better do something about that. And besides, I don't embarrass easy." His eyes hadn't left her lips. She could tell he desired her. It was a nice feeling. Better than nice. She hadn't felt this feminine in ages. She couldn't remember if she'd ever spent time with such a big good-looking man, who was so essentially masculine, so attuned to the outdoors, so unconcerned with law and with business.

She was permitting herself to relax on this vacation. No tensions, no rat race, no thinking every minute, no rush.

She looked around and said, "I feel like I'm in a different world. This can't be America."

"Honey," Scott said, "this *is* America. Where you come from, that's fake. This is the real one. This is where life's worth livin'."

She finished her drink just as the waitress brought a taco salad. "Well, for sure you're not like the other men I've known."

He nodded. "I take that for granted. But we're even. I've never known a woman lawyer, or any woman with a couple of degrees behind her name. I'd have thought that would turn me off." He attacked his salad.

"It hasn't?"

He grinned. "Looks like it's done just the opposite. With my grand-mother, too. She hopes you'll have time to come visit her. Asked me to bring you to tea tomorrow. Think you can fit that in?"

Cat felt a rush of pleasure. She'd liked the older woman immensely. "I'll make time."

The fiddler stopped for an intermission and a jukebox began to play music from the forties and fifties. "Come on, let's dance," Scott said.

Cat glanced around. There was a big dance floor, and probably on Saturday nights the place was packed with dancers, but now it was empty. "No one's dancing."

"What's that got to do with anything?" Scott asked, sliding his chair back and standing. Reaching for her, he said, "I make it a practice never to be limited by what others do or don't do."

Cat stood up and let herself be led to the empty dance floor. Scott took her right hand and pulled her close, his arm encircling her. She barely came up to his shoulder. He moved easily and gracefully as though the dance floor were his second home after the range. "You're good at this," she murmured.

"Just wanted an excuse to hold you in my arms."

He held her close, so she could feel the movements of his leg and follow his lead easily. She liked the feel of his hand in the middle of her back, she liked the way she felt with his hand surrounding hers, the sense of security and simultaneous excitement he engendered in her. She liked their legs moving in synchronization, the smell of him— like the outdoors. Her whole body felt alive.

"You have without doubt the most inviting lips I've ever seen," he whispered into her hair.

Why was she having difficulty swallowing? This was just harmless flirtation.

"Do you accept all invitations?" she was surprised to hear herself say. Flirting had not been her forte.

He laughed, a loud joyous sound that made the other diners glance at them and smile. "I like women who are quick on the uptake."

The song ended, and they walked back to their table.

"May sound funny, but their New York cheesecake is terrific. If you like cherries, that is."

"I do."

"Remember those words, lady."

I do?

Coffee arrived before the cheesecake. Scott drank his black. Cat poured Half & Half into hers.

"You married to the East?" he asked.

She shrugged her shoulders. "I've never really been anywhere else."

"Well, you're here now." Scott delved into the cheesecake.

"It's very good," Cat said, though she didn't think it could hold a candle to cheesecake made in New York City's delis.

They danced again, and Cat let herself dissolve in Scott's arms as Tony Bennett left his heart in that city by the Bay. She hadn't heard music like this since she was a kid, and her mother played tapes from the era in which she'd grown up.

"When's the last time you were kissed?" he murmured in her ear.

Without opening her eyes, she said, "It's none of your business."

"I have news for you. Everything about you is going to be my business. I want to know everything about you."

"I hear you act like this with all the girls."

He pulled her tighter and laughed like it came from inside and didn't quite get out. "Annie's building my reputation. Don't pay any attention to that kind of talk. It's just you and me right now, okay?"

"Okay," she murmured into his chest.

"Lemme warn you. You're not going to bed tonight without being kissed so's you'll remember it for a long time."

"Is that a threat or a promise?"

He stopped dancing and took her by the hand. He paid the bill, left a five on the table, grabbed his white Stetson, and pulled her behind him, out the door, over to the Caddy. He propped her against the door and put his hat on the roof. Then he gathered her in his arms and lifted her off the ground, his lips meeting hers with an urgency and force that made her weak.

He tasted of coffee and warmth as his tongue searched hers. Her feet were off the ground, her back against the car door, and he was being true to his promise. She had never been kissed quite so thoroughly before.

"They teach you something aside from law back East," he said as they broke apart.

Cat's feet touched the ground as he opened the door on her side and gestured for her to get in. He turned the key in the engine and the car glided out of the parking lot. He didn't say anything for a while. Cat opened her window and gazed up at the stars.

"I've never seen so many," she said as though to herself.

After they'd driven up the hill outside of town and had gone about ten miles, Scott glanced over at her and reached for her hand.

"When it comes," he said, "it comes like a sack of cement, doesn't it? Hitting you right over the head."

She wasn't sure, for a moment, what he was referring to until she realized it was them. Her. She wondered how often he'd acted this way before, how many times he pretended he'd been hit by Cupid's arrows. For a flash of a second she was angry with him, and then she relaxed. *Hey, have fun,* she told herself. *You're only here another ten days.*

"Don't tell me this is the first time you've felt . . ." She let it dangle in the air. Two could play at his game.

He smiled. "Only time I thought I was in love I was in the tenth grade and she was in the eleventh. She didn't give me the time of day."

"I bet she's the only woman in your life who reacted that way."

He held her hand tighter. "You know what I'm wond'rin'? I'm thinking maybe you don't have a clue what you're doin' to me."

"This must be the most beautiful night I've ever known." The ridges of the mountains were a shade darker than the starlit sky.

"Tomorrow," Scott said, "we'll go out to Miss Jenny's about four." He didn't ask her.

"I'll pick you up 'bout three-thirty." He reached his right arm out and put it around her shoulders, pulling her close. "You don't stand a chance in hell of not seeing me every day. Better warn Annie."

"She and I see each other all the time in Boston. I'm sure she has things to do other than entertain me all the time."

"Day after I'll take you around the Big Piney ... your choice: helicopter or jeep. Thursday if it stays this hot, we can go swimming up at the lakes."

"Don't you ever work?"

"Sure. I'm at work hours before you even wake up, I bet."

Cat sighed contentedly with his arm around her.

She was looking forward to his good-night kiss.

This was turning out to be a far more interesting vacation than she'd thought it would be. This was what vacations should be. A change of pace and scenery. A bit of flirtation, different people. All women dreamed of meeting a dashing handsome man on a vacation, of having a bit of romance along with the scenery. She thought she'd probably hit the jackpot.

"And you're going to teach me to square-dance, too," she said aloud.

"Too?" he held her tighter. "That sounds promising."

He gathered her in his arms and kissed her as he'd promised. It would be a long time, like forever, before she forgot that kiss.

Five

Cat wondered what would happen if a car came the opposite way. The road to Miss Jenny's was a narrow dirt track that wound up the mountainside. "There," Scott said, pointing. "That's her place."

Miss Jenny's was a huge log cabin nestled among the trees. A wide porch ran along the front of it, overhanging the valley. From there Miss Jenny could rock and watch the deer and birds through her binoculars.

"Sometimes she's snowed in for a couple of weeks at a time," Scott told Cat. "She says it's like having a vacation when that happens."

He parked the car in front of the cabin, and Cat jumped out before he could help open her door. Miss Jenny came from the house, wiping floured hands on a long muslin apron. "I was beginning to think you'd forgotten." She stuck her cheek forward, and Scott kissed it, giving his grandmother a hearty hug.

Cat kissed her cheek, too.

"Come on," Miss Jenny started back up the steps. "I've popovers just ready to come out of the oven."

"That's right, spoil our appetites for dinner."

"I'll never live to see the day your appetite is spoiled," his grandmother said, laughing.

The aromas wafting from the kitchen smelled wonderful, but Cat paused to look over the living room as grandmother and grandson walked toward the kitchen. The whitewashed walls were hung with Indian handwoven rugs. Others were scattered across the shining wooden floor. An eight-foot couch, covered with a rich floral print, aqua and cream with splashes of cherry, faced the fireplace. On each side were deep comfortable chairs in the same cherry shade. Although the room was dark, it was inviting and comfortable.

Cat followed voices through a wide archway to find a modern kitchen, replete with microwave and built-in oven, an oval oak table and six captain's chairs around it. Scott was sitting in one, already sipping a cup of coffee while Miss Jenny, hot pad in hand, lifted the popovers from the pan onto a large china platter.

"I'm hoping, Scott, you'll look at my generator. The lights kept flickering last night."

He grinned. "You just want me out of the way so you can have woman talk."

Miss Jenny nodded. "No one's ever accused you of being dumb."

"Well, not quite true," Scott said as he buttered a popover and smeared it with raspberry jam. "Mm, this is good. Some of my teachers did."

His grandmother shook her head. "Of not paying attention, maybe. Of gazing off into space, probably. Of not concentrating. But of being dumb, never!"

"These are delicious," Cat said.

"You like baking?"

"I've never really done much. Seems to me I've been too busy all my life to do a lot of the things women have proverbially done."

"Guess this is where I go look at the generator," Scott said, standing up and grabbing a couple of popovers.

"I do envy you," Miss Jenny said, sipping her coffee. "In my day, women couldn't do things like practice law. You like it?"

"I love it," Cat said. "Oh, these are so good. Scott's right. I won't want any dinner." She stared out the window, at the valley so far below them, dotted with Herefords. "Do you ever take this view for granted?"

"Once in a while, but not often. I moved up here a year after my husband died. I figured it was time to let Sarah run the big house. Maybe I was wrong."

"You all lived there together?" Cat thought she'd get mighty tired of living with in-laws.

Miss Jenny nodded. "Red brought Sarah home, and they just stayed. Jock and I were in the south wing and Red and Sarah and the kids in the north. But I did think Sarah might like to take over, and besides, I felt nearer to Jock up here, alone. I can talk to him, you see, each night. He's with me more here than he would be if I were still down there, surrounded by people."

"Don't you get lonely?"

"I was stark raving crazy lonely for a year or more after Jock died. I missed him so sorely. But you mean because I'm so far away from people, don't you? I'm never lonely. I enjoy my own company, and I always find something to do. Even if it's just studying the jays in the pines. No, I was lonelier in St. Louis when I was young than I've ever been here at the Big Piney."

They were silent while Cat finished her coffee, then Miss Jenny said, "I'm sorry you'll be here such a short time. I'd like to take you riding back in the mountains."

Cat laughed. "I have a feeling once on a horse was enough for me. I've been stiff ever since we went riding Sunday."

"You'll get over that given enough time."

"Ten more days?"

Miss Jenny nodded, her eyes dancing. "You could take a stab at it. Ride for an hour one day, one and a quarter the next, et cetera." Then she changed the topic. "What made you become a lawyer?" She got up and walked over to the stove, bringing the coffeepot back to the table and refilling their cups.

"I wanted to be important and make a bundle of money. Make a difference. Show the world women are as good as men."

"Hmph," sniffed Miss Jenny. "The only people who don't know that are men. And even some of them don't have an inkling. They have such fragile egos, you know, that when they realize our true worth their egos may not recover."

Cat laughed. She looked over at the desk built into the kitchen wall, overlooking the woods. "You look like you do something important. What do you do up here with all those ledgers?"

"I keep the Big Piney's books. Have for close to fifty years."

"Why don't you have a computer?" Cat asked.

"Heavens, I'm too old to learn something that complicated."

"Nonsense," Cat told her. "It would simplify your work."

"Might be. But there's no one around to teach me. It would scare me silly."

Cat let it go. After all, what did it matter to her?

"Gives me something to do and makes me feel I'm still important. Same reason you went into law." Then, "I hope you won't let Sarah scare you off?"

"Scare me off? She was lovely to me at dinner the other night."

"Good. One never can tell."

What an odd thing to say, Cat thought.

"You haven't met Torie yet, but you'll love her," Miss Jenny went on.

"I'm sure I will."

Miss Jenny stood. "Let's go see how my generator is faring."

Scott looked up as the women appeared in the garage. "Needs a new part, Miss J. I'll bring it up in the morning, unless you really are desperate for it tonight."

"Nothing worth watching on TV tonight anyhow. I'll knit by candlelight if the lights go out again."

"Are you ever scared up here all alone?" Cat asked.

Miss Jenny laughed. "The place to be scared is in a city surrounded by people. Not up here. Not ever."

"Torie promised to come to dinner," Scott said. "I'd like Cat and her to meet."

"It'll be good to have her home after four years away," her grandmother said.

"She only came home to be near Claypool."

"Claypool?" Cat asked.

"Joseph Claypool," Miss Jenny answered. "One of the respected families around here. Father raises Appaloosas and people come from all over, once even from Australia, to buy them. Joseph's a fine young man."

"Come on," Scott said to Cat. "Not that we'll be hungry, but come on down to dinner."

Miss Jenny reached up to brush her cheek against Cat's. "My dear, thank you for coming. I've a feeling we'll be seeing more of each other."

Scott tossed his arm around her shoulder until they got to the car. Once he was in his seat and had purred the motor into action, he waved to Miss Jenny. "You've impressed her," he said to Cat.

Cat didn't know how. She hadn't even said that much. "I'm impressed by her. Is she one of Oregon's rugged individualist women?"

"We've had many," he said, steering to avoid a quail and her brood that trotted across the road. "Maurine Neuberger, a senator. Woman governor." He glanced at Cat and smiled. She thought his smile was irresistible. "We like women out here."

She gazed at his hands on the steering wheel. They looked strong, powerful yet graceful. Like his dancing. Like all of him.

*   *   *

Standing on the porch, waiting for her brother, was a young clone of Sarah McCullough. Her ebony hair was longer and flowed around her shoulders. Her eyes were like her mother's and brother's, obsidian black. Glittering. She'd obviously spent the summer out in the sun, for her tan was golden, accentuating the whites of her eyes and her smile. She wore no lipstick, probably no makeup at all. She was dressed in the ubiquitous boots worn by nearly everyone in this part of the world, faded jeans, and a yellow cotton checked blouse. Torie was startlingly beautiful and tall, taller than her mother, who was an inch or so taller than Cat, who had never felt short at five-six.

Victoria McCullough stretched out a hand to greet Cat. "I've been hearing glowing things about you," she said.

"Easy to impress with just a few days."

"Come on in. It's over the yardarm and time for a drink. I'm prone to mineral water and lemon. What'll you have?"

"Torie's our teetotaler," Scott explained as they walked into the house, the three of them fitting through the wide front door simultaneously.

Sarah was already seated in her favorite chair in front of the floor-to-ceiling fieldstone fireplace.

As Scott headed toward the polished wood table on which stood glasses and ice as well as bottles of spirits, Sarah held out a glass, and said, "I could stand another."

Cat noticed a brief glance between brother and sister and wondered if she sensed something there.

"You stay much longer, we'll have to put in a supply of red wine," Scott told Cat. "We usually can have a bottle last for ages around here. This isn't wine-drinking country."

"I can always settle for a Coke," she offered.

"A girl after my own heart," Torie said.

"You don't have to go that far." Scott's fingers touched hers as he handed her a glass of cabernet sauvignon. Whatever they had in this house, Cat noted, was first-class, no matter what it was. She fleetingly wondered how it would feel to live in a house with twenty-six rooms and twelve bathrooms, where the glasses were crystal and even the everyday silver was sterling. Where jeeps and pickups proliferated, but the two cars were a Cadillac and a Lincoln Continental. Where having a Cessna and a helicopter was a way of life, and no one thought anything of flying four hundred miles to Portland to Christmas shop.

What Cat particularly found attractive was the family's gathering for drinks before dinner every evening, of actually chatting vivaciously, of the warmth generated when they were together, the laughter. A family that liked each other, that loved each other, that found pleasure in each other's company. It was what she'd yearned for ever since her mother died, through all those years at boarding school, those years of living alone.

Torie told them she was getting her apartment together, having fun buying furniture and decorating for the first time in her life. She'd relished the summer vacation but was anxiously looking forward to her first job. She knew most of the teachers, the majority of them having been *her* teachers when she went through school not that many years ago.

"I hear you're coming dancing Friday night," Torie said. "You'll get to meet Joseph then. We'll be at the Grange, too."

Thelma, the cook who wore jeans, announced dinner.

When they were seated at the long dining-room table, Mrs. McCullough, obviously making the effort to be a good hostess, said, "Tell me, Catherine, what kind of cases do you have?"

"Mostly research, since I'm low man on the totem pole. I've only had one court trial."

"You mean like Perry Mason?" Torie leaned forward, arms folded on the table, waiting for Thelma to bring in the leg of lamb. "Do you ever solve cases in court, like he did? Does a life hang in your hands? Isn't that a terrible responsibility? What do you do if your client is sentenced to death or life imprisonment?"

"Don't you think," countered Cat, "that you're facing an awesome responsibility? Educating children. The future of the world hangs in your hands. I mean isn't responsibility one of the reasons to work?"

"No, I've never solved a case in court. I've only had one case, and he got off. I don't know how I'd feel if I had a case where someone I defended and truly believed was innocent got sentenced to death. I can't let myself even think of that prospect."

"You must have had to face that when you considered becoming a lawyer," Red said.

"No," Cat answered, "I haven't. I mean I'd appeal and appeal. I just don't let myself consider that."

"You've got to lose a case sometime," Scott said. "What then?"

Cat closed her eyes. "I'll hope that person is really guilty."

"Are you good?" Torie asked.

"I'm very good." Cat smiled as she answered.

They all laughed.

Red was carving the lamb and passing around the plates.

Scott, sitting next to Cat, pressed his leg against hers and smiled at her. Suddenly all thought left her mind and she let herself be immersed in the pressure of his leg against hers, and while they were sitting here having a conversation about what she thought, all she could really do at this moment was feel, and she realized she'd like to lie in a haystack, naked, with Scott's tongue running over her body, and give herself up to the sensation and not think of another thing.

"You're smiling," Scott commented. "The food and the conversation must agree with you."

"Haying starts tomorrow," Red said.

"Does it take long?" Cat asked.

"Days," Scott answered. "We sell hay all over the state, even to the Willamette Valley. No better hay anyplace. Don't worry. I won't be too tired to dance."

Cat hadn't been worried.

"Ah, youth," Red said.

Cat gathered that meant she had days free the rest of her vacation. At least Annie wouldn't feel ignored.

But Scott did take Thursday afternoon off. He appeared at three-thirty and said, "Grab a bathing suit. It's too hot to be out in the sun."

He took her swimming in a frigid mountain lake, and afterward she lay on her back and looked up at a snow-covered mountain while he kissed her breasts.

Six

"Tell me that falling in love with Scott McCullough would be the stupidest thing I could do."

Annie looked over her coffee cup. They were sitting in the kitchen, lingering over breakfast. She just smiled.

"Okay. So I'm on vacation. I'm relaxed. I'm in the midst of some of the world's most gorgeous scenery, with people who have time for each other and aren't running all the time, who talk about other things than work, and a handsome guy kisses me and dances with me and has me to his family's house for dinner and I'm impressed with all the land they own and their planes and cars and a life like I've never known . . ."

"I hope you're hearing yourself."

"So how could a girl not be in a vulnerable position with all this?"

Annie shrugged. "I guess I knew that first day when he drove us home. On the other hand, Cat, you don't have to see him all next week . . ."

"Not learn to square-dance tonight?" Cat's voice squeaked.

"Or have fun. So, it's a summer romance. You'll get over it when we get back to Boston. You'll get immersed in work and won't even have time to think of him and you'll be left with romantic memories of a once-in-a-lifetime vacation."

"I don't want to move here!"

Annie laughed. "Hey, slow down. You haven't known him a week. Besides, I warned you. Scott's a big-time romancer. He loves them and leaves them. He'll try to seduce you, and if that interests you, fine. No harm done."

"Yeah, two weeks can't hurt me, can they? I mean even if I fall head over heels, I'll get over something that just lasts two weeks, won't I?"

"If you don't think so, I suggest you get the next plane home."

"Uh-uh. I'm having too much fun. I hope you don't think I'm ungrateful because I'm not spending more time with you."

Annie laughed. "I'd wondered what in the world we'd do to entertain you, so this is fine. As long as you don't get hurt."

"But isn't getting hurt part of life?"

"Oh, God, now you're getting philosophical. Okay, if you want to know you're really alive, if you want to feel the pain and anguish of unrequited love, by all means let yourself fall in love."

"I bet every girl who meets him falls for him."

Annie grinned.

Cat was exhausted and exhilarated by her first square-dance. She didn't think she'd ever laughed so much in all her life.

She stood alone by the punch bowl while Scott was talking to several men when a voice beside her said, "You seem to be enjoying our neck of the woods."

She turned to face a square-jawed, clean-cut, stocky man who wore a badge on a dark green Western shirt. He wore the requisite jeans and high-heeled boots.

"I *am* having a good time. A fine time. A great time. Are you here on duty or . . ."

"I always wear a badge. One only wears it when on duty, but I'm on duty twenty-four hours a day three hundred sixty-five days a year."

"Don't you ever take a vacation?"

"Sure, I take my son fishing up in the mountains. Who wants to go any other place than here?"

"I didn't catch your name," Cat said.

"Jason Kilpatrick." He stuck out a hand. "And I know yours. Everyone in town knows about Annie's Eastern visitor."

"I certainly do like your town. I bet you hardly have anything to do, do you? It's so peaceful here."

"Well, if you're talking about crime, you're right. You don't have much when everyone knows everyone else. It's why I like it here. Great place to bring up kids."

"How many do you have?" He was nice-looking. Maybe just a couple of inches taller than she was, solid. Broad shoulders, erect stance. Not much of a waist. In his early thirties.

"One, a son. He's seven now, and he sure likes this better than Seattle."

"How long have you been here?"

"Bit over four years. I was a cop there. I began to get disillusioned with life. All I saw were the seamier sides of it. The bottom of the barrel. And then I discovered Cougar Valley." He sighed as though just short of ecstasy.

Cat laughed. "Don't you ever get bored? That's what I've been wondering. What is there to do here?"

"Have you been bored yet?"

She shook her head. But then she was having a concentrated romance. She'd let Miss Jenny talk her into getting back on a horse that morning. She inhaled air purer than she'd ever tasted. She had just to look out of any window and there was a panorama to excite the most lethargic, jaded person. She was meeting the friendliest people imaginable. Swimming in icy mountain lakes, having tea in a lodge that just about hung out over the valley, surrounded by gigantic pines. Birds she'd never even heard of. An owl hooting in the dark. Even, one night when Scott was driving her home through the valley, the far-off cry of a coyote.

But if you lived here, you'd get so used to all that you'd hardly be aware of it and then what to do?

Scott sauntered over to them and draped an arm across Cat's shoulders. "Hi, Jason."

The sheriff stretched out his hand to shake Scott's and smiled. "The McCulloughs," he explained to Cat, "just about adopted us when we moved here. Nicest people in the world."

"I've already figured that out," she said. Her heart flipped. She actually felt it jump within her.

"Where's your wife?" Scott asked.

"Home with one of her migraines."

"You weren't at the wedding Saturday, either."

"Well, I made the wedding. Just sat in the back but couldn't make the reception."

Scott didn't ask why. "Ah, the fiddler's tuning up again. Ready?"

Cat nodded. "I think I have my second wind. Come on, Sheriff, you going to dance, too?"

"I am that." He walked to the circle with Scott and Cat. "Hey, Miranda, how about it?"

A pretty young girl still in her teens grinned. "Sure, Sheriff. I just been waiting for you."

"The law doesn't seem to intimidate here," Cat said to Scott.

"Jason Kilpatrick doesn't even have a close contender for being the most liked—trusted—guy around."

The music began and Cat do-si-doed into the arms of a man she'd never seen before. But no matter who she was with or where, her eyes found Scott, laughing with his partners, towering above most of the men. The girl in his arms glanced across the circle at Cat and nodded, listening to something Scott was saying. She smiled across the room. He might have had his way with half the women around here, but they seemed to hold no grudges. She bet he'd give the sheriff a run for his money in a popularity contest.

A few minutes before eleven, Red McCullough appeared in the doorway. He walked through the crowd greeting each one with attention yet smoothly working his way to the dancers.

She could tell he was watching her. When the next set of dances was called, Red said to his son, "My turn."

"Sure, Dad." Instead of asking someone else to be his partner, Scott stood on the sidelines, observing.

"Your wife doesn't like to dance?"

"Sarah went to bed," he said. "I sat there, not paying much attention to whatever was on TV, and decided it was too beautiful a night not to be dancing with a pretty girl."

The way he said it made her feel good. He was nice. If he wanted to go dancing while his wife slept on a Friday night, why not?

For such a big man he was light on his feet. She was aware that ever since he'd entered the large hall, the room had changed shape. Wherever Red McCullough was, so was the center of the room.

"I'm glad you came," she told him.

He smiled at her. The same smile she had seen on his son's face. "And I'm glad you're glad." They whirled across the floor.

He danced with several different women in the next sets, and then disappeared. At midnight the fiddlers played "Good-night, Ladies."

As he drove her back to Annie's, Scott said, "I don't want to take you back yet." He'd held her hand the few blocks they'd driven.

"The moonlight *is* wonderful."

"It's not the moonlight. It's you." He drove to the curb, far from any streetlights, and cut the engine.

"Well, you have me for another week."

"That's not what I mean and you know it." He reached to gather

her in his arms. "Goddamn bucket seats. They don't make 'em for necking anymore." His mouth found hers, and she sighed as he parted her lips with his tongue.

She didn't answer, enjoying his holding her.

"Do you know how long we've known each other?"

"Sure."

"One week and thirty-two hours."

She laughed. "And eleven minutes?"

"All I know is I've never felt this way about anyone, ever. I can't think of anything else. I go to sleep with you on my mind, I wake up thinking of you. I'm not focused on my work." He kissed her again. Her toes curled.

"You're just attracted to older women." They'd discovered she was eleven months the elder.

"Do you think that's it?"

"Mm-hm." She kissed his neck, and his arm around her tightened.

"I don't want you to leave."

"I'm not ready to yet, either. This is certainly a very special vacation, thanks to you."

"Come back for Christmas."

"You're really good for my ego, but *this* is all the vacation I get for a year."

"Quit."

"Yeah, sure." He didn't know what an enviable position she was in, that she'd worked so hard for.

"How am I going to get to know you if you won't come back?"

"Oh," she sighed, loving the feel of his arms around her. "You could come visit Boston. We can e-mail each other."

"Shit, I can't work a computer."

"You could, easily. But if you won't, you can phone me."

"It's cheaper than buying a computer or coming to Boston. I better warn you, I'm not likely to show up there."

"I didn't think you were a candidate for that. So, you better kiss me again. They don't kiss like you do in Boston."

"I didn't expect you back before the wee hours," Annie said. She was sitting at the kitchen table in her pajamas, sipping cocoa.

"If we'd stayed together any longer, we might have disintegrated. I thought it safest to come in."

"You didn't want to sleep with him?"

"I haven't been to bed with a man in over a year. It was a great temptation."

"Does he ignite passion and desire?" Annie laughed.

"Well, I must admit I'm aware my glands are functioning."

When it happened, Cat was surprised. It was shortly after noon, in the bright sunlight, beside a rushing creek back in the mountains, two days before she and Annie were to leave. Scott had taken the afternoon off from work, telling her she should have one final horseback ride among the eastern Oregon mountain trails.

They had seen each other every night. They had gone to a picnic, and to a barbecue, and dined in Baker's best restaurant, which surprised Cat with its sophistication and gourmet dining. It was the only restaurant in town like that, Scott confessed. Sunday they drove over to Hell's Canyon on the Idaho border, where he took her white-water rafting.

On Wednesday he took her up for a helicopter ride when they were trying to rescue a cow and its calf out of a canyon.

"I've had more excitement and thrills poured into a two-week vacation than I've had in most of my life," Cat told Annie.

"You've done more here than I have," Annie told her.

When they went horseback riding the last Thursday of her visit, Scott had asked Thelma to pack a picnic lunch, and he halted by a stream that cascaded down the mountainside.

"The way I eat here in the mountain air, I'd get fat if I stayed here long."

He leaned over to run the back of his fingers across her breast. "Then stop eating. You're just right now."

"That feels good," she told him, but he took his hand away and finished his beef sandwich. He had dunked the bottles of beer in the stream, and they were cold. He took a big swallow.

"You know what I've done?" he asked, looking up at the tall trees. She shook her head.

"I've gone and fallen in love with you."

A bird chirped in the trees as a cloud skittered across the sky.

Cat lay down, her hands pillowed under her head, and looked at him. She was sure he'd said that a dozen or more times. "I've had the most wonderful two weeks of my life with you. I haven't laughed as much in months. Maybe years. I haven't had the thrills you've shown me, ever."

He moved over to her, lying down next to her, his hand slipping down the vee of her blouse, touching her nipple. He leaned over to kiss her. Her arms wound around him, and she could taste the horseradish from his sandwich. He unbuttoned her blouse as his tongue played with hers.

"How come when you touch me there I'm on fire all over," she murmured.

He laughed and didn't stop.

"I'll remember these two weeks for a long time," she said as his hand moved across her belly.

His mouth was on hers again and her fingers began to unbutton his shirt. She wanted to feel his skin next to hers, wanted his tongue on her breasts, wanted him . . .

She wriggled out of her blouse and as his head moved down her body she gazed up at the sky, through the pine needles that seemed to reach unto forever, and thought she'd never known anyone like Scott McCullough. Never been kissed the way he knew how to kiss. Never felt her insides churn with yearning the way he was making her feel. And then she stopped thinking.

An hour later, when they lay naked in the dappled shade of the trees, with only the murmur of the rushing brook as background music, his arm around Cat, she said, "I must say, you know how to show a girl fun."

"That was more than fun, and you know it. That was as good as it gets. Better than most people ever experience it, I imagine. That, babe, was one helluva fucking good time."

"Going back to work will be a letdown after this."

His fingers ran across her left breast. She was still amazed that such a big man could be so gentle, that he coaxed from her passion unknown to her before.

"Stay. I can show you things you've never done before, I bet."

"You make it sound irresistible. Couldn't we crowd it all into the next day and a half?"

He laughed. "When you let down your reserve, you're willing to go all the way, aren't you?"

"I don't know. I've never done it before."

"We could drive to Portland and spend the night and all tomorrow in a hotel and screw ourselves silly."

"Sounds inviting."

He sat up and stared at her.

"You serious?"

She smiled up at him. "I don't know. What would your family say? And Annie?"

"Tell her to meet us at the airport. You want to? We could be in Portland by dark. Stay at the Red Lion, overlooking the Columbia River."

They didn't leave the Red Lion's hotel room for twenty-four hours, and then only to get dinner.

"Why didn't we do this before?" she asked. "If I'd known it would be like this, I'd have given in last week."

"Given in?" he said, when she was on top of him. "I was waiting for you to want me as much as I've wanted you."

"I was at that point days ago. I just didn't want to seem too easy."

"Babe, easy or not, you are the best lay I ever had."

"And vice versa."

"Well, we can do it that way, too."

On the plane going back to Boston Cat was aware of her body as she had never been in her life. She wondered if there were any other positions left to try. She felt charged with energy.

Until they changed planes in Chicago it didn't dawn on her that it would be a long time, if forever, before she saw Scott McCullough again.

Instead of crying, she just smiled.

Scott McCullough. She tried on the name just to see how it looked behind her closed eyes:

Mrs. Scott McCullough. Catherine McCullough.

"What are you frowning at?" Annie asked.

"I could never live in Cougar."

"Honey, you would curl up and die of boredom in little ole Cougar Valley."

But, on the other hand, she'd never been so alive anyplace.

Seven

"The sun's shining," Scott told her from three thousand miles away at ten o'clock Boston time Sunday night, "but the light's gone out of my life."

"It's hot and humid here, or maybe my low spirits are due to leaving Cougar. I miss the mountains and the air and . . ."

"And me, I hope?"

"And you." Yes, she missed him. She missed his kisses and the way her body felt as his hands played over her.

"I spent a couple hours up at Miss Jenny's this afternoon, and we spent the time talking about you."

"I had the most wonderful two weeks I can remember," Cat told him.

Though she felt warm and cozy when she hung up from talking with him, it did run through her mind that she might never see him again. She told herself not to be depressed. He had given her a time like she'd never known. She still tingled from those thirty hours spent at the Red Lion.

The next morning she'd barely been back at work twenty minutes when two dozen yellow roses arrived from Scott. The card read, "So you'll think of me all day long."

No "Love, Scott." No "Scott." No name at all.

Tuesday morning, a gardenia plant, with shiny green leaves and full heady aroma, was delivered. Cat wondered if Scott chose the flowers or if it was the florist's selection.

He phoned her Tuesday night.

But Wednesday there were no flowers and no phone calls. Nor Thursday. No flowers Friday, but when she came home from work, there was Scott sitting on the steps of her brownstone, a soft leather suitcase, more like a large duffel bag, next to him, a wide grin on his face.

He stood as soon as he saw her appear, laughing when he saw the expression on her face. He picked her up and caught her in a bear hug, swinging her around, kissing her to the amusement of those passing by.

She hugged him, astonished.

He set her on the steps and picked up his bag. "I couldn't stand not seeing you," he said, following her into the foyer.

She laughed all the way up the stairs to her second-floor studio apartment that overlooked Newbury Street.

"You've got dynamite legs," he said from behind her, his finger running up her leg.

Once in her apartment, he looked around hastily, and said, "What do you pay for this?" but didn't wait for an answer. He caught her in his arms and kissed her, a deep hungry kiss.

Cat stood back and studied him. "I'm in a state of shock."

He looked sure of himself. "I told you, I've never felt this way before."

He gazed around the room, at the teal Naugahyde sofa that opened into a bed, the flowered chintz chair, the antique rolltop desk littered with papers, the seventeen-inch TV screen on a table in the corner of the room. His eyes quickly roamed to the tiny kitchen at the end of the room, the dining table which could barely seat four and had never had to.

"You live or just exist in this?"

Cat had felt fortunate, to have found this on Newbury Street and had lived here for just over a year and a half.

"Annie live in one like this?" he persisted.

"She looks out on an alley, but hers is larger. She has two rooms."

"Jeez," he said as though it were pitiful. Then, "I'm starving. That stuff that tasted like cardboard on the plane didn't do a thing for me."

"I can't believe you're here."

He walked over to the window and looked out at the summer-evening crowd.

"We have all sorts of restaurants around here," she said. "There are several Italian, a Greek, my favorite Indian . . ."

"India Indian?" His face screwed up.

She nodded.

"Your favorite, huh? Okay, lead me to it. I might as well experience new things while I'm in the big city."

"Let me wash."

"Babe, I will let you do anything you want. Absolutely anything."

There was a knock on the door. Cat, heading to the bathroom, said, "Answer that, will you, while I wash up."

It was Annie. Her jaw dropped open. "Scott McCullough!"

"Hi." He stood back and gestured for her to come in.

"Well, you never cease to surprise. When did you blow in?"

" 'Bout an hour ago."

"I guess Cat's not available for dinner."

Cat walked out of the bathroom, drying her hands. "Sure. Come along with us. We're going to that Indian place you and I like. I think maybe Scott's never eaten Indian food before."

Annie's eyes met Scott's. "No, I don't think so. Three's a crowd, and I'm not in the mood to be crowded."

Cat didn't insist.

"How long are you staying?" Annie asked.

He shrugged. " 'Til I succeed in my mission."

The women looked at each other, but neither asked what his mission might be.

He wasted no time in telling Cat, though.

The restaurant, twelve steps down from the street, was in the basement of one of the brownstones that lined Newbury Street. Large planters of riotously colored petunias decorated the steps. The sloe-eyed hostess wore a sari and the waiters were all from India. A quarter-toned musical instrument could be heard in the background, and the aroma of sandalwood incense floated faintly through the air.

"You better order for me. I wouldn't know what I was getting," he said after he'd glanced over the menu.

"Their lamb dishes are great."

"Okay." He nodded.

Cat ordered dishes that weren't too spicy, not knowing Scott's tolerance for such. The restaurant did serve California wines, and Cat ordered a Vouvray.

"I better start acquiring a taste for wine," Scott said. "In Cougar men don't much cotton to wine." He looked around appreciatively. "Fancy place."

"Don't kid me." Cat smiled, filled to overflowing with happiness. "You're no dude."

"Actually," his gaze came back to her. "I've even been to Hawaii and San Francisco and England."

"England, too?"

"And Florida."

She laughed again. "How extraordinary that you're here."

The waiter brought their wine and poured it, filling Scott's glass with about an inch of it.

"Taste it and pretend you're a connoisseur," Cat suggested.

He gulped it down and nodded at the waiter, who poured their glasses two-thirds full and left the wine on the table.

"I came to talk you into giving up your job, leaving Boston, and marrying me."

Cat plopped her glass down on the table, looking at it to see if she'd broken the stem.

"You what?"

Scott slid out of his chair and knelt on one knee. The other diners looked at him, their eyes filled with merriment.

"I have come, my dear, to ask you to marry me." He stayed in position.

Cat looked around at their audience. He certainly was impulsively irresistible.

"I don't know what to say."

"For Christ's sake, it's the first time in my life I've proposed to a woman. How long do I have to stay down here?" He didn't look embarrassed or uncomfortable. He reached for her hand. "My darling, I can't imagine that it's escaped your attention, but I have fallen completely, utterly in love with you. I flew across this vast continent of ours because I cannot live without you. I want to share my life with you, and want you to be the mother of my children . . ."

The audience burst into applause.

Now Cat felt herself blushing with embarrassment. "Scott, get back in your chair. I can't give you a quick answer. We have to talk about this."

"Do you love me?"

"I think so."

"She thinks so?" He turned to his audience. "She *thinks* so?"

"You're the most exciting man I ever met," she admitted, finding herself so embarrassed she didn't know whether she wanted to fall through the floor or laugh.

"Okay." He raised himself back onto the chair, but turned to the other diners and said, "I'll keep you posted."

He poured himself another glass of wine.

"You're supposed to sip it, not down it like beer," Cat said.

"If I did things the way others do, you wouldn't find me the most exciting man you've ever met," Scott countered.

"I can't just give up my job. I've spent too many years getting educated for it."

Scott's eyes bored into her.

"I can't move to Oregon."

"I thought I heard you say it's the most beautiful place you've ever seen."

Cat nodded.

"Nicest people you've ever met."

"That too."

"Best lay you've ever had."

Cat looked around to see if the other diners were listening. They'd gone back to their conversations.

Laughter spilled out of her. "I hardly know you. Three weeks ago I'd never heard of you."

"You can have me every day and night for the rest of your life."

"You're nuts."

"About you. Jesus Christ, you're sure hard on my ego. Here I hoped you'd jump at this opportunity, that you felt about me like I do you."

The waiter brought naan.

"What's this?" Scott studied it.

"A spicy crisp bread." Cat took some and nibbled on it. "Well, we could get engaged and . . ."

"Engaged? I meant like let's get married next week. Or this weekend, though my parents and Miss Jenny sure would be pleased if we'd do it at the Big Piney."

"You've talked this over with them?"

He nodded. "Miss Jenny's the one who said if I wanted you to come get you."

What would she do with herself in Oregon?

An image of lying in Scott's arms every night floated through her mind.

"What a temptation," she said, her voice but a whisper. "Sounds like an offer I'd be stupid to refuse."

"You better believe it," Scott muttered, as the waiter brought a steaming bowl of basmati rice to go with the muglai lamb with turnips, mushroom pullao, spicy green beans, and a cucumber/mint raita. He studied it with raised eyebrows and a skeptical look on his face.

Courageously he heaped a mound of rice on his platter and covered it with the lamb dish. He tasted it, cocked his head and smiled. "S'not bad."

"Oh, good, you like it."

"Not for every night," he said, helping himself to more, "but it's pretty tasty."

Cat studied him. His eyes met hers and he smiled, a tender, love-filled smile that melted her heart.

"Oh, Scott," she leaned forward, "I am crazy about you, but we hardly know each other. You've never seen me with my hair in curlers or we haven't seen each other in bad moods. We don't know anything about each other."

"What's to know? Hey, remember I have a family history. Look, I've known plenty of women . . ."

"That I understand."

". . . and I've never even for a minute had the urge to wake up with any of them for the rest of my life."

Cat began to eat. "It's crazy."

"So?" This didn't seem to disturb him. "You need to get married in Philadelphia to please your father, I will. Though Mother and Miss Jenny are just waiting for the word to plan a big wedding. Miss J says it's the ideal time of year."

"I don't even know anyone in Philly anymore. I don't care if I ever see it again." What was she talking about?

"Well, that settles it. After I get through making love to you tonight—though"—he grinned as he heaped more rice onto his plate—"I don't ever expect to get through making love with you, well we can start packing up whatever you think you can't live without though frankly from looking around that hole you live in, all you need to take is your clothes.

"You wanna drive across the country or sell your car and fly back?"

Cat was having difficulty breathing. She laid down her fork and stared at him, then reached for the wine bottle and poured herself a big slug. She gulped it down before she could talk.

He laughed. "I thought you told me you don't drink wine like that."

"How often do I get swept off my feet?"

"Is that what I'm doing?" He half stood and leaned over the small table to kiss the end of her nose. "I like that. Well, it's settled then, it's to be at the Big Piney."

Cat looked at him and felt herself tremble. Within hours she would be in his arms, they would be wound around each other, he would devour her with those kisses that dissolved her, and after he had played her like a virtuoso does a violin he would enter her and they would explode with passion together.

"Oh, yes," she breathed, not caring if she ate any more. "Let's fly."

Scott stood up and said in a loud voice. "She said yes."

Amid laughter and smiles, the other diners applauded.

The wedding took place the second Saturday in August, a week after Cat returned to Cougar Valley. Scott had flown back after the long weekend in Boston, while Cat stayed to resign her job, splurge on a wedding dress that had been featured in one of the women's magazines and cost her what had been a month's salary, sell her car and furniture.

Annie said she couldn't be her attendant, she'd just had a two-week vacation and couldn't take more time off, so Cat phoned Torie and asked if she'd stand up with her. She phoned her father, too, to ask if they'd all come out to Oregon for the wedding, but he wasn't home. His answering machine said they were in Maine for three weeks vacation and to leave a message. He'd never told her. But then she hadn't told him she'd flown out to Oregon in the first place.

She packed boxes and realized all she'd take were her clothes. She sold her furniture to the young woman who had immediately appeared to rent the apartment, and decided she'd ship her law books, but couldn't figure what for, except they represented so many years of struggle and learning, and one never knew. She could store them in the barn or someplace. Certainly there was enough room out there. No matter where she and Scott would live, there was room to store books at the ranch house, she was sure.

He called her every night of the ten days that they were apart.

"Where do you want to go on a honeymoon?"

"Someplace that has a big bed."

He laughed. "A woman after my own heart."

"It's not your heart I'll be after."

"Shit," he said, "you can't even see what you're doing to me." He went on, "You've never seen the Tetons, have you?"

"I want to go someplace neither of us has ever been."

They finally settled on spending a week at Glacier National Park. Cat would have preferred a luxurious tropical resort or an exciting city, instead of an introduction to the wilds, but she might as well dive right into this new life she was choosing. He told her he'd bring a double-sized air mattress since he knew she wasn't used to sleeping on the ground.

A honeymoon sleeping on the ground? Well, it didn't really matter, did it? He told her they'd go white-water rafting, and they'd hike to where there were views so you could see to tomorrow.

"How do you know if you haven't been there?"

"It's West," was all he answered.

Hike up mountains? She usually drove from one end of a shopping mall to the other.

"How about Tahiti?" she suggested. "Neither of us has been there."

"You'll love Montana," he told her.

Eight

Miss Jenny insisted that once Cat arrived she stay up at the lodge with her while preparations for the wedding were in full force down at the main house. An open invitation had been extended to the townspeople. The ceremony itself would be performed in the living room and would be attended just by family and a few close friends, but the reception would be held on the sprawling lawns in front of the house and hundreds were expected, since Red had run an announcement in the weekly newspaper. An immense barbecue pit would hold a whole hog, and a catering company from Boise would barbecue beef and take care of all the details except the wedding cake, which Miss Jean Featherly would bake just as she had baked wedding cakes for whoever got married in Cougar, in the whole valley really, for the last twenty-seven years.

Sarah commented that she didn't think a barbecue was what she imagined Cat had ever envisioned for a wedding reception.

Cat said all the arrangements were just fine with her. She knew that the whole family was delighted that Scott was getting married at home, where everyone they knew could attend.

"We're just having a few to the wedding itself. The doctor and his wife, Chazz and Dodie Whitley. Have you met them yet?" Sarah asked.

She insisted that Cat call her Sarah, yet there was a formality about her that belied intimacy. "Then the sheriff and his wife and their son. The Bollingers, the bank president and his wife, Nan. They went to college with us. Of course they and Red were from here, and I was from Southern California."

She looked up from the notepad on which she'd been jotting notes.

"I was married here, too, you know. Miss Jenny and Jock talked my parents into letting them have the wedding here. I don't know why Mama gave in. She never forgave herself. Though several of our friends came up for the wedding, dear souls that they were, and heaven knows there were enough rooms for everyone, but it was just such a hardship. I suppose Mama thought after three other weddings—my older sisters—it would be heavenly not to have to go through all the expense and trauma of another big wedding. My sisters came but, do you know, none of their husbands bothered. Said it was too far, and they couldn't take time off from work. Don't you think that's odd?"

"My father's not coming," Cat said. In fact, he didn't even know she was getting married.

"Yes, well." Sarah gazed off into the distance. Then she shook her head and exclaimed, "My heavens! We almost forgot about the flowers. What would you like to carry?"

"Maybe they should be yellow roses. They're the first flowers Scott sent me." Was that just two and a half weeks ago?

Sarah shook her head. "Oh, no, let's get something really elegant. A spray of orchids for you to carry, then you can cut one off and wear it with your traveling outfit."

Cat laughed. "Scott told me my traveling outfit should be a pair of jeans and a cotton shirt. With a sweatshirt for cold evenings." Come to think of it, she'd better go down to Davis's Western Clothing Store and buy something that would be adequate for her honeymoon.

Torie, Sarah, and Miss Jenny had gone to Portland before Cat arrived and bought the dresses they'd wear in the wedding. Sarah's gown was a pale lilac chiffon, so simple and elegant that Cat thought more people would stare at Sarah than at the bride.

She and Torie had consulted long-distance about the bridesmaid's gown and Cat told her future sister-in-law to buy any color she liked. It was all happening so fast that she hadn't time to participate in her own wedding. Torie bought a vibrant turquoise gown that would have been more suitable on the cover of *Vogue* than the lawn of the Big Piney Ranch in Cougar, Oregon. Cat had the distinct feeling that attention was going to be focused on the McCullough women rather than on her. She smiled to herself. In just a few days she would be one of those McCullough women.

Miss Jenny told Cat she imagined there'd be a big argument about whether or not to invite the Claypools. Strong-willed Torie would fight her mother until one of them would give in from sheer exhaustion. Red would side with Torie, Miss Jenny knew. In the end, Scott said,

"It's my wedding, and Joseph is my oldest friend. If he's going to be my best man, certainly his parents will attend the ceremony."

Sarah turned on her heel and left the room.

Sarah McCullough hated those Indians. "Damn heathens," she called them. Ridiculous, because Samuel Claypool had been born thirty miles from here, and though he was directly descended from the Nez Perce's Chief Joseph, he had ranched around here, he and his brothers and sister had gone to school here. "They're as American as you and I are," Miss Jenny told Cat at breakfast one morning. Her kitchen smelled of the delicious cinnamon puffs which Cat was consuming, along with the best coffee she'd ever tasted.

Cat pointed out, "They're more American than we are, aren't they? Wasn't this their land that our ancestors stole from them?"

Miss Jenny narrowed her eyes and studied Cat. "I knew you and I were going to get along the minute I laid eyes on you. I knew that, too, the minute Scott said he was going to go get you and bring you home."

"Did it ever dawn on him I might say no?"

Miss Jenny shook her head. "That he won't succeed never enters his head. He's an arrogant young man, that he is. He's right. Always. Doesn't get that from his father, that's for sure. Red allows to doubts and admits to mistakes. Not Scott. And so far he's been right. He and his father had a big to-do over his quitting college five years ago. Red thinks education is necessary. Scott doesn't. He's bright enough; just doesn't like book learning."

"Oh, Miss Jenny." Cat was sipping coffee across the kitchen table from her. "There's so much I don't know about him."

The older woman smiled and reached out to put a hand on Cat's arm. "Same as me when I married his grandfather. Made for an exciting marriage, discovering new things all the time. I never grew tired of him, or he me. Til the day Jock died our passion knew no bounds."

"Was Red your only child?"

"Talking of passion, you mean?" A film formed over the older woman's eyes, and she gazed out the windows, at the big trees reaching to the sky. "I had five miscarriages, one after another, after Red. Finally the doctor told me to stop trying and performed a hysterectomy. It was a real regret for years, but you know what? I don't mind now. I'm not sure children really bind a couple to each other. Why Red and Sarah were all the time arguing over their two, especially Torie. She's the apple of Red's eye, and sometimes I swear Sarah seems to resent the girl. I suppose it's jealousy, don't you think? Red loves that girl so much maybe Sarah resents her. I suppose that happens often. He'd be happy to have her marry Joseph Claypool, but Sarah says over her dead body. She's helped by Samuel, Joseph's father. He claims Joseph can't marry anyone but an Indian or the blood will be diluted and Joseph won't be able to be a shaman."

"A shaman?"

Miss Jenny tossed her head. "Joseph *does* have remarkable powers."

"Is that like a witch doctor?"

"You've seen too many movies."

"Explain, then."

Miss Jenny leaned forward. "Shamans can enter altered states of consciousness. Samuel Claypool, Joseph's father, is one of the best."

Cat was perplexed. "What's an altered state . . ."

"A shaman can go into a trance at will. His soul leaves his body and ascends to another world. He works that way to heal a patient by restoring vital and beneficial power."

Cat was incredulous, and it showed.

"If a shaman wishes to recover someone's guardian power animal, for instance, he must know how to do it and how to bring it back safely."

"Power animal?" Cat asked.

"His experiences are like dreams, but waking ones that feel real and where he can't control his action and adventures and gain access to a whole new universe, which is really eons old. Those waking dreams provide him with answers to the meaning of life and death and the relationship of the universe."

Miss Jenny stopped and looked at Cat. She gave a sharp laugh. "Look at you. You don't understand a thing I'm saying, do you? Well, open your heart and mind and understanding will come."

Did Miss Jenny believe something like this?

"Shamans work only for the good. You don't need details now. But his being a shaman is what stands between Joseph and Torie. His father and his father's knowledge that Joseph can be a true shaman. A shaman's blood must not be diluted or his powers will be lost. Samuel is against the marriage, though he loves Torie—she practically grew up out at his place—because Joseph must have children that are pure Indian."

"So"—Cat was having trouble following this—"Joseph won't be able to cure people if his children aren't full Indian?"

Miss Jenny shrugged. "Something like that. Or maybe it's that his children will have diluted blood and cannot carry on the strain of shamanism that the family uses for the good of their people."

"Can they use it on others than Indians?"

"Oh, my, yes. Samuel has cured me many times."

"You like the Claypools." Cat could tell.

"I love Joseph. I would dearly love to have him for a grandson, yet I understand the strong tribal obligation."

"Can't Torie and Joseph just go get married and say to hell with all that?"

"The old chestnut about love versus duty and honor. Which is overruling. We've been watching this struggle since Torie was seven and Joseph was—well he and Scott were in the same class, so he was three years older. The old man, though-old man, ha, he's young enough to be my son. He was in school with Red. Samuel didn't see what was coming. Not until they were in their teens. I guess when Torie must have been a freshman and Joseph a senior was when Samuel suddenly realized they were male and female and that they knew it. He's been fighting it all these years since. As for Sarah, she's about as prejudiced as they come. She hates anyone who isn't as pale-faced as she is."

"She almost looks like an Indian, with that dark hair and those eyes."

Miss Jenny nodded. "She and the kids. But she's got that pale skin. And that makes all the difference. When she first came here she wore her hair parted in the middle and long like all girls were doing in the sixties. She looked like an Indian, except for that complexion of hers. I don't recall anything about her being so narrow-minded then. I guess she'd never met an Indian, a full-blooded one anyhow. Of course most Indians have been acculturated and nowadays people are proud to have some Indian heritage, tiny as it might be. Not Sarah."

Cat wondered if Sarah and Miss Jenny were friends.

Just then they heard a car in the driveway. A door slammed, and Red's voice shouted, "I've come to kidnap the bride."

He stomped up the porch stairs and banged the front door as it swung behind him. "Smells good here. Got any left over?" He appeared in the doorway, dwarfing everything else in the room.

"Sit down. Want coffee too?"

Cat could tell Miss Jenny was glad to see her son.

"I've got to go down to the True Value and thought Cat might like to get indoctrinated and meet the gang at Rocky's. So, no, I won't have coffee, much as I'd prefer yours. It's Thursday, and I meet Jason for breakfast there every Thursday. But I will steal one of those muffins." He looked at Cat. "You want to come?"

"Sure." She stood up, ready for any new experience.

Red reached and caught two of the small round muffins in his hand and threw a kiss to Miss Jenny.

"Wait'll I get my purse, and maybe I can buy some jeans and boots."

"Charge it," he said, grabbing her hand and leading her across the living room, down the porch steps to the Ford Explorer.

Once he started the engine, she smiled at him. "This is nice of you."

He grinned. "Well, in two days you're going to be one of the family, and besides, I'm getting to enjoy your company."

"Will you have time to stop at Davis's?"

"Honey, I have time for whatever you want. I save my errands til Thursdays so Jason and I can have time together. Friendships take nurturing, you know."

It seemed funny to hear a big man talk like that.

The bank, the highest building on Main Street, was two stories tall, but most of the buildings were only one story. Rocky's Cafe was lit with a blue neon light, even in the bright sunlight. Pickups proliferated in the head-on parking areas, with most of the trucks featuring a gun on the rear window and a cattle guard on the front of the vehicle.

Cat asked, "Why do all the men here wear high-heeled boots?"

"So they can grip the stirrups."

"I have so much to learn," Cat sighed.

Red looked over at her and smiled, reaching to touch her arm. "To start with," he said as he got out of the van, "in the East a man takes his hat off in a restaurant. No one takes his hat off here."

Most of the hats were Stetsons. Real cowboy country. Cat couldn't help smiling. Actually she felt like turning cartwheels. She had left reality behind in Boston, and the only thing that seemed familiar was the English language.

The cafe was crowded and filled with smoke. The restaurant was paneled in dark wood and lit by dozens of lightbulbs set in wagon wheels which hung from the ceiling.

"My daughter-in-law-to-be," Red called as they entered. "Cat."

Someone meowed, and everyone laughed. Red took her hand and led her to a table in front of the window, where the sheriff sat in full uniform, star on his pocket, big hat pushed back on his head. Dark glasses lay on the table next to his coffee cup, and he looked up at Cat, not rising, but the warmth of his smile made her welcome. Strength of character showed in his face, Cat thought, even though he wasn't really good-looking. She liked the clear gray eyes that met hers.

She couldn't remember his last name.

She sat in the chair Red held out and then, when he was seated, Jason said, "So, you're going to become a McCullough."

"Cat's a lawyer," Red said. "Can you beat that?"

"Hey, it's almost the millennium," Jason said. "Women do everything."

A skinny woman with dyed blond hair, a sharp chin, and a friendly smile approached. "Hiya, Red. I know you want coffee first." She glanced at Cat. "So, you're the lucky lady who's caught Scott McCullough. Hearing about this is breaking a bunch of hearts around here."

"I recommend the blueberry pancakes," Red told Cat, but she had eaten four of Miss Jenny's muffins and decided pancakes would be too much. "Just coffee for me," she told Ida, the waitress.

Red ordered ham and hash browns and scrambled eggs with toast and jam.

Ida brought coffee and left the glass carafe on the table. "I know you guys. You'll want even more." She poured three cups full.

"McCulloughs are the big shots around here, in case you haven't figured that out already," Jason told Cat.

Newcomers who entered the restaurant waved to those at the front table. One man wove his way through the tables to be introduced to Cat.

"Going to be a crowd at the reception," Jason said.

"Jason," Red said, nodding toward him, "and Scott started Little League here 'bout four years ago."

"That was the summer after I came here," the sheriff explained.

Jason talked in a laconic manner, and Cat found herself liking him. His sandy-colored hair was a bit long for the cops she was used to seeing, and if he hadn't been in a uniform of the law, he could have been taken for a construction worker. He was solid.

"What sort of crime do you have here?" she asked.

The two men looked at each other and grinned. "Some of the kids light firecrackers in the rural mailboxes. Hank Snowdon comes in to the jail every Saturday night, dead drunk, and locks himself up. People passing through go too fast. Neighbors get mad at each other. Someone steals someone else's cow. Once we had a murder."

Jason must have read the look on Cat's face because he said, "Challenge isn't what I want in life. Cougar Valley is. I've found a life that's right for my son that can't be equaled. All I know is I'm comfortable here. I know everyone in this town and most people in the valley. And what's more, I like most of them."

"I notice that *most*," Red said, as Ida brought their breakfasts.

Jason continued. "You don't look for excitement here. You look for quality of life, for people who care, for schools that still think teaching is important. You looking for sunrises to take your breath away, then this is the place for you."

Cat hadn't been up early enough to see a sunrise. At this time of year the sun rose well before six.

"You sound like the president of the Chamber of Commerce," she said, sipping her coffee. She hoped she'd like the valley as much as the sheriff did.

After breakfast, she and Red wandered over to Davis's store. With Red's advice, Cat bought two pair of jeans, a couple of cotton shirts, and her first pair of Western boots. Red tossed her a straw hat. "Like mine," he said, "only lightweight, and just right for summer."

She pushed it at a jaunty angle on her head and studied herself in the store's mirror. "I look like a Marlborough ad," she quipped.

"Except you're a woman. And that reminds me, now is about as good a time as any to give you my wedding present." Red reached in his pocket and brought out a square box.

"I love presents," Cat enthused. She opened it to find a silver-and-gold Rolex. "Oh, my." She'd never had anything more expensive than a hundred-dollar watch. She flung her arms around Red and kissed his cheek. "How perfectly lovely. I adore it." She slipped her old watch off and into her pocket and clasped the Rolex around her wrist. She held her arm at a distance to study it.

Red watched her face with obvious pleasure. "That's from Sarah, too, of course."

Her dazzling smile was his reward. "Does Scott know about this yet?"

He shook his head. "No. By the way, he flew over to Portland today. Said to tell you he'll be back midafternoon."

"He flew to Portland?" *And didn't even tell me?*

Red just smiled.

*   *   *

When Scott did come home, he looked like a Cheshire cat. One that had swallowed a canary.

His surprise came at the dinner table, when everyone was gathered together. It accompanied dessert. Thelma had just brought in the mountainous angel food cake dripping with strawberries and whipped cream when Scott announced, "I know Cat wanted to be engaged, so I thought I'd give her two days of it, anyhow." He handed her a gray velvet ring box.

She gasped when she opened it and saw the diamond. "My heavens," she exclaimed, gazing at the largest square-cut diamond she'd ever seen.

Everyone laughed.

"Wait til you see the wedding ring." Scott was obviously pleased with her reaction.

Miss Jenny clapped her hands. Sarah had tears in her eyes.

Thelma, standing in the doorway to the kitchen, said, "My, my."

"All this and you too." She looked up at Scott.

He laughed and gathered her in his arms. As he swung her around her eyes met Miss Jenny's and Red's. "You too," she mouthed silently.

People who said you weren't marrying someone's family were wrong. She already felt that this was her family.

Nine

The night before the wedding, Torie came to stay overnight at Miss Jenny's, for she decided Cat and Miss Jenny sounded like more fun than being involved with caterers and florists down at the big house. Red and Miss Jenny had spent hours with the florist in Baker, who'd probably put in the biggest order he'd ever had. Miss Jenny had contacted the caterers in Boise, and was worried because it had all been done over the phone and was it going to be just as she wanted.

Miss Jenny spent the morning of the wedding down at the big house making sure the caterers arrived. Pits had been dug the day before, and the pigs had been cooking since dawn.

Cat had finally been able to contact her father, right before the rehearsal. He'd finally returned from his vacation and responded to the repeated messages she'd left on his answering service, and actually didn't seem dismayed that she was getting married without him to give her away. He talked more of his vacation at Bar Harbor and how many fish the kids caught and how they all had sunburns. He asked her if she'd like eight place settings of sterling.

When she hung up, Cat felt empty. But when she looked across the room at the McCulloughs, she told herself she was acquiring a new family, and one she'd belong to more than the one in Philadelphia.

Torie left at one-thirty to go down to the big house, and Miss Jenny brought out her dress. She had gone to Portland shopping with her daughter-in-law and granddaughter. Her dress was a soft coral.

When Cat pirouetted for Miss Jenny in the gown she had bought in Boston, Miss Jenny said, "I suppose all brides look beautiful, but none could be more so than you right this minute."

Cat gazed at herself in the long mirror on Miss Jenny's bathroom door and thought she looked pretty good, too. She guessed maybe Sarah and Torie wouldn't outshine her, after all. Though the dress had tight sleeves nearly to her elbows, it was off the shoulder, and she knew she had great shoulders. She'd thought having a long train would be a bit ostentatious for a ranch wedding, and, besides, she could never wear such a thing again, so she did without a train, but the skirt flared out in yards of satin and lace. She wore a single strand of her mother's pearls around her neck and Red's Rolex on her left wrist.

She was surprised the diamond ring didn't weigh her hand down. She'd stared at it constantly for the last two days, holding it at a distance, watching it sparkle in the sun, aware it was there even in the dark. It was the most gorgeous ring she'd ever seen. She had just the tiniest sense that Sarah thought it a bit obscene, too flashy, but she didn't say so. Cat thought it was marvelous. And now, studying the total effect in the mirror, Cat said, "I think I could purr."

Miss Jenny, donning her gloves, smiled. "I like your name, by the way. Not that I'm a cat lover, far prefer dogs, but I like the name. So much stronger than Cathy, and not as common as Kate."

"My mother gave me that," Cat said. "When I was about three or four and she was reading me a bedtime story about cats and dogs, she said, 'Good night, my little cat.' And it stuck."

Miss Jenny walked over to her and took one of her hands. "My dear, in case you haven't sensed it already, I'm delighted we're going to be family." She leaned over to kiss Cat's cheek. "I hope you're going to be happy to be a McCullough."

"Catherine McCullough." Cat had been trying it on for two weeks. "It still doesn't seem real. Why, I'd never heard of Cougar a month ago. And now I'm going to live here."

Then she cocked her head. "My goodness, I don't even know where we're going to live. We haven't even talked about that." In town? At one of the various houses spread across the ranch?

"At the big house, of course," Miss Jenny said as though there were no other option.

"At the big house?" Live in the same house with Red and Sarah? Not have her own home?

"Where else?" Miss Jenny asked. She glanced in the mirror, too, and after nodding her head, sailed out the front door and down the steps to the jeep.

Cat turned to look and broke into laughter. Dressed as ceremoniously as they were, she was going to her wedding in a jeep. Just then she heard a car approaching and, without having to be told, she guessed it was Red in the Cadillac. He wasn't going to have her arrive for her own wedding in a jeep.

A moment of panic came over her. What in the world was she doing here? She was being thrust into a life she wasn't prepared for, tossed into the lap of luxury in a remote corner of one of the country's least known states, with people unlike any she'd ever met, in a valley named after the wild animal which still roamed these forests.

"Well, you do look lovely." She heard Red's voice from behind her. He was staring at her reflection in the mirror. She turned to face him, and he held out a trailing bouquet of white orchids with lavender centers. "Sarah sent these."

One thing for sure. She certainly was glad this man was going to be her father-in-law. She stretched up to kiss his cheek. He put an arm around her waist and grinned at her. "You up to this?"

"If not now, I never will be."

"Well, then let's get going. The band's tuning up, and we want this over with before the mob descends on us. Chazz and Dodi are here and so're Jason and Sandy. You haven't met her, have you?"

He turned and started out the door. Cat followed him. Miss Jenny was already seated in the Caddy. Red had brought her a corsage, too, for she sported three large white camellias on her shoulder.

Once down at the big house, Cat and Torie were sequestered in Red's office until the strains of the "Wedding March" could be heard. Then, Miss Jenny appeared, smiling, gesturing for them to follow her.

The living room looked beautiful decked with what Cat guessed were all the white, purple, and yellow flowers the Baker florist could order in all of Oregon.

Cat had met the Whitleys when she and Scott had their blood tests in order to apply for the license earlier this week. Chazz Whitley was a thin stoop-shouldered man whose blue eyes always seemed to twinkle and who was in a perpetual state of motion. Though his hair was chestnut, his pencil-thin mustache was flecked with gray. Cat knew that he and his wife, Dodie, had met when he was interning, so he had to be younger than he looked, for Dodie certainly was in her early thirties. Maybe just thirty. Whereas Chazz always seemed to be moving, Dodie had an air of calm about her. No one saw her in anything but shorts all summer and nothing but sweats in winter. If she went to a wedding or funeral, she donned a dress, but she only had two, one black and the other a blue that matched her eyes. She assisted her husband in any emergencies, could sew up a cut, advise what to do for a wound, deliver a baby, prescribe for a sore throat. Since Chazz spent the majority of time in his car making calls as far as forty miles away, Dodie stayed at home to take care of any of the townspeople's ailments. Chazz had office hours ostensibly on Monday, Wednesday, and Thursday mornings, but as often as not, Dodie was the one who took care of you if you dropped in at the office when Chazz was out on an emergency, which is what all the house calls seemed to be. His claim to fame was that he'd dined at nearly every house in the whole county in the five years they'd been here.

Maybe the Whitleys had just been too busy to get around to having a child. They'd been married seven years, and people wondered. Certainly Dodie loved kids. And kids loved Dodie. But then so did adults. She was right up there in popularity with Jason Kilpatrick.

Outside of people, Dodie's particular penchant was flower arranging. She won all the blue ribbons at the county fair every summer. The most any other woman could hope for was second place. So, Sarah had asked her to come arrange the flowers, and Dodie had done herself proud. That the living room didn't look like a funeral parlor with as many flowers as Red had ordered was thanks to Dodie's artistic sense.

The only other people were the Kilpatricks and David and Nan Bollinger. Bollie had not only gone through elementary school with Red here in Cougar and high school in Baker City, but they'd been roommates all four years at the University of Oregon. Their friendship had never wavered. Aside from Scott, Bollie was the most formally dressed man in the room. He wore a three-piece dark blue pin-striped suit and a conservative solid navy tie. He looked like a banker was supposed to look, including an expanding waist as a result of his sedentary life. He was the palest man in the room, the only one whose work kept him indoors. His formal appearance belied his sense of humor. And he was a born raconteur. One could not be in a hurry and do business with First Cascade.

The word that first came to mind when being introduced to his wife Nan was class. She always wore tailored clothes, always, and spent the majority of her waking hours on a horse. She had a stable of horses and spent vast amounts of time and money traveling over the West, and sometimes even to Texas, to enter her horses in shows.

The only woman Cat had not met was seated beside a tow haired seven-year-old boy whom she knew must belong to Jason Kilpatrick. The woman looked fragile, as though she might burst into tears if a harsh word were said to her, and her straight blond hair was cut short.

She wore a white flower in it, behind her ear. She sat apart from the others, on a couch against the wall. The little boy, Cody, was obviously having difficulty sitting still. His bright eyes grew round when he saw Cat enter the room in her long elaborate gown. Torie came before her, marching regally as though there were a church full of guests.

Red, Sarah, and Miss Jenny stood as Cat passed them. She wondered where the music was coming from.

And then all other observances and thoughts left her mind as she focused on Scott and Joseph, waiting for her in front of the minister. Sarah had insisted on the Baptist minister when Red suggested his friend from Baker, Judge Dan Oken.

"Any son of mine is going to be married by a man of God," she'd declared. That ended that discussion.

Scott was indeed handsome. Maybe the best-looking man she'd ever seen out of the movies. His black eyes glittered in his tanned face, and his white teeth shone as he smiled at her. He looked at her as though he'd been waiting for her all his life.

They hadn't made love since Boston, since she'd stayed up at Miss Jenny's all week. Scott had spent much of the daylight hours working so he could take off ten days for a honeymoon. Cat thought he could probably take months off, since he worked with his father. But there was much to do on a ranch in the summer, he'd told her.

At five feet eleven Joseph was dwarfed by Scott, who was the same height as his father. Joseph smiled at her, and she thought it quite the nicest smile in the world. He would be her friend, she could tell that already.

Torie stood to the side, and Cat glided into place next to Scott, who took hold of her arm and turned to face the minister.

Cat didn't hear a word he said, and she certainly hoped he hadn't slipped the word "obey" in there. He'd started to use it in the rehearsal last night, and she said, "I won't marry anyone who insists I obey him. I'd like to delete that word."

The minister looked puzzled.

"It doesn't mean anything," Scott said.

"I don't care," she insisted. "Take that word out."

She hoped he had, for all she could think of was that she was becoming someone else. Mrs. Scott McCullough. Catherine McCullough. Cat McCullough. And that's who she'd be the rest of her life.

Scott's elbow twitched at her arm. She looked at him and could see he was waiting for something. "I do," she said, hoping that was the right place.

Joseph handed Scott the ring. Someone laughed when they heard her gasp out loud. It was a gold band of diamonds and sapphires, designed to match the engagement ring. She thought she hadn't earned that much in all the last year of working.

Scott wore a grin over his whole face as he placed the ring on her finger.

"Oh, my," she whispered.

"That's what you are. Mine," he murmured.

The minister said, "I now pronounce you man and wife," and told Scott, "You may kiss the bride."

Being surrounded by people did not inhibit the way Scott kissed her, long, deep, hungrily.

When they broke apart, her eyes could hardly leave him, but she did have to look at those rings again.

Red clapped his son on the back.

Joseph said, "The best man is the first one who gets to kiss the bride." He kissed her cheek.

Torie threw her arms around Cat, and said, "I've always wanted a sister."

Sarah disappeared.

"I already hear cars coming down the drive," Miss Jenny said, and quickly followed Sarah from the living room.

"Come meet Mrs. McCullough," Jason said to his son.

The boy let his father throw an arm across his shoulder and lead him to Cat.

"I heard that," she said to Cody. "Don't be formal. Call me Cat."

He laughed. "Do people kid you about that name?"

"Sometimes," she smiled at him. "I hope you and I are going to get to know each other better."

"Do you play baseball?" he asked. At that moment Cat wished ardently to tell the boy she did.

"I'm willing to learn," she told him. "If you'll teach me."

"My dad's the best teacher there is." He looked quickly at Scott. "Well, Mr. McCullough's pretty good, too."

Scott just smiled, holding a drink in his hand.

"My dad's the best fisherman around," he said as though he were pretty sure of that statement.

"Well, I hope we're going to be friends," Cat told him as Scott began to edge her away, toward another group of people who were arriving.

By five-thirty there must have been at least five hundred people

gathered on Big Piney's front lawn. Cars and pickups extended down
the long dirt road three-quarters of a mile. The wide front porch had
been cleared of furniture so that dancing could follow the dinner, and
the orchestra—a group of teenagers who had formed their own dance
band and specialized in music from the sixties—was tuning up. She
thought they looked darling, the boys in white dinner jackets and the
girl singer in a long formal apricot-colored dress. There was a carnival
atmosphere, and Cat wondered if this were the biggest blowout the
county had ever seen.

"Cat McCullough," she heard Jason behind her. "This is my wife,
Sandra."

Funny to hear her new name. She smiled at his wife. "I'm already
fond of your husband," she said.

The woman shook her head. "Amazing, isn't it? Everyone seems
to be."

What an odd response, Cat thought, and looked at Jason. His
eyes showed nothing. Not a thing. He and his wife could have been
strangers.

Sandra gazed beyond Cat, and whether she was looking at the
far mountains or into nothingness Cat couldn't tell. She didn't say
anything. Cat decided conversation with Jason's wife was like pulling
teeth.

Finally Jason's wife pulled her eyes back to Cat, and responded,
"I hope you'll be happy here."

Scott grabbed her arm and steered her toward Bollie and his wife.
Nan looked as elegant as Sarah and Torie did.

"We're already being invited to dinner by nearly everyone in town.
I tell them to wait until we come back." He laughed. "We need a
calendar for all the invitations."

"We need a moving van for all the presents," Cat said, gazing at
the gaily wrapped packages that were piled high on seven tables.
When would they have time to open them? They were leaving tonight
on their honeymoon. Scott had told her they'd drive up to Pendleton,
maybe just spend Sunday in bed—he laughed—before driving on to
Montana.

One of the first things she wanted to discuss was where they'd
live. Where to move this mountain of wedding presents to. They hadn't
had time to discuss that any more than they'd spent time making love
this past six days. So, she was not only surprised but shocked when
Sarah took her by the arm, and said, "I'll have your rooms arranged
by the time you return. I thought the ones down at the end of the

hall, the ones with adjoining doors, then it could be like a suite. And you'll have complete privacy. We never have guests anymore."

Cat was too astonished to say anything. Certainly Scott couldn't be planning for them to live in the same house as his parents. They undoubtedly could afford a place of their own. Why her engagement ring alone could buy a house! There were lots of those cute little ranch houses scattered around the Big Piney. Thelma, the cook, and her husband, Tom, lived in the nearest one. Tom, a farrier, spent his days traipsing around the county shoeing horses. The foreman, Glenn Morris, and his wife and three kids lived in another one, out of sight of the big house. Farther out the Basque sheepherders lived, two brothers who were only down from the mountains in the winter. The carpenter and his family lived in another one. Why there must be a dozen houses scattered around the ranch. Surely they could commandeer one of them. Or build one. Or even buy a house in town. She thought she'd like to have neighbors. Certainly she wouldn't countenance living with Scott's parents, no matter how large the house.

Scott grabbed her arm. "Come on, it's time to eat." Cat realized she hadn't eaten since breakfast. She looked down the long tables that looked like a cruise ship's advertisements of luscious meals. Fruits were piled high, and artfully, enormous platters overflowed with barbecued beef and thin slices of pork. Cat was thankful there were no Jell-O or potato salads. It was not a typical country picnic. No money had been spared to make this the event of the year, if not the decade. She imagined that until it was time for Torie to get married, this would go down in Cougar's memory as the wedding to remember. She'd never seen such a splendid spread. The Boise caterers wore tall chef's hats and starched white aprons and red bandannas around their necks.

In the center of the table was a wedding cake at least three feet high, intricately decorated. Scott nodded at it. "Miss Featherly knows how I love chocolate, and I'll bet you dollars to donuts inside it's her rich chocolate cake."

Cat doubted it. "Wedding cakes are always white."

"Wait and see." He prodded her along the table. "Come on. About five hundred people are waiting for you to help yourself so they can begin to eat."

Despite not having eaten for over eleven hours, Cat wasn't hungry and didn't pile her plate high, as Scott did. She was too excited to think of eating.

"Your parents certainly know how to throw a party." She looked around for them and saw Sarah standing on the porch, alone, a glass in her hand, looking out over the lawn at the mass of humanity traipsing across her grass. "Let's go eat with your mother."

Scott followed Cat's gaze and grabbed another fork. "She can eat from my plate."

They walked across the lawn, stopping to accept congratulations. Cat knew she would never remember meeting even a tenth of these people.

"Hey," Scott called to his mother, "come eat with us."

Sarah walked over to the steps. "You shouldn't sit on the stairs in that gown," she told Cat, who went ahead and sat on the top step anyhow, holding the plate balanced on her knees.

Sarah sat in a nearby chair.

"I brought an extra fork so you can help me eat all this," Scott said, handing his mother a fork.

Cat told her mother-in-law, "This is the most beautiful wedding. I appreciate all you've done."

Sarah sipped her drink. "You're a McCullough now." She reached out to slip a small slice of pork onto her fork but let it dangle in the air rather than eating it. "You'll be made aware of that every day for the rest of your life."

Cat blinked and looked at her mother-in-law. Strange thing to say.

She looked out at the crowd and observed Torie talking to Joseph. She was already fond of Torie and wanted to know what this man she loved was like and wondered what their chances for a life together were. It didn't seem fair. She'd known Scott for five weeks and here she was married to him, and Torie had been in love with her Indian for years and they were denied each other. If she were Torie, she'd just pick up and marry him, regardless of their parents' opposition. Move away, if necessary.

Joseph worked for the Forest Service. He could ask for a transfer.

The orchestra began to play just as she and Scott finished eating. He reached out a hand. "Come on. We have to start it," and led her along the porch. The whole veranda had been cleared for dancing. The orchestra played "Chances Are."

Cat moved into Scott's arms, "I didn't know kids today even knew of music like that. That's from our parents' era."

He held her close and kissed her hair. "Well, how do you like being Mrs. McCullough so far?"

"So far, so fine. In fact, I'm pretty impressed. Your mother's done a wonderful job. She's very kind."

"Mother? That's not the word I'd use for her. But I think she likes you. She hasn't approved of any girl I've ever dated, including girls in high school. But she hasn't said a word against you, and I think she's really enjoyed helping Dad and Miss Jenny get ready. She's risen to the occasion."

Risen from where? But Cat didn't ask. More couples were joining them, and there was much laughter.

She danced with more men than she ever remembered meeting later, but she did remember dancing with her father-in-law and with Jason. And the only thing she got to say to Joseph Claypool was, "I hope we'll get to know each other. I've been hearing about you from Torie."

She told Scott, "I like him."

"Everyone likes Joseph, except Mother."

When she cut the wedding cake, Cat discovered Scott had been right. It was the first chocolate wedding cake Cat had ever seen.

It was after ten when Scott tapped her on the shoulder, and said to whomever Cat was dancing with, "Sorry, old man, but we have to get going."

She made sure when she threw the wedding bouquet that Torie caught it. Miss Jenny had already slipped a purple-centered orchid from the bouquet, and whispered, "I'll press this for you to keep forever."

Cat couldn't quite make herself wear jeans, but she did wear a casual green slack suit with a white silk blouse and tan sandals that were but straps across her feet.

She'd thought they'd take the Caddy, but Scott's pickup had been gaily decorated with crêpe paper streamers and tin cans.

Once in the truck, she sank back onto the headrest and let herself relax for the first time all day. She exhaled.

"Tired?" Scott reached for her hand.

"Exhausted," she admitted. "Aren't you?"

"What I am is horny. It's been nearly three goddamn weeks, you know."

"I do know." She closed her eyes. She was too tired to feel a thing, actually.

"Fall asleep if you want," he suggested glancing at her. "It only takes a bit over an hour and a half to get to Pendleton. It's not quite a hundred miles. Just be awake once we get there."

She fell asleep before they'd gone ten miles. The next thing she knew Scott had opened the door and was sliding her into his arms, carrying her from the car to the motel room. She snuggled against him.

"Wake up," he said. "I plan to fuck your brains out."

That awoke her. No one had ever talked to her like that.

He jiggled the key in the lock.

"The bridal suite?" she asked.

He nodded, setting her on the floor and kissing her nose. "I'll get the bags."

Before she'd had time to awaken completely, before she could do more than slip out of her jacket, Scott was dropping his clothes to the floor and ripping the spread off the bed. "Christ," he said, "I have used the most enormous willpower of my life to stay away from you this past week. Come here."

She slipped out of her clothes, leaving them on the floor, and walked toward him. He reached for her, flinging her on the bed and kissing her so that within seconds her body came to life.

"Nobody's ever touched me the way you do."

"It's a damn good thing," he said, kissing her left breast, running his hand across her stomach, down her thighs.

He took his time. Scott McCullough did not rush through lovemaking. He made sure she was as eager as he was, that she was not one of those women who faked orgasms but that she exploded with pleasure seconds before he came.

"You're mine," he grinned, still on top of her. "Mrs. Scott McCullough."

Funny, she'd tried Catherine McCullough, and Cat McCullough on, but not Mrs. Scott. But that's what she'd be known as from now on. That's how the world would think of her.

"You sure are one uninhibited lady," he said, taking her head between his hands and gazing tenderly into her eyes. Her heart melted. "Babe, let it be known, and remember this for the rest of your life. I've never loved anyone like I do you."

Ten

Cat was so scared she clung to Scott, who put a finger to his lips to tell her to be silent as they stared out the tent flap at the big brown bear trying to reach the pack of food he'd tied high to a tree branch.

Afterward, she remembered it as a thrilling moment.

She caught her first fish, which Scott cooked over an open fire, where potatoes, wrapped in aluminum foil, had been baking for nearly two hours.

She hiked, her heart thumping so loudly she was sure it was going to burst, up a mountain trail that made her breathe so hard she had to stop every few minutes. The view, upon reaching the top, was worth every bit of it. Mountain peak after mountain peak stretched into infinity.

They took a two-day trail ride back into country that could be reached no other way, and here she spied elk, deer, bighorn sheep, and her first cougar.

She saw three of the more than fifty glaciers that fed the lakes and rivers. She found making love on an inflated pad over the hard-packed earth addictive.

She felt herself expanding, participating in activities that had been totally alien to her. They canoed on Mary's Lake, staying close to the pine-edged shore so that Cat wouldn't be nervous. Scott was very good that way. They sat for hours by the edge of a little mountain lake and watched various ducks, Scott explaining the difference between mergansers and canvasbacks, astonished that she couldn't identify even mallards and wood ducks.

He taught her how to gather kindling for their nightly fires, telling her that early settlers called it "squaw wood," because the women were sent out to gather it, the narrow, low-hanging branches that they could reach. They gathered it outside the park one afternoon, for it was illegal to cut or break anything within the park's confines.

After a surfeit of lovemaking, they lay looking up at the stars. "I feel at peace with the world," Cat told her husband. "Does this ever have to end?"

Forever after, Cat would be grateful to Scott for introducing her to the wilderness. "I wonder if anyone else has ever had so wonderful a honeymoon."

He just laughed and reached for her hand.

"I'm glad we didn't go to any of the places I would have chosen."

"Me too," he said.

The night before they were to leave, she said, "Can we talk about where we're going to live."

"Sure," he said, roasting a marshmallow on a long stick.

"Well, where? Where are we going to put all those wedding presents?"

"We haven't even opened them."

"It'll take me weeks to write thank-yous," she thought aloud.

When Scott didn't respond, she said, "Can we look at houses when we get back?"

He pulled the charred marshmallow from the fire. "Why, we'll live at home." As though he'd had no other thought.

"But I want *our* home."

"Hon, it'll feel like your home soon, I promise."

"But I want my own things, my own kitchen, my . . ."

"What do you need a kitchen for with Thelma and Roseann around? Hey, you don't even have to make our bed. You don't have to iron or do any of those things women complain about."

That was tempting. But the idea of a home of her own was dear to her heart.

"Ask Mother. Miss Jenny. God, I'd think there are a million things you'll want to do. You won't be bored. You have so much to learn."

She sat up straight, offended.

He leaned over to pat her hand. "I mean you don't know a helluva lot about riding a horse, or doing any of the things done around ranches. I'd think you'd welcome the opportunity to have time to learn all the things you'll need to learn."

She hadn't thought of it that way.

"Look, Mother's been redoing the rooms at the end of the hallway.

It'll be a mile from their rooms. No one'll bother us." He laughed. "No one'll even hear us."

Cat walked over to the creek and watched the water rushing over stones. She wished they'd talked about it before. She didn't want to create a scene on her honeymoon. "I'll try it for a month," she said, not knowing whether or not Scott heard her.

At the end of a month, wild horses couldn't have gotten her to move.

Scott was up and out of the house long before she awoke. She lay in bed looking out the window facing the valley where herds of cattle grazed as far as she could see. In the distance, the Wallowas's jagged snow-covered peaks were the eastern horizon. Someday she'd like to drive over and see them close up.

She was dressed and downstairs for breakfast by eight, but the men were long gone. Thelma had a different breakfast every day. Pancakes with homemade blueberry syrup, waffles with homemade strawberry or raspberry jam. Scrambled eggs and popovers, hot cereal and cinnamon rolls, muffins and omelettes, dutch apple pancakes. Cat had never eaten such breakfasts.

Thelma left at noon Saturdays, leaving a refrigerator full of pre-pared food for Sunday. It was customary for Miss Jenny to arrive Saturday nights, and stay overnight. Cat especially looked forward to weekends, because she enjoyed Miss Jenny so much and usually Torie appeared for Sunday breakfast. Torie was still excited talking about her teaching.

Sarah had turned three rooms at the end of the south hall into an exquisite suite for the newlyweds. A king-size four-poster bed didn't even begin to fill the bedroom that faced out over the mountains. The other room Sarah had furnished with a forest green sofa and two cream-colored armchairs and a small desk with a Tiffany lamp. A TV stood in the corner. The plush carpet was a paler green than the sofa but blended with it marvelously well. The windows overlooked the long, low horse barn and the mountains, which Cat considered in their backyard. The views from any of the windows filled her soul. It was an altogether cozy room.

Next to the bedroom, in the front of the house facing east, was a large bathroom, in which Sarah had installed twin sinks; it looked as though it had been copied from a magazine, maybe *Architectural Digest*.

Cat would never have thought of rust, cream, and dark blue as being bathroom colors, but she was ecstatic over a bathroom so beautiful.

Sarah turned another of the bedrooms over to them, one which was not connected by an adjoining room, and there she placed an exquisite antique desk and needlepointed chair, which she had done herself, and lined one wall with bookcases. It still looked largely empty, but tastefully so.

Cat realized no home she furnished could be so beautiful, but it was not just that which she relished. It was being a part of a family for the first time in over a dozen years. It was being offered new experiences daily, and it was Thelma's marvelous food. It was meeting people each Thursday when Red always invited her to accompany him to town to breakfast at Rocky's with Jason. It was rodeos in La Grande and Pendleton. Though Torie no longer participated in them as she had when a teenager, she and Joseph invited Cat and Scott to accompany them to Enterprise, back up in the heart of the Wallowa Mountains, to a local rodeo in September, and Cat reveled in new scenery. The ride through the little towns that dotted the La Grande and Wallowa Valleys was a pleasure.

Cat liked Joseph. She would not have known he was an Indian if she'd met him in Boston. He told her he'd graduated from Cornell, and he'd enjoyed those years, except for being apart from Torie. They'd used those years as a test. They dated others, and if by some chance they could manage to fall in love with someone else, then they'd satisfy his father's requirements and Sarah's prejudices, but neither of them ever found anyone who threatened the love they shared.

"I'm not sure he's a shaman," Torie said. "He is strange sometimes, not like other guys. But I think that's what I love about him. His father is convinced Joseph inherits the strain that Samuel has inherited from his father and grandfather."

Cat hoped they were at least sleeping together after all this time. Why they would let Mr. Claypool rule them, she couldn't understand, though neither of them seemed unhappy.

"We can tell what each other is thinking by just looking at each other. Finish sentences the other begins . . ."

Scott and Joseph had grown up together. Joseph had an older brother who was a captain in the army, and a younger sister, just a month or two younger than Torie, who was married and lived in Wyoming. In high school Joseph had been captain of the football team and Scott of the basketball team.

In the conventional sense, Joseph was not charming. He was not outgoing, not gregarious, he didn't smile often, yet he emanated a warmth and a genuine interest in whomever he was talking with. There was something different about him, which Cat couldn't quite pinpoint. He was serious yet compassionate; he enjoyed working with kids, teaching them to ride or to play baseball.

Scott said, "If he'd wanted, he could have been pro."

"You didn't want?" Cat asked Joseph.

"It's fun. That's all. No, I want to do something that matters and will benefit people. Baseball would benefit me."

"Is that so awful?" she asked.

"I benefit more when I'm doing something that . . ."

". . . he thinks is larger than himself," Torie finished for him.

"I wouldn't have put it quite that way."

"I know." She smiled at him. Cat was aware of their love and respect for each other every minute they were together. There was something special about their relationship. Much as she was in love with her husband, she and Scott didn't have what his sister had with her Indian. Torie and Joseph together seemed as one.

Despite his quiet manner, Joseph was a leader. Scott told her that in Little League someone called him the Pied Piper. Kids followed him wherever he went; they did whatever he suggested.

He knew the history of the Grande Ronde and Wallowa Valleys, and, as they rode along, he recited it to Cat. The way he told it made it the most exciting story she'd heard, yet he was not dramatic in his telling. This had belonged to the Nez Perce Indians, of which he was one of the remaining less than two thousand.

"It's a tragic story," Torie said.

"Tell me," Cat urged, enjoying listening to him. She'd never heard of the Nez Perce.

Joseph needed little urging. As he drove, he told Cat of Chief Joseph and his tribe.

"This whole Wallowa Valley belonged to the Nez Perce, who were, and still are, famous for their Appaloosa horses. You'll see my father's horses sometime."

"I've heard about them," Cat responded.

"The Indians in this valley at first were friendly with the white man, who first appeared around here in the early 1850s. By 1855 the government offered the Nez Perce a treaty, which the tribe initially refused. They couldn't understand the concept of owning land. All land belonged to all people, but the new white settlers were encroaching, taking over land. The federal government promised the

Nez Perce a large reservation in this part of Oregon and extending into Idaho, promising they would have that land forever. The Indians accepted.

"However, during the Civil War, in the 1860s, gold was discovered around here on reservation land, and the government refused to honor its treaty. It didn't want the Indians to have the gold, so they demanded that the Nez Perce give up this part of the reservation and just keep the land in Idaho. Chief Joseph . . ."

"Joseph? That couldn't have been his name," Cat exclaimed.

"No, his name in his language meant 'thunder coming up from the water over the land,' but the white settlers called him Joseph. It wasn't until 1877, though, that some young rebel warriors killed some whites for what they considered intolerable actions. Chief Joseph was an extraordinary military strategist, and in the war that followed he defeated the larger U.S. forces in numerous battles. However, he saw the handwriting on the wall as the army sent more troops, and in an heroic attempt he led his people over a thousand miles through Idaho and Montana on the way to Canada, where his people would be free.

"But thirty miles from the border the army caught up with him and attacked. The Indians endured a five-day battle before Joseph was forced to surrender. By then most of his warriors were either dead or wounded. His people were starving. He surrendered with the words, 'I will fight no more forever.'

"The army then forced the Nez Perce to walk thousands of miles to the Oklahoma Territory, until only a few hundred Indians were left. They were put on a reservation in country unlike any they had known, and had to live there for six years, at which time they were allowed to return to Idaho, walking all the way. Chief Joseph, however, was not allowed back here in the Wallowa Valley, but he lived another twenty years, dying on a reservation in the state of Washington in 1904."

Cat sighed. "The history of American civilization seems to be man's inhumanity to man, doesn't it?"

"That's the history of the world," said Torie, the history teacher.

"Americans think we're such a compassionate people, reaching out to help various countries of the world, but in reality we've committed horrible crimes against other people. I think enslaving blacks, kidnapping them from their homes in Africa, and what we've done to the Indians is fully as terrible as the Holocaust," Cat said.

Scott took her hand in his. "We generally are nicer to white people, aren't we?" he murmured.

Cat leaned forward in her seat, and asked Joseph, "Well, what are you? Aren't you white? I know, I know, you're supposedly *red*, but it seems to me you and I are the same color. And besides, what has color to do with what's underneath the skin?"

No one answered her as they drove through the small town of Enterprise, on their way to the even smaller village of Joseph, which was nestled at the foot of the mountains she could see from her bedroom window. Cat figured it had to be one of the more remote regions of the whole country. Two little towns completely encircled by mountains.

"It's an arty place," Scott told her as they walked, arm in arm, along the one main street in town. "It's famous for its brass foundries."

This little town of Joseph famous?

As the four of them lunched in a restaurant in the little town where tables stood under umbrellas on a deck that ran along Main Street's sidewalk, Cat asked, "Do you people take all this grandeur for granted?"

All three of them said, "Never."

Cat was content for perhaps the first time in her life.

Eleven

Though she loved days spent in the saddle—and each day she felt more at ease on Chlöe—Cat particularly cherished those afternoons when she rode up to Miss Jenny's and they rode together on the narrow winding trails through the woods. Every day was filled with new experiences. Cat's favorite time of the week was Thursday, when Red took her to Rocky's Cafe for breakfast with him and Jason. She didn't know whether it was because, being a city girl, she relished being with other people or whether she savored the rides themselves and her talks with her father-in-law.

Every Wednesday night Red asked if she wanted to go to town with him the next day. And every week she enthusiastically said yes. With fall in the air she watched the leaves drop from the trees and change to gold and then a pale yellow. There was not the wild abandon, the vibrant reds so dramatic in the East. But that was the only thing where the East had it over the West as far as Cat was concerned.

"I think I was born on the wrong coast," she told Red.

"You're here now. That's what counts."

"I feel like the luckiest person on earth," she said.

"Maybe you are." Red grinned. It was obvious he enjoyed her company as much as she did his. "Except I'd been thinking it was us. You're like a breath of fresh air, you know."

"Did Scott tell you I was upset when he told me we were going to be living at the Big Piney? I wanted a home of my own."

Red cocked his head, taking his eyes from the road to look at her. "And now?"

"Now . . ." She reached over to touch the sleeve of his suede jacket. "Now I am so content it's awesome."

"So, we don't turn you off, huh?" He knew the answer.

"Oh, Red, I just love you all. I don't know what I ever did to deserve you. But I feel a bit guilty. I've never not worked. All this free time to do just as I please."

"So, you're not restless?" He thought he knew the answer to that, too.

Jason was not waiting for them as he usually was, but Ida had saved their front table for them.

"We'll order anyhow." Other days Red breakfasted at sunup, so he was always starved by nine on Thursdays when all he'd allowed himself was coffee at home. "I've a hankering for Rocky's blueberry pancakes."

Cat, who seldom ate large breakfasts, had now become addicted to them, thanks to Thelma and Rocky. "Me too."

Just then Jason entered, not saying hello to anyone as he wound his way across the room to Red and Cat.

"Trouble?" Red asked.

Jason sat down, slouched in his seat, pushed his hat back on his head, nodded to Ida when she placed coffee in front of him, and said, without preamble, "Sandy's gone."

Red pulled at his mustache. "What do you mean gone?"

"She's left Cody and me."

Cat didn't know what to say. She knew Jason wasn't talking to her.

Red stirred his coffee and looked Jason in the eyes. "For good, you mean?"

"That's what she says."

Another silence.

"How are you feeling?"

Jason scrunched up his face. "The funny thing is I don't feel anything."

"How can a woman leave her child?" Cat asked.

For the first time Jason looked at her.

"She's never liked it here." Not that that answered her question.

Cat wondered whether Jason had volunteered to leave Cougar in order to preserve the marriage. But there must be more to it than where they lived. Millions of women moved to wherever their husbands' jobs took them and adapted, maybe not gracefully or happily, but at least they made a valiant effort. She wondered if Sandy had. She'd only formed a fleeting impression of her at the wedding. Pale. Fragile. She'd looked out of place then. Maybe unhappy.

"Where's she gone to?" Red asked as Jason ordered French toast.

Jason shrugged. "Back to Seattle, but she thought she might head to California, San Francisco maybe."

Neither Red nor Cat said anything. Cat couldn't figure whether or not Jason was crushed. He was solemn, but she didn't know what else.

"How's Cody taking it?" she asked.

A half smile flitted across Jason's face. "So far, so good. He said, 'Well us men are just going to have to batch it, Dad.' Where he ever got something like that I've no idea."

"How are you going 'to batch it'?" Red asked.

Jason cocked his head to the side and began to pick at his breakfast. So, Cat thought, he *is* affected more than he shows. "At least I know how to cook. I've been doing most of that all along."

"Anything you need, let me know. Including talking."

"I know that." For a minute Cat almost thought Jason was going to reach across the table and touch Red's hand. "Aside from Chazz and Dodi you're the first one I've told. She just left at three yesterday. Told me at lunchtime when I was home. She was gone by the time Cody got home from school. Didn't even say good-bye to him."

"Oh, my God," Cat heard herself say.

Red looked at Jason quizzically. "You going to be able to handle this?"

"In a way it's a relief. I woke up this morning and you know what? For the first time in as long as I can remember, there was no tension in the house." With his last piece of toast, Jason scooped up the maple syrup on his plate.

Ida appeared with coffee for the three of them.

"You look awful, Sheriff," she said.

"Thanks, Ida."

"What's wrong?"

Cat wondered if Jason was going to spill his guts. He did answer truthfully. "Sandy's left. For good."

"Oh, I'm sorry, Jason." She put a hand on his shoulder. "No one'll be sorry, you know. She wasn't half good enough for you."

Ida started to walk away with the glass carafe in her hand before turning around to say, "You know, Katie Thompson's thinkin' of going to Portland to her daughter's now that Fred died. She doesn't want to, but can't afford to keep up her home. She might be interested in housekeeping for you and the boy. Might even be cheap if you could give her a room. What about that space above your garage? You could make that over."

Jason burst out laughing. "See," he observed to Cat, "something like this would never happen in Seattle. Here, everyone's going to try to look out for me." He smiled up at Ida. "I don't know what I'm going to do yet, it's too soon. But that's not a bad idea at all."

"She's a real good cook," Ida went on. " 'Course I don't know if she'd cotton to the idea, but it's there anyhow." Her sharp chin jutted out as though to inform Jason it was a damned good idea whether he did anything about it or not. "You fix over that space above the garage and put a satellite in there, why she'd love to stay around here, and she'd be out of your hair nights. You and Cody can raise cain, and she wouldn't even know. On the other hand, you want to go out on the town nights, she could baby-sit."

Red was laughing. "I couldn't come up with anything near that good, Jason."

Jason rubbed his chin. "I could probably afford her. Sandy said she didn't want alimony. Didn't want anything."

Including her own son, Cat thought. She glanced out the window. A pickup had just drawn up in front of Rocky's and a young man in overalls and a straw Stetson jumped out and went around to the back of his truck. He picked up a tan-and-white furry ball and held it high. She could tell he was shouting something, but couldn't hear what.

She nodded toward him. "Look," she said.

"That's Jeb Smart," Jason said. "Heard tell his collie had a litter awhile back. He's in town trying to make some money from them."

"Just look." Cat's heart had already leapt through the window. She pushed her chair back and stood up. "I'll be right back."

There were seven pups in a box in the back of the pickup. The mother sat in the passenger's seat up front. "Hey," said Jeb Smart when Cat peered over the side at the little dogs. "You're Scott's wife. I came to your wedding, betcha don't even remember."

Cat's eyes didn't leave the puppies. "May I pick one up?"

"Hell, you can pick 'em all up." A blade of grass stuck out of the farmer's mouth.

The ball of fur cuddled into her, but the one who really caught her attention was the most rambunctious. He looked at her and tried to climb out of the box, practically wiggling out of his skin. She reached for the pup and heard Red's voice beside her. "Now, if I ever saw love on anyone's face, this is it. I don't think a woman ever looked at me that way."

The puppy bit her finger gently, then tried to crawl onto her shoulder.

"Just look, Red."

Red, looking at the puppy, asked, "How much, Jeb?"

Cat gazed up into his eyes. "Are you going to? Really? Let me run in and ask Jason if it's all right."

Red fished twenty-five dollars from his pocket, and said, "I thought you wanted this for yourself."

Cat reached up and threw her left arm around Red's neck and kissed him. "Oh, you wonderful man."

Jeb said, "Hey, Red, it'd be worth it to buy the rest."

"It would at that." Red laughed. "In fact, I will buy another. She seemed so in love with them. Let her choose it when she comes back."

Cat and Jason emerged from Rocky's, Cat pulling Jason by the arm.

"This would give Cody something to love," she said, picking up the pup and holding it toward Jason.

He raised his eyebrows and glanced at her before taking the puppy.

"Sandy never wanted a dog in the house. Cats, yeah, but no dog."

"Red's paying for it. But not if you'd rather not, if it's just one more thing . . ."

"It's perfect. Not just for Cody either. I've found it hard to live without a dog all these years," Jason said, nuzzling the little dog. "Sure, Cat, it's wonderful."

Red winked at Jeb and nodded his head toward the rest of the puppies in the pickup. "What one would *you* like?"

Cat glanced up at him, not sure she understood his meaning. "You mean for me?"

"Mm."

Her eyes lit with pleasure. "Oh, Red, really? You dear man!" She leaned over to study them and chose one who wouldn't leave her fingers alone, whose tail waggled with delight just looking at her.

The puppy curled into her as they drove to the Farmer's Co-op and bought Purina Puppy Chow and a black collar and leash.

"She looks like the color of brandy," Red commented.

"That's it. That's her name. Brandy."

Red told Clark at the cash register to charge the items.

As they drove back through town, Cat said, "Will you stop just a minute, Red?" and leaving the puppy with him she dashed into the sheriff's office. Jason was on the phone. When he saw her rush in, he ended the conversation and looked at her questioningly. "Jason, I'm ashamed of myself. Here you are in pain and needing some comfort, and I rushed out like that. I sort of couldn't help myself. But I want you to know my heart's going out to you as much as to that puppy. If you'd like to talk, though I know you don't know me that well, or if I can do anything to help with Cody . . . well . . ."

"Hey, Cat, that's real nice of you. But you know right now I'm not in pain. Maybe a bit bewildered. Maybe I'll feel some pain later, but right now . . ."

She reached across his desk to touch his arm. "I'm sorry, Jason. If you're unhappy in any way, I'm very sorry. Why don't you and Cody come out to the ranch for dinner tomorrow night?" It was the first time she'd invited anyone. She didn't know if it was her place to, but she was sure no one would mind. They'd all want to help Jason in this time of trouble. Whether he thought he was upset or not, he looked sad. "Bring your puppy, and they can play together."

The sheriff smiled at her. "Cody'll go wild over it." Jason had already put it in a box next to his desk. "Sure, we'd love to come out."

"We dine . . ."

"I know. I've been out there often enough. Six-thirty with drinks at 5:45."

"Goodness, I'll have to do something about all that regimentation. The same hour every night?"

"Night after night after year . . ."

"Okay, Jason, but next time it'll be at least a little before or after. I can't live with a time clock like that."

"Good luck."

As Cat turned to go, Jason said, "Lucky man, Scott."

She turned to dazzle him with her smile. "Why, thank you, Jason."

When she told Red what she'd done, he patted her shoulder. "Catherine McCullough, I can't tell you how glad I am you've become a McCullough. I never dreamed my son would luck out with someone like you."

She beamed and kissed the puppy's head.

"But then I never knew there was anyone like you around."

"Go on!" She laughed and felt marvelously happy.

Sarah took one look at the puppy and declared it was not welcome in the house.

Cat, having lived in cities all her life, never dreamed that a dog would not be welcome indoors. All the way home she had envisioned the dog sleeping at the foot the king-size bed. But such was not to be.

So Red and Cat arranged a bed for Brandy in the horse barn, on an old horse blanket, in one of the stalls where she would be safe.

"We used to have several dogs around here as the kids were growing up," Red said. "Frankly, I think it's pretty difficult to live without a dog, but once the kids grew up and when they were both away at college, Sarah talked me into not replacing them when they died. It's seemed sort of lonely around here without dogs."

"If they were never in the house, why did Sarah mind?"

"Torie was always sneaking them in. Sarah just doesn't like animals."

"Then this is a fine place for her to live!"

Red looked at Cat, whose eyes were devouring the puppy, who was gobbling puppy chow.

"We forgot to get bowls," Cat said.

"Next time."

"If you'll let me use one of the cars, I'll drive in town tomorrow and get some."

"Of course. But, I don't *let* you use cars. You're a McCullough now. Use any whenever you want. We always leave the keys in them."

Scott used his pickup to drive out to wherever they might be working that day. Cat didn't quite dare ask for the Caddy or the Lincoln. But she guessed she could. They just seemed so big for one person to drive into town.

When she showed Brandy to Scott and bemoaned having to keep a puppy in the barn, he grinned. "We'll get around that. Mother doesn't even know what goes on at our end of the house. I'll fix up a box, don't you worry about it. We'll leave it in the barn til after dinner. She goes up to bed early anyhow."

She threw her arms around him.

"You know," she told Scott while they were undressing for bed that night, "the smartest thing I've ever done in my life is marry you."

"Yeah, I know it." He grinned.

They'd made love every night, and often days, in the seven weeks they'd been married. Weekends, when Scott would take her to see mountain lakes, they'd find a sequestered place under tall trees and make love there or in a hayfield. Or even in the barn, when the added threat of discovery added fillip to it. There wasn't a part of her body that Scott didn't know. Now, just seeing him take off his shirt excited Cat. She loved his body.

"It's not just you," she said, slipping her blouse off and hanging it in the closet. Scott just dropped his clothes on the floor, sure that someone would pick them up and miraculously wash and iron them and put them in the closet for him. "Your family has become mine."

"C'mere," he said as he lay down on the bed, reaching an arm out for her.

She walked toward him. "I still feel like I'm on a honeymoon," she said as she stretched the length of her body on his.

"Let's make a baby," he said, kissing her breasts.

"I wouldn't mind. I think I'd like a dozen of them. I'm twenty-six. We better get started."

"Hey"—he bit her but gently—"trying's going to be more than half the fun. Come on," he murmured, stroking her belly.

"I can't think of anything more wonderful than having part of you growing inside me."

He rolled her over, his mouth sliding down her belly, his tongue running up her thighs.

"I'm ready."

His voice was muffled as he said, "Babe, ready or not . . ."

Twelve

It wasn't as pleasant to be outdoors now that winter was approaching. Scott had always been home by midafternoon and, while it was still warm, had taken her riding, or into Baker, or hiking wilderness trails. She had never had such a physical lifestyle. Whereas in August it had been difficult for her, by the end of October she was in much better shape and was able to follow where Scott led without having difficulty with her breathing.

She spent several mornings a week up at Miss Jenny's, where the older woman taught her to bake bread.

Cat suggested again that Miss Jenny get a computer. It would make keeping the books so much simpler.

"I'm too old to learn something that complicated."

"Nonsense. You have as sharp a mind as I've seen."

"I wouldn't even know what to get or how to start."

Cat made a face. "Come on, Miss Jenny. You have me. I don't know how good a teacher I'd be, but it'd be fun. I'd love it."

Maybe Miss Jenny and Red didn't want her to know the state of their finances. After all, she was a newcomer to the family.

"A computer could help the whole ranch operation, really. There are programs that benefit a farmer and rancher ..."

Miss Jenny peered at her.

"And you could do all that?"

"Sure. Actually I'm sort of addicted to the damn things and rather miss having one."

Miss Jenny seemed to be thinking. "We'd have to go to Portland to look at some."

Cat shook her head. "We'd buy one of the best ones by mail. I'm partial to Dell. You can only buy them by mail. They're marvelous. I know just what I'd get. A 486 with a six-speed CD-ROM and a . . ."

"Whoa!" Miss Jenny reached out an arm as though to stop Cat. "You're talking Greek to me."

"I admit they're sort of intimidating at first, but soon you'll wonder how in the world you got along without one."

"You really think someone my age . . ."

"Don't give me that." Cat walked over to the stove and poured herself a cup of cold coffee, zapping it for a minute in the microwave. "Your mind is razor-sharp."

Miss Jenny smiled. "I've always thought so, too."

"Is it okay if I talk to Red about it?"

Miss Jenny shrugged, her eyes reflecting interest in something new that would be a demanding challenge for her. "If you really think I could . . ."

"Okay, I'll talk to him tonight."

As Red, Sarah, Cat, and Scott sat around the fire that evening, having cocktails before dinner, Cat said, "I was up at Miss Jenny's today, and we got to talking computers."

Scott laughed, but Red looked interested.

"And?" he prodded.

"Well, she spends so much time keeping the books by hand. I could show her how to do it more easily and without as much chance of error. I'd think she'd enjoy the challenge. There are programs that could benefit you as ranchers, too."

"Like what?" Scott asked.

"Well, I'm not sure of the exact ones, but I got to thinking that maybe I could go over to the state university and they'd know about computer programs for us. Certainly the agriculture college in Corvallis would be up on something like that."

When the men seemed hesitant, Cat said, "I mean, if you'd rather I didn't get involved with the financial end, I don't have to know everything. I can teach Miss Jenny without knowing what you'd rather I didn't."

Sarah stood up and walked over to the tray which held the liquor and poured herself a shot of whiskey, straight. "I don't know a thing about the finances, and I've lived here twenty-seven years."

"That's because you've never wanted to know," her husband said, not looking at her but gazing into the fire.

"Money matters aren't a woman's province," Sarah said. "I remember my father saying that when I just couldn't learn math."

Cat protested, "I'm not much good in math either. I'm a failure at anything with arithmetic without a calculator. But you don't have to be mechanical to learn computer programs. You do have to study and learn."

Scott laughed. "See, Dad, tell me my taste in women isn't terrific."

"If your grandmother can learn it, so can you," Cat said.

"If you and my grandmother are going to learn it, I guess I don't have to."

Thelma appeared to announce dinner.

Cat couldn't sleep. She tossed and turned and realized she shouldn't have drunk coffee after dinner. Even late-night coffee had never bothered her before, but lately caffeine after midafternoon kept her awake until long after midnight. Maybe hot milk or cocoa would help. She slid out of bed and found herself staring out the window at snowflakes she could see even in the dark.

She threw a robe over her nightgown and tiptoed down the hall and stairway.

The light was on in the kitchen, and Red was sitting at the kitchen table, cup in hand.

"What are you doing up at this hour?"

Instead of answering her, he said, "There's hot cider on the stove."

She poured herself some cider and came to sit opposite him. "It's snowing," she said. "I don't even have any winter boots."

"What time is it, anyway?"

"One-thirty. I don't know why I couldn't sleep."

"Full moon," Red said. "I notice that influences me."

"Are you serious?"

He nodded. "Better go get yourself some boots tomorrow. That is, if the road's not too icy."

Cat suddenly realized she must look a mess. "It's not fair," she commented. "Men can wake up in the middle of the night and their hair isn't mussed, and they don't look wan for lack of makeup . . ."

"I didn't just wake up. I haven't been asleep yet."

"Oh?"

He made no response, but stood up and took his glass over to the counter and said, "I'll go upstairs now. Turn the light off." He patted her shoulder.

She sat finishing her hot cider, wondering what had kept him awake until such an hour. When she crept silently into her bedroom, tossing her robe on a chair, and slid between the covers, Scott didn't move. Cat lay there, staring into the darkness, wondering if Sarah lay awake at night wondering why Red hadn't come to bed.

Why did Red sit up until one-thirty in the morning, hours after everyone else had gone to bed?

Ranch work came to a halt, barring an emergency, at noon on Saturdays, and Scott roared in for lunch. While the weather was still good, he and Cat took off in his pickup. At the ski resort he took her up in the gondola that skiers used in the winter, and one weekend they drove all the way over to the coast, four hundred miles west. They found a motel that had a Jacuzzi and luxuriated in that while listening to the ocean waves break on the shore just feet away from them. They walked down the beach, holding hands and waded in the frigid water. "We'll come whale watching next spring," he told her, taking pleasure in her delight in everything.

They didn't get home until midnight, but Scott was already gone by the time Cat awoke at seven Monday.

Sarah sometimes amused herself by tole painting. She never had to worry about housekeeping, for Thelma oversaw the maid who came in five mornings a week. Thelma had been in the Big Piney kitchen since before Red got married, and she knew the family's tastes. She had an old pickup and went into town weekly to grocery shop; she kept the pantry and two enormous freezers filled. She seemed to enjoy Cat's company.

It seemed to Cat that Sarah had abnegated any duties in life though she always fitted around, too busy to enter into conversation until late in the afternoon, when she settled in by the fireplace, a glass in one hand and a book in the other. Her books were always old classics.

However, she did look forward to accompanying Miss Jenny and Cat on the annual Christmas shopping pilgrimage to Portland the week after Thanksgiving. Cat wondered why they hadn't chosen a weekend so that Torie could accompany them, for she scarcely saw her sister-in-law. She volunteered to do the driving, to the relief of Sarah and the pleasure of Miss Jenny, who sat in front with her.

Miss Jenny booked rooms at the Benson, Portland's oldest luxury hotel, and they spent three days in the city, enjoying the restaurants, the crowds, seeing movies each evening, which seemed to give Sarah the greatest pleasure. Cat realized how deprived she herself had felt at not seeing movies regularly. She'd have to talk Scott into driving to Pendleton now and then for dinner and a movie. Maybe even on a Sunday afternoon. That would be a nice thing to do on a winter weekend.

Cat purchased far more than she'd planned to. It was quite exciting, buying things for her new family. The whole trip exhilarated her. Hardest to shop for were the guests who would be coming to Christmas dinner. She didn't know them well enough. She bought Jason a soft wool scarf from Scotland, and wondered what in the world to get Cody. She knew so little about seven-year-old boys. Would he like clothes, or would he rather have something to play with?

They returned to the Big Piney before dark on Thursday, the trunk and part of the backseat piled high with boxes and bags. Cat knew she'd enjoyed wrapping the presents in gaily colored paper. She wondered when Scott would be free to buy her a gift and what he'd give her. She'd spent hours looking and thinking before purchasing a camera for him. She had no idea if he had one, but she'd seen no evidence of it. What did you get a man who had everything? She hoped he'd like it.

Scott promised not to peek into any of the boxes she piled in a corner of their sitting room.

On Friday Cat drove the Caddy into town to do some errands. She also wanted to see Torie, have more connection with her sister-in-law than she seemed to have.

Torie seemed delighted to see her, throwing her arms around Cat. "I don't know why we haven't gotten together more before this, except I always seem so busy. We should do more things together on Saturday nights."

Torie poured Cokes. "Should have offered you coffee in this weather. Brr. I hope snow holds off til after Christmas, or I may not get out to the ranch."

They had chatted for an hour when Cat noticed it was beginning to get dark. As she stood, readying to go, they heard a key in the lock, and Joseph Claypool walked in. *My God, he is good-looking,* Cat thought. Not in the way Scott was, but his finely chiseled cheekbones and his sensuous mouth were riveting. Cat imagined wherever he walked people turned to look at him.

So, he had a key.

He reached out both hands as he approached her. "How nice to see you. You're leaving just as I arrive?"

"I have a couple of errands to do, and it's already getting dark."

*   *   *

As she headed home in the twilight she saw a light still on in Jason's office. She pulled up in front and jumped out of the car.

"Just thought I'd say hi as I'm passing by," she said, sticking her head into the office.

He waved her in. "Good. I'm in the doldrums, and I don't know why. How about a cup of coffee?"

"Let me phone home and tell them I'll be late." They'd soon be gathering around the fire for drinks.

He picked up the phone and held it out, but as she started to take off her gloves, he dialed the number for her.

Red answered. She told him it would probably be another hour and a half before she got home.

"Thanks, Cat," Jason said.

They walked across the street to Rocky's, which was beginning to fill with the dinner crowd, though that never equaled the number who came in mornings.

Cat didn't even know the waitress who was on the evening shift.

"Just coffees," Jason told her.

"I think it's the longer days. I get gloomy when it's dark."

"Would you like to talk about her?"

He raised his eyebrows. "Sandy, you mean?"

"If it would help. You're keeping it bottled up unless you have someone to talk to."

"I talk to Torie now and then."

Cat reached out and put a hand over his. "Why don't you tell me about your marriage, Jason."

"You said you'd be home soon. It would take longer than that."

"Well, how about making a date to talk it over. I bet I'm one of the best free shrinks around. I'm a good listener, Jason. I've been thinking that though I really don't know you that well, you're keeping a lot inside. It's not just the early darkness, I bet it's loneliness."

"Cat, I was lonelier when I was married . . ."

"Yeah, yeah, you said that. Okay, Jason, let's make a date to talk." She glanced around the restaurant. "And not with so many people around."

Their coffee arrived. Jason leaned back in his chair and studied Cat. "You're serious, aren't you?"

She didn't say anything.

After a minute Jason said, "I have to drive over to Ukiah tomorrow. I'll buy you lunch if you'll come along."

"It's a date," she said.

They had waited dinner for her. Thelma said she didn't mind. "It's not like it was soufflé or something."

While they devoured Thelma's meat loaf with mustard sauce, Cat told them she was going to drive to Ukiah with Jason in the morning. She didn't see Red and Scott smile at each other across the table, over her head.

Thirteen

Jason started to light up a cigar.

Cat said, "Sorry, Jason. But it's either me or that."

Jason made a face. "How come none of the women I know like cigar smoke?"

Cat left the question unanswered, but Jason put the cigar back in his pocket.

He was driving with one hand on the wheel, having chosen to take the back road, which was considerably shorter. The sky was pewter, filled with rolling clouds. Jason predicted snow by nightfall.

"After all, it *is* December," he said.

They were quiet for a while until Cat said, "I came along to listen, you know."

Jason nodded. "I don't know where to start."

"How about when you met Sandy. At the very beginning."

"Okay." Jason nodded. "I'd been out of college a couple of years. I'd toyed with going on to law school, but we didn't really have that kind of money. I didn't know whether I really wanted another three years of school, anyhow. So, while I was considering it I joined the Seattle police force. I'd grown up in the little town of Anacortes, a couple of hours north of the city, but I'd gone to U. Washington, so I was familiar with Seattle.

"I met Sandy at a party. One of the guys I worked with had been telling me about her. She was a friend of his sister's. She was lovely then. Quiet, and sort of unreachable, but somehow that seemed mysterious and appealing. She never gave of herself, so I guess I felt challenged. I was young and didn't realize the havoc that could create. She liked to do the same things I did. We'd hike into the Olympics or take the San Juan ferry weekends. She got me into cross-country skiing, and I got her into kayaking. I thought we had so much in common that I never realized we hardly ever talked, I mean really talked about anything other than mountain trails and health foods and where we'd go hiking that weekend. I thought here was a woman who shared all the things I liked."

"Were you in love with her?"

"I thought so, though—I hope this doesn't embarrass you—it wasn't really physical. When I'd put my arms around her it was almost as though she wasn't there. I'd kiss her, and I wondered if I was the first person to kiss her, she was so inexperienced, so lacking in knowing what to do. Kissing, being held, seemed to embarrass her. I should have had an inkling then. Instead, for reasons that now escape me, unless I was just ready to get married and I'd been spending all my weekends doing things with her, I asked her to marry me.

"She didn't say yes right away. When she did, she said, 'My mother thinks you're the best thing to ever happen to me. My father likes you, too. So, yes, I'll marry you.'"

"She never said she loved you?"

"Never." He was quiet for a minute, staring at the road, but Cat was sure that wasn't what he was seeing. "My mother, however, warned me. She told me I was going to give more than I'd receive. I didn't even understand what she meant by that. I think now that because I was always giving to Sandy, I thought that was love. I wanted to protect her, keep her from harm, bring her out of whatever shell she sometimes seemed to be in.

"You'll find it hard to believe in this day and age, but we hadn't made love when I proposed to her. We began to after she said okay to marriage. She'd never been to bed with a man, so I thought her lack of enthusiasm was due to self-consciousness and that my powers of lovemaking would waken her libido or something. It didn't.

"She conceived about a week before we got married. Sandy enjoyed her pregnancy. It was as though nothing else existed. All her focus was centered on the child growing inside her.

"I was pretty happy. I thought I was lucky to have a marriage where my wife was waiting for me when I came home from work, a good meal prepared, and we were expecting a baby. Once in a while I have to admit I felt guilty to find myself bored, because Sandy and I never talked of anything else. She didn't want to read, and when I'd read something that I thought would be fun to discuss, her eyes became unfocused, and I knew she was off somewhere else, certainly not with me, even though her body was.

"When Cody was born, Sandy had to be the best mother there ever was. But she wasn't a great wife. When I showed any physical interest in her it was as though she suffered it, and more often than not just pushed me away. So much for my powers of lovemaking. It wasn't a great time for my ego. I told myself, however, that after Cody was a year old she'd pay attention to me. But she never did. We still hiked weekends when the weather was good, and I carried Cody on my back like a papoose. But we didn't kayak and ski anymore, because Sandy wouldn't leave Cody."

"Did you resent him?"

Jason shook his head. "Not for a minute. And, in fact, I thought Sandy was a perfect mother, but I did yearn for closeness, physical and mental. I missed that. Looking back I realize I'd never had that with her, but you know the old saying, love is blind, and I hadn't realized it. I sure felt thwarted, though, and I knew something was lacking in our marriage, but I only see it objectively in retrospect.

"Then, one day I got a sore throat and felt so miserable, I left work about three and came home."

He stopped talking for a minute, and when he resumed, his voice was choked up. "At first I thought no one was home, but as I went up the stairs I heard murmurings from the bedroom. When I opened the door, Sandy was naked, and making love with someone who was moaning with ecstasy. I couldn't move. Neither of them heard me. And I suddenly realized the person underneath her was another woman."

For a minute Cat wouldn't speak. Finally, she said, "Oh, my God." She reached out to touch Jason's arm. He nodded.

"You haven't gotten over that yet, have you?"

He sighed heavily. "Yes, I think I have. In fact, a long time ago." They drove in silence for a while.

"It shattered me for months. Sandy claimed she loved me as much as she could love any man, but she'd always been attracted to women. She knew that her lesbian tendencies would dismay her parents, and she begged me not to leave her. But I told her I couldn't live like that. I urged her to go to counseling, and she agreed. We went together a number of times, and it sure made me feel like shit to learn that when I touched her she cringed inside." His laugh was not pleasant. "So much for my macho image."

"Oh, Jason," Cat said, her hand on his arm. "You must know that it wasn't *you*. It was just any man."

"Sure, my head knows that, but inside I was torn to pieces. I started drinking too much. Going to a bar with some of my friends instead of going home after work. At the same time, Sandy seemed to lose interest in Cody. Poor kid. It took me a couple of months to realize that. That made me sit up, I can tell you. I started coming home and stopped drinking and just then I heard about this job. I thought moving away from the city would help. Give us a new start. Be good for Cody to be out of a city, to be in a small town where everyone knows everyone.

"I came out for an interview and they offered me the job ten days later. I told Sandy that Cody and I were coming, and I hoped she would, too.

"It took her a couple of weeks to decide, during which she saw her counselor daily. She didn't want her parents to know about any of it, of course."

"It must have been a time of great strain for all of you."

Jason didn't say anything. After another five miles, he resumed his story. "The change in Cody once we moved here was evident. He was three, and we moved into a house that had a four-year-old on one side and two-and-a-half-year-old twins on the other. It was summer, and he was outdoors with his friends all day. From the day I moved to Cougar, I've loved it. It felt like coming home. I don't ever want to live anyplace else. I want to spend my life here. And I do think Sandy tried. When people invited us to dinner, I think she tried, but she just couldn't hack it. She knew within a week that a small town like this would reject her if they knew the real her. Back in Seattle, thanks to counseling, she had tried to enjoy lovemaking, but it was so obvious that it was an effort I just stopped trying.

"When there was a social event in town, she'd get a headache at the last minute or some gastric upset. They might even have been real. When I'd try to talk to her about it, she'd say, 'I'm nobody but the sheriff's wife.' I tried to tell her with a little effort she could be more, could be her own person, and she'd say, 'Not in this redneck town.' Cody never brought kids home, but would have lemonade and cookies or whatever at the homes of the neighbor kids. Sandy wouldn't get together with other mothers."

"Sounds to me like you would have wanted her to leave."

Jason shrugged. "I think now maybe that idea was there, sitting, not letting myself think it consciously. I was enjoying my job so much and the town and . . . I was getting closer to Cody than other fathers seemed to, because I was assuming Sandy's role, too. She just seemed to retire behind some wall she built around herself. The only time she came out of it was when we'd go visit her parents on my vacation. She wouldn't come out and hike in the woods like we used to. She lost weight. I didn't know what to do. I contacted her shrink, but got no satisfaction there.

"And then the day before she left I came home and there she was again, in bed with a woman. I don't know who she was, she wasn't from here, and I doubt from Baker. I think Sandy wanted me to discover them, or she wouldn't have been doing it in our home.

"Before I could say anything, she pounced on me as though I were at fault, telling me she hated this goddamned town that was stifling her, I was extinguishing her desire to live, Cody imprisoned her and kept her from freedom. She screamed at me that she couldn't stand to have me touch her, which seemed irrelevant as we hadn't made love in well over a year. Hadn't touched each other, even. So, as calmly as I could, I suggested she leave. That it was about time she told her parents the truth so that she could be free to live whatever life she wanted.

"She just stared at me and began to cry, 'I can't help myself.' I knew that. But being married to her had made my life a hell for longer than I care to remember. I needed more than I got from her. I needed something. You know what? I kept expecting something more so I was always disappointed. Crushed, even. Alone, I don't expect anything, so I'm pretty happy most of the time. Not fulfilled, mind you. I'd love a home, warmth, someone to share my life with. But just Cody and I make for far more contentment than I'd known the years Sandy and I lived together."

They pulled into Ukiah, in front of a one-story building that needed paint. Jason stopped, and said, "I'm going to be gone about half an hour to an hour. There's a restaurant over there if you want a Coke or something. I'll buy you lunch when I'm through."

Cat nodded. She was emotionally drained from listening to Jason. Such a fine man to have been denied so much.

She was starving, yet she felt slightly queasy. She crossed to the restaurant and ordered a Coke. No one else was there at eleven in the morning.

How awful for Jason . . . such a warm-hearted man to have been denied love and affection. No one would ever know from his actions. No wonder he seemed glum yesterday. No one to laugh with, no one to share the day with, no one to touch.

She knew there was no advice she could give. He just needed to talk.

That night Cat told Scott Jason's story. When she finished she said, "Why don't we go up to Pendleton for dinner and a movie Saturday and invite Jason. He's lonely."

Scott was always ready to do something. He nodded agreeably, and said, "Good idea, hon. Know what's playing?"

Cat shook her head. "There's got to be at least one movie we wouldn't mind seeing." She wouldn't mind seeing *Little Women*, but she knew she couldn't drag Scott to that.

"Hey, Cat," Jason said when she phoned him. "You're just taking pity on me, but it sounds great."

"We can have an early dinner and catch the seven o'clock show. I'd say to bring Cody, but I haven't the foggiest what movie is showing."

"He's going to sleep over at Jerry's anyhow. I was going to be all alone."

While Scott and Sarah watched TV, Sarah with the ubiquitous drink in her hand, Cat wandered into Red's office. He was sitting in a high wing chair, a book on his lap, the dying embers of a fire fizzling in the fireplace.

"Mind if I sit down?" She didn't wait for an answer. "I have an idea I'd like to discuss with you."

He cocked his head as though waiting, his eyebrows raised.

"Last week we were discussing Miss Jenny's learning to keep the books on a computer. I'd love to get her one for Christmas. What do you think?"

He made a sound that was a mixture between a laugh and a cough. "Pretty extravagant, isn't it?"

"I have money," she said. "I was a working woman."

"Actually, ever since you mentioned a computer a couple of months ago I've been thinking it might be a good idea for both of us to learn. I wouldn't even know what to look for though."

Cat was pleased not to be getting an argument from him. "I know exactly what I'd want. I thought of asking Dodie if we could have it delivered there so no one'll see it arrive. Probably FedEx or UPS. I'd just love to do it. And I'll be pleased as punch to teach you as well as her. I really think anybody who's in business can save hours and get much more information in the electronic age. Do you have a stock portfolio?" She hesitated, "Not that it's any of my business."

"Of course I have a portfolio."

"We can get daily stock reports. We can . . ."

"You don't have to talk me into it. I think it's a fine idea. But how about going half and half. I hadn't come up with anything for Mother, and this'll benefit me as much as her. I'm willing to try it too."

Cat looked at him, and his eyes met hers. "Red, would you like to come to the movies with us tomorrow night. You and Sarah?" They never seemed to go anywhere.

His eyes lit up. "That's a nice thought. Can I come even if she won't?"

"She won't come, will she? Well, Jason's coming, too. I have to tell you I can't think of a more enviable position than being accompanied by three men such as you, Scott, and Jason."

"I suspect you're making all our lives happier."

She smiled at him. "What a nice thing to say."

"At least you're lighting up my life."

Before she left the room she leaned over to kiss the top of his head. He grabbed her hand and pressed it.

Sandy and Sarah had rocks in their heads not to appreciate Jason and Red.

At least she appreciated Scott . . . madly, passionately, quite totally happily. The more she got to know him, the happier she was.

Fourteen

Despite or perhaps because of Sarah's absence, the four of them found themselves laughing all the way back from seeing a movie whose title none of them could remember.

It was nearly eleven when they arrived back in Cougar, which was lit up like it was already Christmas.

Chazz Whitley was on his knees in the middle of the street, bent over a body surrounded by a widening pool of blood.

"Jesus Christ!" whistled Jason. He was out of the car before it stopped. "What happened?" He rushed over to Chazz.

Chazz, his eyes intent, didn't even look up. "Look around. There are four bodies." He stood up. "All dead."

Jason pushed his hat back on his head and looked around. "What the hell . . ."

"Darwin Clee went on a rampage. Killed his wife, then just started shooting anyone who was on the street."

Jason looked around. A crumpled body was in front of the door to Rocky's.

"That's Melba," Chazz pointed. "She was just leaving the last shift. Over there is Frank Demshaw. I don't know what he was doing downtown at night." Frank was a wheat farmer. "Over there's Henry Bellatoni." He owned the Alhambra.

"Julie's in her car." He pointed to Julie Clee's battered Dodge, the door swinging open, one of her legs protruding from the car, the window in smithereens.

"Where's Darwin?"

"In Rocky's. He's not even trying to get away. Just sitting there."

"Jesus H. Christ," Jason said, starting for the restaurant. The one night he was out of town. He stopped by the car and leaned in to tell the astonished passengers what had happened.

"I got problems." He strode on to the restaurant, walking through the open door. Rocky was behind the counter, wearing a wide-eyed expression.

The only other person in the place was Darwin Clee sitting at a table, his hands palm down, staring into space, a pistol next to him, right on the table. He'd always been an introverted person, even back in his school days, and he eked out a living on a couple of acres of land back in the mountains. Shot rabbit and deer and lived a hand-to-mouth existence. The town had always been amazed that Julie Garr, one of the prettiest cheerleaders they'd ever had, had married quiet old Darwin. But five months after they married, they understood, because Julie gave birth, back there in the mountains, to a boy. The town smirked. Well, Darwin Clee had more in him than they'd given him credit for.

Darwin was obsessed with Julie. The sun rose and set on her. But Julie got to town whenever she could, which wasn't often. She was one of the few women who went into the Alhambra. Everyone in town knew that whenever Julie was in there, she'd come out with some man. It was late at night when her car could be seen slowly moving onto the back road that led to Darwin's farm.

Darwin Clee looked up with bloodshot eyes. "Just once too many times," he said. He didn't have to explain to Jason what he meant.

"Where's the baby?" Jason asked.

Darwin just stared straight ahead, as though he hadn't heard the question.

"I've got to arrest you, Darwin," Jason said.

He was wondering how to tell Mary Bellatoni and Grace Demshaw and Gus Johnson, Melba's boyfriend. He put a hand on Darwin's shoulder. The young man stood up and walked along with Jason, as though in a trance.

"Do you know where the Clees live?" Jason asked Scott, who was standing beside the Caddy.

"Sort of," Scott answered.

"Well, get Dodie. She'll know. The Clee baby must be out there. Go get it." He turned to Red. "You take Cat on home."

"I'm staying. I'll go out to the Clees, too," Cat said.

Jason said to Scott, "Chazz and I'll take care of things here. You go find the kid."

Dodie was in bed. She answered the door dressed in a flowered robe and her hair in curlers. One look at Scott's face told her something was seriously wrong.

"Get dressed," he said, walking into the house, "and I'll tell you what's happened." While Cat stood in the doorway, Scott followed Dodie down the hall and stood in the doorway while she grabbed slacks that were thrown over a chair. As Scott talked, Dodie kept saying, "Oh, my God," and, tearing the curlers from her hair, ran a brush through it. "I'm ready.

"Nothing like this has ever happened here," Dodie said. Tears sprang to her eyes.

She practically jumped into Scott's car. Then she slid out. "This beauty doesn't have four-wheel drive. Let's take the pickup. We'll need it to drive out to the Clees."

She backed out of the garage and Cat hopped in to sit between her and Scott. It was not a comfortable position. All the forty minutes that it took to drive out over the dirt roads they discussed what had happened over and over.

The Clee house was a blaze of lights. When they entered the house through the open front door, they discovered it was neat and tidy. While Scott walked to the kitchen, Cat and Dodie glanced in the first bedroom, but all they saw was a brass bed with a wedding-ring quilt covering it. The baby was not in its crib in the other darkened room. They searched in closets and under beds and out in the swaying barn.

As they drove back to town, Dodie asked, "Where could that baby be?"

Cat noted the strange tone of Dodie's voice. "You think something's happened to it? That he killed the baby, too?"

"His name is Danny," was all Dodie offered.

Despite the hour there were more people milling around downtown than there had been at six o'clock. They stood at a distance from the dead bodies which had been gathered together. Sheets were stretched over each one. The mortician, Frank Elliott, stood beside them.

"Oh, God," Dodie whispered, "there are Mary and Grace." She parked the pickup and practically leapt from her seat, not actually running but walking fast in order to do what she could to comfort the two grieving widows. Kneeling in front of the dead bodies was Gus Johnson, his arms spread over Melba's inert body.

It was after two o'clock before the bodies were taken to Elliott's Mortuary. Despite his profession, Frank Elliott was popular in the town. He was the third generation to run the mortuary. His grandfather and his father had been leading citizens before him. He was a handsome man, with black curly hair and Irish blue eyes. He loved poker and people, and when one of the townspeople died he took it personally. It hurt him every time he had to bury a friend.

Most of the town, of course, didn't hear about the murders until later in the morning. At five, Torie woke from a deep sleep, responding to the alarm clock, which was set to go off at that hour every morning so that Joseph could get dressed and slip out of her apartment before anyone in town knew that he was there. However, this morning he didn't move when she touched him. She turned over in bed. "Hey, sleepyhead, up and out," she whispered. But he lay there on his back, his arms outstretched.

Torie raised herself on her elbow and turned on the light. Joseph did not open his eyes. "Hey," she said louder.

For a minute she was panicked. He looked dead. But he was breathing regularly even if slowly. She sat up in bed and studied him.

She usually turned over and went back to sleep until six-thirty, when she had to get up for school. She didn't know what Joseph did until he turned up at Rocky's for breakfast.

The trouble was that Torie would not give Joseph an ultimatum. Marry me or else. She understood his position. Torie wanted children, but she wanted those children to be Joseph's. She would like Joseph to have proved to his father that he could not become a shaman. Just because he was Samuel's son did not mean he had inherited Samuel's abilities.

Yet, all the time they were growing up she and every one else in the Cougar Valley knew there was something different about Joseph. Now, looking at him lying in what she could only define as a trancelike state, she was sure. Joseph lay in her bed, but she knew he was not there.

She padded out to the kitchen and brewed coffee. While waiting for it, she stood in the doorway of her bedroom, arms folded, studying her lover. Samuel would win. She felt it in her bones. In her blood. A shiver passed through her.

The sun was trying to poke through the overcast sky, shortly after seven, when Joseph opened his eyes. He saw Torie standing in the doorway, and for a moment bewilderment covered his face. Then he shook his head. "Did I oversleep?" he asked, in no hurry to get up.

Torie shoved her cup of coffee at him. "You're going to have to make an honest woman of me if you don't hurry."

Joseph arose and walked into the bathroom. When he returned to the bedroom, he said, "If I slip out the back way, no one'll see me on a Sunday morning. And Rocky's will already be open."

Torie nodded.

Rocky's was not only open, but crowded. The conversation was hushed; there was one topic.

"Where's the baby?" Joseph heard people ask.

He looked around. Jason was not there. Without paying for his half-eaten breakfast, Joseph got up and walked out of Rocky's, strode across the street to the sheriff's office, and opened the door. Jason sat behind his desk, on the phone. He waved at Joseph and, after hanging up, said, "Good morning."

"We'd better hurry," was all Joseph said.

Jason studied him.

"If the creek rises, the boy will die."

Jason grabbed his hat and shot out the door. He didn't even ask a question. He slid behind the wheel of his pickup, waited a second for Joseph to get in the passenger's seat, keyed the engine, and asked, "Where to?"

He raced all the way out to the Clees. As soon as he was out of the car, Joseph started off on foot, Jason following him through the underbrush. Joseph seemed to know exactly where to go.

They hadn't walked twenty minutes when they came to a creek that Jason hadn't even known was there. Joseph pointed downstream. "There, under that cottonwood."

Jason guessed what they'd find.

The eighteen-month-old boy was lying on his back, whimpering. Beside him, whining, was the black Lab that Darwin Clee loved almost as much as he loved his wife.

"He didn't have the guts to kill his son," Jason observed. "So he was going to let nature do it?"

Joseph picked up the baby, made a face at its smell, and said, "Dodie will know what to give him."

Jason wondered why Dodie should. She was the one woman in town who was childless.

As soon as Torie heard what had happened, she sat at her kitchen table staring into space. An ice pack surrounded her heart, so cold was the center of her being.

She knew irrevocably that Joseph was what his father wanted him to be, what she had prayed that he was not. How else could he have known where to find the Clee baby?

Fifteen

Jason took Darwin Clee over to the county jail.

The entire town turned out for the quadruple funeral. Both Frank Demshaw and Melba had belonged to the Baptist Church. That service was held at eleven. Loudspeakers were set up outside because not everyone could squeeze into the little church that ordinarily held fewer than two hundred souls. The crowd left there and walked up to the end of the block on Church Street, which was only two blocks long, for the service at the church where Henry Bellatoni had been a pillar. The Catholic Church was the smallest in Cougar, so all but a handful stood outside in the pale winter sun. Julie Clee hadn't belonged to any church, so the Methodist Church held a service for her. The whole thing lasted over two hours.

En masse, the townspeople marched to the Riverview Cemetery, where four graves had been prepared.

For three days afterward hardly anyone could hold a conversation without breaking into tears. Darwin Clee was charged with first-degree murder on one count and three counts of second degree.

Dodie Whitley kept Danny. She drove over to Baker City to buy a crib and baby blankets and new clothes for the child. She told Cat, "I don't know how happy most married couples are, but Chazz and I have something special. We're aware of it, even when we disagree. The only thing that's marred our happiness is being childless. Do you think it's a miracle? I feel so guilty to find happiness when four people are dead because of it."

"Have you talked to Julie's parents?"

"Chazz talked with them. They feel too old to take care of a baby. They have seven others of their own, anyhow. They barely scrape by.

Mrs. Garr said she was sure the baby would be privileged to live with us. But we have to wait for the trial. If he's judged not guilty . . ."

"Oh, come on," Cat protested. "Not a chance in hell that'll happen."

"But, nevertheless, if such should happen, the father would get custody."

"Let's you and me and Chazz drive up to visit him. Meanwhile, whether you think it's too soon or not, I'll work on adoption papers, if that's what you want."

"Want? Oh, my dear, I'm having a romance. We've fallen in love. Chazz and I just look at each other nights and think Danny is a gift from heaven. Such a sweet, responsive child."

It was a Christmas Cat would never forget.

They'd invited Cody and Jason to stay overnight Christmas Eve, to enjoy the Christmas tree that Scott and Red had cut back in the mountains. Over eight feet tall, it didn't begin to touch the high ceiling.

Miss Jenny baked cookies, dozens of iced gingerbread men and stars and Christmas trees, and when Cody reluctantly went upstairs to bed she told him to come down after he was in his pajamas and they'd make up a plate for Santa Claus and he could put it by the fireplace or under the tree, wherever he thought best.

They sang Christmas carols and Torie, who had also come out to stay overnight, played the piano. They drank eggnog and devoured little sandwiches which Miss Jenny had spent the morning making and basked in the warmth of the fire and friendship.

"Our first Christmas together," Scott murmured as he held Cat close when they'd come up to bed. She wished he'd had the camera so they could have taken pictures tonight. Well, she'd have to see that it was one of the first things opened tomorrow. Once Cody was asleep, Scott and Jason spent nearly an hour placing gifts under the tree. Cat had never seen so many. They were piled high.

"I've never had so much fun getting ready for Christmas," she told Scott as he nibbled her neck. She knew she'd been extravagant, but then she wanted to repay these wonderful people for making her feel a part of them. It was the first time since her mother died fifteen years earlier that she had a sense of belonging.

Chazz and Dodie arrived with the baby, Danny, about nine-thirty Christmas morning. Cody had already been allowed to open a present, which happened to be a new baseball glove. He jumped up and down, hardly able to contain himself at the slowness of the adults in getting around to opening presents, devouring all the candy and fruit he'd received in his stocking. Cat hoped he wouldn't be ill.

They sat in front of the roaring fire, drinking orange juice and opening gifts. The sky looked as though it were going to pour forth snow, but it held off and was just gray and cold. Cat knew that the brightest place in the world was that living room. She hugged herself with happiness. She said the proper oohs and ahs at the fur-lined gloves Sarah gave her, and the handknit sweater from Miss Jenny. And she did love it. "No one's ever spent so many hours making something just for me," she said, kissing her grandmother. That's how she thought of her. Not as Scott's grandmother, but as her own.

Dodie had bought about a hundred gifts for Danny. "I've wanted to shop for a baby for as long as I've been married," she said, glowing with happiness. The way Chazz's eyes followed her he looked as though he were in the early stages of love. Cat hoped the adoption would go through. The trial wouldn't be until next month, but Darwin had already given his permission for them to adopt Danny. Cat had spent hours investigating adoption procedures in Oregon. She'd enjoyed getting back into the legal world. She hadn't been aware she'd missed it.

In the midst of the festivities, Scott picked up his new camera and said, "I've got to take a photo of something, so come on outside, Cat, and let me take a picture of you."

She'd been snapping pictures with his camera all morning.

Everyone stood and followed them out of the living room, through the immense foyer, and out onto the porch. She didn't know how he'd done it without her seeing it, but at the bottom of the steps, with a big red bow on it, was a yellow snowmobile.

"Well?" Scott said, grinning.

She looked at him. "For me?"

He nodded. "Go on down so I can take a picture."

"Oh, how wonderful!" she exclaimed. She knew he had an old one in the barn, and he'd promised to take her back up in the mountains snowmobiling come real winter. "Yellow!"

"Like the first flowers I sent you."

She skipped down the stairs and over to the little machine. She hopped on it and, a grin on her face, waved at Scott so he could take her photo. Everyone was crowded around him, laughing, taking pleasure in her joy.

Cody ran down the steps to ask, "Will you take me for a ride?"

"You'll be the first one." She leaned down and pulled him up to sit on her lap.

When the last present had been opened, when the living room was littered with torn paper and scattered ribbons, Red said, "Hey, I guess I forgot to bring in the presents I have for Torie and Cat. Now, where did I leave them?" He grinned. "Darn it," he said, "I guess I forgot to wrap them. Must have left them out in the barn. Come on, let's go out and see if they're still there. Better get your coats."

"Oh, Daddy," Torie said, laughing. "I know you. You didn't forget them. They're just out there."

Out back, the mountain behind the barn rose gray and majestic, jagged against the sky. Snowflakes began to fall.

"A white Christmas. I don't remember when I've had one."

Jason said, "I've had the best Christmas since I was a kid."

"Me too." Cat smiled at him.

Red, twenty paces ahead of them, opened the barn door and disappeared into it. When they entered the darkness, with the sweet smell of hay assaulting them, Red, at the other end of the barn, called. "These have your names on them. Catherine. Victoria."

Cat stood and looked at Torie, who was grinning but shrugged her shoulders. They walked together toward Red. At the end of the barn, where tractors were stored in winter, sat a shiny red Mercury Mystique. And indeed, there was a Christmas card about two feet tall, a picture of a Christmas tree and the word "Catherine."

Next to it was a dark blue Ford Explorer, and a sign reading, "Victoria."

Torie squealed. "Oh, Daddy, you knew how much I wanted one." She threw her arms around her father and ran to open the door.

Red stood beaming.

Cat, tears stinging her eyes, sucked in her breath. "You look exactly like Santa Claus," she said, overwhelmed. She went over and put her arms around Red, too. "Thank you," she said, scarcely able to talk, her heart full to overflowing. "I don't know what I ever did to deserve you."

"Funny," he said, holding her tightly for a second, "I thought it was the other way around."

Cat turned to look at the group standing behind her. "You're the family I haven't had. I can't tell you how much I love you all."

"Now you don't have to ask to use a car or wait until one's available. The key's in the car, in case you want to take a spin before dinner."

"Of course I do."

Torie was already opening the barn doors.

Cody said, "I want to be first to ride in the car, too!"

After dinner Chazz and Dodie took off with their Danny. Cat promised to drop in to see Dodie during the week. She liked the Whitleys.

By four-thirty Sarah was smashingly drunk. No one said anything. She had started singing fraternity songs before dinner was over. Then old Frank Sinatra songs. Right after the Whitleys left, she threw a glass at the fireplace and laughed as it shattered. Red, saying nothing, scraped up the splinters.

When he offered to take her upstairs so she could take a nap, she went willingly after snapping at him, "You're so goddamned perfect, aren't you." But she let him lead her up the stairs and put a quilt over her when she lay down on the bed. He stood looking out the window at the snow falling gently and, when he saw she was asleep, he returned downstairs, where Torie and Scott were arguing.

Scott was trying to explain to Cat why environmentalists and cattlemen were at odds. "Environmentalists have their heads in the air and wouldn't understand a dollar sign if they fell over it. They don't care if people are out of jobs and starving as long as they can protect their precious spotted owls."

Red continued, "I think they both have points. We own so much land that if our cattle and sheep can't graze on Bureau of Land Management property in the summer, we can make out, but many ranchers can't. From time immemorial, loggers have been granted rights to certain BLM lands and ranchers to others. It's been a way of life for as long as America's been a country. But then there weren't as many people, and animal and plant species weren't endangered."

"For Chrissakes, Dad," Scott exclaimed.

Torie had to raise her voice to be heard. "Look, let's face it. Indiscriminate logging the way it's been done these past hundred or more years is destroying the balance of nature. The earth's on its way to extinction."

Scott slammed his fist in the palm of his other hand. "My God, you two sound as though . . ."

Red interrupted him. "Scott, I'm not an environmentalist. I'm just saying they have a point or two, but they go too far. You have to admit the earth's resources aren't infinite."

"God, Torie and Joseph have brainwashed you," Scott said, resignation in his voice. "They're not going to run out of oil or forests in our lifetime."

"Oh, Scott." Torie shook her head vehemently. "You just don't want anything to change, and by not wanting to change you're not recognizing the world's become so crowded that . . ."

"Look around." He waved his arm. "We're not even in sight of neighbors."

Jason and Torie exchanged understanding glances. Red, leaning back in his big leather chair, listened.

Torie stood up. "It's already dark. I'm going back to town."

Cat imagined she wanted to spend part of Christmas with Joseph.

"You could stay overnight again," Red suggested.

"I have my own place, Daddy." She leaned down to kiss the top of his head. "I'm a big girl now. Consider yourself lucky to have me in town."

He caught her wrist and smiled up at her. "I consider myself lucky to have you for a daughter."

"I'm taking the Explorer, of course," she told him. "When you come to town someone can drive my car. Maybe I'll sell it, Daddy. I don't need two."

"Don't you want to keep your car?"

"I need two vehicles like another hole in my head." Torie laughed.

Jason stood up and stretched. Cody had fallen asleep in front of the TV in Red's den. "We better take off, too." Jason turned to Red. "We had a wonderful day."

Then Jason turned to Scott and shook hands. "Thanks for inviting us."

Jason woke his son, and they bundled up. Cat put on her new boots and down parka. Snowflakes silvered her hair as they walked out to Jason's car.

"It's beautiful," Jason said. "Lousy for driving but awful nice to look at. Everything seems so muffled when it snows. So quiet."

She noted he was wearing the scarf she'd given him.

"You're a good thing for this family, Cat."

"I'm good for them? My heavens, I never had such presents in my life."

"Does Sarah drink a lot?"

"It's the first time I've seen her like that, but yes, she drinks far too much."

After Jason left, Cat returned to the living room. Miss Jenny was saying, "I'm going to slice some of that turkey to take home."

"It's snowing, Ma. You can stay here."

"It's not that bad yet. I've got four-wheel drive."

"Will you phone when you get there?"

She laughed, and said to Cat, "Isn't role reversal wonderful? I used to worry about him being out all hours of the night."

About eight, Cat fixed turkey sandwiches and brought them and leftover pumpkin pie into Red's study. They ate in front of the fireplace, and Cat said, "I'm so happy I should pinch myself to see I'm not dreaming. I can't tell you how wonderful it is to be a McCullough."

Scott grinned. "We've known that for years. But I'm as happy as you are. You have brought happiness to me, Cat, that I'd never known was missing."

"That goes for me, too," Red said.

"I'm frightened at times," Cat said. "All this happiness makes me scared that something is going to happen to ruin it."

"Don't be silly," her husband said, reaching out to put an arm around her and pull her close.

Sixteen

"Lord, I feel I must really be getting old," Miss Jenny told Cat. "Do a stupid thing like slip on those steps."

She'd refused, at first, to contemplate spending six weeks down at the big house recuperating until Red convinced her it'd be an inconvenience to carry her meals up the mountain every day, and someone would have to go up there to take care of her a couple of times a day. So, with reluctance on her part, they moved Miss Jenny down to the ranch house.

"How am I going to do the monthly payroll and take care of the books?" she asked no one in particular.

Cat answered. "With my help." She turned to Red, and said, "I realize I'm new to the family, and you may not want me delving into your finances."

"They're yours, too, now," Red said. "Be obliged for your help."

Cat reached over and patted Miss Jenny's knee. "You can tell me what to do and look over my shoulder and learn the computer while we do it."

Miss Jenny looked skeptical.

Sarah said, "I wouldn't even want to learn it."

Red gazed at his wife. Cat couldn't read the expression in his eyes.

"We could set the computer up in one of the upstairs bedrooms, couldn't we?" Cat asked.

"No," Red said. "We'll use my office, so Ma won't have to climb stairs."

"My God," Miss Jenny sniffed. "It's my arm, not my legs."

"Well, all the records are in my office or up at your place."

Miss Jenny nodded, giving in.

Teaching Miss Jenny the intricacies of a computer and keeping the
ranch's books made the days pass quickly, even though they were
housebound in January. Cat not only loved Miss Jenny but felt she
was doing something worthwhile, and Miss Jenny was an apt pupil.
She took to the computer with both trepidation and alacrity. "I can
hardly wait to get this goddamned cast off so I can attack this computer
myself," she said.

Cat was amazed at the fortune involved in the McCullough holdings and investments.

"I've done it all," Miss Jenny said. "The investments, I mean. The
men have done the hard work, but I've put their sweat into a portfolio
I'm proud of."

"I'm impressed," Cat told her.

"You should be. We're worth nearly seven times as much as when
I began taking care of the finances twenty-some years ago."

Cat studied the older woman with admiration. Miss Jenny smiled
and leaned toward Cat. "I don't know that anyone else appreciates
it. How glad I am to have you around."

Cat had known they were wealthy, but the extent of their fortune
amazed her. She wondered if Scott knew. He seemed so careless and
uninterested in money.

Shortly after Miss Jenny and her computer moved back up to her
lodge in the middle of February, Cat began to suspect she was pregnant. She'd been feeling queasy in the mornings, and the sight of
Thelma's wonderful breakfasts made her feel nauseous, though she
felt fine by midmorning. She made an appointment to see Chazz, who
told her that Darwin Clee had been sentenced to life in prison with
the earliest hope for release twenty years. The Whitleys had been
granted permanent custody of Danny.

"Congratulations," he said, grinning, after performing the test.

He calculated the baby would arrive in early October. Cat could
hardly wait to tell Scott. When she arrived home, he was already there.
He and Red were in Red's office, and when Scott heard her come in,
he called to her to join them.

"I'm going over to John Day tomorrow," he said. "There's a bull
over there at a ranch in the Strawberry Mountains that Dad wants me
to look at. Wanna come?"

"Of course."

He had never looked more wonderful to her. He was going to be the father of her child, and they would add another generation of McCulloughs to the world. Together, through their love, they had created a human being. She wondered how big the baby was, if it even looked like a human being yet. She knew so little, next to nothing, about having a baby.

Couldn't he tell just by looking at her that something was different? Scott said, "Forecast is clear tomorrow."

Cat said she'd meet him upstairs. But he didn't come up, and she sat down to wait for him. Darkness crept over the land, with its thin veneer of snow. There hadn't been much snow, they'd told her. It wasn't a normal year, not that it ever piled up high around here, but at this altitude the ground was frozen all winter, and although all one usually needed was a down vest, this winter had been colder, with less snow than usual. There'd been enough up in the mountains for snowmobiling weekends, and for cross-country skiing, which Torie and Joseph had introduced her to.

Finally Scott came into the room and, flicking on a light, asked, "Why are you sitting in the darkness?"

Cat came out of a reverie. "I was just thinking."

"Of what?" He walked to the bathroom, turned on the water, and washed his hands, then came to stand in the doorway, drying his hands on a towel.

"Of what your face is going to look like when you hear we're going to have a baby."

She was not disappointed. His eyes widened, and in three strides he was across the room. He knelt next to her. "Are you sure? Really?"

"Chazz verified it this afternoon."

Scott put his arms around her and held her close. "Oh, Cat," he whispered. "Oh, dear, beautiful, lovely mother of my son."

Cat closed her eyes and wondered if there was more happiness than she felt at this moment, engulfed in Scott's arms, anticipating their child.

"Let's go tell the folks," he said.

When they went downstairs, holding hands, Red and Sarah were already before the fireplace with its roaring fire. Scott poured red wine for her and whiskey and soda for himself. He grinned and, with an arm around her shoulders, announced, "You're going to be grandparents."

Red's face lit up with pleasure, and he reached a hand out to shake

Scott's hand, but ended up hugging him. He put his arms around Cat and kissed her on the cheek, murmuring, "Wonderful news."

Sarah looked startled. She stood up, and she, too, hugged Cat. "Thank God," she said. "Thank the good Lord. A McCullough to carry on."

She clung to her son's arm, and kept saying, "I'm so glad. So pleased. I'm happy." But she never looked happy. Cat had never once seen any sense of joy on Sarah's face. She knew her mother-in-law approved of her, but there was no sense of warmth in her being. Not for the first time, she wondered what had attracted Red to his wife.

Thelma showed more excitement than Sarah did.

"You better drive up after dinner and tell Ma," Red said. "She won't just want to hear it on the phone."

On the way to John Day the next morning, Cat asked Scott to stop at the Safeway in Baker so she could buy some soda crackers. "I'll be okay by the middle of the morning," she assured him, "but I feel ooky now."

"Ooky?" He grinned.

"Ooky."

When she got back in the car with crackers and a six pack of Cokes, Scott reached out for her hand.

"Boy, this is beautiful scenery," she said as they headed west on Route 7.

"It's all national forest," Scott said. "It's only a couple of hours to John Day, and until we get to the town itself it's gorgeous, and you have wide-open vistas. The town itself is enclosed between a couple of ridges, and I'd get claustrophobia living there. We'll stop there for an early lunch if"—he looked at her—"you're not feeling ooky, and then head south about three quarters of an hour to the Clintons. Dad never thought they'd sell that bull, but finally he offered them enough money I guess they couldn't refuse. We're just going over to finalize it all, and then, come spring, we'll send a truck over for it. He wants me to take a second look, just to make sure."

Cat felt pride that Red trusted Scott to make such a decision. "I love you," she said.

He grinned and reached for her hand again. "Okay, what're we going to name him?"

"Or her."

He nodded, admitting to the possibility.

"Whatever we choose today, we'll probably change our minds daily for the next eight months."

"That's okay, isn't it?" he asked. "I'm just in the mood to talk about it. What better way?"

"Scott, Junior?"

"I'd never wish that on any kid. The junior I mean. How about Christopher?"

Cat tried it out. "Chris McCullough. Not bad at all."

"Or Matthew."

"Matt McCullough. Hey, you're pretty good at this."

"I take that for approval. Shall I go on?"

She finished the Coke and was feeling better.

"Bet I'm not nearly as good at girls' names," Scott said. "I don't know why, for I sure do like women! I really wouldn't mind a daughter at all."

"Darn good thing. I think it's too late to change it. Would you like me to have amnio—oh what's the name, you know that tells you the sex of the baby?"

Scott glanced over at her. "Do you want to know?"

Cat thought a minute. "Not really."

"Neither do I. Let's leave it to fate and wait to find out. It'll be part of the fun."

Tears formed in Cat's eyes, much to her surprise.

"What's wrong, hon?"

"I'm just so happy."

No other cars were behind them, so he pulled over to the shoulder of the road and stopped the car, reaching out for her and holding her close. He kissed her, and she said, "I don't feel ooky anymore."

There weren't many choices for dining in John Day, but a small restaurant on Main Street offered charcoal-broiled hamburgers on homemade buns, and they munched on them as they stared at each other like silly fools.

They reached the Clintons ranch by one-thirty. Cat was glad she'd worn her heavy boots even though there wasn't snow because they stood out in the cold afternoon after they'd seen the prize bull, talking with old man Clinton, who never did invite them into the house.

It was after three when they left, and Cat was freezing. The sky swirled with dark gray clouds. "Let's stop and get some coffee," she said, her teeth chattering. "He certainly wasn't charitable."

"His wife died right before Christmas, and I think he's lost interest in life. Probably doesn't even think of the social niceties."

When Scott gassed up and bought hot coffee from the mart at the gas station, snowflakes were beginning to come down in soft gentle swirls.

"We can probably make it home for dinner if we take the cutoff," Scott said. He glanced at his watch. "Ought to be there by six or if snow slows us down, six-thirty anyhow. If we take the shortcut it means we don't have to go through Baker. We'll come out behind the Big Piney."

"Wake me," Cat said. She curled up in the seat, not that she could ever get really comfortable in the pickup. She wished they'd brought a blanket.

Scott switched the radio on and discovered the weather report had changed. A cold front was heading in from the northwest, and by tomorrow there should be several inches on the ground, more at higher elevations. Rain was predicted for Portland and the Willamette Valley.

"I'll take snow anytime," Scott said. "With four-wheel drive we can get through anything. A couple of inches won't even slow us down much, but four-wheel drive's no earthly good on rain-slick roads."

"Don't wake me," Cat murmured, taking off her boots and curling up on the seat. "Why didn't we bring the Cadillac?"

Scott ran a finger across the bottom of her foot.

"Do that again, and I'll purr."

He did. She smiled, closing her eyes.

When she opened them an hour later, snow was swirling so thickly Scott had the lights on and was just inching along.

She sat bolt upright. "Oh, my."

"I did a stupid thing about thirty miles ago," Scott said. "I decided to take the cutoff that would shorten the trip by about twenty miles, never dreaming there was this much snow in the back country. Now, dammit I can't find a place to turn around."

It wouldn't be dark for another half hour, but the tall trees and the snow rendered visibility nearly zero.

"I have a snow shovel in the back," he said. "Don't let the motor stop running." He halted the car, got out, and had to reach through six inches of snow to find the shovel. "I think it would be a good idea to turn around and go back the way we came," he shouted.

Cat put on her boots as Scott shoveled snow off the road. It was already piled high. By the time he had finished clearing a space large enough to turn the car around, there was already half an inch over most of it.

"I didn't think to bring gloves," he said, getting back in the car and looking around for something to dry his hands. There was nothing. He rubbed them together and blew on them. "Not the first stupid thing I've done, trying to take that shortcut in this weather," he said, leaning over to kiss her.

"You're cold," she said, hoping the car heater would warm him quickly.

Scott maneuvered the car, turning it to face back south, and began to plow through the snow. He inched forward, peering out his window as though that would increase his visibility. Within minutes it was as dark as a moonless night. He couldn't even see where the road was.

"No sense going on like this," he said finally. "We're just going to have to stop or we'll fall off a mountainside or get mired at the side of the road." He looked at his wife. "Hon, we're just going to have to park here overnight."

"As long as you're with me," she said, feeling no panic, "I don't mind. I have some soda crackers left and a couple of Cokes."

"You must've been a Girl Scout," he murmured, cutting the motor. "We'll just hope no car comes along at this hour to plow into us. In the morning we can see where the road is even if it's covered with snow. And snowplows will be along for sure."

"We can make love all night," Cat said, sliding close to him.

He put an arm around her. "You make being stranded sound like fun."

"Well"—she curled into his arm—"it's a bit of an adventure, isn't it. The three of us together."

He laughed and kissed her. She ran her tongue along his lips, and he muttered, "I wonder if you have any idea what you do to me. I think about making love to you at least twenty-two times a day."

"Is that all?" she breathed into his ear, unzipping her parka and reaching for his hand, guiding it to her breast.

Scott laughed.

"Don't you think since it's only about five-thirty, and we have at least thirteen or fourteen hours with nothing else to do that we might try for the *Guiness Book* of *Records?*" She reached for his belt and undid the buckle. "How many positions is it possible to do in a car?"

"Or how many times in a fourteen-hour period?"

"Mmmm. God, you have the most erotic fingers in the universe."

"How would you know?" Hey, don't take off your clothes. We can't keep the heater on all night or we'll run out of gas."

"I don't give a damn. We can walk home when it's daylight. I am going to take off my clothes, and you are going to kiss every inch of me, and I am going to shout with ecstasy if I want, because no one can hear us."

"Maybe there's a house nearby."

"Fine. We'll have coffee in the morning."

They fell asleep in each other's arms around ten-thirty or eleven. Scott awoke about five, able to see the time from the dials on his watch. He tried not to awaken Cat as he stretched from his cramped position. He opened the window an inch but could hear nothing. Not a sound at all. He was impatient for dawn.

He needed to go to the bathroom. He'd inch the door open as quietly as he could and take a leak from the car. No one would know.

He turned the door handle but the door wouldn't budge. He sat up straighter and pushed. He threw himself against it. Nothing. He rolled the window down and was disturbed to feel snow blowing in his face. He reached his hand out and was alarmed to feel his hand touching piled-up snow. Jesus, God Almighty. Snow was piled halfway up the door.

At least it had stopped snowing. No flakes fell onto his hand.

What the hell should he do if the car wouldn't move?

He didn't believe for a minute that snowplows would come up this road until spring. This was one of those back roads closed all winter, if they were even on maps. How stupid he had been. He should have known better, but when he'd turned off Route 7 the snow hadn't looked like it was coming down that hard. The weather report, which was unreliable at best, had predicted several inches. Except for the mountain roads.

And with Cat in her condition. He wanted to kick himself.

He closed his eyes, but he knew he couldn't sleep. He wasn't exactly frightened, but he didn't know quite what the hell he was going to do. He'd have to set out on foot come daylight and find a way to save his wife and unborn child. He reached out to put an arm around the sleeping Cat and pulled her close. God, if anything should happen to them.

And it was his fault. His own goddamned fault.

He knew damned well there wasn't a house along this road he'd traveled so many times. Just national forest. They'd passed the nearest house thirty miles back.

He mustn't let Cat see his trepidation. He mustn't let his growing anxiety show.

Shit.

Seventeen

"I want to come with you," Cat said.

"Well, I won't let you. It's going to be hard going. It'll take me an hour just to walk a couple of miles," Scott told her. "I don't remember any houses after the national forest began, which was about twenty miles back."

"Are you saying it'll take you all day just to get back there?"

He hadn't wanted to put it that way. "Well, it may be until tomorrow before I can get a wrecker or something back here."

"I don't want to stay here all day without you." *Without food and water, and all alone without anyone or anything in sight except trees,* she added to herself.

"I know, hon, but there's no other choice. I wouldn't let you try even if you weren't carrying our child. You'll slow me down, and you just can't walk through this snow. We'd never get out if I had to carry you." He kissed her, holding her tight. "You've just got to be brave and wait it out. I have faith in you, my love."

Cat felt like crying.

"I'll be back with help just as soon as possible. If you get thirsty, reach out and get some snow." He had crawled out his window and shoveled snow away from the doors so Cat could at least get out to relieve herself. "If it snows again, get out every half hour and shovel it away from the doors. Don't let it pile as high as the roof, or you won't be found!" He laughed.

Cat didn't find it funny.

"Look," he said, cupping her chin in his hand, "I love you more than life itself. I already love this unnamed unborn child of ours that much, too. I'm going to save you. I'll be back."

"I know you will. I just hate being alone here."

"Next week, maybe tomorrow, ten years from now we'll look back on this and you'll feel proud of yourself. I want to get going while I still have ten hours of daylight ahead of me."

"The snow's higher than your boots."

"Won't be the first time I've slogged along with wet feet. You just keep your chin up and wait. Seems to me waiting's harder than doing."

She clung to him, knowing she had to let him go.

"Okay." He kissed her. "I'm off. With luck I'll see you come evening. Just know that even if I'm not back tonight, I'll see you tomorrow. I promise. No later than tomorrow. Just depends how long it takes me to walk through this stuff. Ordinarily I could make it back there today, but I don't know."

She didn't dare ask what he'd do if darkness came and he was still on the road. She wouldn't let herself think of it.

"Until tomorrow," she said, hiding her fear from him. "Don't worry about me. I'll be right here, thinking of you. Waiting to be rescued by my knight . . ."

He grinned, though she could tell by the lack of joy in his eyes that he wasn't happy. He kissed his fingers and touched her lips with them. "So long," he said.

She got out of the car and stood beside it in the little circle he'd cleared. He'd put the shovel in the pickup with her. When he'd gone about twenty yards he turned and waved, calling, "Make it Matt."

"Okay," she called back. "Matt McCullough."

"I'll be back for you and Matt," and he turned his back to her, picking his feet up to move through the snow, already a couple of feet high.

He'd never make it to a house today. She just knew it. Yet, she also knew he'd know what to do if he had to stay out overnight. He'd told her how he and pals camped out in the winter when they were kids, building log lodges from the branches they could find. He'd be all right.

Would she?

She'd make damn sure she was. She wasn't about to let him down when he had such faith in her.

God it was quiet. And cold.

He'd left the car keys with her but told her unless she was freezing not to turn the motor on. Thank goodness she'd worn her boots and down parka. She got back in the car and wondered what to think about. How to pass the time.

* * *

Thelma had held off on dinner until seven. Red didn't begin to feel a sense of worry until nine. They should have been back hours before. If they'd decided to stay overnight in John Day, Scott would have phoned. He knew his son that well. Finally he phoned Dan Clinton, only to be told Scott and Cat had left there by three-thirty. Shouldn't take six hours to get home. No more than two and a half, three at the outside if they'd stopped for gas or food.

He looked out the window. About a foot of snow since dinnertime. Certainly Route 7 wasn't the most traveled of roads, but there'd be cars going through there. Even if they'd gotten stuck, someone was bound to . . .

Maybe not. Maybe the snow was worse up in the mountains, and perhaps the roads were closed. Maybe they were holed up some place for the night and a plow would be along in the morning. He wouldn't let himself worry too much. They might be in a motel, and the phone lines were probably down. Scott could take care of them.

Sarah, her eyes glazed, asked, "Where are the children?"

He shrugged. They'd already discussed this when wondering whether to go ahead and dine. Miss Jenny had phoned, sounding pleased to say, "Looks like I won't get down off my mountain for a few days."

"I guess I'll go to bed," Sarah said. She'd been asleep in her chair, with her needlepoint on her lap, for the last hour and a half.

Red watched her back as she left the room and started up the stairs. Such a far cry from the spirited girl he'd married. What had happened? When had it gone awry? Longer ago than he could remember.

He turned out the light and sat with only the glow from the fire. He seldom was given to introspection, but perhaps it was time.

When had Sarah changed? When had she begun to drink too much? Probably long before he became aware of it.

About the time Torie was born, though he sure wasn't conscious of it then.

Perhaps she never forgave him for not letting her go on that trip to Australia he and his father had taken, looking for prize cattle. She begged to accompany them, but his father—who, he now realized, had never really approved of Sarah, thinking her far too fragile for ranch life and warning him before they even became engaged, "She's not woman enough for you, son"—had said she'd only get in the way during their trek into the Outback. They were going to visit at least three ranches famous for their cattle, and his father hadn't wanted a woman around to impede their discussions or their chance to experience outdoor life as it was lived down under. "No," he'd told his son. "Our wives can stay at home. We'll only be gone three months."

Red had encouraged her to take that time to visit her parents in Southern California, a place she always regretted leaving. She said she might, but she had stayed on at the Big Piney.

Was it when he returned from that trip that she'd changed? While he'd been away, she'd discovered she was pregnant with Torie. There wasn't a doctor in Cougar then, but their family doctor over in Baker reminded him that Sarah had experienced postpartum depression for months after Scott was born, and he suspected she just didn't take well to pregnancy, despite the ease with which she gave birth. Something psychological. Maybe physiological.

For years now, or so it seemed, Sarah sat in a rocking chair and gazed off into space until sometimes he'd thought she wasn't even in Oregon with him. Miss Jenny never said anything, but once in a while Red saw his mother studying Sarah and shaking her head. She was the one who took care of Scott during the pregnancy. And then Sarah devoted herself to her son, ignoring her newborn daughter. She refused to nurse the child, and hardly even looked at her, spending mornings reading to Scott and playing games with him, and her afternoons napping. It was about that time, Red reflected, that he thought Sarah began to drink. Only one drink before dinner with the family, so he didn't catch on for months. Or maybe it was years.

Miss Jenny only once mentioned anything to him about his marriage. It was after his father died, when the kids were still young, and Miss Jenny told Red she thought she'd move up to the hunting lodge if he had no objections.

He'd lived at the Big Piney with his mother all his life. The Big Piney without Miss Jenny wouldn't be the same, he'd told her.

She gazed at him levelly for a long time, then turned and walked to the kitchen and made coffee. When it was ready she called for him. He sat down at the long oaken table opposite her, and she said, "Just because there's never been a divorce in the family doesn't mean it's evil, you know. You don't have to stay in a marriage that takes from you and gives you nothing."

It was the first time in all those years that they'd ever faced the issue together. Aloud.

"I have Scott and Torie."

Miss Jenny nodded.

"Maybe you could have more than that, too."

"And maybe I'd screw them up, a broken home."

"So, you're willing to sacrifice yourself?"

"Is that what I'm doing?"

Miss Jenny poured herself another cup of coffee. "More than any man I know, you're a giver. You get pleasure out of giving. You give naturally, not to get anything but just for the joy of giving. But it seems to me that you don't *get*. You must be awful lonely."

Oh, Ma, he'd wanted to say. So lonely sometimes I wonder how I can stand it.

"Well," she finally said when he didn't respond, "I won't blame you if you go up to Pendleton or wherever and find yourself a woman for a night . . ."

"Ma!"

Miss Jenny waved her hand. "I'm just saying you've got to get something someplace, and I wouldn't blame you. In fact, I guess what I'm doing is giving you my blessing. You're the best son a woman ever had, and it breaks my heart for you not to find happiness."

"I'm not unhappy. I have the kids. The Big Piney. And"—he reached across the scratched table to put his large hand over his mother's smaller one—"I have you, which is no small thing. If I'm a giver, it's an inherited trait. You've never put yourself first for anything in all the years I've known you."

Miss Jenny nodded. "That may be, but I got given to in return, so it was worth it. I've never loved anyone more than you and your pa, and from each of you, I've gotten as much as I've given."

"I know that."

"But"—Miss Jenny stood up and carried her cup to the sink— "it's not enough for you. A mother's love never is."

So, what was he supposed to do?

That was years ago. And he'd never done anything about it.

He'd tried to have no liquor in the house, but Sarah went into town to buy it. He talked to the liquor-store clerk and told him not to sell Sarah any, but she found some someplace. Maybe she went over to Baker or up to La Grande or to Haines or who knew where. He'd find empty bottles in wastebaskets or hidden at the bottom of closets in rooms they scarcely ever used.

Sarah participated in few social activities, seldom attending school activities except when Scott played in a game. She never appeared at

Torie's rodeos. Red always went alone. Not that he was ever truly alone; friends always surrounded him.

As Red sat in the chair, unable to sleep with wondering how Scott and Cat were faring and where they were, he envied his son. Scott had gotten a winner there. Cat was like a breath of spring—no, spring itself—to this household. Her infectious enthusiasm about everything and everyone never ceased to delight. She buoyed them all up, and Red suspected she didn't even know it. He hoped she wouldn't get squirrelly thanks to childbirth. Of course, most women didn't. Or was it drinking and had nothing to do with childbearing? Like the chicken and the egg. Which had come first? Had Sarah begun to drink first, or was it postpartum depression that led her to drink? She refused to acknowledge it, of course. Wouldn't even talk about it. Not with him, not with Chazz, not with Torie, who had tried any number of times. He himself had given up. He could never tell whether she was sober enough to understand or not. During the day she appeared quite normal except that she kept to herself. It wasn't until dinnertime that her words began to slur, and that glazed look came over her eyes. She seemed spaced out more often than not. Any conversation they had was about the most superficial of things.

She had rallied for the wedding, taking charge in a way he wouldn't have believed possible. She was more gracious to her daughter-in-law than to her daughter. But though it was apparent that she liked Cat, she never seemed to quite connect with her, either.

His own life had gotten a lift from the woman who had entered his son's life. Now there was dinner-table conversation that he spent the day looking forward to. There was laughter in the house. There was a vital woman who was interested in the people she met daily, in riding out on the range with him and Scott, who offered Miss Jenny the camaraderie she'd been denied since his father had died. He smiled when he remembered the way she had thrown her arms around him when he'd given her that car for Christmas. He'd have given Sarah the world if she'd been that enthusiastic about his gifts. If she'd even acted as though his work and his conversation stimulated and interested her. As though she cared. As though his touch didn't freeze her up.

If just once in the last twenty-two years she'd looked at him the way Cat and Scott looked at each other, how different he might feel—about her, about himself, about life.

But he thought he'd come to terms with his fate in life, made peace with it. Was grateful for what he did have. The ranch. The Big Piney rewarded him daily, gave both his mind and body a challenge. And his children. He had not let himself have dreams for his children as they grew up. He wanted them to do what they wanted, in whatever way they could find fulfillment. That Scott chose the ranch and that the two of them were able to work so harmoniously together more than made up for the high jinks shenanigans of the boy's youth. Sowing his wild oats, a little wilder than most. As wild as he himself had been when he was growing up on the same ranch. Of course his own generation had been the first one tempted by drugs and indiscriminate sex. He'd indulged in both in his teens, for which he was glad now. But he'd been pretty square by the sixties' standards. It wasn't until the Beatles were ready to break up that he began to appreciate them, for heaven's sake. It wasn't until a decade after Elvis's death that he began to enjoy *his* singing.

Both Scott and Torie had had streaks of wildness in them when they were in school, but they'd settled down now, and they were the rewards for his marriage. The love he felt for those two filled him to overflowing. He couldn't have chosen two more wonderful kids, and he'd been aware of that all their lives, even when he helped change their diapers. He'd done it more often than Sarah had. Torie was the apple of his eye, and he didn't care who knew it. She was like him in so many ways—stubborn, muleheaded about whatever she deeply believed in, passionate about life, attuned to nature.

Oh, would that he had been able to live a life wherein that passion had been allowed to flower. He gave his passion to the land and to his family, but he was ever aware that there was much fire within him that was still eager to burst into flame.

How long had it been since he and Sarah had shared a room? He either slept in the adjoining room or on the sofa in his study. Neither of them mentioned it. They never mentioned anything of importance to each other.

He was surprised at her apparent delight in the news that they would be grandparents. She drank three glasses of Scotch that night, for she no longer tried to hide her drinking. He'd noticed that when they went in to dinner, she stopped to swallow the wine Cat had left. She couldn't leave undrunk spirits, just couldn't.

After dinner, he had to help her upstairs. There she shook off his hand from her arm, and he went back downstairs while Cat and Scott were up telling Miss Jenny the great news.

Where were they now, his son and daughter-in-law and grand-child? It had been at least four years, since Torie graduated from high school, that he was kept awake because his children weren't at home. Was it because he was to become a grandfather that he couldn't sleep and worried more than he wanted to admit?

He knew they'd be all right. Scott would take care of them. He'd know what to do. Red had complete faith in his son.

So, then, why the hell couldn't he sleep?

Eighteen

Cat started the motor about every hour, when she could no longer stand the cold. She only ran the engine for a few minutes, until heat penetrated the cab and she slapped her hands together to keep warm. Before she did that she opened the door and got out in the area Scott had cleared and stamped her feet and ran in place.

She began to understand how the worst enemy in jail might be boredom. She tried to think of other things, but after a few minutes of forced concentration her mind came back to her present predicament.

In the middle of the afternoon it began to snow again. This time it was accompanied by wind that blew snow so badly she couldn't see out the window. Visibility zero. There was no use getting out of the car to brush the snow away, because she was covered with it in seconds and couldn't see anyway. She was sure snow was blowing into the space Scott had cleared. It pelted against the windows until it might as well have been midnight, for she could see nothing. When she ran the motor, the windshield wipers stuck and wouldn't budge.

She yearned for something to eat, hunger pangs beginning to gnaw her innards. What would this do to her baby? Would it starve? She could still wind the window down—thank goodness they didn't have those electronically operated windows—and get a fistful of snow, so she wasn't thirsty. But she began to feel nauseated and dizzy.

She slept.

Red paced in Jason's office.

He'd put chains on the jeep and forged his way into town. Jason contacted the state police, the department of roads, everyone. Route

7 through the Wallowa Whitman National Forest was impassable. It was still snowing so hard in the mountains no plows could get through. Electricity and phones were out.

Red wished the wind would die down so he could take the helicopter up. It wasn't so bad here, though it had taken him an hour to drive to town.

"They're okay," Jason reassured him. "Scott's not gonna take any chances. He knows this country as well as anyone."

Red knew that. They both knew all the back roads and the trails for a hundred or more miles around. But Scott wouldn't be on a back road. He'd be snowbound on Route 7. Or safe in a motel in John Day. One or the other. Nothing dire was going to happen either way. As soon as the snow stopped the snowplows would be out and 7 would be cleared and all would be well.

"Come on," Jason said, throwing an arm around Red's shoulders, "I'll buy you a cup of coffee."

Red nodded, and they walked out into the blowing snow, crossing the street to Rocky's, which was packed with people even at two-thirty in the afternoon, an hour when it was usually all but empty.

When they'd sat down and Myrna, the afternoon waitress, brought them coffee, Red told Jason, "Cat's pregnant."

Jason raised an eyebrow. "Ah, now I see why you're acting this way. So, you're going to be a grandfather, huh? Do I say congratulations?"

Red grinned. "Is that what one says to a grandparent?"

"I dunno. Doesn't seem quite right, does it? What did you have to do with it?"

"I had Scott."

"Oh." Jason glanced out the window. He had word that it was much worse than this at higher elevations, but he wasn't about to share that information with Red. He'd never seen the older man so worried. To keep Red talking, he asked, "And when's the blessed event?"

"October sometime."

"Chazz going to deliver it?"

"Guess so. Say, you know what? I better find Torie and tell her. School's certainly closed, isn't it?"

Jason nodded. "No school bus could move."

"I should've known from all the sleds in the streets."

"Keeps on like this, you're not going to get back to the ranch. We've an extra room, if you need it."

"I've got to get back home. Scott may call." And Sarah wouldn't know what to do all alone. She might just sit in the darkened living room and drink herself senseless with no one around. Maybe that's what kept him with her. She might not want him, but she needed him to take care of her. She couldn't function alone. He'd known that for years. There was no one else to care for her. No one at all.

He sighed.

Jason said, "Now look, Red, I'll let you know first thing we hear anything. You go see Torie and go on back home."

Red finished his coffee and stood up. "Try Torie's first, and then the Big Piney."

"Sure," Jason said, staying where he was.

Torie was sitting in the kitchen drinking peppermint tea when her father knocked on the door.

"Daddy," she said, hugging him, "what a nice surprise."

He shrugged out of his snowflake-covered jacket and hung it over the back of a chair.

"Want coffee or tea?"

He shook his head. "No, got to get home, but thought I better stop by. Scott and Cat are caught in the snowstorm, and we don't know where they are."

Torie wasn't upset. "They're probably in some farmhouse or a motel. They're okay, Daddy."

"And Cat's pregnant."

Torie's eyes danced. "Oh, how nice. How wonderful! I'm envious."

Her father studied her. "You know you have my permission to marry Joseph, don't you?"

Her eyes clouded over as she sat down at the kitchen table. "I do know, Daddy. And we'd do it even against Mother's wishes because they're just based on narrow-minded prejudice, but we can't go against Mr. Claypool. You know that, Daddy."

Red shook his head. "I know how Samuel feels, but those days are dead and gone. No one in America can be pure-blooded. So what if Joseph can't be a shaman. How are the powers that be going to know that his children . . ."

"That's what it's all about. Our children. It won't affect Joseph, but our children . . ."

"Your children will be like everyone else. If they want to cure people and can't because they are no longer shamans, let them go to med school."

Torie smiled. "I wish it were that easy."

"Get pregnant," her father said.

"Why, Daddy!" But Torie was laughing.

"Well, then Samuel couldn't stop you. It would be a done deed."

"If I could talk Joseph into it, I would."

"None of my business, but I sure as hell hope the two of you are sleeping together."

Torie reached out to touch her father's hand. "I didn't know fathers made such suggestions."

"One thing this family hasn't done right is communicate. Let's start rectifying that, shall we? Your happiness is the most important thing in the world to me."

Torie studied him a minute. "Yes, Daddy, Joseph and I have slept together since we were in high school."

This made Red cock his head and whistle. "Well, I didn't know that. So, what happens if you do become pregnant?"

"Joseph won't let that happen. Not until he comes to terms with himself. You know, duty versus love. Honor versus desire . . . those old chestnuts."

"He's a fine young man," Red said. "An honorable man, but is he so honorable he'll deny you and himself happiness?"

Torie couldn't answer.

"You may have to find happiness someplace else."

"I can never find happiness anyplace else, Daddy."

Red nodded. He envied his daughter her ability to love so completely. He told her, "I not only love you, darling, I admire you."

"Me you too, Daddy." She leaned across the table and kissed his cheek. "I'm the luckiest daughter in the world to have you for a father."

"That my blood runs in you is my path to immortality," said her father. "Best thing I ever did with my life was create you, that's for sure. You and Scott are the constants for happiness in my life."

"What's come over you, Daddy? You've never talked like this before."

"I don't know. But I'm going to talk like this more from now on. It's about time we are open and honest with each other."

"Like about Mother's drinking?" Torie asked.

"Like about your mother's drinking."

"How do you stand it?"

Red had no answer.

He stood up and walked over to put on his still damp jacket. Just then Joseph walked in.

The two men shook hands.

"It's a pisser out there," Joseph said, tossing his head and shaking drops of wet snow onto the floor.

"Daddy's worried because Scott and Cat are out in it somewhere." Joseph studied Red. "How long have they been gone?"

"They left a ranch south of John Day about three-thirty yesterday. Haven't heard from them since."

"Probably holed up in John Day," Joseph said, hanging his wet jacket in the closet.

"Yeah, I think that, too." Red wrapped himself in his jacket. "I'll let you know when I hear."

He walked down the stairs and out into the cold. It had started snowing again. By the time he reached the edge of town, he'd turned his headlights on and still had trouble seeing oncoming cars. Half an hour later, he couldn't tell where the road began and ended. He inched along, unable to see landmarks or even the side of the road.

Sarah was wringing her hands with worry. Thelma had supper ready for them to zap in the microwave and had left so she could get home while she could still sense the right direction.

Red slept fitfully on the couch in his office, getting up frequently to look out the window into the darkness, where he could tell the snow was piling up like it hadn't in years here.

Be safe, he told his son. *Be cozy in a motel in John Day and not stuck in a car that by morning could be covered with such snow we won't find you until spring.* It wasn't reassuring to him to realize spring was just a month away.

Cat had never been more scared in her life.

Okay, Scott told her he mightn't be back tonight. Even if he'd arrived at the nearest house, they couldn't get a truck or jeep or anything up the road in the dark, not with snow piled this high. She couldn't even open the car door now. And she felt ill, like she'd throw up. She could still open the window, so the car wouldn't smell bad if she had to do that. How would she go to the bathroom, though? Maybe she was just ill with fright, not with the nausea of pregnancy. What would this do to the baby, just starting out in life? Would it die in her belly from malnutrition? Would it become dehydrated?

Dear God in Heaven.

She was so damn cold. But there was still plenty of gas, so she turned the engine on again for a few minutes until she was no longer shivering. Her mouth felt dry and fuzzy. How long could she last without eating? It must be days. As long as she had something to drink. Snow. Melted snow might save her.

What about Scott? Was he safe? Had he found a comfortable warm bed for the night or had he built himself some protection from low-hanging tree branches? She knew he was safe, she just knew it. And he'd be back tomorrow with help, some way to pull this truck out of the snow. And she and the baby would be safe.

The baby. She'd think of names, though she liked Scott's suggestions. Liked Matt McCullough. It sounded strong and masculine. It was alliterative and rolled off the tongue nicely. What about a girl? What names would she have ready to offer Scott for a daughter?

Debra? Lisa? Patricia? Candace? Janice? She discarded them all. They didn't sound right with McCullough. She understood, deep within, that right now nothing would sound right.

She opened the window a crack. There was no sound at all. Not even a snowflake dropping on millions of other snowflakes. Silence surrounded her. She had never heard it so quiet in her life.

She hugged herself and closed her eyes.

Scott, come. Please, darling, come.

Morning dawned with skies so clear Red thought he could see to the center of the earth.

It was frigid, but calm. The first thing he did was phone the state police for a weather report and to check on any sign of Scott. He told them he was taking his helicopter up and going to search for his son and daughter-in-law. He'd be heading down Route 7. They told him cars might be buried, that it would be difficult to see anything.

Red grabbed a cup of coffee but couldn't eat breakfast. Thelma wasn't there anyhow. She probably couldn't get up the road. He couldn't remember when that had happened.

He phoned the sheriff's office, but Jason wasn't in yet, so he called him at home and told him what he was planning to do.

"Let me go with you, Red. If you find them stranded, you'll need help. You can't fly and rescue at the same time."

"I'll meet you at the athletic field," Red told his friend. "I'll land there in twenty minutes, give or take."

"Give me forty minutes," Jason asked. "The streets in town aren't all cleared yet. And you can bring a thermos of coffee."

Red hung up, grateful that Jason had volunteered to accompany him.

Sarah came down the stairs, still in her dressing gown, her hair disheveled. She ran a hand through it and asked, "Any word yet?" She looked like death warmed over. She mustn't have slept well either.

"I'm going to take the helicopter and fly over Route 7 to John Day. State police say phone lines are open."

"There are so few motels in that town I'd think you could call them and see if Scott's been there."

Red looked at her with respect. How come he hadn't thought of that?

Twelve minutes later he had learned that no McCullough had been at any motel in John Day.

"We may be gone all day. I'll try to land someplace by noon and phone to see if they're home yet or you've heard from them."

Sarah grabbed his arm, her eyes frantic with worry. "Don't let anything happen to our son, Red. Do you hear me?"

He wondered if she'd be all right, alone here. Well, he couldn't worry about that now. He had enough to worry about.

He put on his jacket, got a thermos of coffee, flashlights, blankets, and walked out to the barn, where he loaded the snowmobile and then took off over the fields to the hangar where he kept the copter.

The frigid air was as still as death.

Nineteen

Route 7 wasn't cleared even by the middle of the afternoon.

Red flew low, between the rows of pine trees that bordered the road, and was sure he could at least see the roof of a car or truck had one been there. No sign of any stranded automobiles or pickups. No sign of much of anything. He flew on into Prairie City, which had a population hovering around a thousand and didn't deserve the name City. From there he spoke to state police and those in John Day, eleven miles farther up the road with nearly twice as many inhabitants.

Nothing.

He refueled and flew back along Route 7, as close to the ground as he dared.

There weren't tracks of any kind. Snowplows had been partway up the road. It was about eighty miles from Baker to Prairie City, and between the two towns there was no sign of life on the road. Most of it was national forest, so there were very few houses along the roadside. They didn't even see deer tracks.

"What's worst," Red said to Jason, "is that I feel so helpless. I don't know what else to do. I keep telling myself Scott camped out in the wilderness in the snow over and over again when he was a kid. He'd know what to do."

Jason peered out the window. They'd been gone all day.

* * *

Red dropped Jason off at the school's athletic field and whirred into the air again, wondering if there were just anyplace left to look before he beat darkness home.

Cat couldn't understand why Scott hadn't returned. She'd waited all day. Maybe there was no way to get up the road. Snowplows were probably busy clearing streets in towns and certainly nothing less could plow through all this snow. It would take an army with shovels to go a mile, she thought. Scott was no doubt as worried about her as she was about him.

She'd had no food all day. Despite swallowing snow, her mouth was dry. At least no one could walk along here to rape or rob her. She was uncomfortable, cramped up in this seat all day and night. And she was colder than she'd ever been in her life. If only she could get the door open and at least stamp her feet on the blacktop, do something to exercise and warm herself. There was still over half a tank of gas, but she turned the heat on sparingly. What if Scott didn't get back for two or three more days?

She tried to think of something else. Michelle. Shelley McCullough. She sort of liked that name, but Scott wouldn't. Michelle sounded rather too French for Cougar Valley, Oregon.

She wondered if her father ever thought of her. He phoned her maybe monthly, but they didn't have much to talk about. He asked her each time if she was happy and if there were Indians in Oregon. She said yes to both and then didn't know what to say. He'd forget, at least about the Indians, and ask her the same thing again. How would he react to the news he was about to become a grandfather when his youngest wasn't quite eleven. Cat couldn't even remember her youngest stepsister's name.

She thought of food. She'd give her eyeteeth for a ham sandwich on some of Miss Jenny's homemade rye bread, slathered with mayonnaise and mustard. Kosher dill pickles, a helping of Thelma's cole slaw, and Pringles potato chips. A glass of cabernet sauvignon, some grapes and a slice of melon, as though she could get the latter two at this time of year. Nevertheless, she salivated at the thought.

She rolled down the window and reached out for a handful of snow. She didn't want the baby to become dehydrated, born wrinkled and already deformed because of malnutrition. Could her going without food for two days—actually it was two and a half days since she'd last eaten—starve the baby so that it would die within her? How would she know whether it was dead or alive? Could Chazz hear heartbeats this early in its life?

She'd learn to knit. She'd spend the spring and summer knitting bootees and little sweaters and maybe crochet a crib blanket. She wondered if the McCulloughs had an old-fashioned crib in one of the barns. She'd love that. She could refinish or repaint it. She hoped Scott wouldn't mind its sleeping in their room the first few months.

She didn't even know how to hold a baby. What kind of mother would she make? Would she be patient and understanding, would she demand too much or not enough?

She looked up through the tall trees at the darkening sky above and thought that in six weeks it would be light at this time. Daylight saving time would be here, her favorite time of year. She loved the long languorous evenings of summer when it didn't get dark until nearly ten. What she'd missed last summer was fireflies. No one seemed to know what she was talking about. No fireflies to glow in the evenings, for kids to put in jars in which they'd punched holes in the top and watch them beam erratically.

"Daddy called," Torie told Joseph when he appeared as she was peeling onions. "No sign of them."

Joseph walked over to her at the kitchen counter and, standing behind her, put his arms around her. "You are the single most gorgeous woman in the universe." He kissed her neck. Gooseflesh traveled down Torie's left arm.

"Behave yourself or you won't have dinner til nine."

His hands cupped her breasts. "Threat or promise?"

Torie finished peeling the onion and leaned her back against him. "How many times do you think we've made love?"

"Hm." Joseph thought, kissing the top of her head. "Several thousand, anyhow."

"How come I never get tired of it? Shit, you walk in the door and I'm ready to tear my clothes off, even after all these years."

"I'll help you, if you're propositioning me." He began to unbutton her sweater.

"Joseph Claypool, nobody in the whole world can do to a woman what you can."

"You've never even tried anyone else."

"Wouldn't be fair to them, would it? After you?"

He turned her around to face him and caught her face in his hands, staring deeply into her eyes.

"You are my world," he whispered.

"And you are mine," she said, raising her mouth to meet his.

They didn't eat dinner until after ten.

There would be no school the next morning, for the roads still had not been cleared. There had not been snow for two days, but the snow on the dirt roads that were serviced by school buses was piled high.

"Maybe I'll stay all night," Joseph said with a smile.

"You won't get an argument from me," Torie said, blowing out the candles on the table.

She awoke to Joseph's bouncing out of bed, standing, naked, at the foot of the bed, saying, "I have to phone your father."

"My father?"

He nodded and picked up the phone.

"It's not even light," Torie said. "He won't be awake."

"I think he hasn't slept much." Then into the phone, "Mr. McCullough, it's Joseph. I'm heading out your way right now. I'll be there by the time it's light. You know that cutoff from Route 7 that goes off the road between Granite and Sumpter? It's just a Forest Service road and we hardly use it even in the summer. Scott's truck's up there. Only way we can get in is helicopter."

Torie, also naked, sat upright. Neither she nor her father asked Joseph how he knew.

Joseph nodded his head as Red said something and hung up the phone. He reached for his shirt, which was lying on a chair. "Any chance you can make some coffee in a hurry? Instant's okay. I want to be outta here in five minutes."

Torie grabbed a sweater and slipped into it, practically running to the kitchen. She found some peanut butter and slathered it on bread for sandwiches.

While the microwave was heating water, she ran back to the bedroom and pulled more sweaters out of a drawer. She grabbed a couple of towels and found a nearly empty bottle of Scotch. She threw them all into a drawstring bag and filled a thermos full of instant coffee. She stretched out an arm to hand it all to Joseph, who leaned over to kiss her, but his mind was elsewhere. She could tell.

"I'd go with you, but the copter won't hold more than three."

"Your father may have to come back for me once we find them, but don't worry."

He was gone.

Torie walked back to her small kitchen and ground coffee beans for herself. While water boiled she went into the bathroom and drew on panties and a pair of sweats. She walked on the shellacked floor barefoot.

So, would it be so awful if their son, or daughter, couldn't tell things like that? Would Scott and Cat die if Joseph didn't have this awesome ability, for she knew he was going to find them. Wouldn't she, herself, die if she couldn't have Joseph, if she couldn't live out her life with him, bear his children—though she would willingly give up children if it meant living with Joseph. She would risk anything, dare anything, give up everything else to be his wife.

Cat could hardly move. She knelt on the seat, she tried to lie across it, but bucket seats weren't conducive to stretching out. She couldn't stand. She was tempted to crawl out through the window even if it meant standing in four feet of snow, but she was worried she could never get back in.

Her heart jumped in her chest when she heard the helicopter's whirring. She opened the window and stretched out as far as she could, waving her arms, searching from her disadvantaged viewpoint. The minute she saw it, she recognized it as Red's. Oh, thank God.

It was following the road, coming from the opposite direction, and she waved madly, hoping they could see the roof of the cab even if it was covered with snow. Could the helicopter land on the snow or would it sink in and not be able to take off?

As it moved closer, she saw Joseph waving from the craft. Oh, thank goodness. Thank heavens. She felt tension dissolve from her body.

The helicopter did land, but Red did not cut the engine. Joseph jumped out and, with a shovel, began to dig the snow from in front of him so he could reach Cat. He couldn't traverse the distance otherwise. Red followed him from the helicopter with another shovel, but it took them over fifteen minutes to clear a path to the pickup and pry open the door. Cat broke into tears as she fell into Joseph's arms.

Red peered into the cab. "Where's Scott?"

"He didn't tell you where I was?"

The men looked at each other, though Red reached out to encircle Cat in his arms, holding her close.

"He left two days ago to try to find help. He headed back the way we came."

"No one could walk through this," Red said, his voice thick. He looked down at Cat. "You all right?"

She sniffled. "I am now."

He kissed the top of her head and said to Joseph, "We'll have to shovel out under the copter in order to take off. We can pick this truck up when the snow melts."

Might be another month, or even longer, back here in the high country.

The men retraced their path through the snow, which was above Cat's waist.

"Where can Scott be?" she asked, but neither of them answered.

The peanut butter sandwich and coffee tasted like ambrosia. Cat donned three of Torie's sweaters, trying to throw off the chill that had captured her body. Red said, "Take a sip of that Scotch. It'll toast you."

Cat hated the taste of Scotch but did as she was told. It did warm her, even as it went down.

Red glanced at Joseph. "Let's follow the road down to Route 7. Look for any signs, of anything."

Cat knew Scott was safe and warm some place.

There were no telltale tracks, as it had snowed since he'd left the truck. But it hadn't snowed again for about twenty-five hours. If he'd been trudging since then, there would be some traces. Joseph did not take his eyes from the road that they knew was below them, in the lane between the towering pines.

Route 7 was passable, if still dangerous. They stopped in Sumpter to talk to police there, who put through calls to houses along the road where Scott might have found a haven. Nothing could have gotten through that road, they claimed. He might still be up the Forest Service road, in a cave or some makeshift protection he'd built.

The police in Sumpter took Red's phone number and promised to call if and when they discovered anything. As soon as they could get up the road, they'd search.

That wasn't good enough for Red, who said they'd fly back over it, retrace the route.

There was no sign of Scott. Once they found the pickup again, Red whirred higher and flew over the mountains to the Big Piney. Obviously Joseph had no clairvoyancy as to Scott's whereabouts. Red looked at the Indian, who shrugged his shoulders at the unanswered question.

"How about calling your father?" Red suggested.

"My father would have called me if he'd had any intimations," Joseph said, "but I'll phone him anyway. Maybe I'll drive out there now. First I'll call Torie and tell her I'm safe, then I'll drive out to my father's." The roads at the ranch, while still covered with snow, were passable, and there were just inches of snow compared to the feet back in the mountains.

Red put an arm around Cat's shoulders as they walked to the house. Neither of them said anything, and when they entered the house, Sarah was asleep in front of the fireplace, an empty glass on the table next to her chair.

Twenty

No one could think of anything but Scott. Cat fell asleep during the day from sheer exhaustion, but she couldn't sleep nights. She wandered down-stairs in her robe, and Red was always awake. Always waiting, it seemed, for the phone to ring or the door to open.

Life came to a standstill. Two days passed. Three. A week.

Sarah didn't eat a thing. She started drinking before the breakfast she didn't eat. By noon she was out of it. She babbled, muttering that Red should never have sent her son over to John Day. That Red should be out looking for him instead of . . .

Red kept going out to search for him until there were no other places to look. Red and Jason and Joseph, and all the able-bodied of Cougar spent hours and then days looking for Scott.

"God is punishing me for my sins," Sarah declared, weeping.

"Oh, Sarah, you can't believe that," Cat said. "If there's a God, he's not vengeful." Besides, what sins could Sarah have possibly committed? "He's a God of love."

"That's all you know." Sarah cried like a banshee. "He's taken my baby from me as punishment."

"Punishment for what?" Cat asked.

Sarah just waved her hands and reached for another Scotch. It was eleven in the morning.

Red had stopped responding to anything Sarah said. Cat thought she should, too.

Miss Jenny had come down to stay until they received word of Scott. None of them was any comfort for the other.

When ten days had passed, Jason came out to the Big Piney. It was early March, one of those rare winter days when you could tell spring was in the air. He knocked on the front door, and Miss Jenny answered.

"Morning, Miss Jenny," Jason said, hat in hand. "Red around?"

She nodded toward Red's office. It was as though all those at the ranch had stopped speaking.

He walked through the vast foyer and down the hall. He looked up to see Cat coming down the stairs. He stopped.

She came over and held her hands out. He took them, shaking his head. "No word yet."

Cat nodded, no tears left. She was pale and haggard-looking. She spent her mornings throwing up and her afternoons crying. The panic had subsided into a dull heavy ache that sat on her chest twenty-four hours a day.

Red's door was closed. Jason rapped lightly and entered. Red was standing staring out a window, the white glare of the snow blinding.

"Just thought I'd come see how you're doing."

Red nodded, his eyes reflecting his exhaustion. "Not well, I'm afraid. It'd be easier if we knew *anything* for sure. This uncertainty . . ."

"I could use a cup of coffee," Jason said, not really caring whether he had one or not. "And a sandwich." He bet no one here had eaten a meal since Scott's disappearance.

Red acted as though in a trance. "He's my only son, Jason. It's not just that he's the only chance of our name going on, but I love that boy. He's a part of me . . . and I don't know where the hell he can be. Is he alive or dead? Is he waiting someplace, with a broken leg or something, hoping to be rescued . . ."

"Red, we've searched everyplace. The Forest Service, the state police, the Sumpter and Granite police, the Boy Scouts, people have come from as far as Bend and Portland, you, me . . ."

Red waved a hand in the air as though to halt Jason. "I know. I know."

"Well, guess I'll go ask Thelma for something to eat and drink," Jason said when Red made no move to do so.

He walked to the kitchen and found Thelma, who wasn't in any better shape than the family. "Come on," Jason said, "fix us all some coffee and sandwiches, will you, Thelma?"

"No one'll eat."

"I will. And they'll have to, to keep up their energy."

Thelma took out a coffee grinder and hazelnut beans from the freezer. She ground them noisily and placed them in the coffeemaker.

Her shoulders sagged as she opened the refrigerator door. "What kind of sandwiches?" she asked, peering in.

"Surprise us, but make it substantial," Jason suggested.

With bread and mayonnaise in hand, Thelma said, "Sarah won't eat."

"Make one for her anyhow. And potato chips and pickles."

He walked back to Red's office. Red looked up. "He's dead, Jason. I know it."

Jason knew it, too.

"I wish the goddamned waiting were over. I wish we knew for sure."

"Thelma's making sandwiches. If I may make a suggestion, don't let Sarah have a drink at lunch."

"What difference does it make? It's one way of escaping."

"What's she been escaping from up to now?"

But Red's mind wasn't on Sarah's drinking.

Three days later, Joseph appeared at the door at ten-thirty in the morning. Miss Jenny had been staring out the window and saw Joseph's Forest Service car approaching. She had the door open, waiting to welcome him. He took his hat off and stood staring at her.

"I've come with bad news, Miss Jenny."

She sucked in her breath and said nothing, closing her eyes. "Where's Mr. McCullough and Cat?"

Miss Jenny didn't hear him.

Joseph called out, "Mr. McCullough?"

Miss Jenny pointed down the hall, to his office. Joseph walked across the foyer and down to Red's office. He was in the adjoining bathroom, shaving for the first time in three days. Joseph stood in the doorway.

"Come in," Red called, and when Joseph continued to stand there, Red came out of the bathroom, razor in hand, face half-lathered and said, in a monotone, "They've found him."

Joseph nodded. "I'm afraid so, sir. This morning. The snow's melted enough that they found his body just to the side of the road, about ten miles down from where the pickup still is."

"Jesus, God," Red said, sitting in the nearest chair. "Are you sure? Are they positive it's Scott?"

"Body's in pretty bad shape, but no doubt about it, sir."

Red felt that his chest might cave in.

"I'm sorry, sir. He was my best friend, you know."

Red nodded. "Yes, I know that, Joseph. I know how you must feel." He wondered if parents survived the death of a child. It wasn't supposed to happen that way. He guessed the worst thing in the world, the very worst thing in the universe, was having a child die before you did. He couldn't even envision a life without Scott. He couldn't imagine not breakfasting with his son, making plans for the Big Piney with his son and partner, doing much of anything without his son in the world.

They heard Cat's voice, Miss Jenny telling her that Joseph was here, not quite being able to break the news to Cat herself. The staccato sound of her boots on the shining floor made Red square his shoulders, and say, "I'll tell her, Joseph."

Joseph moved into the room and stood aside so that when Cat arrived the first person she saw was Red. One look at his face and posture told her.

She glanced briefly at Joseph and let out a keening cry, running to her father-in-law's outstretched arms. She gazed into his haunted eyes, and cried in a strangled voice, "No, tell me it isn't so!"

Red pulled her close as she burst into tears.

A blaze of light centered in back of her eyeballs, light so bright and glaring she couldn't see anything. She stopped breathing. She thought her heart had stopped. Red's hand on her shoulder moved, pulling her closer.

Behind her she heard Sarah's voice, "What is it?"

Joseph reached out to hold her.

"Get your hands off me, you heathen!" Her eyes were fastened on Red and Cat. She sank to the floor. "Dear God in Heaven, tell me it's not so!" But her frantic eyes, seeking Red's, told her it was so. She beat the floor with her fists, until Joseph reached down and put his hands under her arms and raised her slowly. She gave him a look of loathing. "Why couldn't it have been Torie?" she spit at him.

Red started out of his seat, letting go of Cat for a moment. "Sarah!"

There were no tears from Sarah; instead, she strode out of the room and in a minute they heard the sound of breaking glass.

Both Joseph and Red rushed from the room. Cat had to hold on to the chair because the room was revolving around her. She was too dizzy to walk.

Sarah had found Scott's old baseball bat in the umbrella stand, where it had stood for a decade, and was systematically bashing the glass out of the windows along the front porch.

Joseph reached her first, grabbing the bat from her hands while she beat her fists on his chest.

Red pulled her away, trying to hold her, to calm her. She wrested herself away from them and tore down the steps, running across the snow down the hillock and out along the driveway.

"Call Chazz," Red called to his mother, who was standing motionless in the living room. "Tell him to get out here with a sedative."

"I'll get her," Joseph said, heading toward his car.

"No, not you. Let me."

Joseph handed him the key to his car so that time wouldn't be wasted.

"Wait," Cat cried, running out onto the porch. "Let me come. You may need help." She jumped into the passenger seat as Red gunned the motor.

They were upon Sarah in a matter of minutes, but when she saw them approaching she veered away from the road and into the fields, mushy from melting snow, sinking in to her ankles. She stood mired in mud, her hands flailing the air.

Cat bounced out of the car before Red came to a complete stop. She ran through the fields, her arms outstretched to her mother-in-law. Sarah fell into them, sobbing uncontrollably, holding on to Cat as though she'd never let go. Red had started toward them, but seeing them wrapped in each other's arms, he stood by the car, his hand on its roof, looking at the weeping women and wondering why he wasn't allowed to do that.

An emptiness as large as the universe welled up inside him. If he lived to be a hundred he would mourn the death of Scott, and he knew it would be years before he could stop grieving. He had just lost a son.

Sarah had lost a son.

Cat had lost a husband.

Their lives would never again be the same.

Not ever.

Twenty-one

Sarah wouldn't come out of her room, even for the funeral. They had to use the school auditorium, for none of the churches was adequate. It seemed as though everyone in the town and the valley turned out. Norah Eddlington wrote the nicest obituary Cat ever read.

Cat went through the funeral as though sleepwalking. She and Torie and Miss Jenny clung to each other. Scott was buried in the family plot, under a spreading oak tree in a little square of land surrounded by a picket fence, about a hundred yards up the mountain, where McCulloughs for the last three generations were laid to rest. She and Red rode out on horses every day to the grave.

Spring came and went. One day melded into the next.

By the time summer was upon them Cat felt stirrings of life within her. A part of Scott would go on. She would always and forever have part of him. She was carrying part of him within her, and this was her only solace. She could scarcely stand the thought that his arms would never encircle hers again, he would never make her laugh, nor come up with crazy ideas, or take her snowmobiling or cross-country skiing. He would never share a Christmas with his child. She would never feel his kisses again. She often woke up crying. She was sure she would never feel whole again.

Sarah came downstairs only for dinner.

Red was forced to run the ranch, and had to take on the duties that Scott had performed, so he worked twice as hard as he had before.

He moved his clothes permanently to the bedroom down the hall, the one that used to be Torie's. Thelma took a tray up to Sarah at breakfast and lunchtimes, but Sarah barely tasted the food. Chazz suggested a psychiatrist, but when Red suggested this to Sarah, he couldn't reach her. She seemed deaf. It wasn't until midsummer that she came out of her trancelike state.

"At least she hasn't been drinking," Red said. "Maybe she's broken the habit."

But she hadn't.

She became obsessed about Cat's pregnancy. She wanted to touch Cat's belly and feel the baby move. She wanted Cat's assurance that, if it was a boy, he would be named Scott.

Cat shook her head. "Scott wanted him named Matthew."

Sarah began to knit. She knitted bootees and jackets and sweaters and crocheted blankets. She knitted caps and mittens and then more.

Torie came out to the ranch a couple of times a week, in spite of her mother's refusal to see her. Sarah acted as though Torie were to blame for being alive while Scott was dead.

Torie felt her brother's loss keenly. She played chess with her father in the evenings, and spent time up at Miss Jenny's.

Cat couldn't imagine feeling intense joy at the birth of this child, even though it was Scott's, because she knew she would never find happiness again. Yet as she felt it kick its feet she did feel life surge through her.

One Wednesday night in July, Red said, "Jason phoned. He thinks it's time to resume our weekly breakfasts. Want to come to Rocky's with me tomorrow?"

"I guess that's his way of telling us we have to get back into the mainstream of life . . ."

". . . whether we want to or not." He smiled and patted Cat's shoulder.

"It's so hot," Cat said, wiping perspiration from her forehead. "At least there's not the humidity of the East, but I wish there were a swimming hole or something around here. I don't suppose I can go into town in shorts, can I? Not in this condition."

"My dear," Red said. "As far as I'm concerned you can do anything you want to. You want to wear shorts, I'm not going to be embarrassed, no matter how big your belly."

Though they were greeted cordially and enthusiastically, no one in the restaurant acted like it had been months since either of them had appeared.

Jason had news for them too. "Sandy wants to come back."

Neither Red nor Cat said anything for a minute. They glanced across the table, their eyes meeting.

Ida brought them coffee, and said, "We have new kinds of muffins, Red. Carrot, orange, and coconut with nuts in them."

"Sound great," he said, winking at her. "Will they go with a Denver omelet?"

"They go with anything." She put a hand on his shoulder.

He reached up to touch it. "Better bring me a dozen if they're that good, and I'll take some home."

"Aren't a dozen left."

"Bring me whatever's left."

"How do you feel about it?" Cat asked Jason, sipping her coffee. For the first time since Scott's death she found herself *caring* about how someone *else* felt.

"I don't know," he said.

"Does Cody need her?" Red asked.

"I don't know. I thought we were doing pretty well, even though I can't take her place. He's done all right in school all year. He's got friends and doesn't seem to have been emotionally affected."

"How do *you* feel?" Cat asked again.

Jason took a minute to answer. "I've been happy."

"Do you want her back?" Red asked. Cat had told him the story of Jason's marriage. He'd be damned if he'd want a wife who preferred sleeping with women.

Jason shook his head. "I wish I knew. I sort of don't think so, yet don't I owe it to my son and even to our marriage to try everything? She says she'll go to a counselor."

"Where's one around here?" Red asked.

"Hear tell there's a really good one in Pendleton."

"Does she hope that consulting a shrink is going to change her sexual orientation?"

Jason looked around to see if anyone had heard Cat. "I don't know. Can it help?"

"People still tend to treat homosexuality"—Cat lowered her voice so that no one beyond their table could hear their conversation—"as an aberration that could be cured if one really wanted to. But I'm not convinced of that."

"What do you know about it?" Jason asked, almost accusingly.

"Jason, all you have to do is read a bit and listen to TV and the movies and take psychology courses in college. No one around here ever talks about it, but in cities, people are more open about it. Sandy may feel tortured, trying to fit in to a little community that frowns on anything that wouldn't be approved by a *Father Knows Best* script."

Red was staring at Cat as Ida appeared with his omelet and Cat's granola and muffin. Ida poured more coffee for them.

"Why does she want to come back?" Cat asked.

"She misses Cody." Jason poured cream in his coffee. "And though she didn't say it, I think she's having trouble making it financially."

"Do you want a woman who wants you just so she doesn't have to struggle to make ends meet?" Cat asked.

"There are more reasons than romantic love to stay in a marriage," Red said.

Jason and Cat both looked at him.

"I imagine there are as many reasons for getting married and for staying married as there are people," Jason answered.

"Are you lonely?" Cat pursued.

He shook his head. "I was lonelier when Sandy was here than I am now. I guess when you're in a relationship you expect something and when there's just about nothing you get lonely. I'm happy now. I wake up happy every single day. I don't even mind being mother and father. It makes me closer to Cody, I swear it does. And if he wants to run barefoot around the house, that's okay. There's no one to tell him to put shoes on. Or to tell me what I'm watching on TV is junk. There's no one always looking sad and longing for something that I can't supply."

So why couldn't Sandy have died instead of Scott? Why did a happy marriage have to end in tragedy? It didn't seem fair. Cat couldn't control her thoughts.

"She's trying to talk me into coming back to Seattle, or moving to Portland or San Francisco. She's a fish out of water here and doesn't fit in, she says."

Red waved to Ida. "Some orange juice," he called.

"What are you going to get out of it?" Cat wondered if he was sleeping with anyone now.

He shrugged. "Well, I'm thinking of trying it, for the boy's sake. His eyes lit up when he heard his mother might come back. You know, she calls him every Sunday. She didn't when she first left. I guess she just had to feel free of us for a while, but ever since Easter she's called him very week. He went to Seattle for two weeks in early July to be with her, and they had a fine time."

"Couldn't that satisfy her? Holidays and part of summer vacation?"

* * *

On the way back to the ranch, Red and Cat discussed Jason's predicament. It was good to have someone else to think about.

"He deserves the best," Red said. "So does the boy. I wish there were someone around here who was good enough for him, who appreciated him the way he should be."

Three days later Jason called and told Cat he had to drive over to Ontario on business and wondered if she'd drive along. He'd buy her dinner, and there'd be a full moon to drive home by.

"I think he needs someone to toss this around with," Cat said. Her inclination would be to advise him to say no. She thought that would be Red's advice, too.

But Jason had something else on his mind.

Twenty-two

"How come more people don't visit Oregon?" Cat asked as Jason drove seventy miles an hour toward the Idaho border. "Not that I expect you to have an answer, just wondering out loud."

"Because we're lucky, for one thing. Secondly, we're as far away from the centers of population as you can get, so it's not as easy to get here. There hasn't been much PR about what Oregon offers. What did you know about it before you moved here?"

Cat thought. "The Oregon Trail. Crater Lake. It rained, and there were mountains."

Jason drummed his fingers on the steering wheel. "Hey, not even Oregonians who mainly live in the Willamette Valley know how beautiful it is over here. Their weekend excursions stop at the Cascades. Bend is about as far east as they come. They have the Cascades and the coast where they can camp and fish, places nearby in which to get away from the world. They think the rest of the state is high desert and forget about it."

"That doesn't explain why the world isn't vacationing here. Is Washington as pretty?"

"Washington is every bit as pretty. In fact, Washington is outrageously beautiful. I don't know why we're not as famous as Wyoming and Colorado and Montana. Certainly we're as beautiful and have as much wilderness. We're just lucky that the world hasn't discovered us."

The windows were open and the afternoon heat blew hot on them. "You know, Jason, this is the first time I've been able to look at anything and appreciate it since . . . well, you know."

He nodded and reached out to put a hand over hers. "I'm glad you came."

"Me too."

Ontario was a bit over half the size of Baker, and about five times the size of Cougar, but it lacked Baker's Victorian charm.

"You want to get a Coke or something while I'm in the court-house?"

"I'll just walk around and take in the sights."

Jason laughed. "Won't take you long."

She watched his back as he walked up the courthouse steps and thought what a great friend he'd become. His erect stance and the formality of his uniform gave no indication of the warmth and sense of humor within. He was straight. Straight as an arrow. A good person to have around in times of trouble. And any other time.

It was good of him to have brought her along. She hadn't realized how much she'd needed to get out, have a change of pace. She knew he wanted to talk about Sandy, but he was taking his time, letting Cat relax and shift moods.

She walked down one side of Main Street and up the other, just a few blocks long. She walked into what passed for a department store and was drawn to the baby section. She couldn't resist purchasing two soft flannel receiving blankets, the first things she'd bought for the baby. She purchased a dozen diapers, too. It felt good to have something positive to look forward to, though she nearly burst into tears while paying the salesclerk at the thought that Scott would never see his child.

She stuck a note under the windshield of Jason's car and went down the street to a Dairy Queen, where she indulged in a peanut buster parfait. Nothing had tasted that good in months. She sat, staring out the window, watching the few people on the street. They nodded to each other or waved across the street or to a passing car. She wondered if small towns back East were as friendly as the Northwest. She imagined they were—when you lived in a place where you knew everybody you didn't throw up defenses, and you were open to the neighborliness that small towns seemed to engender.

It was another half hour before Jason appeared, sliding into the booth opposite her and ordering lemonade. "Business attended to," he said.

"Does that mean you're off duty?"

"What did you have in mind?" He looked interested.

"I've never been to Boise. How far is it?"

Jason glanced at his watch. " 'Bout forty, fifty miles."

"Do you have to be home at a certain time?"

He shook his head. "No, I can phone home and tell Katie I'll be late. She won't mind putting Cody to bed. You want to go over to Boise for dinner, is that it?"

"Well, what's another hundred miles? And it feels so good to be out and about. I'm enjoying myself so much I don't want today to end."

He gave her a look she couldn't decipher, and said, "Sounds good to me. I'll call on my car phone. You finished? Let's go." He reached out and took her hand.

They arrived in Boise about five, too early for dinner. Cat said, "I'm just yearning to visit a bookstore, Jason. Do you mind? I don't even know what's new in the book world."

He couldn't believe it when she bought twenty-two books. One was the updated Dr. Spock, but the rest were current best-sellers.

"Hey, most of these are adventure, how come? Aren't you a typical woman?"

"Boy, are you a sexist! Do you mean if anything's out of the realm of romance and homemaking, it's not typically feminine? Well, I hope not. What's wrong with adventure? And Dick Francis. Do you know him?"

Jason shook his head. " 'Fraid not."

"I ought to remedy that. Dick Francis is an ex-jockey who writes a best-seller a year, always something to do with horses, but you don't have to like horses to like Dick Francis. His heroes always have some flaw, like one has an extramarital affair, but you forgive him because his wife is in a wheelchair and they haven't had sex in ten years and he loves and cherishes his paralyzed wife, so he explains to the other woman that he's not going to leave his wife. A thoroughly nice guy."

"The hero or the author?"

"I suspect Francis is as nice as his heroes."

"As nice as you are."

She turned to smile at him as they each carried a bag of books to the car. "I haven't felt I was much of anything these past months."

"We'll talk about you at dinner."

"We will? And where are we going to eat? I'm starving. After all, I'm eating for two."

Jason opened the car door, and they piled the bags in the rear seat. He closed the door and locked it and took Cat's arm. "Up the street here. I've eaten here a couple of times and the steaks are great."

"Oh, Jason." A warm breeze came up and riffled Cat's hair. "I feel better than I've felt since February."

He squeezed her arm, pointing to an awning that jutted out into the street. Scrawled across it in bright red was the name of the restaurant.

There were a few customers already even though it was barely six.

A waiter led them to a secluded table which had fresh flowers and dim lighting. "How come," Cat asked, expecting no answer, "in fast-food places and in restaurants where the bill's about $4.95, there are waitresses, but in more expensive restaurants it's men?"

Jason raised eyebrows. "I certainly hope you're not expecting me to answer such a question."

"I want pork chops," Cat said, scanning the menu. "I have a pregnant urge for two extremely large well-done thick juicy pork chops with applesauce."

"French fries or baked potato?"

"Baked. And I want two or three glasses of wine, but since I'm pregnant I'll settle for one. Do you think they have a Merlot?"

"We'll see."

Cat sighed as the waiter brought two wineglasses of a French Merlot. She took a sip, and said, "You chose good, sir. The food's got to be good if the wine is this divine."

Jason smiled.

Cat sank back into her chair, glass in hand. "For months I've thought I could never enjoy anything again. This is such a treat. And the timing's right. I wasn't ready before this."

He put his elbows on the table and leaned toward her. "I'd like to talk about something you may not be ready for."

"Jason, I'm ready to talk about anything you want to. Just realize I'm slightly prejudiced. From what you've told me, I don't think Sandy will be good for you to have around. Cody seems to be doing fine, better than that. If I've seen any normal, well-adjusted, really nice boy it's your son. I only hope I have a child half as nice."

Jason took a big swallow of his whiskey. "That's sort of what I want to talk about. Not Sandy so much but Cody . . . you . . ."

The wine warmed Cat as it went down.

"Look, I know you're not ready to hear what I have to say, but I'm going to say it anyhow. Cat, I've been in love with you since the night I met you."

She nearly dropped her glass. She did set it on the table.

"Your heart isn't ready for me, it's still got grieving to do, and I'm aware of that."

She stared at him.

"Sandy and I hadn't been getting along for years, and there you were . . . and I wanted you so bad I had to fight to control it. Getting to know you, becoming your friend, has only strengthened my feelings. Don't get me wrong. I never wanted Scott to die. I mourned his death. Still do. I had settled for being your friend, knowing I'd see you several times a week, that I could be near you . . ."

Cat reached out to put a hand on his. "Why, Jason."

His other hand closed over hers.

"I don't want Sandy to come back. You're the only one in my heart. I want you to marry me, let me be a father to your child, you be a mother to Cody. He loves you, too. Even though your heart isn't ready for love, for another man yet, get on with life, Cat."

Cat was blinking hard. Her mouth felt dry, and she had trouble swallowing. She closed her eyes, her hand still surrounded by Jason's.

"Oh, Jason, that's just about the nicest thing . . . I had no idea. But I can't feel anything yet. Today's the first day that I've felt any interest in anything. I'm not ready for my emotions to be engaged. I didn't even think I had any emotions anymore, I've been operating on such an even plane of depression. But yesterday and today, I feel glimmerings of glad to be alive, of interest in something beyond myself and my grief. But I'm not yet ready to take on any responsibility for anyone other than myself. I hope that come October, I'm ready to take on motherhood. I'm determined I will be. But it *is* too soon."

"I know that, but I want you to have it in your mind. And hopefully, your heart. If you won't marry me now, will you think about it? Carry my love around with you, Cat?"

She didn't know how to respond.

The waiter appeared with their salads. She slathered on ranch dressing until she could hardly see the vegetables. She studied it as though it were the single most interesting thing in the universe.

"I'll be there when the baby's born, if you like, and I'm ready to be a father to it, Cat. He, or she, could keep the name McCullough, but I'd be happy to adopt the child. Nothing in the world would make me happier than to have you as my wife."

Cat waved a hand in the air. "Don't press it, Jason. I can't even think of anything like that. Not yet. Give me time. I'm flattered. I really am. Certainly you're one of the nicest people in my life. I cherish you . . ."

"Well, that's a beginning."

"All I can think of now is the baby. I hope I'm up to giving it what it needs. I couldn't be any kind of wife to you or mother to Cody at this point."

"I'm glad you added 'at this point.' Understand, though, that I am going to begin to be an active important part of your life."

"You've been important all along."

He cut into his rare T-bone. "Not on a daily basis. You're not going to be able to ignore me from now on."

Cat smiled at him. "Jason, you're about the last person I'd ever want to ignore. I do appreciate what you're saying, and I'm quite pleased, really. Here I thought you brought me to talk about Sandy."

"No. I don't want her back in my life. I'm sure of that. I want you in it."

"If I weren't around, would you take her back?"

"No." He shook his head. "I asked Cody how he felt, and he said, 'We're pretty happy, aren't we, Dad?' which I think was rather adult for an eight-year-old. And we are happier and freer than we ever were with his mother in the house. You know what I think she'll do when I tell her? I think she'll go to San Francisco. She's wanted to live there for years. Seattle's pretty liberal, but she'd feel far more at home in California. I know it. She's a nurse, you know."

"No, I didn't know that." Cat noticed the green flecks in Jason's eyes.

"She hated it, though. But she could get a job in a hospital, or a hospice, or privately. There's always a demand for nurses."

"Most of the world works in jobs they don't like."

"Yeah," Jason agreed, breaking open his baked potato and covering it with sour cream and chives. "I am lucky, I know it. A job I love."

"I think that's a career rather than a job."

"Did you like being a lawyer?"

"I loved it. My adrenaline flowed. It demanded problem solving and creativity and intelligence and . . ."

"And you were good at it, I bet."

Cat smiled. "I think so. I got dressed up every day and went out to compete with men. I think I grew up wanting to work in a man's world. When I was a kid I never spent time thinking of getting married, though heaven knows I was interested in boys, but I wanted to be *doing* something. I wanted to be an *active* part of the world, a foreign correspondent in Argentina or someplace in Europe . . ."

"Argentina?" Jason's voice cracked.

"I don't know why there. Or I toyed with being a doctor, a surgeon so I could make megabucks . . ."

"And help save people, too, I imagine . . ."

"That was somewhere in there, but I was mainly thinking of doing something that women had traditionally not participated in. And now, here I am, becoming a mother, and that's all I think about."

"That's probably happened to women since the beginning of time."

"You mean women giving up dreams to become mothers?"

"And wives. When I was in school it seemed the smartest and most creative were usually girls, but then they sort of dropped out of sight after they got out of school, to get married."

"Like that's the end of the line? Well, Jason, I have to tell you that despite feminism, I still think that's what men want. A woman to come home to, to keep his house neat, to take care of his children, cook his meals, and look up to him."

Jason grinned. "Sounds good to me."

When he saw the look on Cat's face, he reached out to touch her across the table, and said, "It *does* sound good and boring as hell. I wouldn't want that to be the limit of your life. Me and Cody and the new baby."

"Who would have time for more?"

"Winston Churchill helped to win World War II, was up half the night in conferences, wrote a raft of books, and painted impressive paintings."

Cat sat back in her chair and studied Jason.

Jason grinned. "And he took naps after lunch, too."

"He couldn't have done it without a wife who brought up the kids and kept his clothes pressed and food on the table."

"Fortunately, I'm a pretty good cook, I even iron my own shirts, and pay Katie Thompson to do everything else. She does most of the cooking now, but I *am* a good cook."

"You'll have to invite me to dinner some night."

"That's an offer I can't refuse."

"I hoped not."

"How about Saturday?"

"Sure," she answered.

"Would you like me to invite Torie and Joseph, too?"

"That's be nice."

"You like lasagna?"

"Who doesn't?"

They finished eating at the same time.

"No dessert for me," Cat said. "No coffee. I'm full."

Jason asked for the check. As they walked from the restaurant to the car, Cat said, "I like you, too, Jason."

"I know that. But I want more from you."

"Give me time."

"I'll give you all the time you need. But whether you're ready for it or not, I'm going to kiss you good night."

Cat didn't know how she felt about that.

It was just getting dark when they arrived back at the Big Piney a bit after nine-thirty.

"You want me to drive out and pick you up Saturday?"

"No, I'll drive into town. Just because I'm pregnant doesn't mean I'm incapacitated." She opened her door.

Jason leaned over to hold onto her arm. "Uh-uh. You're not getting out of here without a good night kiss."

"Jason . . ."

He pulled her close, his mouth moving onto hers. His lips were gentle as his arms wound around her. Cat sighed.

"That was nice, Jason."

"It was that," he said, unwilling to let her go.

"Just go slowly, please."

"I'll try," he said.

Though the house was dark, there was a light on in Red's office, but Cat didn't follow the beckoning light, going straight upstairs to her room instead. She wanted to be alone to consider the events of the day.

She felt guilty to have enjoyed another man's kiss. It was as though she was being unfaithful to Scott, who had only been dead five months. Yet she felt stirrings of life, and it was not only the little creature growing within her.

She wondered if Scott would approve, how he'd feel about her getting on with her life. She would never forget him. He would always be a part of her. But she was twenty-seven years old and would live for many more decades. Today showed her there was still something of interest in life.

She smiled as she crawled between the sheets, and tried to push away feelings of guilt.

Twenty-three

On October tenth Cat awoke feeling more energetic than she'd felt in weeks. Months. She'd wakened several times during the night with cramps in her legs, but she felt refreshed.

She waddled as she walked, but that bothered her not at all. The idea that she was about to bring a child into the world was a marvel to her. The thought that Scott would not disappear from this earth gave her life meaning.

She had been surprised to find herself able to enjoy life again. She and Joseph and Torie had gotten into the habit of Sunday night suppers at Jason's. She could tell sometimes, by the expressions in Torie's and Joseph's eyes, that they'd approve of her liaison with the sheriff.

Though he never said anything, Red approved of her seeing Jason, but not Sarah. Sarah had only one topic of conversation, and that was Scott's baby. She probably didn't even know Cat was seeing Jason. It wouldn't dawn on her that an ungainly, waddling, very pregnant woman would have a man interested in her. Jason hadn't said anything about marriage since that day in July, but he made it obvious that he cared for her. He did not pressure her, for which she was grateful, and she enjoyed his company.

"I'm starving," she told Red, who hadn't yet left for the day.

"I'm planning to be up at the Spring Creek area today," he said. "I'll have the cellular phone with me. Need me at all, phone. Okay?"

"Of course." She bent over to kiss the top of his head as she headed to the sideboard to help herself to scrambled eggs and crisp bacon, Thelma's buttermilk biscuits and raspberry jam. "You know what? We eat better than anyone else in the world, I bet."

Thelma stuck her head around the kitchen door. She grinned. "I heard that."

"I'm glad. You were meant to."

"If you're going to have that baby today," Red proclaimed, "maybe I won't go as far as Spring Creek."

"What makes you think today's the day?" Cat asked, plopping into a chair.

"You're glowing. You look positively beautiful," her father-in-law told her.

Cat blinked and felt herself blushing. She laughed self-consciously. "Beauty must be in the eye of the beholder, because no one else but family would call me beautiful in this condition."

"Well, you are today." Red poured himself another cup of coffee and poured cream into it. "You are every day," he said in a lower tone of voice.

"Ha!" Cat said. "That's just because you've grown to love me. When I compare myself with Torie and Sarah . . ."

"Don't ever do that!" Anger shot from Red's eyes, his voice was unusually loud. He stood up, coffee cup in hand, and said, "I'll stay home today. I'll either be in my office or the barn. I'm trying to find someone to help Glenn." His foreman. "I'll work on that. Make some phone calls."

Cat was surprised at Red's reaction. He turned around in the doorway, and said, "Sorry I shouted," but didn't wait for a response from her.

The phone rang. It was Chazz, calling to ask how Cat was and to tell her he'd be west of town, out at the Murchisons', but he had his cellular phone with him and could be at the hospital or in contact whenever she wanted. For the last three days he'd kept in close touch with her, letting her know where he could be reached. He'd phone again about noon.

"I feel great," she said. "Wonderful."

"Uh-oh." She could tell the doctor was smiling. "Then it's likely to be today."

"That's what Red said."

"Okay, I'll keep in touch. But you phone if you're in any doubt."

"It would be nice to have it on such a beautiful day."

Adrenaline surged through Cat. Funny, because she felt so great, both men had decided this was to be the day. She hoped they were right.

The phone rang again.

"That you, Cat?" It was Miss Jenny's voice. "I hope I've arrived in time."

"Where are you?" Cat was thrilled to hear her voice.

"I just arrived in Portland. I'll be home this afternoon."

"Why didn't you call Red? He'd have flown over to get you." Miss Jenny had been gone six weeks, during which time they'd received three postcards from England and one from France, all of which only told them that the traveler was having a marvelous time. It was the first time Miss Jenny had been out of the country.

"You aren't a mother yet, are you?"

"No. I'm still enormous and fat and waddling like a duck, but you better hurry home if you want to beat the baby. You had a wonderful time?"

"I can't even begin to tell you. Is Red there?"

"Just a minute." Cat walked, not very gracefully, down the hall, calling, "Red, Miss Jenny's on the phone."

She heard him pick up his phone and hung up. How wonderful to have Miss Jenny home before the baby was born.

She walked upstairs, took a long oil-scented bath, and dressed. She was in a hurry for nothing. All she had on her agenda was giving birth, and that would come in its own time.

She went back downstairs and walked out on the porch, looking across the valley at the mountains sharply etched against the cobalt sky. Falling leaves had scattered from the tall oak trees and crackled under her feet as she walked across the lawn. She inhaled deeply.

She walked all the way down to the mailbox, nearly half a mile, even though she knew there would be no mail this early. Then she walked back to the house via the road. If she could have run, she would have. Energy spilled from her. She felt the baby's movements, readying itself to enter the world.

She had the wild urge to turn somersaults. Maybe today she'd become a mother, and it might be years before she'd have another morning just to herself. Twenty years, maybe.

Red found her standing in the leaves, hugging herself. He stood in the doorway, gazing out at her, silhouetted against the distant mountain range, and felt his heart turn over.

Three hours later she came to his office, smiling. She knocked three times on the already open door, and said, "You're right. It's today. My water's broken, and I'm getting regular contractions."

"I'll call Chazz."

Chazz's phone didn't answer. He'd no doubt left it in the car and was in someone's house.

"He was going to be at Murchisons'," Cat volunteered.

Red found the phone book, leafed through it, and called their number. Mrs. Murchison said Chazz had been and gone, and didn't know where he was heading next.

"Well, we can head to the hospital anyhow," Red said.

"My pains are about every ten minutes. Isn't it too early to head there?"

"I'd rather be early than late," Red said, standing up. "Do you have to pack anything?"

"I've had a suitcase ready for two weeks," Cat said, then doubled over as a pain seared through her. Red rushed to her and put his arms around her, holding her. She straightened up. "Wow. That was a good one."

"Let's get going," Red said. "I'll get the car and pull up in front. Okay?"

Cat nodded.

"I'll go get your bag. I can bring anything else you need later."

"Do you want to tell Sarah?" Sarah had not appeared all morning. Thelma had taken tea and toast and left it on a tray in front of her bedroom door, but it hadn't been touched.

Red just looked at Cat. Then he bounded up the long stairway, two at a time, and was back in a minute with her overnight bag. "Wait on the porch for me. I'll have the car around quick as I can."

While waiting, another sharp pain shot through Cat. She sat on the top step, unable to move, huddled over, her arms around her knees. She began to shiver. Shit, no one had said it was *this* bad. Or at least she hadn't believed what she thought were old wives' tales. Ah, that was better. Once the pain left, it was as though it had never been.

When the Caddy pulled around the side of the house, Cat picked up the suitcase and walked down the steps slowly.

"No one knows."

"I do," Red said, helping her into the seat and placing the bag on the backseat. "And I'm as related to this baby as you can get and not be the absolute father."

"That's true." Cat smiled. He walked around the front of the car and got back in. He hadn't turned off the motor, which purred so quietly Cat hadn't been sure it was on.

"I'm glad you're here," she told him.

He drove with his left hand and reached out to take her hand in his right one. "I am, too, my dear."

"Ouch," she said, squeezing his hand and curling her legs up. "They're coming really quickly now."

"I'll take the back road. It'll be quicker."

But before they'd gone three miles a sharp stone cut the left rear tire and the car swerved. Red stopped, saying "shit" quietly, and got out to see what was wrong. One look told him.

"You're going to have to get out while I change this tire. Of all times for this to happen."

The nearly midday sun warmed Cat. She lumbered out of the car and walked back to where Red was opening the car's trunk.

"Damn," he said. "This won't take long."

She stood and watched him until another pain hit her. Then she doubled up and sat down in the middle of the dirt road. Red continued working but looked at her, worry furrowing his brow. "You okay?"

Cat didn't respond. She didn't know whether or not she was. She felt terrific pressure in her lower back, and that pain didn't go away. It sat there, rendering her incapable of talking, so severe was it. Red jacked the car up and began to loosen the lugs.

"Red!"

He continued working but looked at her.

"It's coming."

"It just feels that way. It wouldn't happen so quickly." Sarah had been in labor four and five hours. "I'll be through here in a jiffy. You get up now, and go get the car phone and phone Dodie. If she can't get Chazz, she's delivered about a hundred babies herself." He thought that would give Cat something to do, something to think about other than the pains that were coming too fast.

But Cat didn't budge. She just kept sitting in the middle of the road, hugging her belly and rocking back and forth, as though to alleviate the aching. She tried to remember how she'd been taught to breathe, trying not to hyperventilate.

Red had the tire off and now got the spare from the trunk, working as fast as he could. When Cat cried out again he stopped, went to the front door, opened it and reached in for his cellular phone.

It wasn't there. And he suddenly remembered he'd taken it out the previous afternoon, when he wanted to make a call from the barn, and that's where it was now, sitting on a stack of hay. Shit a brick!

He went back to the tire, to hear Cat moaning. "Oh, Red, it's coming!"

It couldn't be. She hadn't been in pain for even an hour and a half. It couldn't be this quick. She just felt that way. After all, it was her first time.

He finished, stowing the gear in the trunk. "Okay, honey, we're ready," he said. He walked over, leaning down to help her stand.

"I can't," she said.

"Come on," he urged.

"No," she said.

He put an arm around her, and she collapsed against him. "Red, I can't help it. I feel it coming. Oh, Jesus Christ!"

He opened the back door, so she could lie down as he sped to the hospital. It would take another thirty or forty minutes at least.

Cat stretched across the length of the seat. "Hurry," she said, gasping for breath. She swore she could feel a head bursting out. Red started the car.

She reached down to feel between her legs and whispered, "Red, I feel something."

He stopped the car, got out, walked around, and said, "Cat, do you want me to look?"

"Oh, dear." After a second, she nodded. "You'll have to. Red, I think you're going to deliver your grandchild."

He pulled down her panties and whistled. "Sure enough, there's a head. Well, Cat, you're right. You're having your baby right here, and looks like I'm going to deliver it."

He tried to think. He had his Swiss Army knife, so he could cut the umbilical cord. As long as the baby came headfirst, he thought he could handle it. He couldn't remember how many calves and piglets and lambs he'd helped into this world. But his heart hadn't pounded for them, and he could hear it thumping so loudly he wondered if Cat heard it, too.

In the trunk there was an afghan Sarah had crocheted long ago. He opened the trunk and pulled it out.

"Cat, let me put this under you." No sense in ruining an expensive, relatively new car. He lifted her and placed the blanket under her.

"Don't be shy," he said. "I am related, you know. It's my grandchild. My blood, too. Here, jackknife your legs, yeah, like that, so I can see what I'm doing."

A severe pain shot through Cat, so severe that her whole world blackened. She heard a scream and realized it must be her own voice. *Oh, Jesus God,* she thought. *Let it be all right. Dear God, don't let anything be wrong with Scott's baby. Let me be all right. Let this pain . . . oh, Jesus Christ Almighty.*

"Swear all you want," Red said, "and push."

He'd been there with Sarah when each of their children was born. The doctor had permitted him in the delivery room, so he'd seen it all twice, but being an observer and actually delivering were two quite different things. He tried to remember how babies came out. "Push," he said again. He reached out his arm and said, "Hold on to me, Cat, and scream as loud as you want."

Perspiration dripped from her face. He leaned into the car, knelt on one knee, and said, "I'm here, honey. Red won't let anything happen to you. We're in this together. Come on, hold on to me when you feel that pain. I see the head, come on, not too hard, but push, we need your help to get him out . . . there, there." He leaned over to kiss her hand, his eyes on her face.

She pushed, and he let go of her to help gently pull his grandson into the world. He couldn't help grinning, as he caught the baby and immediately wrapped it in his suede jacket. The red blotched baby cried.

"It's a boy," he told her, "and looks as healthy as can be." Was it? He laid the baby on the floor of the backseat. "You can rest a minute, honey."

"Hold him up for me to see. My baby."

He was so ugly she could hardly believe it.

"He's beautiful," Red said, laying him back on the floor, in the suede bassinet.

Cat closed her eyes, exhausted. Another pain overcame her. Red reached out his arm, and said, "Come on, clasp it. Hold on to me."

What would she do without him? He wasn't even nervous. He seemed to know exactly what to do.

"Okay," she heard her father-in-law's voice, "here it comes. Push again, Cat, come on, that's it. Let's get rid of the afterbirth."

Cat's exhausted voice came through. "I think there's another."

"It's just the placenta."

How did he know so much? Cat thought she was too tired to push anymore, but with Red's urging, the afterbirth followed. Red caught the liverish-looking stuff and tossed it at the side of the road. He wiped his bloody hands on his pants. He debated whether to return home and wash up or drive on like this to the hospital. Cat and the baby seemed fine. He heard it make gurgling sounds. Maybe they didn't even need a hospital. He'd go back home, phone Chazz or

Dodie and have them decide. He wondered if his chest had swelled out noticeably. He'd delivered his own grandchild. And he'd seemed to do a pretty good job.

Cat sprawled in the backseat, partially sitting so she could accept the bundle he held out to her. After looking at her son, she closed her eyes and lay exhausted, breathing regularly but heavily. Her hair was stringy with sweat, her face still damp with perspiration, her skirt blood-spattered and gooey. Red thought he had never seen anyone more beautiful in his life.

He'd better get back home so he and Thelma could wash them up and get Dodie out here pronto, and hopefully Chazz, too.

He leaned over and kissed Cat on the forehead.

"I love you, Red," she said.

"I love you too, honey," he told her. At the moment he thought he loved the two beings in the backseat as much as he'd ever loved anyone in his life.

Twenty-four

Chazz decreed that as long as there was someone to take care of Cat and the baby, he saw no need for a hospital. Red had done a superb delivery.

Cat couldn't understand why she was so exhausted. It was all she could do to get out of bed and get to the bathroom. Thelma ran up and downstairs, Red insisted on bathing Matt. Cat lay on the bed watching it all and sleeping. Sarah, for all her interest in Scott's progeny, did nothing except stand over the baby, cooing.

Miss Jenny, home from Europe, moved into the big house and took charge of everything. She was almost unrecognizable. She had had her hair cut in a Parisian salon. Cat laughed, and Red gasped when they first saw the glamorous woman she'd become. Though she was still prone to slacks around the ranch, they were now couturier-cut and she looked like she was dressed in clothes from a Hollywood horse movie. She'd had her ears pierced and wore dangling earrings that shimmered when she tossed her head.

She was wearing eye shadow and had drawn fine lines above her eyes so that she looked mysterious and glamorous.

"Funny," she told Cat when they were alone in Cat's room and the baby was asleep, "but I'd always thought no place could compare with America. I'd felt sorry for all these billions of people living in someplace other than the good old United States. My, have I changed my mind!"

She'd spent three weeks in England and two and a half in France and couldn't decide which she liked better. The food in England was so bland that France won in that category. She felt at home in England because everybody spoke English and she, who ordinarily didn't like cities, loved London. She never did get to see as much of the English countryside as she wanted. She'd met some people who'd invited her to their estate in Cornwall, so she did go there, and it was lovely, just lovely. Hilly and on the coast, and tranquil.

"You broke through the famous British reserve?" Cat asked, as she nursed Matt. She really enjoyed being by herself when she nursed, but Miss Jenny was like a breath of spring air, and Cat was exhilarated by her presence. "They invited you into their home and you were just there three weeks?"

Miss Jenny nodded. "It was funny. I sat next to this brother and sister at *Les Mis* and we got to talking, and then we went out together for a late supper after the theater, and one thing led to another and we lunched the next day and one or the other of them took me all over London in the next few days and then we went to Cornwall for four days.

"In fact, he flew over to Paris the last three days I was there." She laughed self-consciously and touched her hair. "He hardly recognized me!"

Cat cocked her head and studied her grandmother-in-law. "Do I notice some male-female stuff here?"

Miss Jenny laughed, not at all the way Cat was used to. A faint blush crept over her cheeks.

"Ah, that's why you did all this glamour routine, isn't it?"

Miss Jenny didn't quite answer Cat, but she said, "Wait until you see my new wardrobe!"

"Where are you going to wear it?"

Miss Jenny took Matt and cuddled him against her bosom. "I've been thinking about that. In January, when it's's so bitter here, I thought maybe I'd toddle over to Thailand or India or Australia."

"Toddle over?" Cat broke into laughter.

"Must be the British influence," smiled Miss Jenny, managing somehow to look mysterious. "Well, anyhow, I'm glad I got back in time for all this." Holding Matt, she sat in the chair next to the bed, letting the baby grasp her finger. She kissed his forehead. "This is the most beautiful baby."

Cat agreed. In four days he'd filled out and was no longer blotched and squirrelly-looking. She knew Red and Miss Jenny both were pleased as punch at the color of his red hair.

"I'm going to come down for dinner tonight," Cat announced. "I've lollygagged and been waited on long enough."

"It's Friday. Torie said she'd be out tonight, that she'd take over my duties for the weekend. Let her, Cat. Make her feel a part of all this."

Torie had rushed out after school on Tuesday as soon as she knew Matt had been born, and come out the next day, too, her arms filled with toys and clothes and a little bicycle, which wouldn't be used for several years.

Miss Jenny had brought tiny sweaters and snowsuits and soft cashmere blankets from England.

Red sauntered in half a dozen times a day. He was proud of his role in the delivery. Last night when he'd come in about nine, he'd been carrying an old Stephen King novel, *Christine*. "Just starting it," he told her. "This guy's good. Things happen in his novels you know can't happen. A little girl gets upset and her anger starts fires. A car has a personality. I mean you know these things are impossible, but King makes you believe in them."

"Are you averse to reading to me?" Cat asked.

Red looked surprised. "TV's got better actors."

"Maybe, but their stories are lousy. I'd rather you'd read to me, unless you hate doing that sort of thing."

"I'd love to. You want me to begin now?" The house was quiet, and Cat wasn't nearly ready for sleep. She was recouping her energy and was slept out.

"Mm," she murmured, getting comfortable under the covers. "I have to be awake at eleven to nurse anyhow."

He pulled the chair closer to the bed and sat down, opening the book. Then he looked at her. "Want a glass of wine or hot milk or cocoa or anything?"

"Oh, cocoa sounds great. With marshmallows."

He smiled and got up. "I'll be right back. Don't go away."

"As if I ever would."

He looked back at her over his shoulder before heading downstairs to make cocoa for her. For the first time since his son had died, Red was aware of experiencing a feeling of happiness. Of joy, even.

Jason had come out to see the baby the day after he was born. He waited until late afternoon, after school got out, so he could bring Cody with him. Cody looked with round wide eyes at the tiny human being lying in its bassinet, and asked, "Would he like a puppy to play with?"

"Not yet," Cat assured him.

Jason brought a bouquet of flowers for which they had no vase large enough. Miss Jenny divided it into three smaller ones, and decided she'd keep the smallest one in her room, nobody would know.

Sarah said, "Thank you, Jason," as though the flowers were for her. She sat in the rocking chair in Cat's room, humming to Matthew, her eyes riveted on him, though one was never sure if that's where her attention was.

Chazz had tried to interest Sarah in AA, but she'd looked shocked, exclaiming, "Why ever do you think I need that? One or two drinks before dinner doesn't call for that," but ever since Scott's death, she'd started drinking before breakfast. Or a drink was her breakfast. She spoke in slurred speech all day. She thought no one noticed. Perhaps she was the only one who didn't. The only reason her clothes were neat and cleaned was that Thelma took care of them. Cat was afraid to let her pick up the baby. But Sarah only tried to do that when she sat in the rocker next to the bassinet and leaned out to pick up her grandson, crooning to him as she rocked back and forth.

In the year and a half that Cat had known her mother-in-law, Sarah's looks had changed drastically. She was no longer stylishly dressed; often she forgot to apply makeup, and her mouth always seemed slack, her eyes fastened on some faraway place.

Red finally talked about it, saying, "We can't make her stop. She has to want to."

But Sarah denied there was any problem.

When Cat began to feel stronger, Miss Jenny and Red tried to limit her to taking care of the baby. Not that she had ever done any of the housework. Cat made her bed, but that was the extent of it. She suspected Sarah and Red didn't even do that. She didn't know about Miss Jenny. When Miss Jenny was up at her lodge, she had no help at all, except in the spring when she hired someone to do a thorough job of spring cleaning.

The first week after Matt's birth, Jason drove out three times. Cat took great pleasure in his attention. She began to look at him in a different way.

And then, though he had told her he did not want her back, Sandy moved to town. She waited after school for Cody and took him to her little house and gave him cookies and milk and invited his friends there, but it didn't click. Cody told his father, "I love her, Dad, but my friends don't enjoy going over there. We like to do other things."

"Can't you tell her that?"

The boy shook his head. So Jason took himself over to see Sandy, and told her Cody needed more freedom. If she wanted, Cody could stay with her two nights a week, but he told her that Cody hoped she'd stop trying to possess him.

"Mothers always get custody," she said. "Maybe it's time to file for divorce and go through a custody battle."

Jason studied her. "So, your son is not more important than your desires?"

"Maybe they're the same."

"Sandy, you don't stand a chance. If you want to make him a pawn in divorce proceedings, you'll be the loser. Do you know how many people I can call to court to vouch for me as a father? These same people will say what they think of a mother who leaves her son. And yes, I do think it's time for us to file for divorce. It's been a year."

"Jason, can't we try again? I'd like a second chance."

"And whenever I'd make love to you you'd wish I were a woman?" He shook his head. "Nope. You've killed any love I had for you. You did that before you even left."

"You're in love with that McCullough woman," she accused.

"That has nothing to do with us. If I have fallen in love with someone else after you left me, no one would blame me. My emotions are no longer any of your business. When they were, you ignored them."

"I'm not going to leave. I'm going to have my son."

"I'm not asking you to leave. I'm asking you not to insist he come with you after school every day. He doesn't want it. He needs the freedom to play with his friends."

"You know one of your big problems? You think you're perfect. You think you know the answer to anything . . ."

Jason held up his hand. "Hey, that's not me you're describing. Maybe that's how you see me, but that's not how I see me."

"You have no ambition! You're willing to spend your life in this little backwater, denying your son opportunities, denying me a social life and an interesting job . . ."

"None of that had anything to do with why you were discontent with our marriage. You're still unable to accept yourself as you are. You need help, Sandy. More help than Cougar, Oregon, can give you."

Sandy studied him and suddenly burst into tears, sitting down on the couch and putting her hands over her eyes. Jason walked down the hall to the bathroom and found some Kleenex, which he handed to her. She did touch his heart. He felt achingly sorry for her.

"I can't afford that kind of help," she sobbed. "I've always known I was different. But I don't know how to get along in either world. I feel guilty when I'm trying to be in either."

"It's nothing to feel guilty about," Jason said, sitting beside her and reaching for one of her hands. "Society has made you feel guilty for feelings you have trouble accepting. Sandy, you have to find a way to get in touch with these feelings so you can exist with some degree of happiness."

"But I love Cody."

He shook his head. "And so you should. I couldn't understand how you could walk away from him, not even saying good-bye to him."

"Oh, shit, Jason," she said wiping her eyes, "there you are again, too goddamn understanding. Why don't you get mad? Hit me? Throw something? Weren't you angry and hurt when I told you I didn't love you?"

He thought a moment. "I think I'd stopped loving you years before, my dear. I didn't get what I needed from you. I think I was living what Thoreau called a life of quiet desperation."

"And now?" Her voice cracked.

"Now I find life quite sweet."

"So what do you do for sex?"

He shook his head again. "Just what I did when we were married."

"Nothing?"

He smiled. "Whether it is nothing or a lot, or with whom, is absolutely none of your business anymore, Sandy. I have no desire to share any of my life with you."

She burst into tears again. "I want to be loved. What do I do about that?"

"Exactly what I've been asking myself for a long time."

"I don't want one-night stands," she wailed. "I don't want to pick some one up in a bar and just go to bed with her without knowing her. I want something more."

"Don't we all," he murmured, standing. Getting ready to go.

"Can you and Cody and I spend Christmas together if I stay?"

"No. We're already spoken for. We're spending it where we did last year, at the McCulloughs."

"Damn."

"I'm sorry, Sandy. But it's over. Go get a job someplace, someplace where you'll feel at home. Small towns are hard on people who don't fit in, I understand that. But a small town is where I belong, and Cody seems to like it, too. I'll help you, Sandy, as much as I can on the salary I earn. Until you get on your feet. I'm not willing to pay alimony for something that's not my fault. I don't earn that much, as you well know, but I'll do what I can."

She stood up and turned her back to him, staring at the wall. "Oh, Jason, I'm so sorry."

"I know you are. But don't take it out on Cody. You won't win a custody battle, not here in Cougar."

He heard her sniffling. "You're right."

"If you'll leave this week, I'll manage to get you a thousand dollars. It's all I can spare now."

Her shoulders sagged. "You want me out of your life, don't you?"

"Look, I know we'll always be part of each other's lives, because of Cody. I don't hate you, Sandy . . ."

"I know, you feel sorry for me."

Jason didn't say anything for a minute. "It's too late to go to the bank now, but I'll go first thing in the morning . . ."

She turned to face him, and he could see agony reflected there. "I don't want to go back to nursing. I hate it. Hate it."

"Then sick people don't deserve you. Sandy, I can't tell you what to do with your life. People have been asking themselves how to earn a living from time immemorial. I imagine most people don't like their jobs. They do it just to keep a roof over their heads and food in their bellies. You have to find answers from within. Try different jobs . . ."

"I can't even get one."

"I don't believe that. You're just thirty. You have a nursing degree. There must be other jobs where you don't have to work in a hospital, where nurses are wanted. In industry. I don't know where, I can't make life right for you."

"I don't like you, Jason."

"I've known that for a long time, Sandy. A long time. But for years I wondered why. At least now I have a reason."

"It's not just sexual. I mean," and her voice took an angry tone, "you're always so understanding, so goddamn right, so perfect! Living with you was tough, even if I didn't suffer your touches. I mean, no one can live up to you. You cooked when I didn't. You ironed your own shirts, you never lost your temper, you could always fix everything from a john that didn't flush to your own carburetor. I mean I don't like you. I really don't."

Then why, he wondered, had she wanted to start over, live with him again?

"I'll be over in the morning with the thousand. You better begin packing." He opened the door and started to leave. "I'll start divorce proceedings. Send me an address when you know where you'll be."

"You're cold," she cried after him. "So goddamned unfeeling and cold!"

His only feeling was of relief. If he reached out, he thought he could touch it. And it felt good.

He could go to Cat as a free man.

Twenty-five

Cat wouldn't leave Matt for the first three months, but she awoke one day in late January suddenly stir-crazy. She hadn't been in anyone else's house, except Miss Jenny's, since the baby's birth. She'd done all her Christmas shopping by way of catalogs, after Red had had a long talk with her one evening about finances.

"You've taken over the books when Miss Jenny's been away," he said. "You know how well off we are. I want you to buy anything you want. Instead of always having to be beholden to us, I thought I'd put a thousand dollars in your own account every month and if you need or even want anything else, charge it. There's no limit, Cat."

"I can't do that," she protested.

"You would if Scott were still alive. You're family, Cat. You're the mother of my only grandchild. You're a McCullough."

"You're very generous."

He smiled. "Fortunately, I can afford to be. But I don't feel generous. If I were generous, I'd buy you a fur coat and a Porsche and . . ."

Cat laughed. "I don't want either of those, thanks."

"Also," Red was sitting at his desk, the fireplace warming them with its glowing coals across the room, "I think you need to get out. See people. Do things. Don't become like Sarah," he said. It was the first time she'd ever heard him say anything like that. "She never participates in the town. Doesn't have a single friend. She's become gray, and I don't mean physically. Don't do that to yourself, Cat. In fact, come back to our Thursday breakfasts. Everyone always asks about you."

"And leave Matt?"

He nodded. "Yes, leave Matt. You'll feel imprisoned pretty soon if you don't get out, do things. Come on into town with me tomorrow. Life goes on, my dear. I feel Scott's loss, and will the rest of my life. For a few months, none of us cared whether we went on or not. Well, we're going on. Don't cling to Matt. There's more in life out there, just waiting for you. We'll ask Thelma to see if her niece, Lucy, would be interested in coming several times a week. She can use the money, I know, with that no-'count husband of hers not working over half the time. She can take care of Matt when you're busy or just when you need some relief."

"Relief? I don't feel that way . . ."

He nodded. "I know. I know."

"You know, Red," Cat walked over to him and leaned down to put her arms around his neck, "I don't know why Sarah drinks when she has you around. You are absolutely the nicest person in the entire world."

He reached up to put a hand around hers. She started to kiss his cheek, but he had turned his face toward her and her lips brushed his. For a second, she was startled. That's not what she'd meant. But he pressed her hand, and she knew it was okay. Everything was all right with Red around.

"Yes, sure, I'd love to have breakfast at Rocky's tomorrow. If you have errands, I'll stop in and see Dodie. I haven't seen her since they were here for Christmas, though I talk on the phone with her a couple of times a week. Did you know she and Chazz have adopted another child? She won't say who, but one of his patients out in the country had an illegitimate child, and her parents insisted she put it up for adoption, I guess she's a wild one and just sixteen, so Chazz and Dodie are going to adopt it. A little girl."

Red nodded. "Yes, I know. Funny, isn't it. Of all the women in the world who should have children, it's Dodie."

"Maybe this is nature's way of taking care of those who need love and wouldn't have it if Dodie had children of her own to take care of."

"That's one way of looking at it. Sure, I have to go to the Co-op and I want to see Bollie at the bank . . ."

"Good." Cat crossed the room. "For the first time since Christmas I have to think about what I'll wear."

"You always look good in whatever you have on."

"You're better than a mirror," she said. *You're better than anything,* she thought.

*   *   *

Driving into town the next morning, with the ground covered with a light crust of snow, Cat said, "You know, I'll be nervous every minute I'm gone from Matt."

"It's a beginning. Maybe a month from now you'll be used to it. You want to go out evenings, I'll personally take care of Matt, how's that?" Perhaps this was his way of evidencing approval for proceeding with a relationship with Jason. "That should alleviate your worries. Go to basketball games with Joseph and Torie, even away ones. Go skiing."

Cat couldn't think of doing anything that concerned snow. She hated it with a passion. It had robbed her of her husband. She didn't even enjoy looking at it on the mountain peaks. She had stored her snowmobile under hay in the barn. When it snowed she pulled the drapes in her bedroom so she couldn't see it, but she heard it. Heard the muffled sound the world inhabits when snow falls. Heard its silence.

"I'd sort of like to invite Jason and Torie and Joseph to dinner sometime," Cat said, "but Sarah has such a fit about Joseph."

"Cat," Red said, reaching out to touch the sleeve of her parka, "I've spent the last twenty-some years catering to Sarah. Giving in to her every wish or what I thought was her wish because I didn't want to antagonize her. I walked on tiptoes when she'd be in a drunken stupor. I'm tired of it. Having you around, seeing how a normal woman is, gives me the courage to stand up and say 'Hey enough. Your neurotic drunken ways do not rule this house.' I have a life to live, too, and I've not been doing it for far too long."

His voice was cool and calm, but he was saying things to his daughter-in-law he had not dared to admit he even thought. "I'm tired of living life to appease a woman who doesn't even know what's going on. We'll change things. I think it'd be great to have a little dinner party. Do you want to ask Chazz and Dodie, too?"

"No, let's make that another time. We could ask the Bollingers then, also."

"And if Sarah passes out, so be it." He said it as though his coming to that conclusion were a triumph. They had not entertained in years because of the embarrassment Sarah might cause. She'd become worse since her son's death.

"As long as we're going to start doing such things, what about another dog?" Cat asked. "I'd love to breed Brandy."

"Another collie, you mean?"

"Would you mind?"

"You want puppies."

Cat smiled.

When they entered Rocky's, Jason knocked over his chair, standing up to greet Cat. "This is a nice surprise."

Red noted the look in his friend's eyes.

Cat slid into her seat. Before Ida handed her a menu she poured Cat a cup of coffee. "Well, how's motherhood?" she asked.

"It's wonderful," Cat responded. "But it's good to see you all again. I want that Mexican breakfast, but not too spicy. I love the way those potatoes are done."

"Gotcha."

Jason had been out to the Big Piney Sunday afternoon, with Cody. Red had taken the boy snowmobiling.

"Good to see you back in town," Jason said.

"Red's a good influence." She smiled at her father-in-law. "He told me I had to get out."

Jason cocked his head and looked at Red. "Life's more exciting anyplace when she's around."

"I'll agree to that," Red said, raising his coffee cup in a toast.

"You guys are great for my ego."

Ida brought Jason the waffles he'd already ordered.

Just then Norah Eddlington came into the café. She seldom wore makeup, but the vivaciousness of her face counteracted that. Cat thought with just a bit of color she'd be a really handsome woman. Her hair was pepper and salt, and her blue eyes wide-spaced under thick dark lashes. She was losing her waist, but she looked good. Cat wondered if she could really be as content as she always seemed, married to a man who'd been in a wheelchair sixteen years. The few times she'd seen them together, Norah treated Stan as though he wasn't disabled at all. But she'd spent all those years taking care of him as well as gathering all the valley's information, which he then wrote up. Norah's way of making him still feel necessary?

They didn't even need a printing press now that they were computerized.

"Hi," Norah said, sitting. "Mind if I sit?"

Red moved over to make room for her.

She nodded to Cat and Jason, and told Ida, "Just coffee."

"What's new?" Jason asked.

"Simon Oliphant is retiring."

"Can't say as that makes me unhappy."

"Who's he?" Cat asked.

Jason lathered strawberry jam on his English muffin. "You know Simon, he's the town's lawyer."

"Oh? He was at the wedding, I think."

"Everyone was at your wedding," Norah said. "He's been here about thirty years. I imagine he was barely adequate when he came, but after his wife died about eleven or twelve years ago, he just lost touch with everything. I mean he's the justice of the peace in town, too, so he's married a bunch of people who didn't want to get married in churches, and he's collected fines and he's done deeds and arranged mortgages and wills, that sort of thing. I think he even took care of the Clarkes' divorce." There hadn't been many divorces in the county.

"We better think of recruiting someone," Red said. "Of course, we can go over to Baker, but it's nice to have someone around."

"We need one here," Nora said.

Jason agreed. "I need one on call at times, and he'll have to go to school board meetings."

"Let's give it some thought," Red said. He knew, and Jason knew, and over half the town knew that what got done in Cougar usually started at this table at Rocky's on Thursday mornings.

After Norah drank her coffee and left, Cat finished her Mexican breakfast, and asked Red, "How long are you going to be?"

"How long do you want?"

"Well, it'd be nice to have an hour to chat with Dodie."

"I'll pick you up there"—he glanced at his watch—"at eleven-fifteen, okay?"

"Great." She stood up and wiggled into her parka. "Walking's good for me. I need to get some of this weight off. I swear I still look pregnant."

The two men looked at each other and grinned. She probably looked better than she'd ever looked in her life.

After she'd left, Red said, "She wants another dog."

Jason raised his eyebrows. "Any particular kind?"

"Another collie. She has a yen for pups."

"Seth Brown's bitch had pups sometime before Christmas, but of course they're halfway down to Baker."

"Got his phone number?"

"Sure. Come on over to the office."

* * *

Dodie always wore an apron. Over her jeans, or her slacks or a dress, which she hardly ever wore. She whipped up the aprons herself, and they were about the size of a serving napkin, always trimmed with lace and embroidered with little flowers.

She showed Cat the new baby, as proud as though she'd given birth herself. She was three weeks old, and they'd just gotten her three days ago. Danny wouldn't even look at the family addition.

"He pretends she's not here," Dodie said, only a bit of dismay in her voice. "My heavens, motherhood agrees with you. You look great."

"I feel guilty. I don't have to do anything but feed Matt, play with him, and change his diapers. Someone else does all the dirty work."

"I don't mind doing all the dirty work, as you call it. I'd be happy to have half a dozen more."

"The great Earth Mother."

"Want some coffee?"

Cat shook her head. "I just had two cups. Any more and I could float home."

"Well, it's rather past time that you got out and joined the mainstream of life," Dodie said, putting the baby in the bassinet. "I guess Chazz and I've been wondering if you're going to stay here."

"Stay here?" Cat had no thought of leaving.

"Well, you're what, twenty-seven, and living out at the ranch, or even in Cougar, what kind of life is that for you? You're from a big city. We wondered if you'd go back East."

"Dodie! And take their grandson away from the McCulloughs? I keep busy. Miss Jenny's heading to Thailand next week, and I take care of the books when she's gone and—hey, this is my home!"

"But you don't have any young people to talk with or do things with . . ."

"I talk on the phone with you a couple of times a week and with Torie. She comes out to the ranch at least once a week to see the baby and we talk."

"Doesn't sound like much of a life for someone your age."

"I bet there are new mothers all over the world who find satisfaction in the kind of life I lead. You wouldn't think it peculiar if Scott were still alive . . ."

"That's true," Dodie admitted. "But what are you going to do, live alone out there without a man? How are you going to meet men in Cougar?"

Cat thought of Jason. "I'm not sure I'm ready for another man."

"You will be," Dodie said, who couldn't imagine living life without a husband.

"It's too soon." That's what she'd been telling Jason.

"It's nearly a year."

"Look, I'm content for the moment. Do I have to look beyond now?"

Red appeared exactly an hour later, grinning. "Hi, Dodie, well look at that new little girl," he said, reaching out his hands to hold the baby.

"Red, you're one of the few men I know who does that gracefully. Most other men don't even offer to hold her."

"I'd have had a dozen." He smiled at the baby, whose eyes were unfocused. "I'm going to have to steal Cat. We have a busy day ahead of us."

"We do?" Cat asked. She'd thought they were going home.

"You wanted another dog, right? I found six puppies, just six weeks old. Thought we'd drive down and look at them. Just about fifteen miles. That is, if the idea interests you." He grinned.

"If it interests me?"

"Call home and ask Thelma to give Matt a bottle." Cat had been weaning him at midday, just nursing him in the morning and at night. "Thought we might drive on into Baker and have a hamburger at McDonald's."

"McDonald's? Aaaargh!"

"Or someplace else."

Cat phoned Thelma, who said she'd be not only happy but delighted to give Matt a bottle and maybe some applesauce, too.

When they got in the car, Cat said, "Hey, all I have to do is say something, and you get it for me? What about a fur coat?"

He looked sharply at her. "You want one?"

"No,"—she laughed—"but don't spoil me, Red."

"And why not? What else do I have to do with my money? I get pleasure out of your pleasure. You must know that."

"Who gives to you?"

He sped south. "You do. In ways you don't even know."

The collie bitch was handsome, regaining her hair after birth, and each one of the puppies was irresistible. It took Red and Cat over an hour to narrow it down to a black-and-white ball of fur who licked them and seemed to carry joy within him. Red paid for it, and said, "Let's go on into Baker and we'll get a collar and dog dish and some toys at Kmart."

The puppy settled down happily on Cat's lap and promptly fell asleep as soon as the car started.

"I think I'm in love already," Cat said, her eyes devouring the fuzzy pup.

Red looked at Cat. He reached over to pat the dog's head. "We better think up a name."

"I've no ideas. This was so sudden," Cat said.

"When I was in Australia that time one of the places we visited was a ranch near a tiny hamlet in New South Wales. Kerrybree. I don't even know if it's there anymore, it was so small. What do you think of Kerry or Bree?"

"I like Bree," she answered immediately.

"Okay. Bree it is."

"That was too easy." Cat smiled at him.

They went into Baker and through the town to Kmart. Red bought half a dozen toys while Cat chose a dish and collar. "Do we need a leash?"

"I don't think so. But get one anyway. You might need it for some training."

"I don't know a thing about training a dog."

"You're in luck, then, because I do." Scott had been training Brandy when . . . "Come on, let's find a box so the puppy can sleep in the car while we have lunch."

"I feel I've been eating all morning."

He glanced at his watch. "It's almost one."

"Do we dare leave him?"

"We won't be long."

"I've another proposition to talk over with you." She wondered if he'd react as positively and as quickly as he had to her suggestion for another dog.

"A proposition? That sounds exciting. Something you want me to do?"

"Some advice," she answered. "I don't know how I feel about it yet, but I've been thinking about it ever since breakfast."

Twenty-six

"You've never been here?" They were seated in a booth in the dark restaurant. "We'll have to get you out more often. Let me recommend their charcoal-broiled hamburgers, which can't be beat."

She smiled. "I *am* having a delightful day. I guess I'll have what you're having. Charcoal-broiled sounds fine. And I'd like some red wine. If it puts me to sleep this afternoon, that's okay."

The waitress took their order.

Cat hunched her shoulders and, resting her elbows on the table, leaned forward. "What would you think of my buying Simon Oliphant's practice?"

For a second Red looked perplexed. "You mean . . ."

"I mean become Cougar's lawyer. I was a damned good lawyer."

Red studied her. After a few minutes he said, "I'm sure you could pass the Oregon State Bar easily."

"I like to think I could. I know, I'm a new mother, and that should occupy my time. And if I were an average American housewife it *might*, but it's not enough to take up my whole day. I've been thinking about this ever since Jason told us. Red, the fact is, much as I'm passionately in love with my son, being a mother isn't going to be enough for me. I'll get restless and think of leaving Cougar Valley." She smiled at him. "You wouldn't want that, would you?"

"The very thought chills me."

"Look." She reached across the table and absentmindedly ran her fingers across the back of his hand, gazing intently into his eyes. "I can't bear the thought of leaving, but I'm twenty-seven and changing diapers and watching my son grow is just not enough to occupy my mind. My heart, yes."

"And even in that area you'll need more eventually."

"Dodie was saying the same thing."

The waitress set a glass of red wine in front of Cat, and coffee for Red.

"Okay," he said, thinking as he went along. "If you have a business in Cougar, you're more likely to stay around. And even without thinking of leaving, you need more in your life. You need something to think about. A challenge." He grinned. "Not that being a lawyer in Cougar will be a challenge like being a lawyer in Boston was. As Jason told you, it's small potatoes in comparison. But the school and the town both need a lawyer . . ."

"I could work just half days, and spend half the day with Matt. I wouldn't be under a lot of pressure, but it'd give me something to do and to think about . . . I could take Miss Jenny's computer down there." Cat was keeping the books permanently, even when Miss Jenny was home.

Red studied her as she sipped her wine.

"When I woke up this morning it certainly wasn't even a glimmer in my mind, but I've been thinking about it ever since I heard."

"If you do it," he said, swallowing his coffee, "I don't think you should stay in that office over the bank where Simon's been for so long. It's cluttered and a mess. It'd take you two months to clean it out. Buy any books of his you want, but we'll look around for another place."

"*We* will?" She smiled at him.

The hamburgers arrived, with side orders of crisp french fries and a salad. Cat poured Roquefort dressing on her salad.

Red stared. "What do you do? Order salad so you can have dressing?"

She nodded, a twinkle in her eye for the first time in longer than he could remember. "Pretty much so."

Excitement coursed through her.

For the first time since Scott's death she was aware of her body. And that sitting across from her was the most interesting, thoughtful man she'd ever known.

"I've never thought of having my own office," she said, mulling the idea over.

"You won't have any big cases to make you famous out here," Red said between bites. "Hey, even Thelma can't do this to a hamburger."

"It *is* good." She wiped ketchup from the corner of her mouth.

"It'll get you caught up in life in Cougar. Not just at the ranch, but in the town . . . why, in the whole valley."

"I can just be open four or five hours a day."

"I bet Simon didn't even have enough work for that."

"I'll have to find out when the next bar exam is, and get books to study." She finished her hamburger and leaned back in the booth to study her father-in-law. "I don't want you to underwrite this."

He raised his eyebrows.

"I have to do it on my own. I have ten thousand that I could put into it, which means I'd have to borrow some, from either you or the bank. But I'd want to pay you back. Whatever it costs to set up an office would be a loan. I don't want to take and take and take from you, Red."

He gave her a look she didn't quite understand. "Of course. I understand that well enough. But borrow from me," he urged. "I'll give you better interest than Bollie will. Let me feel a part of it."

"What do you think Sarah and Miss Jenny will say? They'll have fits, won't they?"

Red sighed. "Miss Jenny's in Thailand. By the time she returns this will be a done deed. Do you really think Sarah's aware of anything? All she can think of now is that her son is gone. Nothing else even enters her tunnel vision."

Cat didn't respond to that until they were in the car again and Bree was curled on her lap. The weak winter sun shone on the puppy. "If he were a cat, he'd be purring." After they'd pulled out of the parking lot and were on the road through town, she said, "I mean, I know it's none of my business, but how can you stand it? All these years . . ."

Red didn't say anything until they were on the road north. "It was so gradual that I didn't realize . . . then there were the kids, and Miss Jenny . . ."

"So, you have thought of divorce at some time?"

"A long time ago. But I've gotten used to it."

"How can you be happy?"

"Happy?" Red looked straight ahead.

He never did answer the question. They rode in silence for half an hour, until they were nearly in Cougar, and he asked, "You want to go talk with Oliphant now?"

Cat shook her head. "No, this is more than enough for one day. Let's talk more about it tonight."

He drove on home.

When they arrived and he pulled up in front of the house, Cat leaned over to kiss him on the cheek, telling him, "It's so wonderful to have you to talk with about everything. About anything. Despite losing Scott, Red, I want you to know that having you in my life I feel incredibly fortunate."

She slid out of the car and bounded up the veranda steps, anxious to see the son she'd left for so long.

She did not look back to see the expression on Red's face as he watched her disappear through the door.

Then he turned the car toward the barn, where they kept it winter nights, and found himself whistling. Because he was happy or because he was nervous he wasn't sure.

Twenty-seven

Jason said he knew just the place. Three doors down from the sheriff's office. "See." He pointed across the street from their table in front of the window of Rocky's. "Over there."

There was fine snow swirling down. Cat's hair was plastered close to her head, and she wiped a sleeve across her eyes so she could see. She'd dropped by his office and said she had an idea she'd like to discuss with him. It was shortly after the lunch hour, and Rocky's was pretty empty.

"My heavens, the weather caught me off guard," she said, but she sounded more enthusiastic about life than he'd heard her in over a year.

He'd ordered coffee, but Cat was sipping Cherry Coke through a straw. The idea of Cat's being in town every day filled him with joy, but he wasn't sure how Cougar was going to react to a woman lawyer. He didn't voice his doubt.

He agreed with Red. She should not rent the space above the bank where Simon Oliphant had had his office for over twenty years. The bank owned the building across the street, so they should be happy to rent that space to her. "Come on," he said, "let's go get a key from Bollie, and you can look at it."

Bollie nodded his head, though Cat could tell he wasn't sure her buying Oliphant's practice was a great idea. He handed the key to Jason, and said, "Take your time."

The storefront was dingy, recently vacated after having been a mercantile store for what Jason said was probably fifty years. It was bare.

"I'd paint the walls white," Cat said as she scanned the place.

Right now they were a faded mustard color. If there was no warmth, there was no clutter either. "This front room could be the reception area." It opened into a larger room which would be her office. There was even a fireplace in the corner.

"That'll warm you up on winter days and add coziness," Jason said, studying Cat as she surveyed the room.

"Brightly colored braided rugs will look nice against this wooden floor planking."

"I'll come help polish it. I'm pretty good at that kind of stuff," he volunteered.

There was a small room off the office which could house a copier and other office supplies. A small dreary bathroom was beyond. "I'll have to modernize and brighten that."

"Shouldn't be too difficult."

None of the glamour and glitz of a big-city law office, that was for sure, but she was excited at the thought of making it comfortable and attractive.

She'd study for the bar and spend the meantime decorating the office. She'd always wanted to have the time to really decorate a place. She'd have several months before she could even begin to practice, and she'd give time and thought to just how her own law office should look.

Her own office. She'd never even imagined having one. Her dreams had centered on making her mark in a big, prestigious firm that reeked of money.

She'd get a nice sofa and comfortable chair and coffee table for the reception area. Something that would allow people to feel at ease. To assure that white walls wouldn't have a hospital effect, she'd add vibrant warm accents, bright spots of color.

She doubted, really, that there would be much business. She'd just plan to be open from, say, ten to two, and wondered if there'd be enough business to warrant that. Oliphant had been surprised and rather overcome when she approached him about buying his practice, saying he'd just thought he'd shut down and walk out. He was making it easy for her, offering her all his books and a list of clients he'd had over the years. She wondered if anything short of a wrecker could ever clear his office. One had to walk carefully through narrow lanes between stacks of magazines and bric-a-brac. She didn't know how he ever found anything.

"I didn't even ask what the rent was on this place," she said to Jason.

"Does it matter?"

"I guess not."

"You know you'll pass the bar, don't you?"

"I appreciate your confidence," Cat said. "I don't expect it'll be too bad. Oregon will have some things peculiar to it, each state does. I'll have to bone up a bit. If I can get back in the routine of studying a couple of hours a day I shouldn't have any trouble."

She walked back through the room she'd chosen for her office. "I don't want it to look masculine," she mused. "But not too feminine either. I want it cozy and not impersonal, but not like it's strictly a woman's bailiwick. I don't want to spend a fortune on it, either."

"Red can afford it."

She looked at him sharply. "Red's not bankrolling this. He's supporting me emotionally, but not financially. This is me. Not McCullough." Yet she was Catherine McCullough. "I have to buy a copier, and a fax machine and I'd love a big long desk. I'll need bookcases from floor to ceiling to make room for Mr. Oliphant's books."

Jason reached out a hand to touch Cat's arm.

"I'm awfully glad you're doing this. I think maybe I had this hope in the back of my mind when I heard about Simon."

"You did?"

"Cat." He moved close to her, looking down at her. Even with wet hair flat against her head she looked lovely. He put his arms around her, and his mouth moved onto hers.

"Come to dinner tomorrow night? Cody was saying he'd like to see you." When she didn't respond, Jason added, "I would, too. You can bring Matt."

She hadn't been out of the house for an evening since the baby was born.

"Sounds nice. Meanwhile, let me go see what Bollie wants for this place."

"Take it, no matter what."

"I plan to," she said, sailing past him and walking out into the cold gray afternoon.

Miss Jenny came home from Thailand, and said she'd been disappointed in it. It could have been any third world country, it wasn't distinctive, and except for the King's Palace in Bangkok she'd been mighty let down, despite riding an elephant. "That was too hokey."

However, she'd stayed six weeks longer than planned because that man she'd met in England last fall, Sir Geoffrey Forrester, had invited her to visit India with him and his sister.

"But," she admitted to Cat with a sly smile, "Amelia only stayed for two weeks. Then Geoff and I traveled through the most exotic place in the whole world, I'm sure, Rajasthan in northwest India, and we had an absolutely exquisite time." It didn't even sound like Miss Jenny talking.

"Think maybe I'll go to Kenya in the fall. They say the weather's marvelous there then. I suppose September and October are near perfect the world over."

She drove to Boise to get her hair done and polished her nails with a frosted pink. She wore eye shadow even when she was alone in her lodge.

"You look like you could pose for the cover of *Vogue*," Cat told her.

"My dear, you know what. I'm sixty-nine years old. I have a forty-nine-year-old son. I have a great grandson, and I feel beautiful. Now, that's got to be a state of mind."

"It's a fact."

Miss Jenny grinned. "I knew I loved you from the very beginning. Now, tell me. What about Jason?"

"What about him?"

"He's getting divorced. You like Cody well enough."

"I love Cody."

"So . . ."

"Well, he's making overtures," Cat admitted.

"He's a fine young man. And you have your whole life ahead of you. Don't mourn too long. Scott will always be part of you. But get on with life, my dear."

"You didn't. Your husband died . . ."

". . . over ten years ago. And I didn't think I was lonely at all. In fact, I enjoyed myself. Felt free. But I'd forgotten how good sex can make you feel."

Cat's jaw dropped open.

"Oh, don't look like you're in shock," Miss Jenny said, pouring tea. "You think people my age don't have it? Geoff's a year older than I, but I can tell you, good sex makes you feel physically great for days afterward." She smiled wickedly. "Not that many days passed in between."

Cat still sat, openmouthed, staring at the older woman.

Miss Jenny laughed. "I must be lucky. I've only been to bed with two men, and they've both been good in the sack."

"Miss Jenny!"

Miss Jenny's eyes sparkled. "I said it that way to shock you. I guess I'm in my second childhood, except this doesn't feel like being a child."

"Are you in love with him?"

Miss Jenny shrugged. "I must be changing with the times. I grew up thinking women only went to bed with men they loved, and I only went to bed with Jock. I never even had a hankering for another man. But, I don't know. I think I've lived alone too long and am used to my own ways. Besides, do I want to live in a drafty English country house? I couldn't leave the Big Piney. I don't know if it's love, but I do like him a lot, and he makes me laugh more than I've done since Jock. And he's very affectionate, aside from sex. You know, not all men know how to be affectionate. Well, Geoff does. He's very nice that way. Not what I'd thought a British lord would be like, not stuffy and stiff upper lip sort of thing, though there is an arrogance about him that sometimes embarrasses me. I don't know why. My democratic spirit, I suppose. He's horrified, but I think also charmed, by my egalitarian American attitude."

Cat had never heard Miss Jenny use the vocabulary she was throwing around lately.

Miss Jenny leaned forward and waved a finger at Cat. "It wouldn't hurt for you to at least sleep with him."

Cat swallowed. "Jason, you mean?"

Miss Jenny nodded. "Or someone else who takes your fancy."

Cat exhaled. "I think you're becoming Continental."

"Is that what it is?" Miss Jenny changed the topic. "Well, I approve of your going into business in town. Too few women in business there. Too few anywhere. That nice women's clothing store in Baker is run by that delightful woman, but not too many others. You show 'em."

Cat smiled. "I doubt that making out deeds and wills will show anyone anything, but it'll keep me busy."

"Anything to keep you here, my dear. Now that Scott's gone you're the only thing that keeps my son from desolation."

"He never acts that way."

"No, he doesn't. And never has. He keeps it all within. But you and Torie are the only people he has to love who give him any joy."

"Do you think he still loves Sarah?"

Miss Jenny shook her head. "I don't think he's loved her for well over twenty years. She changed. When he brought her here, fresh from college, she lit up the place. She took to riding and hunting and hiking and skiing with an unmatched enthusiasm. We all fell in love with her. Then in that second pregnancy, something changed. Hormones, or what, I don't know. It was like a postpartum depression before she even gave birth to Torie. I don't recall seeing her smile since. She turned to alcohol and God. Funny kind of God, though, hers.

"For years, Red threw any liquor down the drain, but it didn't help. She secreted it in places where no one could find it. She's denied having a drinking problem, claiming she just has one or two before dinner, like the rest of us. We stopped doing even that for a long time, but that didn't help Sarah. When we did drink, she'd be the last one to leave the living room, stopping to finish off any liquor anyone had left in a glass, even a sip.

"She's ignored Torie from the minute that girl was born. I brought her up. Me and Thelma. Well, Red did, too. He was the best father I've ever seen. Now, Jock, he wouldn't change a diaper for anything, but Red did that, and bathed the kids, and fed them, and did everything for them when he was in the house. He was the one who taught them to ride, though once Torie was in school and discovered Joseph, she was over at Claypools as much as here. Mr. Claypool taught her to ride bareback, and that girl went like the wind. Nothing frightened her. She won rodeo after rodeo."

"Why doesn't she do that anymore?"

"Guess she passed through that phase. Now, she's into saving youth. I've never seen her in a classroom, but I just know she's one of those rare ones who'll make a difference to the lives of those students of hers.

"Personally, I think what she should do is get her tubes tied, then Samuel couldn't keep them from marrying. There'd be none of this folderol about Joseph's children. Or, maybe he should get a vasectomy."

"Oh, Miss Jenny!"

"Well, d'you see how they're tortured? I'm sure they're sleeping together, and they're not getting younger. What's she now? Twenty-three or so. They either need to get married and get all this over with, or one of them should leave, never to come back, so they can both get on with life."

"You said before it's not that simple."

"Nothing worthwhile ever is, is it? I'm just saying what I think, but then we can always give advice about things in other people's lives that we can't accept in our own."

Cat sipped the coffee and stared out the window at the little green-gold buds on the trees. Spring, at last.

"I really came up here to ask you to go shopping with me. Red said he'd fly me over to Portland to shop for office furniture, and I'm hoping you'll come along to give me advice."

Miss Jenny's eyes lit up. "Of course. I'd love to."

"How about either tomorrow or Thursday?"

"Going to take Matt?"

Cat nodded. "Sure. Red said he'd take care of him while you and I shop."

"He'll be in good hands," Miss Jenny said, shaking her head up and down. "And"—she reached across the table to put her hand on Cat's wrist—"so will you be, my dear."

"I never doubted it for a second."

The only furniture they disagreed on was Miss Jenny's suggestion of expensive Persian rugs when Cat wanted brightly braided cotton ones. Cat won.

She and her father-in-law had been sitting on the porch after dinner. It wasn't completely dark yet, and they could still see the outlined ridges of the Wallowas across the valley, though the stars were beginning to dot the sky like diamonds. Red sat in an Adirondack chair and Cat swung gently back and forth on the wooden slatted swing that hung from the ceiling. Only its creak and the sound of frogs down by the creek could be heard. Cat fanned herself with a magazine but sweat beaded down her face and between her breasts.

"God, it's hot."

"When the kids were little we used to go down to the creek and swim. Not at night, of course."

"I'd give my eyeteeth for a place to swim right now. I'd put a pool right out there." She pointed to the front lawn.

After a while she said, "Look at those stars."

Red murmured, "Want to reach out and pick one?"

"You know I thought I could never be happy again, but I am. Not to the same degree, perhaps, but I find life worth living."

Red nodded.

Another comfortable silence. Then, "You getting anxious to hear about the bar?"

"Not really. I feel confidant. We should hear soon."

"You want to go fishing this weekend? That's something you haven't done. You and Matt. We'll camp. Some pretty rivers up in the mountains."

"That sounds nice."

"You don't have to do anything." Excitement was reflected in Red's voice. "I'll get Thelma to pack food, and we'll see about getting you a fishing license. You just see to Matt."

She had weaned him, and he was eating food now. He was the center of attention of the entire household.

Red came home the next day with a knapsack that fitted her back, especially made to carry a child.

They left at dawn Saturday morning, planning to return Sunday evening.

Red drove up through the Grande Ronde Valley, into the mountains where villages sprinkled over the landscape. He turned onto a dirt road that zigzagged up into the jagged peaks, still covered with snow. Patches of it dotted the sides of the road.

A breeze rustled the leaves high in the trees, where the sun dappled shadows down onto the narrow road.

"This is an old logging road," Red told Cat. "Not in use anymore."

"Looks like we're the only people in the universe."

"Would that that were true."

Cat looked at him. He stared ahead at the road.

Matt was asleep in the backseat, in his basket, with the dogs on either side of him.

"You know, Red, you're the most comfortable person in the world. I don't think I could have gotten through this last year without you."

"Works both ways," he said.

"Do you ever want to get away?"

He glanced at her. "That's what we're doing now."

"No, I mean, go someplace else. At least for a while."

He shook his head. "Never."

"You work so hard." Once winter was over, Red left the house at dawn and was not back until dinnertime, except for Thursdays, his day in town.

Since she'd been furnishing the office and being downtown a couple of hours a day, she met Jason for coffee each day at ten, unless he was out of town. They'd hired Lucy Carpenter, Thelma's niece, to take care of Matt.

Lucy was a quiet girl. Girl? About thirty. Older than Cat by two years. When school was in session, her six-year-old son got on a bus before eight, and she drove a battered pickup out to the ranch.

"Lucy's husband has been a first-class bastard from the time he was little. I'm sure she has a tough row to hoe. Thelma practically brought Lucy and her brother up. The boy's the one who's the manager at Ace Hardware in Baker. Turned into a responsible young man. Lucy's responsible, too, but once Matt gets growing and she can be an influence, I think we better look for someone else. Lucy's afraid of her own shadow."

A stream came tumbling down the side of the road, silver foam breaking over smooth stones. Red halted at a curve in the road, where there was a turnoff. "We'll leave the car here and hike back into the woods."

"Here looks nice."

"Wait'll you see where we're going," he said.

Cat hoisted the pack he'd bought onto her back and Red lifted Matt into it. The dogs jumped around, sniffing every place, running across the narrow road to drink from the cascading stream.

Red leaned down to shoulder his backpack, containing the tent, food, and fishing gear. "Not as young as I once was," he said as he stood up. "Used to be a piece of cake."

"You're still young," Cat assured him. "You're not yet fifty." She half wanted to tell him what Miss Jenny was doing at sixty-nine.

She followed him through the woods as he went up a narrow walking trail. They only walked for three-quarters of an hour, but she could hear her heart pounding. She had to stop a couple of times to catch her breath.

"Boy, am I out of shape."

"You could fool me." He turned to look at her.

Bree and Brandy, undaunted, bounded both ahead and behind them, their tails wagging. Bree followed Brandy wherever the older dog went. And whatever she did.

They came to the crest of the hill and Cat found herself literally breathless, not just as a result of hiking upward but at the beauty of the spot. Nestled among the tall pines was a jewel of a lake, shining azure under the blue sky, reflecting one white cloud that hung above it.

Red watched the look on Cat's face. "We'll camp here, but we'll fish in the stream." He knelt down and unshouldered his backpack, then came to take Matt out of Cat's.

"That's better," she said. "I didn't know how much longer I could carry him."

"We'll have to do this more often so you get used to it."

Matt started to fuss, unimpressed by the grandeur that surrounded him.

"You feed him, and I'll set up the tent."

Red had the tent set up before Cat fed Matt three mouthfuls. He opened the bag of lunch that Thelma had packed and set it out on a flat rock.

"Fish aren't going to be out at this time of day. We'll wait til later, but we can walk around and you can see how pretty it is. We'll fish about five. Evening is a good time and so's early morning."

Cat had only fished once with Scott. They were downstream of the lake, Matt sitting in his jumper seat, cooing at the leaves that rustled above him and watching Bree pounce around after Brandy.

"Here, this is how you hold the rod," Red demonstrated.

Cat tried.

"No, like this." He showed her again, how to hold it, how to throw the line into the water. "Real technique involved here."

She still didn't get the hang of it.

Red came over and stood behind her, putting his arms around her, holding her hands in his and moving them with grace, giving her the feel of it.

Giving her the feel of him.

It was a shock.

She'd hugged and kissed Red for close to two years now. He'd delivered her baby. He'd seen her nurse Matt. She had shared myriad intimate moments with him. They'd held each other when Scott's body was discovered. But now, he stood with the length of his body against hers, his arms around her, his breath riffling her hair, and she was aware of him, of his body, as she had never been before.

He was talking, telling her how to toss the line, where the fish would be, and she hardly heard a word he said. Against her back she could feel his heart beating, felt the safety he represented, yet she was also aware of his masculinity, of his vitality and his power.

"You're not getting it," he said.

He moved away from her, suddenly. Let go of her arms, and backed away. She turned to look at him and could tell by the look on his face that he had been aware, too.

"Try anyhow," he said, bending down to pick up his fishing rod.

Her heart fluttered in her chest. His back to her, he walked down the stream and cast his line into an eddy.

She tried to clear her mind. Not let herself think of the moment that had just come and gone.

She caught three fish to Red's two. "Beginner's luck," he teased her.

But something had changed.

She was pretty sure Red knew it, too.

Twenty-eight

Red fried the fish for supper, and they sat in the gathering darkness by the campfire after Cat had rinsed the dishes. Matt fell asleep, and Red carried him into the tent, where he set up an air mattress for Cat. He said, "Think I'll sleep out under the stars."

Bree curled beside Cat while Brandy lay with her nose on Red's knee. Little animals skittered around in the grass.

"You know what I've been wondering," she said, thinking this was the perfect time to bring up the idea she'd been tossing around in her mind ever since she started moving furniture into her new office.

Red gazed at her. "I haven't the faintest."

"I think Cougar needs a library."

He sat back on his heels and studied her. Then he looked out over the lake, at the reflections of the stars that were beginning to appear in the sky. He smiled. "You do, do you? I already know what that means."

"You do? What does it mean?"

"It means by fall, or Christmas at the latest, Cougar's going to have a library."

"Whoa. Don't overestimate me. I don't even know how to go about starting one. I don't even know if the idea . . . "

"Come on, Cat." He laughed and stood up, walking over to skip a stone into the lake. "You get interested in something, it gets done. You start off well. You approach me, and of course I'll help get it off the ground . . . "

"Red, that's not why I mentioned it . . . "

"I know. I know. And then Bollie. You'll talk to Torie and see what the school wants, and to Nora. If Nora's interested, any opposition wouldn't stand a chance. Nora is the one to get everything done in town. There'll be bake sales and car washes and solicitations . . ."

"Apparently I did approach the right person. I wouldn't even have thought of those ideas."

"Cougar's needed a library forever."

"Then why isn't there one?"

"No one with the passion and energy and time to devote to it, I'd guess. It takes all that to get something done around here, you know. People tend to be satisfied with the status quo."

"The only thing around is the rack of books in Vlahov's Pharmacy. Not much of a choice."

Red turned and came back and sat opposite her, across the fire. "I'll do what I can," he said. "Whatever you want or need . . ."

"Oh, goody," she clapped her hands. "The idea began to grow in the winter when all I did was sit around and nurse Matt and stare out the window."

"Nora will have a hundred suggestions if the idea appeals to her."

"How do the kids in school do research projects? Is everyone content to look at the junk on TV . . ."

"Hey, not all of it's in that category," Red protested, even though he didn't spend many evenings looking at television.

Cat shrugged. "I like to curl up in bed at night with a good novel."

"Okay, talk to Nora, to Torie, to the Latin teacher at school who is also the school's librarian. Talk to Bollie, and I'll talk to some of the businesses in town to see how far they'd go to helping out. Jason and I'll take care of that part."

Two days ago she'd have gotten up and gone over and put her arms around him and kissed him for his suggestions and willingness to help, but now, for reasons she couldn't quite define, she was glued to her spot on the grass.

She wasn't ready for sleep, yet she stretched and stood up. "Long day. Guess I'll join Matt."

"Are you nervous?" Red asked.

About him or being out in the wilderness? "Hey," she smiled. "Not all big-city girls think they're going to be attacked by wild animals. No, I'm fine."

"I'll keep the fire going for a while." He stood up and unrolled his sleeping bag, laying it not far from the fire. Brandy immediately lay on it. "I'll gaze up at the stars til I fall asleep."

She started for the tent. "Thanks, it's been a wonderful day."

"Luck of the beginner," he said, referring to her fishing fortune.

She bent down and picked Bree up, crawling into the tent, listening to Matt's even breathing. "I'll take the little one with me."

"Leave Brandy with me. I need some company."

Cat lay down, fully clothed, on the air mattress, her hands folded on her stomach, the puppy curled by her side, and stared into the darkness.

Maybe it was her imagination. Perhaps Red wasn't as aware of the change as she was. The awkwardness since that moment was in her imagination.

He was her father-in-law, a married man. Not that married men didn't fool around, but Red wasn't the type. He had withdrawn as soon as the electricity surged through them. Electricity? So that was what it was.

He was a man caught in an unhappy marriage, and had been unhappy for over twenty years. Yet she knew as she lay with only the canvas of the tent between them that she wanted him, wanted her father-in-law's body next to her, wanted his arms around her again, wanted his hands on her breasts, his lips on hers.

She moaned softly, ashamed of herself. It was practically incestuous, wasn't it?

Would he be disgusted to know her thoughts, or was he having similar ones as he stared into the universe beyond the stars?

She awoke in the morning to the smell of bacon frying and coffee brewing. She awoke with a start, from a dream she couldn't remember but which she knew was painful, whatever it had been about.

Matt gurgled. She reached out for him and crawled out of the tent.

"Rise and shine!" Red called. "Breakfast's nearly ready." He walked over and reached down to take Matt from Cat's arms.

She stood up. "I have to brush my teeth before I can be nice."

"Bottle of water there," he pointed. "Take your time. Wash your face, whatever. I'll take care of him." He held his grandson close and smiled into his dark eyes.

Cat walked into the woods.

When she came back, Red said, "Tell me when you're ready, and I'll crack the eggs."

"I didn't know you had these talents."

"Just because we've lived in the same house for near two years doesn't mean you know all about me."

Matt was playing with a piece of bacon, crunching it in his fingers
and licking it simultaneously. Bree didn't leave his side, hoping that
he'd drop a bit.

"Here, girl," Red said, flipping the pup a piece of bread that he'd
fried in the bacon grease.

"Smells good."

"It may just be the best breakfast you'll ever have eaten. Come on,
you don't have to comb your hair before breakfast." He cut holes in
the center of the frying bread and dropped eggs in them. "Hope you
can eat two and hope you don't want more."

Cat sat cross-legged, reaching for the coffeepot and pouring the
coffee into a tin cup Red handed her. "This smells strong enough to
make my hair stand on end."

Red shook his head and smiled. "That'd be novel."

"What time is it?"

"Does it matter? Sun's up and fish are biting. Be good to catch
enough to take a string home and have Thelma do things to them
that'll make you salivate."

"I'm doing that looking at *your* cooking."

Red expertly flipped two slices of bread, with the eggs in the center,
and four pieces of bacon onto a tin plate and handed it to Cat. He
dished his own out and sat down on a log. "Now, isn't this the life!"

"You like the wilderness so much, how come you don't go hunting
in the fall?"

His mouth was too full to answer right away. Finally, he said, "I
hunted all my youth. In fact, beyond that. And then along came a
new word—ecology—and we began paying attention to the environ-
ment and the balance of nature, and I didn't need to shoot animals
in order to eat . . ."

"So you stopped killing animals?"

"Not really," he admitted. "After all, I raise cattle and sheep by
the thousands. But the last few times I went hunting I got no joy from
it. I enjoyed the company of the men I was with, and went even a
year after I determined not to hunt, but I just gave it up since it doesn't
give me pleasure anymore."

"Talking of pleasure, Miss Jenny's certainly having fun at this point
in her life."

"I don't even recognize my own mother. I thought I knew her as
well as one knows another human being, and she ups and surprises
me."

"You know she has a boyfriend? A British lord or something."

He shook his head, and Cat could tell he was mystified by the turn of events. "I told her to invite him here."

Cat laughed. "So you can decide whether or not you approve, or whether he's after her money?"

Red didn't find it so amusing. "Something like that. She's sure not going to marry him, but is the guy for real?"

"We could find out. There are ways. You want to know if he's got money or is after hers?"

"Something like that."

"I can make inquiries."

"How'll you do that?"

She smiled mysteriously. "I used to be a big-city lawyer. I can have someone run a check on him."

"Can you really? Is it legal?"

"Now, Red," she teased him, "would a lawyer ever do anything illegal?"

He did laugh at that. "Okay, Cat, go ahead, but let's never let Ma know."

She caught absolutely no fish that morning, and Red brought in five. She could tell he derived satisfaction from both those facts and laughed to herself. Typical man, after all.

They arrived home at four-thirty, and Sarah was wringing her hands.

"Jason's been calling you all day," she said. "I've been worried sick. Where have you been? Thelma's not here."

"It's Sunday. I told you we were going fishing."

Sarah looked confused. "You did?"

They both knew she had been in no condition to remember.

"No one's been here to get my breakfast. I'm starving."

"Give me a couple of minutes, and I'll get something going," Cat said.

"Oh, good, that's nice of you. Then phone Jason."

Cat phoned Jason first.

"Cody and I are going up to La Grande to the movies and want to know if you'll come. We'll have pizza first."

Cat was tired. "Give me a rain-check, Jason. We just got back from camping in the Wallowas, and I'm a mess."

"Oh, okay." She could hear the deflation in his voice. "When?"

"Well, maybe not movies, but dinner anytime this week. Tell Cody I'm sorry, and we'll get together . . ."

"Tuesday?"

"Sure, Tuesday's fine."

"Want me to invite Torie and Joseph?"

"It's up to you." What was she going to whip up for Sarah, who hadn't eaten all day?

"Okay, then just us."

She hung up and went to the kitchen. There was cold chicken that Thelma had left and which Sarah could so easily have found. There was potato salad, and a tossed green salad just waiting for dressing. A string-bean casserole. Well, they could all have that for supper. Sarah couldn't find this herself? Cat found herself more and more impatient with Sarah's self-imposed limitations.

"Anything important?" Red stuck his head in the kitchen.

"No, he just wanted me to go to the movies."

"You want to? I'll take care of Matt."

Cat shook her head. "No, I'm tired." She fixed a tray and took it in to Sarah, who said, "Oh, it's nearly five, isn't it? Over the yardarm. Time for a drink." She was pouring herself a Scotch.

Cat and Red looked at each other.

"Do you want some ice?" Cat asked.

"Oh, darling, that would be nice."

Cat went back to the kitchen and loosened ice from a tray, walking back through the hall to the living room.

"I really was worried all day. It was like there was no one else in the world."

"You could have phoned Ma," Red said.

"Is she back?"

"She's been back nearly a month."

"Oh, my, where does the time go? Well, I do think I called her, but there was no answer. Or maybe that was yesterday. How long have you been gone?"

"Just since yesterday." Red poured himself a drink.

Cat poured herself a glass of cabernet sauvignon.

"That looks good." Red studied Sarah's tray.

"I'm glad, because that's what Thelma left us for supper."

"What would we do without her?" Red asked rhetorically.

"What did Jason want?" Sarah asked.

"He just wanted me to go to the movies."

There was a silence and a look of abject shock on Sarah's face. Finally she said, "I hope you told him certainly not. What nerve!"

Red's eyes met Cat's and then he turned to his wife. "Sarah, Scott's been dead over a year and a half."

Sarah burst into tears. "If anyone knows it, I do. God never stops punishing us for our sins, does he?"

Red just shook his head and got up from his chair, walking out onto the veranda.

Sarah barely touched her food.

After Cat changed Matt's clothes and gave him a bath, she put him in his pajamas and fed him. Sarah had turned the TV on and was watching *Murder She Wrote*. Cat walked out to join Red and the dogs on the porch.

"Cat," Red said, gazing out over the valley. "Don't let Sarah inhibit you. It's time you do things with another man. And there's not a finer one in the valley than Jason."

"I know," she said, and was surprised to hear herself add, "He says he's in love with me."

Red nodded, and after a minute he walked down the steps and disappeared around the corner of the house.

Cat sat on the steps for half an hour, but there was no sign of Red.

She went back to the kitchen and set the oaken table with red-and-white-checked table mats, placing the bowls of green salad and potato salad in the center, heating the green-bean casserole in the microwave, and finding the gingerbread that Thelma had baked the day before.

She went into the living room to find most of Sarah's supper still on her plate. "Come on," Cat said, "come eat in the kitchen with us."

Sarah's eyes were glazed. "In the kitchen?"

"In the kitchen," Cat reiterated. She reached a hand out to help her mother-in-law up. Sarah docilely followed, this time with no glass in hand. Cat noticed she had not combed her hair at all. *She may not have even looked in a mirror since Scott died,* Cat thought. She'd have to start doing something about that. Maybe brushing Sarah's hair every day. Seeing that she didn't wander around in her robe all the time. Such a gorgeous woman letting herself go to seed. Drinking her life away.

Red did not come in for dinner. Cat walked out to the barn to let him know it was ready, but he wasn't there. She called, but no answer.

When she went up to bed at ten, he still hadn't come in.

She got under the covers, and with Bree at her feet and Matt in his crib beside her, she lay with her hands pillowed under her head, knowing why Red had not come in.

Twenty-nine

Monday morning after breakfast—Red had already eaten and was long gone—Cat waited for Lucy to arrive, and then she took off for town. She stopped in the office just to look at it, wondering what in the world she'd do if she didn't pass the bar.

Not much chance of that, but one could never tell for sure.

Since it was nearly ten, she walked across the street to Rocky's, thinking she might broach the library idea to Jason. He wasn't there. Instead of going to look for him in his office, Cat walked the five blocks to Dodie's.

Dodie opened the door, an apron over her shorts. "What a pleasant surprise."

"It just seemed like such a lovely day."

"Come on in, I've news I'm dying to tell."

Her baby was asleep in the playpen, and Danny was playing in a sandbox out back with the neighbor's two kids.

Cat followed Dodie down the hallway and into the kitchen. It seemed Dodie was always baking something. "It smells heavenly in here."

Dodie poured coffee and placed a blueberry muffin on a little plate, shoving it across the counter to Cat.

"How come you and Chazz aren't fat?"

"Metabolism," Dodie answered. She seemed ready to burst with news. "After eleven years of marriage I'm pregnant. Not only that, but I'm pregnant with twins!"

Cat threw her arms around her friend. "I envy you," she said. "I'd have liked at least three."

"You've still got many childbearing years ahead of you!"

Cat didn't talk to her about the library. Later, she walked over to the newspaper office where Stan was in a trance in front of his computer and Norah was eating a peanut butter sandwich and sipping a Coke as she made phone calls.

"Hi." She waved.

"I've an idea, and Red suggested I see what you think of it."

Norah got up and pulled a chair over to her desk. "Hope you don't mind if I go ahead and eat. It's always on the run, it seems."

Cat explained her idea about the library and, as Red predicted, Norah was enthusiastic. "However," she said, "I can't help with all the work, but I'll suggest who to contact and do some phone work. First of all, go talk to Bollie. Get him in on it and we'll be off to a good start." Cat noticed the we. "And no one's lived in that Meyerson house for years. It's a white elephant. The bank's trustee for that. It'd make a perfect library."

"You mean that big Victorian one at the corner of Maple and Elm?"

"It'd be great, don't you think? Could stand some paint and fixing up, but it's the biggest house around, and we can find volunteers, easy. Get a place first, then we'll find a way to raise money. You ought to be chairman, Cat. It's your idea."

"I'd sort of like that, but aren't I too new to town?"

"You're a McCullough," Norah said as though that eliminated any doubts. "Bill O'Rourke . . ."

"The principal?"

"And one of the high-school teachers, either English or history . . ."

"Of course, Torie's the history teacher."

"Well?"

"Is that too many McCulloughs?"

"Get Lois Vlahov then. Or Ed. Seems to me Ed's even a closet writer. And Bollie, for heaven's sake. Go right over there, Cat, and tell him what you want and ask him about that big house and about being on the board. Him or Nan. Get the powers who be behind us."

Us. Cat liked that.

"This will give me something to do while I'm waiting for the exam results," she told Norah.

"I must admit what you're doing is what I had in mind when I came over to Rocky's that day to tell you all that Simon was retiring. I hoped you'd pick up on that."

"Oh, you did, did you?"

"Don't want you to leave Cougar. You sure make a difference in Red's life."

How would she know? Or did everyone see it?

Norah put an arm around her as they walked to the door. "Bollie and your father-in-law have given more to this town than anyone else. The two of them and Jason make whatever happens happen."

Cat never thought of Red that way. When did he do it all? Were there more to those Thursday breakfasts with Jason than she'd been aware of? When did Red and Bollie get together except once a month to play poker with a couple of the ranchers, something they'd done every month for over twenty years. Cat had heard them when they'd met out at the Big Piney, and it certainly sounded like they talked poker more than power.

On her way back to the office she stopped in at the bank. As usual, the door to the president's office was open. Bollie sat at his imposing but littered desk, his shirtsleeves rolled up. When he saw Cat standing in the doorway, he gestured a welcome with his left hand while his right held the phone to his ear. He pointed to a chair and she sat. As he continued his conversation, he pointed to a table by the wall where a coffeepot and cups sat.

Cat shook her head. Too hot for coffee.

"Well, my dear, you're a sight for sore eyes. Haven't seen you in weeks. You heard yet whether or not you're Cougar's new lawyer?"

"I keep hoping each day."

"Not worried I hope." He pulled out a cigar and snipped off the end.

"Just anxious. I already have my first client."

Bollie raised his eyebrows.

"Thelma," Cat explained. "She wants to make out a will and insists on being my first client. I told her we could do it at home, but she said no, she wants to go down in my memory as my first client."

Bollie nodded as he lit and relit the cigar.

"I'm here on business, though. Well, not my own business but something for the town."

His eyebrows remained raised but he said nothing. He had about the warmest brown eyes Cat could remember. She leaned forward, and asked, "Do you ever have to foreclose on mortgages?"

"What brought that on?" he asked. "Sure. I've had to do a couple over the years."

"I bet you hate doing it."

"Not easy, but sometimes necessary."

"I was just thinking you're not a typical banker."

"Do you know a typical anybody? Typicals are for statistics. You're not a typical lawyer, at least not in my book."

"Just because I'm a woman, you mean?"

"That, and knowing you, I suspect you're going to be as unlike Simon Oliphant as it's possible for two human beings to be."

"Is that good?"

Bollie smiled. "It's different."

"I spent all winter holed up at the Big Piney, and I figure there are lots of women, and men, too, out on the ranches, who would love to have something to read. The only reading material in this whole town are the magazines and the one book rack at the pharmacy." She paused to take a deep breath. "I think we need a library."

Bollie sat back in his big swivel chair and studied Cat.

She went on. "You're the town's leading citizen . . ."

"You mean I hold its purse strings."

She cocked her head, and said, "That's not all, and you know it. I've talked to Norah and Red about this idea. They're both enthusiastic."

"I'm not surprised."

"Anyhow, they both think it's a good idea, and I want to get together a committee to work on it and I'd like you on the board. Your ideas will be welcome, I'm sure."

Bollie was nodding as she talked, his mind already busy. "Better take Nan rather than me. She'd be great for this. We subscribe to every book club known to man. Wonder why no one's ever come up with it before."

"I'll call her today. Got any other ideas? Norah suggested the principal and a teacher . . . "

"Gladys Amador."

When Cat looked blank, Bollie said, "Jack's wife. I know she lives about fifteen miles out of town, but she'd be perfect. She used to be head librarian at some college in the Midwest. In fact, she'd know more about setting it up than anyone I can think of. Gladys and I are good friends. Leave her to me. I'll set this in her lap like it's an idea that's been waiting for her. Her youngest is heading to college in the fall, and she'll need something to keep her mind off having all the kids gone."

He made himself a note.

"And, uh, what about the Myerson house?"

Bollie looked over at her, his pencil poised over a pad. He stared at her. After a minute, he said, "You're suggesting instead of selling it we take a loss and donate it to the town?"

"That's exactly what I'm suggesting."

"My God, girl, what gall you have. Do you think banks . . ." And then he shook his head. "It's a white elephant. Young people today don't want a house that big since most of 'em can't afford help. Okay, let me bring it up at the board meeting this month. Don't talk of it yet, the library okay, but not that old house. Let me see what I can do to cut our losses and do a good deed at the same time."

Cat grinned like a Cheshire cat.

"This town and the McCulloughs sure are lucky Scott found you."

"No," she said, standing. "It's I who has the luck. Just think, I could be in a humid Boston summer winning cases that would make me famous and take me to Congress or even the Supreme Court . . ."

"Are those the dreams you had?"

Cat shrugged. "They were sitting in the periphery of my mind, anyhow . . ."

Bollie grinned. "We'll see what little old Cougar Valley can do for you."

He stood up and walked Cat to the door. She was surprised when he leaned over to kiss her cheek.

"The banker with the personal touch?"

"Look at it that way. Maybe now that you're active again, you'll come to the house for dinner some night."

"I'd love to."

"Okay, go call Nan and start on this civic project."

"If I don't pass the bar, it'll give me something to do."

The sheriff's car was in front of his office, so Cat stopped in. Jason said, "I saw your car, and was hoping you'd drop in. You had lunch yet?"

Cat glanced at her watch. It was nearly one. "Uh-uh."

"It's on me."

"I'll accept that offer. I have things I want to discuss with you anyhow."

Jason's eyes danced. "I like hearing that."

"You don't even know what they are."

"I don't even care. Have I told you lately you look good enough to eat?"

"Be careful," she said recklessly. "What you want most you might get."

He stared at her, his eyes wide. "Life is suddenly getting extremely interesting."

Cat smiled to herself. It had been a long time since she'd flirted with a man.

She flirted with Jason all through lunch and didn't even get around to mentioning the library until he was eating strawberry-rhubarb pie.

She even let her leg brush his under the table.

He couldn't keep a grin off his face. His eyes danced all through lunch.

She left him after that, after he promised to do what he could to help get a drive for the library under way, and went home. The meadows were golden with mustard, and herds of cattle dotted the fields at the foot of the mountains.

She told herself Dodie was right. She couldn't be a grieving widow forever. Scott was dead and gone. She would be twenty-nine in the fall and all her life, including what Dodie referred to as her childbearing years, was still ahead of her.

And Jason was one of the nicest men she'd ever known. He was good-looking and he had a sense of humor and he was always finding ways to help people. It about broke his heart when he had to break bad news to someone, like when Jake Clement's car hit that telephone pole last month and it was up to Jason to go out to the farm and tell Jake's wife. Tell her that she and their two young children were alone from now on. Or when Randy Taylor fell off his tractor and it ran over his leg and Jason had to rush him up to the hospital where they took Randy's leg off. He liked being a big fish in a little puddle, more than just being another cop in Seattle, but he suffered when he had to deliver bad news.

In Cougar, he was fond of saying, there was no seamy side of life. Poor, yeah, hardscrabble poor a lot of these people. On welfare a lot of the unmarried single mothers. Collecting unemployment half the year for hundreds of the young men. Ranchland on the dole.

He coached Little League in the spring and fall, and Cody was thrilled to be eight this spring so he was eligible. Scott and Jason had founded the Little League, and now Jason had talked Joseph into helping.

She sighed as she thought of Jason. She wasn't being fair to him, she was all too aware of that. She flirted with him, and ran her toes up his leg under the table because somewhere inside her she thought that would get her mind off her father-in-law.

Just in the last couple of weeks she'd been aware of yearnings—

urges to be held, to be kissed. To see herself reflected in some man's eyes. Six, even three months ago she'd thought she'd never even think of another man, and now here she was, wanting to be touched by a man. She hoped Jason would touch her tomorrow night at dinner at his house. She'd told him she'd bring the dessert.

It'd been forever since she'd baked anything. She'd ask Thelma to let her have free rein of the kitchen tomorrow afternoon and she'd bake her mother's recipe, that tall walnut cake that everyone raved about. That would knock Jason's socks off. She'd bake two and leave one at the house. Yeah, to knock Red's socks off, too?

She said aloud, "I've got to get in control of this." Idly, she wondered what "this" was.

Turning off the blacktop onto the dirt road which eventually led to the ranch, she told herself, "Don't let this go one inch farther."

But she found her heart beating faster when she came in sight of the house and saw Red standing on the porch, holding her son.

It's seeing Matt, she thought. She'd been gone from her son for four and a half hours.

She hadn't seen Red since seven o'clock last night.

Maybe the thudding in her chest was seeing them together. Whatever it was, she could hear the blood pounding in her veins.

She pulled the car up in front of the porch steps and slid out of the car. Red helped Matt wave his hand at his mother. The boy did hold out his arms and moved into Cat's embrace.

"You're in early," she said.

"Had some business to tend to," he said. "Saw your car downtown as I went through on my way to Baker. Have a successful day?" He acted as though everything was the way it had always been.

She breathed more easily.

She was imagining all this. Then how to explain the electricity that shot through her when his hand brushed hers as he handed her son to her?

Thirty

"Oh, boy, a cake!" Cody exclaimed.

"Baking isn't on my list of talents," Jason admitted.

"Your chicken cacciatore certainly is."

"Sounds exotic, doesn't it, but it's really easy."

"You did that to impress me, didn't you?"

Jason smiled. "I told Katie that if she'd clean up tomorrow, I'd get this dinner, yeah."

"I'm glad," Cody said. He gobbled the last from his plate. "Will you play Parcheesi with me?"

Cat glanced at Jason, who nodded as he helped himself to a second piece of the walnut cake. "You baked *this* to impress me, didn't you?"

"Oh, I don't know."

"You succeeded, but then I've been impressed all along."

"My ego is going to swell my head so I won't fit through a door."

"What's an ego?" Cody asked, getting up to go find the Parcheesi set.

"Meaning we make her feel good," Jason said. He leaned across the table and put his hand over Cat's. "Right?"

She nodded, pressing his hand.

She liked him. A lot. Genuinely liked him and Cody, both. She liked feeling desirable. Jason made her feel good. She'd enjoyed his kisses.

At the end of an hour, wherein Cody had won three games to Cat's one, Jason said, "Okay for tonight."

"I'm out of practice," Cat told the boy. "I haven't played Parcheesi in years. You just wait until next time!"

It was just eight-thirty.

Jason asked, "You want to look at that video I picked up today?"

"Yeah, sure," Cody said, turning to Cat. "You want to watch it, too?"

"I don't think so. Thanks."

"You go watch it in your room while Cat and I talk," his father suggested.

Cody disappeared.

"I hope Matt turns out as nice as your son."

Jason nodded. He knew he was fortunate.

"Does he ever miss his mother?"

"If so, he doesn't talk about it. She's in San Francisco, you know. She asked if he could come visit for a week when she gets a vacation the end of August. I don't know how I feel about putting him on a plane. I could drive him over to Portland and he wouldn't have to change planes, I suppose. He's more excited at the thought of flying than anything else, I think."

He led the way onto the porch that ran across the front of his small house. They sat in the plastic chairs there. They were more comfortable than they looked.

The sky was just beginning to darken. It wouldn't be totally dark for another hour yet.

They nodded to Don Christiansen, walking past the house.

Don tipped his baseball cap.

"It'll be all over town this time tomorrow morning that you were sitting on my porch with me."

"Is that the most exciting thing they'll have to talk about?"

"Depends how many heard about Luann Michaels."

"What about Luann Michaels?"

"She just had a baby."

"I don't know of her."

"She's Cissy Sorenson's daughter."

"Why Cissy's not old enough to be a grandmother."

"Cissy's thirty-two, and her daughter's fifteen."

Cat raised her eyebrows.

"Luann had the baby and nobody even knew the girl was pregnant. Turns out Cissy's husband is the father. Cissy and her husband are going to adopt it, and she's going to be raised as Luann's sister."

"Oh, my."

They were quiet for a few minutes. In the distance there were the sounds of dogs barking and the shouts of children playing a game. Cat appreciated the tranquillity.

"Are you ready yet?" Jason asked.

"Ready? For what?"

"Ready for a man in your life."

Cat turned to smile at him. "You mean, am I ready for you?"

"I suppose you won't know that until I make some moves, will you?"

"Are you thinking of making some?" She knew she was toying with him.

"I'm at a point where I think of you all the time. I'm driving out in the country, or I'm going to a meeting, or I'm trying to solve some sort of dispute when what I'm really doing is trying not to see you in front of me, trying not to reach out to touch you whenever I see you. I get into bed at night and whether you like it or not, you're there with me. Can you tell from my expression when you see me in Rocky's that what I'm really doing is thinking about tearing your clothes off?"

"Aha, I've wondered what that expression means."

He laughed.

"You're a man of rare self-discipline then."

"No longer, Cat, no longer." He stood up and reached to pull her to him. He put his arms around her and brought his mouth to hers.

"What will the neighbors say?" she murmured.

"That it's about time."

His warm mouth on hers felt good. His tongue traced along her upper lip until it parted her lips and meshed with hers. His arms around her tightened.

Then he let go of her and suggested, "Let's go inside. What comes next is nobody else's business."

He walked back in the house to tell Cody to turn off the TV, but the boy was asleep in front of it. Jason turned it off and closed Cody's door.

"We're alone," he told Cat.

She walked over to him. "That kiss felt nice."

He kissed her again and her arms wound around his neck. His left hand encircled her breast. She heard herself moan.

"It's been a long time," she whispered.

"For me, too," he breathed into her ear.

He picked her up and carried her down the hall to his bedroom. When he stood her up, she began to unbutton her blouse.

"No," he said. "Let me."

He flicked the switch on the lamp on the bed table. "Sandy hated a light on."

"Looking is half the fun," Cat said as he came to her, finishing the unbuttoning of her blouse. She reached out to do the same to his shirt.

"Do you know how often, and for how long, I've wanted to see you naked?" he muttered. "This is not the first time you've gone to bed with me."

His hands slid her slacks down and he unbuckled his belt, unzipping his pants, and letting them fall to the floor. They stood together, their naked bodies stretching against each other.

He picked her up again and laid her on the bed, looking down at her and saying, "You are every bit as beautiful as I'd imagined. As I'd known."

He lay on top of her, cradling her head in his hands. "I am so crazy in love with you." And he kissed her again.

"You sure are athletic," he said.

"I controlled myself." Cat grinned. "I didn't want to waken Cody."

"Wow," Jason said, sliding off her and lying beside her.

"You can say that again."

"Wow."

"Do you think all the people who will hear about us sitting on the porch will know we did this too?"

"Uh-uh. They'll think it'll take us time to work up to this."

"Work? Didn't seem like work to me."

"It was fun. In fact, I'd say I can't offhand think of anything in my life that ever felt better." Cat looked at the bedside clock. "I have to go. It's after eleven."

"Don't go. Don't ever go."

She laughed. "Well, I do think there's a good chance we can do this again."

"And again. And again. Marry me, Cat."

"Look, Jason. Just because we go to bed together doesn't mean I'm ready for a permanent commitment. Don't rush me and ruin it. Let's just take it a step at a time, okay?" She got out of bed and walked to where her slacks were in a heap on the floor.

"Let's enjoy this. We made love tonight for the first time in what seems like forever, and it's mighty nice. Let's do it again sometime soon. But don't push me, please, Jason. Tonight is all new to me. I liked it. A lot. If Sandy couldn't enjoy sex with you, she had to be out of her mind or just not interested in sex with a man, because you are quite terrific in that department."

"You bring out the best in me. You don't even have an idea what tonight means to me."

She found her bra on the floor and her blouse, a green silk one that clung and which she'd worn just to entice Jason. She'd suspected, perhaps known, that this would happen tonight and had been prepared. She decided she'd ask Chazz for birth control pills. Would he be shocked? Maybe she should go over to the clinic in Baker and get them so no one in Cougar would know what she was doing.

Thirty-one

The next morning at breakfast, Red asked, "You going into town today?"

"I go every day now that I have a mailbox and am waiting to hear from the state."

Thelma, standing in the kitchen doorway, said, "I'll take care of Matt. Lucy's not feeling well."

"Oh?" Cat looked up. "Are you sure he won't be too much bother? I can take him with me. I'll be in the office anyhow. He'll be okay there."

"No bother at all," Thelma said.

"I didn't get around to calling Nan yesterday," Cat told Red. "But I will today. I think instead of my chairing a library board, it might be a good idea if she did."

Red smiled. "You're becoming a politician."

"I have lots of ideas. Norah and Bollie were both enthusiastic, so that means our chances of raising enough money are pretty good."

Red took his eyes from the paper he was halfheartedly reading. "I never doubted it for a minute."

She looked at him. "You have more faith than I do. It'll take ages and a lot of energy to raise enough money."

"Bollie going to give the town that house?"

"He wasn't averse to the idea. He's going to try. Incidentally, I was going over our books and I think I found a way to save you seventy or eighty thousand in taxes."

Red put down the paper, and a look of surprise covered his face. "Legally?" He whistled.

She laughed as she fed Matt in his high chair. "Of course. It has to do with land management. I'm not a CPA, but I think those guys you have doing your taxes down in Baker aren't quite on the ball. Those classes I took at Oregon State in computerizing rangeland management gave me some ideas."

"Seventy or eighty thousand?" Thelma could tell that the look he gave Cat was one of admiration even if Cat didn't see it.

"Maybe I can come up with more, for I think it can be retroactive. I can explain it to you if you want when we have more time."

"Maybe I better let Blackwell & Johnson go and have you do it all."

"I wouldn't mind that, if you trust me. I imagine I'll have plenty of time at the office to bone up on this sort of thing. But we'll have to do some serious talking about your finances."

"You have access to all of it on your computer."

"I know, but I have some ideas." She turned to look at him now. "Nervy, aren't I?"

Matt pushed a fist into the cereal and tossed it over Cat. "Thanks heaps, kid," she said. "I knew I shouldn't have dressed before breakfast."

"I won't mind taking care of him," Thelma said. "I don't have anything extra planned today." Like baking or canning or any of the myriad things Thelma did. "Roseann is coming to clean."

"And I'll be back to the house for lunch," Red said. Which was unusual for him.

"Okay, fine. I'll get him dressed."

Cat knew she was spoiled. No housework. Willing baby-sitters. But no husband either. Not that just any husband would do. In fact, much as she had enjoyed last night, she really had to make it clear to Jason that she was enjoying her freedom. She was starting her own business, she was going to get a library going in Cougar, she was free to come and go when she wanted. She sort of liked what last night might mean. Affection and sex without ties. At least for a while, for she was wise enough to know that continued sex did bring responsibility. Pretty nearly always.

Ah, that's what she'd do after lunch. She'd go see Chazz about birth control pills. He wouldn't tell anyone, not even Dodie, and she suspected he wouldn't stand in judgment of her either. He'd guess it was Jason. And he'd probably be happy for both of them.

She felt good this morning. Miss Jenny was right. Good sex made one feel on a high for some time afterward. So, why was she having trouble looking at Red? She had the definite feeling that were she to confess to him what she and Jason had done last night, he'd nod in approval. In fact, the whole town probably would be rooting for them.

She half expected Jason to appear shortly after she unlocked the door to her office, but he didn't. A painter was there though, lettering on one of the front windows in gold,

Catherine McCullough
Counselor-at-law

"Oh, my goodness," she said, standing back to study it. "Who sent you to do this?"

The young man shrugged and went on with his painting.

When Jason hadn't appeared by ten, Cat wandered across the street for coffee at Rocky's, but Jason wasn't there either. She talked with several of the old-timers and with Ida, and drank a cup of coffee, and walked back across the street to stop in at the sheriff's office. No Jason.

She went back to her office and called Nan Bollinger, whose husband had already broken the ice. "Cat, I can't imagine why I never came up with such an idea. Probably because I've lived here so long and am used to cultural deprivation. Of course, I'll help. In fact, after Bollie told me about it I lay awake til after midnight, coming up with one idea after another."

"I can't tell you how happy that makes me. When can we get together?"

"How about coming over for dinner Saturday. Just us, so we can talk about this. Bring Red why don't you, for I'm sure he'll help back this."

When Cat hesitated, Nan said, "If you think Sarah will come, of course bring her. If not, you two come anyhow. And if you want to bring the baby, that's fine, too. We'll just have supper on the patio. In fact, bring your bathing suit and we'll swim first."

"That sounds great." She didn't even know if she'd fit into her bathing suit, which she hadn't worn in two years. She had gained ten pounds since then, pounds she had no desire to lose. "Can I come even if Red and Sarah don't want to?"

"Nonsense. I'll call Red this minute and tell him Sarah or no, I expect him to see that you get here. Bruce probably won't be home. He's been seeing some girl over in Ontario."

Nan hung up.

Their youngest son, Bruce, was home from Dartmouth for the summer holidays. He had a summer job as a firefighter with the

Forestry Service. The other two Bollinger children were married. One lived in Washington, D.C., and the other in Santa Fe. They'd left Cougar Valley as soon as they could. Funny, Cat thought. She who had always lived in cities, had no desire to leave, and those who grew up here could hardly wait to get away.

Jason didn't appear until almost noon. Then he walked into her office, his sheriff's hat tilted back on his head, a haggard expression on his face. He sprawled into the chair across from her desk.

"You look beat," she said, happy to see him.

"Been down the old mill road all morning. A dead baby. Looks like its head was bashed in."

"Oh, my!"

"Yeah, oh my. That sort of thing doesn't happen around here. Not in Cougar Valley."

"How old was it?"

"Newborn. Probably less than a day. How can anyone do that?" he asked rhetorically, not expecting an answer.

But Cat had one. "Because that seemed preferable to admitting to having it. Someone not ready for the responsibility, who should have had an abortion when she realized she was pregnant, so it wouldn't be a fully formed human being and killing it wouldn't be so terrible."

Jason stared at her. "You better go into politics."

"That's the second time I've heard that. I feel for the mother who did this."

"How do you know the mother did it?"

Cat cocked her head. "Who else?"

"I don't know. But now it's murder, in my county, and it's my problem."

Cat gave him a long, level look. "I don't think you should work too hard to solve it, Jason."

He stood up and walked over to stare out the door. Then he said, "You'd think it would take my appetite, wouldn't you, but I haven't even eaten breakfast. You want some lunch?"

She nodded, and together they walked across the hot dusty street to Rocky's, where the lunch crowd left only one table, in the back by the swinging kitchen door, where it was noisy and dark.

"What I really planned was to pick some of those wildflowers in that vacant lot, two down from my house, and come let you see that last night meant a lot to me."

She smiled. "I liked it, too."

"Liked? That seems an understatement."

"I look forward to a return engagement."

"My office? Your office? My house? A car? Out in the woods? Down by the creek? You name it."

Ida brought their roast beef sandwiches with Rocky's homemade dill pickles.

Cat laughed as she spread mustard and horseradish over the rye bread. She shifted the conversation to tell him about progress with her library idea.

When they went their separate ways after lunch, she spent a couple of hours studying Oregon tax law and delving into rangeland measures. Who would have thought a hotshot Boston lawyer would end up doing this sort of stuff?

End up? She looked up and around her office. She wasn't ending up. She was just starting.

She left for home at two-thirty, and even as she drove up the long dirt road she could see trucks and equipment parked on the side lawn.

A backhoe was digging a hole.

She knew before she was even close enough to read the sign painted on the side of the dusty blue pickup.

A swimming pool. She'd said she'd give her eyeteeth for a place to swim.

Red was standing among the men, watching them dig up his earth. When he saw her, he grinned. "Don't know why I didn't do this years ago," he said.

"I guess I better be careful what I ask for from now on."

"It's not just for you," he said, almost too fast. "Matt can grow up learning to swim, and God knows I'll enjoy it. I'm too old to go to that swimming hole. Haven't been up there in years. And besides, you just saved me seventy or eighty thousand this morning, so this pool isn't costing anything!"

"Sure," she said, and as in old times she reached up to kiss his cheek. He threw an arm around her waist, smiling at her pleasure. "I bet you sent that man to paint that gold sign on my window, too."

He shook his head. "What man? What sign?"

Cat never did discover who had sent him.

But the next morning when she went to the post office, she received official notice that it was now legal for her to practice her profession in the state of Oregon. She phoned Thelma and told her to find a way to come downtown today, if she wanted to be her first client. "In fact," Cat told the cook, "if you want to come down at lunch time, I'll treat you to lunch at Rocky's."

"Mercy," said Thelma. "But let's get it straight. I'm paying you to make out this will."

"Of course," Cat said, deciding she'd charge Thelma twenty dollars.

The following morning a van from the florist in Baker pulled up in front of Cat's office and brought in bouquets of flowers, one from the bank wishing her success, another from Vlahov's Pharmacy, one from Jason and Cody, from Chazz and Dodie (she'd forgotten to go see Chazz about pills. Better do it before another day passed). One from Davis's Clothing Store, another from the Co-op. Must be a local practice to welcome new businesses to town.

And one red rose, with a card that read.

To Cat, who gives me more happiness than I'm used to and of whom I am very proud. Red

Chazz smiled at her when she told him why she'd come.

"That cheers me up."

"Me too."

He wrote out a prescription, and she said, "I almost didn't come to you . . ."

"Because your sex life is not my business?"

"Exactly."

"Maybe your mental health is. Anyhow, your secret is safe with me. Oh, and Dodie told me about your library idea. Great. You're the McCullough woman that everyone hoped Sarah would be."

"Don't say things like that!"

"Well . . . okay, you're an addition to the town, Cat."

"Okay, that's better. Just remember that when you need a lawyer."

"My malpractice insurance is paid up."

"Still . . ." She asked, "Am I going to have trouble being a lawyer here?"

Chazz twisted his lips, thinking. "I don't know. People'll come to you for the small things, like wills . . ."

"I don't expect anything but small things here."

"You are automatically the town's and the school's lawyer. It may take awhile, but people'll get used to you. Now, if you were a doctor, most of 'em would go to Baker or La Grande rather than have a woman look at them, and that's including most women."

Cat shook her head. "Don't people around here know it's the 1990s."

"Hah," Chazz muttered, "look how they've crucified Hillary because she's smart and independent. Last time they had a first lady like that was Eleanor Roosevelt. And then they had to make fun of her looks. Inside was one beautiful lady. Small towns are inclined to resist change and be suspicious of anything their grandfathers didn't approve of. That's why the young people can hardly wait to leave. If you'd decided to practice law when Scott was still alive, hardly a soul would have come to you. You should then be home being a wife and mother. Period."

"So, why do I like it here? I don't even miss Boston. Or the East."

The doctor shook his head back and forth. "Practicing law here may bore you crazy. It's all diddly."

"Isn't that one of the reasons we like it? No crime?"

He nodded. "You better go over to the pharmacy in Baker to fill this prescription if you don't want everyone knowing your business."

Cat took the slip of paper and folded it into her purse. "Good suggestion."

"We're barbecuing Sunday about three. You and Matt want to come?"

"Sounds nice. Yeah, I'd love to." Saturday at Bollingers' and Sunday at Whitleys'.

"Bring Red and Sarah, if you can get her to come out."

Cat reached for the door knob. "I doubt it, Chazz. She's out of it most of the time. I'll ask, though."

"If not, make Red come. We never see enough of him."

Red Saturday night, too.

"Why don't you call and ask him."

"Hey, I can do that." He picked up the phone as Cat left through the outer office.

Later, all he told Dodie was that he'd run into Cat and invited her to come for Sunday hamburgers and hot dogs. "I told her to bring Red and Sarah, and she said she'd try."

"Yeah. Sure," was Dodie's answer to that idea. "But I'll be glad to have her. Jason's coming, too."

Chazz thought of suggesting Joseph and Torie, too, when Dodie said, "Let's invite Joseph and Torie, too."

It was uncanny, he decided. She could read his mind more often than not. She even could unconsciously usually follow his train of thought. Like he was thinking of Joseph and . . .

Thirty-two

Red had savored last night. He'd wondered if Cat was having a good time. She was young enough to be the Bollingers' daughter. His, too, of course. But she seemed to be enjoying herself. She fit in, and certainly added delightfully to the conversation. That was his word, delightfully. She and Nan spent over an hour after dinner plotting to raise money and engender interest for a Cougar Public Library.

Nan, who had grown up in Pendleton, looked as though she would have been at home with the horsey set in Southampton. The closest she'd been to that kind of life was a few days every couple of years when she and Bollie flew to New York to do Broadway. She didn't even shop much in the Big Apple. "Where would I wear the kind of clothes they sell there?"

Nevertheless, she did look as though she shopped at Saks and had facials at Elizabeth Arden. Actually, she ordered her clothes from catalogs and wore a perfect size 10. She looked to the manor born. Elegant. Her soft blond hair fell straight, with a hint of curl about her shoulders. Cat imagined Nan woke up looking that good. Her makeup was applied so artfully one really couldn't tell she wore more than lipstick.

The sapphire on her left hand was noticeable from across a room. She'd told Cat, "Bollie gave that to me as an engagement ring, saying only a sapphire could express his love was as deep as the ocean and as infinite as the sky."

From the way he looked at her, Cat surmised he still felt the same. Bollie, Nan, and Red had known each other forever. Bollie and Nan met in their senior year in high school, when their towns played football and Bollie scored a touchdown for Cougar while Nan led the cheerleading squad rooting for the Pendleton team. From among the crowd of faces, as soon as he walked out on the field, Bollie had seen a heart-shaped face framed with blond hair and an energy that was contagious. She was enthusiastic in a quiet, elegant way, her voice always modulated and her soft, blue-gray eyes luminous. She was what Red referred to as "a really classy lady."

She'd put time in over the years as the PTA president, a Girl Scout leader, a den mother. She led a 4-H equestrian group when her daughter was in school. She'd driven kids all over the state to debates when her middle boy was on that team. She'd taken an automotive class in Adult Ed in Baker and could take a car apart and put it back together.

She traveled to banking conventions with her husband, and Red and Cat were both sure she charmed the socks off the other bankers. Every year she and Bollie took an eighteen-day trip to someplace, as they'd done for the twenty-seven years they'd been married.

Cat had once asked, "Is there anyplace you haven't been?"

Bollie thought for a moment. "The Antarctic and Zimbabwe."

The Bollingers were probably the best-read people in town, and Nan again wondered why she, at least, had never thought of a library here.

"Doesn't have to be big," Cat said. "One room for adults and one for children."

"If we could afford to pay a librarian, I know just the person," Nan said.

"Your husband and Norah mentioned Gladys somebody."

Nan nodded agreement. "Exactly."

"If we could garner enough enthusiasm," Cat thought aloud, "maybe we could talk the town into a library tax."

Bollie stopped whatever he'd started to say to Red, and said, "I heard that. Not a bad idea." He grinned at Red. "That girl's got potential."

Cat looked across the room at him. "I've given this a lot of thought."

Red was gazing at her, too, with what she could only interpret as a look of pride.

On the way home, he said, "You certainly fit into Cougar."

"I want to," she responded, looking out the window at the stars.

They were silent for a few miles. Red said, "The pool should be done this week. Would you like to have a christening party?"

"Aren't we being partied to pieces? Tonight, and then tomorrow at the Whitleys'. That's quite enough for me in one week. Besides, we'll be welcoming Miss Jenny's Brit."

This week her British lord was due to arrive. His mother asked Red if he'd fly his Cessna over to Portland to meet Sir Geoffrey there.

"By the way, my Boston investigator phoned me yesterday, and I forgot to tell you. Miss Jenny's new friend is on the up and up. In fact, he has more money than you and the Bollingers and maybe the Weyerhausers put together."

Red laughed. "The Weyerhouses? How did they get in there?"

"Well, don't they own nearly all the trees in the Northwest?"

"Oh, I see. You mean he's filthy rich."

"Filthy. And he's a doer. He's not just a lord in the House of Lords, but has actually worked at it. However, he really politically belongs in the other house, the House of Commons, politically, because he works for the people. He's rather a maverick. His family used to own coal mines and he's gone down in them . . . I guess he got so upset about working conditions that he got rid of the mines. Then he had a string of newspapers, guess he still does, but he's not active in the management. Chairman of the Board, that sort of thing.

"He has four children, all in their forties. His wife died thirteen years ago."

"So he's not just a stuffy old guy," Red said.

"Doesn't sound it."

"I feel a bit relieved. Funny, isn't it. Wonder how he'll react to the wide-open West."

"I wouldn't call this wide-open. I'd call this the majestic mountainous West."

Even at this hour she could see the darker mountains silhouetted against the night sky.

From a couple of miles away, as they turned from the blacktop onto the dirt road to the Big Piney, she could see the lights from the house. "Red, did you see Lucy yesterday?"

"Not that I remember. Why?"

"The whole side of her face was swollen."

He whistled. "That husband of hers."

"I wondered. Why does she take it?"

He shook his head. "Mystery to me."

When they pulled up at the ranch house, Red said, "I had a good time, Cat. It's nice to have someone to do things with. It seems I've been on my own for so long."

She reached out to touch his hand, but he caught hers in his and just looked at her for a moment.

"I enjoyed it, too."

She slid out of the car and ran up the steps. She didn't stop downstairs, but went right up, glancing in at Matt, asleep in his crib, before going into her own room.

As she undressed, she said aloud, "I'm nuts. There's nothing there, really."

To everyone's surprise, Sarah accepted Chazz's invitation. Dodie had phoned Miss Jenny and invited her, too. So, early the next afternoon all five, including the baby, drove into town.

"My, it's a beautiful day," Sarah exclaimed.

Cat and Jenny were in the backseat. Cat asked, "Are you nervous about what-his-name's visit?"

"Nervous? My dear, not at all. If he doesn't like what he sees, that's the end of a little fun, that's all. He doesn't have to meet me in Egypt, you know, not if he doesn't want to."

"Egypt?" Red twisted his head around to look at his mother.

"Well, not until October," Miss Jenny said.

"Are you becoming a jet-setter?" Cat asked.

"I do think my horizons are expanding," Miss Jenny admitted. "I'm toying with Samoa in January."

"Samoa?" Sarah asked as though it was a word new to her.

"There or Bora Bora." Miss Jenny leaned forward as though talking to a deaf person.

"Ah, Bora Bora," Sarah breathed as though it represented paradise.

Cat thought that Sarah hadn't yet had a drink today. Chazz had told her that if Sarah came, they'd see there was no liquor available. "Not that we drink that early in the afternoon anytime," he said.

When Chazz heard that Sarah had accepted their invitation he suggested to Dodie that they not invite Torie and Joseph.

"Nonsense," Dodie said. "Sarah just has to get used to it. My God, they've been in love for years. They should just go away and get married. Get jobs someplace else. Who gives a damn if his kids won't be able to perform purifying acts for his tribe. How many are left there anyhow? They've all intermingled, and most of them have moved away to get jobs in lumber mills or factories or wherever. There's not even a reservation here."

"Ours not to reason why . . ."

"Maybe not yours, but mine. Two finer young people never lived than Torie and Joseph, and they're being frustrated as hell."

"How do you know? Maybe they're perfectly happy . . ."

"No people in love are happy when they're denied marriage and a family."

"Hey, don't judge everyone else by what you want. Plenty of people don't want kids."

"You know perfectly well Torie and Joseph would be wonderful parents."

Chazz didn't tell her that Torie was on the pill. And had been for longer than he'd known her.

Dodie warned Torie that her mother was coming.

"Well, that's hopeful," Torie said. "I'll tell Joseph and let him decide for himself, but I'll come."

By the time the contingent from the Big Piney arrived, Jason and Cody as well as Torie and Joseph were already at the Whitleys'.

Chazz had assigned Jason the job of barbecuing the hamburgers, so he was across the yard, by the fire, when Cat came out to the backyard. Dodie and Torie and Red all noticed the expression in the sheriff's eyes when he saw Cat. The look on his face shouted.

Cat, however, was setting Matt down in the little jump chair Dodie had waiting for him.

Cody came bounding over. Cat leaned down to kiss the top of his head. "You want me to come see a game soon?"

"Yeah. Saturday would be good."

He'd refused to invite her until he'd played several games, and now wanted to show off, she could tell. "Okay, Saturday it is. What time?"

"Ten."

"Hey, that's pretty early." Cat's eyes were above the boy's head, watching Sarah move like an apparition across the yard. She held out her arm as she approached Jason, smiling her beautiful smile, her eyes shining, her hair coiffed perfectly today. Not at all as she had been around the house since Scott died. Cat noticed Red's eyes following his wife, too.

Jason grabbed hold of Sarah's hand, and bent over to kiss her cheek. Their conversation was animated, and Cat heard Jason laugh.

Miss Jenny involved herself in a conversation with Joseph, whose eyes also followed Sarah.

Cat went back into the kitchen where Dodie put her to work chopping onions and tossing a salad.

"How many lives might be different if your mother-in-law were like this all the time," Dodie commented, looking out the window.

"You know," Cat said, "most of the time it's like she doesn't even live out at the house. She's sort of not there, even when she's sitting in the living room. She's in a different world. I'm not convinced it's always from drinking. I can't tell half the time whether she has been drinking. She's never querulous, or unpleasant. Sometimes she starts to sing old songs and falls asleep during a meal or slurs words, but she isolates herself, and it's as though she doesn't even live there most of the time."

Dodie just shook her head. "Look at her out there, flirting with Jason, looking so gorgeous you can't believe she's nearly fifty."

"She's totally ignoring her daughter and Joseph."

"Honey, that's their problem. Torie knew that would happen. I did too. You didn't tell her Joseph was coming, did you?"

"I didn't even know."

Dodie changed the subject. "When is this beau of Miss Jenny's arriving?"

"Wednesday. Red's flying to Portland to pick him up."

"I think it's simply marvelous."

"I'll reserve judgment til I meet him. He sounds too good to be true."

"Sometimes I think we women tend to screw up relationships by worrying whether or not they're leading someplace instead of just enjoying the present."

"I don't think that's a problem with her. She's enjoying the present to the utmost. I think she likes things the way they are and doesn't want a long-term involvement."

"What about you? Are you ready for one?" Dodie's eyes narrowed when she heard Cat sigh.

"Life is a puzzle, Dodie," was Cat's only response before she left the kitchen with the large salad bowl.

Dodie stared after her, then followed with the platter of deviled eggs.

Miss Jenny had baked a mayonnaise chocolate cake that morning, and it was at least six inches high. Cody was eyeing it.

"I'm waiting for that, too," Joseph told him. "Meantime how about a game of horseshoes?"

"Sure," said the boy, glad to have someone paying attention to him.

Sarah had turned her attention to Chazz. Cat walked over to the barbecue to say hello to Jason and was surprised when he smiled and kissed her on the cheek. She wasn't ready for any public acknowledgment.

"You want yours rare?"

"Ugh," she replied. "Pretty well done."

"Called you last night."

"We were over at the Bollingers' for dinner."

"You look ravishing."

"You probably tell that to all the women . . ."

". . . all the women I've slept with lately, anyhow," he said, his voice low.

"You're pretty handsome, yourself." He wasn't in uniform today, but wore a shortsleeve forest green shirt open at the neck. "Red's building us a swimming pool. You and Cody will have to come out to swim and stay for dinner."

"Sounds good, but not exactly what I have in mind."

Torie sauntered over to them. "You two look deep in conversation."

"Did you know your father's building a swimming pool at the ranch?"

"No! What prompted him to this?"

"I said it was hot." Cat laughed.

"You're good for the family, Cat. You make things happen, whether you know it or not."

Beyond Torie, Cat observed Red watching them. He nodded his head as his mother said something, then walked over to join Joseph and Cody.

"I don't know how you got Mom to come today."

"Just invited her," Cat said.

"How long is Miss Jenny's beau going to stay?"

"I don't think that's been decided," Cat replied.

"Is he going to stay down at the ranch?"

"Not to my knowledge," Cat answered.

"She only has one bedroom up at the lodge."

They looked at each other and burst out laughing.

Red heard them and his glance traveled across the yard to watch them. He grieved for the son who would never know the happiness that Cat brought to them. He listened to his daughter and daughter-in-law laughing, and his heart stirred. He wondered if it were possible to love anyone more than he loved those two women.

He felt a tug on his sleeve and looked down to see Sarah looking up at him. "Red," she whispered, "they don't have anything to drink."

He pushed down a sense of irritation. "Sure they do." He led her to the long table and grabbed a Coke from the ice chest, opening it with a bottle opener, finding a cup with ice and pouring the liquid into it. "Here's a drink, Sarah."

She gave him a brief look and walked away.

He raised the Styrofoam cup to his lips and looked back across the lawn at Cat and Torie, still talking animatedly.

He was not at all surprised to feel a tightness in his chest.

Thirty-three

Sir Geoffrey Forrester had been born in India, where his father served with the Grenadier guards for six years before leaving to found an air force for the rajah of Ranispoore. That air force consisted of six planes, which ferried the rajah and his entourage, sometimes even all his six wives and twenty-three children, to whatever playground the rajah was interested in at the moment.

In this way Geoffrey Forrester's father had met Hollywood movie starlets, heads of state, wealthy hunters who wanted to bag tigers, and his wife. The woman who was to become Estelle Forrester accompanied her father on a safari to Ranispoore and spent more time studying the pilot than how to shoot a tiger. She did not return to London with her father.

Geoffrey's father, Leslie Forrester, was the second son of a lord and thus had no chance of inheritance passing on to him. He had chosen the military as his career because he was in love with planes. He knew he would never starve, but the title and property would pass on to his brother. This bothered Geoffrey not at all.

In 1925, Geoffrey's parents, his brother, and sister-in-law thought it might be fun to sail to India for the Christmas holidays and spend it with Geoffrey and his new wife, whom they had not met. The ship foundered in the Indian Ocean and all aboard were lost at sea eleven days before Christmas.

Geoffrey became Lord Forrester, a title he would happily have done without to have his family back.

He left the maharajah's air force in a depressed state, flying back home in a single-engine plane the rajah had given him as a farewell present. He didn't know a thing about administering the family lands and mines, but set out to learn all that he could. He was thirty-one years old.

He and Estelle chose to live at the drafty castle north of London rather than in the London flat. Here she kept her horses and bore three children, the oldest and only son of whom was Geoffrey.

Geoffrey was always a problem. He hated school, and though he could ace any class in which he bothered to study, he found it boring, found the school full of bullies, who never bothered him but took delight in terrifying the smaller younger boys with sadistic tricks and homosexual acts. When he heard that three of the older boys who came from families well-known throughout England had performed acts which sent the smallest boy in the school, Henry Wilkins, into nightmares night after night, he calmly walked into the room where one of the attackers dwelled, took him by the collar, marched him into the bathroom, and held his head in the loo as he flushed it over and over again, until that young man—terrified—promised never to do such to another student again.

Geoffrey Forrester was kicked out of yet another school for this act, and the young man whose face he tried to flush grew up to be a rather famous barrister.

In desperation, Geoffrey's family sent him to military school, and Geoffrey refused to open a book. He flunked out with the lowest average any student had ever had.

His aunt had recently married an American and, since it was wartime, volunteered to take Geoff to Massachusetts with her and her new husband and see how he reacted to public school there.

Geoff flowered. He loved the free and easy lifestyle. He loved it that no one told him to study, and so he did. He graduated in the top 10 percent of the Amherst high school class of '43.

He enlisted in the Royal Canadian Air Force and flew planes over Germany, being one of those who bombed Berlin. After the war he went on to Cambridge, taking a degree in business and finance.

When Geoff was thirty-three, his father suffered a stroke, and though he lived another eight years, he never spoke again. Geoffrey took over the family mines and the other businesses that had been Forresters' for well over a century and a half. When he sold the mines, he doubled the Forrester holdings.

He married a young woman whom he saw across a crowded dance floor one night and who held his heart forever after. They had four children in five years, and though he toyed with entering politics, he did nothing about it because he alienated big business, and the common man didn't trust a man with that much wealth.

He devoted his life to good works until his wife died, and then he seemed to lose interest in everything. Until his recently widowed sister suggested they start traipsing around the globe and see what the rest of the world was like.

Right before their first trip, they attended the theater—it was the second time he'd seen Les Misérables, but there was a new cast—and sat next to a most delightful, really rather irreverent American woman who must have been about his age. She reminded him of the girls he'd gone to school with in Amherst so long ago, except that she had an individuality quite unlike anyone he'd met before. His sister was charmed, too, and they ended up inviting her to their country place that weekend and, well, before he knew it he was interested in life again.

When he heard Jenny was going to Paris, he managed to be there when she was. When she said she thought she might visit Thailand, he talked her into a side junket to northern India.

They'd rather decided the next meeting place would be Egypt in the fall, but he now wanted to see what she was like in her own surroundings. She'd told him she and her son ran some Herefords on a ranch in the Northwest, and taught him how to pronounce the name of the state, with which he was totally unfamiliar.

Or y gn

He'd seen enough American movies that he thought he knew what to expect. Middle-class America. Dorothy and Toto. Jenny's son might be what movies called a "dude," and his wife probably wore aprons and made jam and didn't care what her hair looked like.

Jenny had told him her grandson died in a freak accident last year and the young wife now had a baby and stayed on to live in the ranch house. He knew that little one-story, three-bedroom tract homes were called ranch houses all over America.

He didn't care. Jenny gave him a new lease on life.

He was old enough to do exactly what he wanted, with no repercussions from his children or friends. Actually, he knew his children were never surprised at anything he did. They had teased him mercilessly when he told them he was flying to the west coast of America to meet the family of this lady he'd junketed around the world to meet at various places.

"Sounds serious, Dad," said his oldest, a twinkle in his eye.

"What's nice about her is she's not serious. She makes me feel like a teenager."

"Oh, then, it *is* serious," the son's pretty wife remarked, laughing.

He knew what they meant. Was papa getting ready to marry in his old age?

Old age? He didn't feel old. At least not any longer. Was seventy *that* old? He and Jenny sure didn't act it. They walked around seeing the sights and lingered over dinners and then spent hours in bed delighting each other.

He'd forgotten how good that could be. He wondered, as he looked out the plane flying over the snow-covered Cascades, if—much as he'd adored his wife—they had ever had as good sex as he was now having in the twilight of his life?

He was glad Jenny was thin and hadn't succumbed to the middle-age spread that afflicted so many older women. Yet here he was, on the portly side. Sir Geoffrey nearly died laughing at her answer when he asked if his weight bothered her.

"I like a man who doesn't get lost in the covers," she'd answered.

The plane began its descent into Portland, and he wondered why he had come. Partly because he thought of her every single day. And he wanted to see where she came from. Where she belonged.

He imagined her family would be a bit intimidated by his title and perhaps by himself. He'd wielded power, and certainly considered himself rather urbane. Something these middle-class Americans in their little towns were not accustomed to.

He was the surprised one, to find that the tallest, most imposing-looking person waiting for passengers was Jenny's son, who grabbed his bag and introduced himself.

"Recognized you from the picture Ma showed me," Red explained. "Come on, let's head for the baggage."

He led Sir Geoffrey, who found he had to hop along to the big man's long strides, down the escalators to the carousel where luggage from his plane was already moving along the ramp.

"That blue one," Sir Geoffrey said.

"We'll grab a cab over to my plane," Red explained, heading out the glass door.

Geoffrey was impressed with the countryside. Certainly spectacular, though brown. He'd been to California in the summer and laughed to himself at the "golden" state. Brown. Tan. Grass like hay with the lack of rain. Oregon must be a golden state, too, for once they'd flown over the green, jagged Cascades, the land was tan.

After an hour, there were green mountains rising again. Red started to descend into what seemed like the middle of them.

"Rather impressive scenery you have here," the man from London said.

"Never take it for granted," Red replied, circling in readiness to land on a long field. "It's not level around the house, so we land here and we'll drive up to the house. I'll take you to Miss Jenny's first, for that's partway up the mountain, but you'll be coming down to the ranch for dinner. Casual."

What was casual in America? In a little town in eastern Oregon? Ordinarily Sir Geoffrey never thought about what kind of impression he'd make. It was up to others to impress him. He liked this son of Jenny's, this down-to-earth though obviously literate ranch man.

Red pointed. "That's the ranch. We land about a mile away."

Which he did as smoothly as though he were parking his Caddy. Geoffrey saw a hangar.

A young man in jeans came running out when Red landed, and after Sir Geoffrey disembarked, Red and the young man pushed the Cessna into the hangar. Red tossed the bags into the back of a jeep and jumped into the driver's seat. "Oh, good show," Sir Geoffrey said, climbing into the vehicle. "I've never ridden in a jeep before." Maybe while he was here he'd buy himself a hat like Red wore. He'd only seen such in cowboy movies.

Red churned up the dust as they barreled along the completely straight dirt road.

"My God, Jenny didn't tell me about these mountains."

Red swerved to the left and headed into them, taking a right onto a narrow dirt road that climbed heavenward through tall fir trees.

The car followed a curve in the road and there, half hanging over a cliff, was a log home overlooking the expanse of valley below. Standing on the steps, in faded blue jeans, high-heeled boots, and a blue-and-white check shirt, with a kerchief tied around her throat, stood Jennifer McCullough. Geoffrey Forrester was aware that his heart was pounding, whether from the altitude or because of the pleasure he was receiving seeing this sixty-nine-year-old woman of the Wild West in front of him.

She waved, and came down the steps.

"Heard you coming up the drive about two miles ago," she said. Her eyes sparkled, and anyone could see she was more than pleased to see this man.

Red's eyes widened when she threw her arms around Geoffrey

and kissed him, not like a welcome kiss he'd expect her to give a visitor, but a real smackeroo. He grinned. He wondered if other people his age had a mother like Miss Jenny. Suddenly he wondered if she might be going to bed with this man. Funny, one never imagined one's parents making love. And especially not at nearly seventy.

"Maybe there's still hope for me," he mused as he turned the jeep around and headed back down into the valley.

Thirty-four

Hearing Red's report of Sir Geoffrey, Cat was predisposed to like him. Actually she hadn't even needed that. Anyone who made Miss Jenny's eyes sparkle that way was someone Cat was going to like, no matter what else.

She thought an outdoor barbecue by the new pool would be just the ticket to introduce the Englishman to the ways of American country life. Without telling Sarah, she invited Torie and Joseph. When something was a family affair, Cat thought, all the family should be invited. Sarah ignored Joseph and acted as though Torie were not visible.

Though he wasn't as gregarious or loquacious as either Red or Jason, people found Joseph mesmerizing. Strangers stared at him, wondering who the magnetic man was. Those who knew him felt warmly toward him, and probably respected him as much as anyone in town. He had the knack, people thought—strangers included—of being able to look behind one's eyes, and into the soul. It was not a frightening thing with Joseph. One felt that he saw you to your very core and liked you despite what he might find there.

Joseph squatted on his haunches and held out his arms to Matt who, holding on to a couch, toddled to him, hands waving in the air for balance.

"Do you like Miss Jenny's boyfriend?" Torie asked Cat. She'd brought caramel cinnamon rolls she'd baked that afternoon.

"He was absolutely charming at dinner last night," Cat said. "He's amusing, witty, and I'd imagine he'd be completely at ease just any-place."

"Does he know the Queen?"

Cat laughed. "Ask him. He thinks Americans are nutty about royalty."

"Well, we sure were about Princess Di," Torie admitted. "Though I'm getting a little tired of it all." She looked at Cat. "I'm thinking of going to California to teach this fall."

Cat nearly dropped the dish she was placing on the table.

"Well, you know it seems like such a dead end with Joseph and me. We thought maybe we should try it apart and see what happens. I applied for jobs in towns around San Francisco, and one has called my references. Walnut Creek wants me to come for an interview next week."

"Oh, Torie!"

Torie put a hand on her sister-in-law's arm. "Don't be upset. I'm afraid Daddy will be. He thinks Joseph and I should just up and get married and forget everything else, yet Daddy has an immense sense of responsibility himself. You must know that."

Cat nodded. "He just wants you to be happy."

"I wouldn't leave if you weren't here," Torie said.

"You're not responsible for your father's happiness," Cat told her.

"I know I alone can't make him happy. Heaven knows, I tried for so many years with Mother. I thought I was the reason for her being like she is. It wasn't until I was nearly out of high school that I realized it's mainly because she drinks. All that time I thought it was me."

"Oh, Torie."

"Sometimes I used to think she was jealous of me with Daddy. We've always been so close. He taught me to fish and to ride, and he even taught me how to read before I went to school. He always had time for Scott and me. I don't ever remember a time when he was too busy for anything we wanted to do. Or when we wanted to talk. Golly, I talked over all my problems with Daddy. He's the one who told me that it was all right to sleep with Joseph. Of course"—Torie giggled—"we'd been doing it for years by the time Daddy gave us his okay."

"You two won't be able to function without each other."

"Joseph and I? We've talked about this, Cat, and talked about it, and think it's time to try. We can't go on forever like this. Some drastic move has to be made."

"Maybe being apart will show Joseph that you're more important than his heritage."

"Who knows?" Torie shrugged her shoulders. She did not look unhappy. "I've got to tell Daddy. Will you be around when I do, please?"

Cat hugged her sister-in-law. "If you think it'll help."

"Your being around anyplace makes McCullough lives easier, I think. What would we ever do without you, Cat?"

"Hey, I don't think I've done anything. It's I who am grateful to all of you."

"Maybe it's mutual," Torie said as they walked back to the house to get more platters. "But somehow you give us, Daddy and me, and I think Mother, too, at times, you've given us a strength. It's not exactly that you've taken Scott's place, but you've made his loss bearable. It's like he left you and Matt in his stead. You give Daddy something to smile about and you talk with him and play chess with him . . ."

"I'm not much of a challenge in that department."

"You want a pool. Daddy gets pleasure in building a pool."

"I'm thinking of mentioning an ermine coat next."

Torie laughed. "If you really want one, I bet he'd get it. You've given Daddy a whole new lease on life."

"I love your father," Cat said.

Torie shook her head. "Isn't he wonderful?"

But Cat didn't hear her. She heard her own words reverberating back to her. The words she'd uttered floated out on the air and stayed in front of her, growing larger and more pronounced every second.

"Speaking of love," Torie went on, "I do think Jason's been bitten by it. He couldn't keep his eyes off you at the picnic at the Whitleys' last weekend."

"I like Jason."

"Is that the extent of it?"

Cat shook her head. "I don't know. I'm not ready for another man yet. Jason certainly is a sterling character."

"He is that. But it's hard to follow a McCullough."

"Unless it's another McCullough." Cat heard herself say those words and could have pulled her tongue out.

Torie gave her a puzzled look, but didn't linger. She grabbed two platters of food and whisked them out of the kitchen.

Cat grabbed the edge of the kitchen table, wishing a chair were nearby. Instead she just clutched it until the dizziness passed.

Sir Geoffrey Forrester charmed the entire McCullough clan, even Sarah, who went upstairs immediately after lunch for a nap, though everyone but Geoffrey knew she was really going to find a drink.

Miss Jenny had never looked lovelier. She sparkled.

They all went swimming, and Cat thought Miss Jenny a fine figure of a woman for any age, much less nearly seventy. She could tell from the way his eyes followed her that Geoffrey thought so, too.

He told Red, "I must say, I'm quite impressed with what you call a spread."

Red smiled. "You can call it that. My father and grandfather really did it, you know. I just keep it going."

"He's being modest," Miss Jenny said. "It never made this kind of money until Red started managing it."

"Did she tell you how it started?"

Geoffrey eyed Jenny, and said, "No, we had other things to talk about."

"My great grandfather came out on the Oregon Trail right after the Civil War. Came from a little fishing town in Scotland, where he had a dozen brothers and sisters and a hardscrabble kind of life. After he arrived in America he heard talk of the fertile land and temperate climate in the Willamette Valley, but when he crossed these mountains he almost stopped, it was so beautiful. Everyone else said he was crazy, the land of milk and honey was over on the more moderate Willamette Valley, where it seldom got really cold or really hot. So, he went on. But much of the good land was already taken by the time he got there, and after three winters there he was depressed. Some people are, without sun, you know. Ten months a year with little or no sunshine nearly did him in. Would me, too. And he remembered this place, where a couple of miles north of here you can still see the wagon marks from the hundreds of wagons that came so long ago. Up mountains, between towering trees."

"I don't know how they made it," Jenny said.

Red shook his head and continued. "There'd been Indian raids, so it wasn't until the late 1870s that it was relatively safe to start homesteads here. So my great grandfather and his wife came back here and homesteaded on three hundred sixty acres."

"That's a lot of land in England."

"It's an anthill here," Red said, and gazed into the pool where Cat and Torie were trying to show Matt how much fun water could be. "It wasn't an easy life. Up the valley about a mile and a half we've preserved the cabin they lived in for the rest of their lives. You'd think they'd have suffered claustrophobia, but they had three children there and lived in it close to forty years. He plowed his money back into land, not in houses.

"His oldest son, my grandfather, built the main section of this

house and added the north wing about fifteen years later. Then Ma"—
he nodded to his mother—"and Dad built the south wing. My grandfather acquired another thirty thousand acres, and Dad added on to
that. By the time I came along we had all the land, including the land
butting up to the national forest halfway up the mountain. Grandfather
built the hunting lodge where Ma lives now. People used to come out
to visit from Portland, no small trip then to cross the entire state. The
women would stay in the big house while the men spent four or five
days up in the lodge hunting."

"What did they hunt?" The Brit asked.

"Cougar, of course. Bear, deer, elk."

"I suppose all extinct by now?"

"Not at all," Red said. "I no longer allow hunting on my property,
but hunting is big time in this part of Oregon."

Geoffrey watched Joseph jackknife into the pool. "A stunning
dive," he commented. "You know, I've never met a real live Indian
before."

"You mean," Cat said, "a real live one hundred percent American."

"Touché." Geoffrey smiled. "I was talking with him earlier and
find his philosophy rather delightful."

"What philosophy?" Red asked.

"Well, you're talking of hunting animals and he said he thought
we're all interrelated. That the bear and cougar and elk you're talking
of are his brothers. Are my brothers, too, for that matter. He thinks
the stars are equal to each of us and we are all a part of the whole. I
suppose carried to an extreme that way of thinking means if we hurt
anything or anyone else we are also hurting ourselves."

Miss Jenny eyed him appreciatively. "I think you've got it in a
nutshell."

"I rather like the idea," Sir Geoffrey said.

"You've gone up a notch." Miss Jenny leaned over and pressed
his hand.

"Oh, rather," he said, and a blush spread over his face. "Anything
to go up a notch. Do I have many more I have to go?"

"You can keep trying." She laughed.

Cat had an idea he tried quite hard later that night from the look
in his and Jenny's eyes when they left.

She laughed at the thought as she walked downstairs after tucking
Matt into bed. She heard the dishwasher whirring and strolled out to
the kitchen to see Red, his shirtsleeves rolled up, cleaning the kitchen.

"I was going to do that."

"You can still help." He glanced at her. "All this food needs to be put away."

Cat reached for the aluminum foil and Handi-Wrap and began putting the leftover food in covered bowls. When she came to the potato salad she looked at it, grabbed a fork, and sat down at the kitchen table. "Not enough of this left to bother saving," she said.

"Wait," Red said. "There's enough for two. I saw some ham in the fridge. Want a ham sandwich, too?"

Cat nodded. "You want a beer?"

Red grinned. He made the sandwiches while Cat fished two pickles out of a jar and found two cold beers.

"Ma seems to be having a ball."

"So does he. I think he likes us."

"What's not to like?" Red asked, sitting down opposite her and pushing a sandwich across to her. She reached over and ladled half the potato salad onto his plate.

"Are you crushed about Torie?"

Red sighed. "I'm crushed about her not finding happiness with the only man she's ever loved. Damn Samuel Claypool."

"It's not just him, and you know it. It's like saying you'll give up believing in your religion. One can't always do that just by saying you want to."

"God damn it, Cat, I know it. I know it. No, I'm not happy Torie's going off. I'm not happy about the reason. Hell, I'd hate to have her go for any reason, but it wouldn't make me miserable. Kids are meant to live their own lives. If she and Joseph were married and going off to Burns or Grants Pass or someplace because of his job, I wouldn't mind, though I'd miss her sorely."

They ate in comfortable silence. Cat glanced out the window. "It's already getting dark early. A month ago at this time it was still light at nine-thirty. Now it's nine."

"It was a good day," Red said. "Maybe I'm going to lose a mother, too. Do you think she'll marry this guy?"

"She told me she thought marriage was only if you were going to have children. She said why get married and ruin a nice romance."

"Hmpf," he snorted. "Marriage didn't ruin her romance with Dad. They were in love, like young kids, all their lives."

"I'm just telling you what she said." Cat stood up and walked over to rinse her plate in the sink. "Look, there's the evening's first star."

Red stood up and brought his dishes over to the counter. She could feel him standing in back of her, though he wasn't touching her. He looked over her head into the night sky. "So it is."

She could hear his breathing.

She was afraid to turn toward him, so she stood still until he moved.

She finished packing the leftover food into bowls and then went through the big hall to the front porch, letting the wooden screen door slam behind her. She walked over to sit on the steps.

Bree got up from where he'd been sitting on the cool grass and sauntered over to sit next to Cat. Her hand idly ruffled the dog's fur.

She knew Red was standing inside the screen door, that he stood there watching the sky darken and she knew, too, that he was looking at her back, because neither of them knew what would happen if any other part of her faced him.

Thirty-five

On Saturday morning, Thelma told Cat, "Lucy can't come to work for us anymore."

"Does it have something to do with her husband?"

Thelma looked away.

"Did he tell her she can't come here anymore?"

Thelma nodded. "He thinks she's getting hi'falutin ideas over here." But Cat could tell that wasn't all.

She walked over to Thelma. "Did he beat her again?"

Tears welled in Thelma's eyes. "He broke her arm and wouldn't let her go to the doctor. If I hadn't stopped over there, I don't know what would have happened. I called Doc Whitley, and we took her to the hospital. They set it and I brung her home, but Pete came over and knelt down and told her how sorry he was and he wouldn't do it again and he couldn't live without her and she went home with him."

"Oh, Thelma, I'm so sorry. Is there anything we can do?"

Thelma shrugged. "How can you help someone who doesn't want help?"

"What about their child?" Lucy had a seven-year-old son, whom her mother looked after when she came out to the Big Piney.

"It's not Pete's, you know."

Cat nodded. The little boy had been eighteen months old when Lucy and Pete married.

"I mean, is the boy safe?"

"He's scared to death of his stepdad, but I haven't heard that he's laid a hand on the boy."

"Any idea who we can get to replace her?"

"I just happen to. Myrna Lee's had to quit work because she's pregnant, but she'd do fine until she's ready to have her baby, and even then, they're pretty hard up for money. I bet she'd bring her baby out here and go on after her baby comes."

"I don't even know her."

"She's my husband's cousin, once removed."

Cat didn't want to figure that one out.

"If she lives in town, I could drive in and see her."

"No, she lives another five miles beyond us, north. But she has a pickup and can run down here real easy. Her baby's not due for another four months, but they didn't want her clerking in the store, looking like she does."

"They couldn't get away with that in Boston, or New York . . ."

"This is Cougar Valley," Thelma said. "If you want to talk with her, we can run out there right now, or I'll ask her to drive in here."

"If you go out there," Red said, standing in the doorway, "you can get a sense of her from her house."

Cat thought that a good idea. "Call and ask her if it's okay if we come out now."

"She loves babies," Thelma said. "She used to have more dolls than anyone I know. All she's ever wanted to do is be a mother."

"Okay, call her."

After Thelma disappeared into the kitchen, Red asked, "Are Ma and Sir Geoffrey coming to dinner tonight?"

Cat didn't look at him but shook her head. "No. Miss Jenny said she'd drive him over to see Sun Valley this weekend. I think they'll stay overnight. They'll have to." She paused. "I won't be home to dinner, either."

Red didn't say anything. Instead, he walked into the dining room and poured coffee before helping himself to bacon and scrambled eggs from the sideboard where Thelma had them warming.

"The sheriff?" Thelma grinned, returning.

"Mm-hm," Cat answered. "We're going to play bridge. I haven't played bridge since I was in college."

And sleep together, she didn't add. *We're going to make love so nicely it'll erase any thoughts of Red from my feeble mind. The very act will unite Jason and me and bind us and I'll remember that Red is not only my father-in-law but a married man, and he's more than twenty years older than I am.*

* * *

Cat changed to pale green slacks and a dark green blouse and the gold dangly earrings that Scott had given her. She'd developed a penchant for Birkenstocks and wore a pair of their jade sandals.

Red knocked on her bedroom door. "You can leave Matt here," he said. "I'll be glad to feed him and put him to bed. You should have a carefree evening now and then. Go out and enjoy yourself."

She turned to face him. "You don't mind?"

His smile was kind. "Of course not. What else do I have to do with my Saturday night? I'll be glad to, Cat. Matt's good company even if he can't talk."

"I thought you'd be tired after the way you've worked today. You've been gone since breakfast."

"It's summer." He held a cup of coffee in his hand and sipped from it. "I don't know why I enjoy summer so much more than winter, because summer's when all the work is."

"Because you love the work as well as the warm weather." Cat watched him, standing there, and wondered if he was aware how good-looking he was, how impressive-looking. How impressive, period.

"Why don't you ask Jason and Cody out to brunch tomorrow by the pool," he said. "We have to get our money's worth."

"Okay. I'll bake popovers."

"With raspberry jam. Thelma just made some batches."

"I think that's an offer they won't be able to refuse."

"Make it ten-thirty."

Cat hesitated. Then, "Do you approve of my seeing him?"

"What right have I to approve or disapprove of anything you do?"

"Oh, come on. I'm part of your family."

When Red didn't say anything, she asked, "Aren't I?"

He stared at her for so long she wondered if he was going to answer. Finally he said, "Yes, you are family. And if I had to choose someone for you, I couldn't find a finer man than Jason, or one more deserving of the happiness that seems to go along with you."

She wondered if he was afraid she'd marry Jason and move into town with Matt. Or if he'd been afraid she'd leave Cougar and move back East. She wondered if he ever thought of her the way she so often thought of him, or if it was all in her mind.

* * *

Red stood on the porch and watched her zoom off, leaving a trail of dust down the road. He kept watching as the car grew smaller and smaller, until it was a dot, until it disappeared from his view.

He'd worked out in the hayfields all day. It was the second crop of the year, and he'd taken off after breakfast to go see how all three meadows were coming along. The day-to-day work he so often left to Glenn, his foreman, but he kept on top of everything. It was a gorgeous day, as most August days were, clear and hot by eight-thirty. The big machines were already at work, and he got out of his truck at each of the fields and watched for half an hour, finding satisfaction in what was going on.

At the third field, though, he rolled up his shirtsleeves and got to work. He stayed there with the men the rest of the day, someone giving him a sandwich and someone else handing him a Coke. He worked until his back ached, until sweat dripped from his forehead into his eyes and he had to wipe the salt away with his sleeve. He thought maybe he could work her out of his system.

He had to get her out of his pores in some way.

Work didn't do it.

Would anything?

"I told you I'd be awful at bridge after not playing since college."

"It wasn't your fault. Not that losing is anybody's fault. But if there is a fault, it's mine. I wasn't concentrating."

"Why? Is anything wrong?"

"Quite the contrary." Jason reached for her hand as they drove to his house. "All I could think of was you lying naked in my bed. I exerted enormous willpower not to reach out and grab you. I've wanted to kiss you all evening."

Cat brought his hand to her lips. "I've been looking forward to making love, too."

"Christ, it's all I think about lately. I went out to the Millers' today to tell them they had to pay for the sheep their dog killed, and when Mrs. Miller answered the door, all I saw was your face. I went into Rocky's for coffee and instead of Ida, there you were. Every woman I see is suddenly you. Even when no one's in sight, I see you."

She ran her tongue across the palm of his hand.

"Jesus Christ," Jason said, "I'll go right off the road."

She took his hand and cupped it around her breast.

He stopped the car with a jerk and turned to grab her, kissing her, holding her tight against him.

"I'm glad this doesn't have bucket seats," she murmured.

"If you're not careful, I'll just rip your clothes off you right here."

"Promises, promises," she whispered into his ear.

He laughed and took his foot off the brake. The car glided ahead half a block to his house. A porch light was on.

Katie Thompson was looking at CNN. "Nothing else worth looking at," she said, "and I've seen this repeated three times." She stretched, rubbed her eyes, and said good night, heading to her loft over the garage.

Jason turned out the lights and took hold of Cat's hand. "Come on," he said, walking down the hall. "I have designs on you."

Cat followed willingly. "I thought it was the other way around."

"Do you know what a turn-on it is to have some woman tell me she wants me?"

"Wants you? Oh, I think that's an understatement."

"Come here," he said, turning to kiss her, picking her up and carrying her through the doorway. He sat down on the edge of the bed, cradling her against him, and began to unbutton her blouse.

"I think I'm a nymphomaniac," she whispered, not wanting to awaken Cody. "I really love this." She could feel her body begin to tremble as his lips encircled her left breast. His left hand stroked her thighs.

"Get me out of these clothes," she told him. "Like, now!"

"Stand up, then," he said, nibbling her belly as she did so.

He stood up and got out of his clothes, then lay down, pulling her on top of him.

She didn't think of Red for the next hour. Not until she was driving home.

She looked up into the inky night, feeling replete and content from the lovemaking. It was after two. Jason had said, "Make an honest man of me, willya?"

But she had not let him pursue that conversation.

She hoped Red had gone to bed. She didn't want to see him tonight. Not after what she'd been doing with Jason. She wanted to get in bed, lie naked in the moonlight and think about Jason Kilpatrick and how he pleased her, the things he did that titillated her body. She wanted to tell herself that this was growing into love. That good sex was important in a marriage, and that she and Jason would make a fine couple. The whole town would root for them, she was sure of that.

And yet when she was away from Jason, she hardly thought of him.

The moonlight danced through the leaves of the big tree outside her window, danced across her naked body as she sighed. She turned on her side so that the moonlight could have its way with her, and it was Red whose body she yearned to have next to hers, Red whose face would not go away even when she closed her eyes.

Thirty-six

"It's strange with Torie gone," Cat said at dinner early in September.

"It is that." Red was home for dinner, one of the few nights in the past week. He'd gone out before dawn every day, riding with his men back into the national forest and into the mountains to round up the cattle. It was time to separate the young ones they'd keep for breeding, the ones they'd send to market, and the ones they'd keep for fattening to sell next year. They culled the old ones then, too. Once Scott had taken over as foreman, Red left that part of the work up to him. Now, even though he'd grown to trust Glenn, he enjoyed getting out and doing some of the hard work, being with the men.

Cat and Sarah had dined alone nearly all week.

"I think she'll have a wonderful time in California. Near San Francisco she'll be close to culture, the ballet, the opera, the symphony, the theater . . ." Sarah's voice faded.

Cat and Red looked at each other. Did Sarah know why Torie had gone?

"I'd have loved that life," Sarah said, talking to neither of them in particular. "Instead of being in this backwater place where they don't even know how to spell culture. Not even a movie theater."

"Well, as of next month, there'll be a library," Red said. There had been a big party Labor Day night, to show the town what had been accomplished in such a short period of time.

Bollie had charged the town ten thousand dollars for the big Victorian house, which was worth ten times that. They were going to float a bond issue next month, and there was no chance it wouldn't go through.

Mrs. Amador had worked all summer ordering and cataloguing books, along with half a dozen volunteers, spurred on by Nan Bollinger and Norah Eddlington. Cat was the treasurer of the board, which met twice a month on Tuesday evenings.

"I had five clients today," Cat announced. It was the most she'd had since she'd opened her office.

"Pretty soon you'll be earning so much money you'll wonder what to do with it," Red said. He was tanned and leathery-looking. Cat leaned across the table to peer at him. He was wearing his glasses all the time now.

Red saw her observing him. "I guess it's about time. I'll be fifty in three weeks."

"Ha," teased Cat. "Is that your subtle way of reminding us? Don't worry, I already have your present."

He grinned. "Okay, what kinds of cases landed in your lap?"

"Let's see. I'm making out a will. Someone from Billings, Montana, is buying the Trevelayan house, and I have to research the deed and set that all up. Means I have to go over to Baker to the courthouse tomorrow."

"Isn't that rather dreary?" Sarah asked.

"I can't say it's exciting, but I'm happy doing it. It may not lead me where I thought the law would lead me, but . . ."

"Where did you want the law to lead you?" Red asked.

"Oh," Cat shrugged. It seemed so long ago. "Maybe to Washington and Congress. I've always thought there were too few women there, and I had visions of being one."

"Senate or House?"

"I had my sights set high. The Senate. However, when I observe the caliber of senators, I think maybe I don't want to associate with guys like that. I have a feeling little ole Cougar Valley is more my cup of tea."

"You could always help raise the standards."

"I don't think so. I do think that most men who run for politics are rather idealistic when they first get elected. They hope to achieve something, to change the system, to battle the corruption, but once they get going they care more about staying in office, and pretty soon they can be bought, if not with money, with the assurance of staying in Washington and having power."

"Too bad you feel that way," Red said. "You're saying the American dream's gone awry?"

Cat explained before running upstairs to find her car keys and look in on Matt.

"I better phone Thelma," Red said.

"Yeah," Cat agreed, coming downstairs at a trot. She didn't stop but ran outside, where her car was parked in front of the porch. She gunned the engine and took off.

Murder. The second time since she'd been here. Murders of passion, both times, but she suspected self-defense was more like it with Lucy. She'd been driven to her limit, of that Cat was sure.

She made the sheriff's office in nineteen minutes, a record for her.

Lucy sat in the chair opposite Jason's desk. Her hair was awry, a dazed expression was on her face. Her eyes were blank. She scarcely looked up when Cat entered.

"You stay here with her while I go back to the crime scene," Jason said. "Chazz is going to meet me there. We have to do something about the body."

"He can't be dead," Lucy said in a faraway voice. "I loved him."

Cat wondered how you could love anyone you were afraid of, someone who got pleasure from hurting you, who kept hurting you over and over and over. How could love flourish in such conditions?

She went over and knelt next to Lucy, putting her arms around the dazed woman, whose eye was already turning purple and a nauseating shade of green.

"I've got to get someone here with a camera," Cat said aloud. The sleeve of Lucy's blouse was torn and there was blood all over her shoes and skirt. Her lips were puffy and there was a smear of dried blood over a gash that started in her lip and ended in the middle of her cheek.

Cat stood up and went to the phone to call home. "Red, call Norah, will you? If she can't get here pronto, bring a camera yourself to the jail."

Red didn't ask any questions, but hung up, and Cat was sure someone would appear to capture Lucy's looks for a jury.

For she was sure that's where Lucy was headed.

Thirty-seven

Lucy curled herself into the fetal position, drawing her knees up nearly to her chin and enclosing her arms within them.

Cat was glad Jason had gone. No one could reach the young woman. She was spaced out. Far.

Cat walked back to the single cell and found a navy wool blanket. She wrapped it around Lucy. She wasn't quite sure what to do next.

Thelma arrived before the sheriff did.

"She killed him," Cat told her. "Stabbed him to death."

Thelma's hand flew to her mouth, her eyes round as saucers. Then she peered at Cat. "Will they arrest her?"

"I'm afraid so."

Thelma sat down on the long wooden bench against the wall. She sighed heavily. "I don't have an awful lot of money, Cat, but I'll give you all I have. Be her lawyer, please."

Cat turned to look at Thelma.

"Please," said the woman. "Please. She's had a hard life. She's been married to him for over six years, and he's treated her terrible bad."

"Let's see what she wants," Cat said.

"I know what she'll want," Thelma said. "She'll want to die. She'll hate herself."

"I hope it was self-defense," Cat muttered.

Thelma's head jerked. "What do you mean? What else could it be? You don't think she'd plan something like this, do you?"

"Let's just wait . . ."

"No." Thelma fished in her purse and pulled out a crumpled ten-dollar bill. "Here, this is a down payment. Take it. Then you have to be her lawyer."

Cat studied the older woman before reaching to accept the money. "All right, Thelma. Your niece has a lawyer."

Women who kill their husbands get sent to prison. For long periods of time. For life, sometimes, even when they were protecting their young children when they killed. These thoughts ran through Cat's mind.

Red arrived with Norah who had a camera slung in a strap over her shoulder.

"I want these bruises on film," Cat said.

Red knelt down in front of the withdrawn Lucy while Norah snapped several shots. "My God," he said.

"She stabbed her husband twelve times." Cat shivered as she said it.

"That mousy little bit of nothing," Red said.

"She's not nothing," barked Cat, her eyes blazing.

Red looked startled. "I didn't mean . . ."

"Okay," Cat said. "I know. She's so slight she does seem as though she'd blow away, doesn't she?"

"That's all I meant."

"I know." She wanted to let him know she understood.

"She needs clean clothes," Thelma said. "Why don't I go get her some."

"Good idea," Cat said, looking again at the blood-spattered young woman.

When Thelma left, Cat held up the ten-dollar bill, and said, "A murder case."

Red nodded. "And in Cougar Valley of all unexpected places. Will it even go to trial?"

"I hope not, but I think it will. Women who kill their husbands are not treated lightly. Do you know that over 70 percent of women in jail for murder had abusive husbands whom they killed?"

"You mean Lucy's chances are slim," Norah commented.

Cat shook her head. "I don't know that that's what I mean. I do know women are not likely to get away with killing their husbands even in self-defense. On the other hand, men who kill their wives because they think they've been unfaithful, are angry at them for leaving or even threatening to leave, get lighter sentences than the women who've killed because they've been abused."

"Careful." Red managed a small smile. "You'll make a feminist of me."

"I would hope you're already one without knowing it," Norah interjected. "Generally, men kill in anger and women kill to protect, either themselves or their children."

"Doesn't say much for men, does it?"

"Hey, we're not talking about all men." Cat put a hand on Red's shoulder. "Not you. Since I like men, I prefer to think it's chemical rather than otherwise. Testosterone. You know, they like boxing and hunting and even war. It's basic to their natures."

Jason came in, his hat tipped back on his head, trouble reflected in his eyes.

"Jason, did Lucy ever call you about Pete?"

"Once. Neighbors did, other times. I've been over there at least half a dozen times in as many years. And I imagine there have been dozens of times when I wasn't called."

"What did you do about it?" Norah asked.

"Nothing I could do. By the next day she either dropped charges or hadn't filed charges."

Cat stared at him. "Can Thelma or I take Lucy home?"

Jason tossed his hat on his desk and looked at Red and Norah, as though imploring support. " 'Fraid not, Cat."

"Oh, come on, Jason. She's not going to run away."

"Sorry."

"I'll take responsibility for her," Red said. "Look at her, the condition she's in. She'll need someone around when she starts talking."

"I want to be there when she does."

"No," Cat said. "As her lawyer I'll advise her to say nothing. Not a thing."

"You her lawyer?" Jason asked. "Since when?"

"Since fifteen minutes ago. Thelma paid me a retainer. She's gone out to find some clothes for Lucy."

"Damn!" Jason grabbed his hat. "I don't want anyone in that house. I don't want a thing touched." He practically ran from the room, and Cat heard his car tear away from the curb.

Thelma and Jason returned together in five minutes. They'd passed each other on the road, and Jason had swerved around to follow Thelma back to town.

Thelma's eyes were red. "I threw up, it's so horrible-looking," she said. "Blood all over the place." But she had a few clean clothes for Lucy. She looked at her sleeping niece. "Come on, Cat, let's change her blouse anyhow so when she comes to the first thing she sees won't be his blood."

Lucy slept through the clothes change as though drugged.

"Jason, tell you what," Red said. "If you have to keep her in custody, all of you come on out to the Big Piney and we'll put you in the room next to her to make sure she's not going to run away."

"Aw, Red, you know that's not necessary. I just want to be there to hear her."

"No," Cat said. "If I think you should talk with her, I'll let you know. You may not question her when she's not in my presence."

Jason's mouth tightened. "Boy, you can be hard-ass, Cat, with your lawyer's hat on."

"You better believe it," she said, hands on her hips.

They stared across the room at each other.

Red walked over and stooped down to gather Lucy in his arms. "I'm taking her home, Jason. Come out as early as you want in the morning."

"If she's still in this state, that'll serve no purpose," Cat interjected. 'I'll call you when she's conscious."

Jason gave her a skeptical glance. Then he said to Red, "Okay."

Whether it was okay or not, Red was halfway through the door with his charge. Cat ran after him, saying, "You better put her in the backseat of my car. That'll be more comfortable than your pickup." She opened the back door to her car, which was at the curb.

"I'm out of here," Norah told Cat. "I'll call you in the morning."

The street was deserted. Even Rocky's was closed.

Jason and Thelma followed them. "I know she'll be safe," Jason said.

They made a caravan, Red's pickup in the lead, Cat following, and Thelma pulling up the rear in her gray Honda Civic.

As soon as they arrived home, Red carried Lucy upstairs to one of the guest bedrooms.

Thelma picked up the kitchen phone and called her husband. "I'm staying here overnight," she said, telling him briefly what had taken place. She debated whether to sleep with her niece or in the adjoining bedroom. She hadn't asked Red about staying overnight. She said, "I guess I'll just sleep in here with her. If she wakens she won't know where she is."

"Let's go down the hall then," Red said, "to the room with twin beds." He picked Lucy up and carried her two doors down the hallway, toward Cat's quarters.

Thelma looked at Red. "You look like you could use some hot chocolate," she said.

"That sounds good." Red placed Lucy on one of the beds, and Thelma covered her niece with a blanket.

"I'll get it," Cat said. "You stay here, and I'll bring you some."

Thelma managed a weak smile. She didn't argue.

Red said, "I'll help," and followed Cat down to the kitchen.

He didn't help. He sat at the long oak table while Cat found the cocoa and cups, zapping them in the microwave. She found marshmallows and put them on the cocoa before heating them another thirty seconds.

"I'll take it up to Thelma," Red said, standing. "I'll be right back. Don't start without me."

When he returned a couple of minutes later, she told him, "I'm beginning to think I daren't start anything without you."

"In the morning, I think it'd be a good idea if I go out there with Norah and have her take photos."

Cat nodded. "Better make sure Jason's with you. We'll call him and suggest that, then he can come out here. I think Lucy should be aware by then. But maybe not."

Red leaned back in his chair. "Well, this is a helluva thing, isn't it?"

Cat sighed. "I think we're in for a peck of trouble."

"How do you mean?"

"You won't find juries sympathetic to spousal murder. Even if it's self-defense."

"Oregon's pretty advanced, you know. Back in about 'seventy-eight Greta somebody sued her husband for rape. First case in the country where a woman sued a husband for that."

"And?"

"Well, she lost and even went back to him. Nevertheless, it was a first."

Cat's eyebrows furrowed. "You know, I do seem vaguely to remember that. It was before I began practice. Even before I went to law school. Set a precedent, didn't it?"

"I don't know that much about law," Red said, nodding his head, "but it does show Oregon is pretty advanced in its thinking, according to the statistics you're throwing at me. We were one of the first states to have a woman senator and a woman governor."

"Yet you have kept reelecting a senator who thinks abortion is tantamount to the Holocaust."

"Where'd you hear that?"

"I once wrote Hatfield a letter, way back when there was talk of repealing *Roe v. Wade,* and he sent me a long answer, a form letter to be sure, saying that he was against a woman's right to choice and that quote abortion in any form is tantamount to the Holocaust unquote."

Red let that sink in. "I voted for him, too. I didn't know. He always had a statesmanlike quality about him. I met him several times and was impressed each time."

"Because you're not a woman," Cat ventured.

"Well, what I'm trying to suggest is that a jury in Oregon is more likely to be socially aware than you might find other places."

"A jury in Eugene or Portland might be more likely to be liberal, you mean, but not in Cougar Valley or, say, Grants Pass."

"You'll be surprised, Cat. We're not typical small-town Americana."

"Oh, I think you are, Red. You've lived here all your life and aren't aware how different it is from the urban centers. They're a lot less beautiful but far more aware of injustice."

Red's lips tightened. "I hope you'll be proven wrong, Cat. I want you to be."

She leaned forward. "You don't even know what racial injustice is. You've never even had African Americans in Cougar."

He raised his eyebrows. "Cat we're coming from different places. I'm merely trying to encourage you, saying that despite your statistics, I think you can get a fair trial in this county."

She stood up. It felt as though she'd just had her first argument with Red. She sounded like big city despite her two years here, and he sounded like most gun-toting Oregon ranchers.

She took her cup and headed to the sink, but he grabbed her wrist and looked up at her. "Cat, we're on the same side."

She leaned down to kiss the top of his head and his grip on her wrist tightened. For just a second it passed through her mind that he was going to kiss her, too, but he didn't. He let go, but remained seated at the table as she left the kitchen and went up the stairs to her room.

Thirty-eight

When Lucy awoke, she hugged herself as though in pain. "Oh, God, I'll never see him again." Then she burst into tears.

When Jason arrived, they sat around in the kitchen. Staring into the distance, once in a while reaching for Thelma's hand, Lucy told what happened. Haltingly, with infinite grief, and some puzzlement.

"I tried to please him. I loved him so much when we got married. He was about the handsomest thing I ever saw."

Cat squinted, remembering the stocky jut-jawed man she'd fleetingly seen.

"He about made my heart melt to look at him," Lucy went on.

Jason's eyes met Cat's.

"He come home last night, and I could tell what was coming. After six years I knew one of those moods when I first saw the little hints of it. He'd stopped on the way home from work for a couple of beers, and that was a usual sign, though it wasn't always. But he'd gotten so nothing I did was right. I mean, I always *tried* to please him or I knew what would happen, but I didn't always *know* what pleased him." She turned to look at Cat and Red. "Like quitting my job with you. He told me hanging out with rich people was spoiling me, that I got tastes beyond what we could afford and was making his life miserable, yearning for things. It wasn't true. It really wasn't. What do I want with a house with this many rooms? But I did say I'd like a microwave once, and all hell broke loose.

"So after he beat me a couple of times, I quit, but it didn't make no difference. I never, in all those years together, figured just what it was that triggered his anger."

Cat turned to Jason. "Jason, what I'm about to get is privileged information. You can't hear it. You have to wait downstairs."

When he hesitated, though he knew she was right, she added, "I'll tell you what you need to know."

When Jason picked up his hat and left the room, Cat shut the door and sat down opposite Lucy, leaning forward. "I know it's painful, but I want you to tell me exactly what happened yesterday, everything you remember. We'll go back later over how often he beat you, but right now I want to know about yesterday."

Lucy's sigh was ragged, on the verge of a sob. "I knew I was going to do it."

Cat didn't want to hear that.

Lucy pointed to her battered face. "This didn't happen yesterday. It happened the night before. I knew I was going to kill him."

Cat put a hand on Lucy's arm. "Tell me."

"The night before last he wasn't home when I went to bed, but I woke up sometime in the middle of the night with something cold at my throat and Pete was on top of me with a knife at my throat. 'I heard you dreaming,' he whispered, so low I could hardly hear him. 'I heard you dreaming of running away.'

"He pulled the knife across my throat and I was so scared I wet the bed.

"I knew then that if he didn't kill me, I had to kill him. Maybe I knew it the night he brought Ricky home from Boise. I couldn't see no other way out of it. I thought living in jail, even if I'm gang-raped like they say happens, would be better than the hell each day with Pete. Not that it happened every day. Sometimes he'd take me and Ricky up to Pendleton to McDonald's and the movies and he'd laugh and be real nice and say wasn't we a fine family.

"But when he wanted sex he was never tender and nice anymore. Sometimes he couldn't even do it. Once, oh God"—and she burst into tears—"once he got a corncob and raped me with it, using real soft sweet words, telling me he wished he was that big and he kept on doing it til I came, and I was so shamed I'd have liked to die. He'd do things like that, and then he'd beat me bloody. He got so he could hardly do it anymore unless he knew he was hurting me. Sometimes he made me lie on my stomach and did it from the rear and almost always I was bloody. He'd use dirty words to me and dig his nails into my buttocks, and I don't know what hell's like but it can't be any worse than what living was for me.

"I knew when he didn't kill me the night before, but kept the knife at my neck for hours, that it was time to kill him. And yesterday morning I knew it was going to be that day. When I saw him driving home, weaving down the street, I sent Ricky out the back door over to the neighbors. Pete wasn't so drunk he couldn't talk, but he was already angry when he walked in the door. I knew there was going to be hell to pay. The neighbors must've known what was going on. I screamed often enough, but they never asked, except once, years ago, and then Pete told them to butt out.

"I looked around for something and saw a couple of Cokes in the fridge. I emptied one as fast as I could and broke the top off in the sink. I was going to keep that bottle in my hand or nearby, and I was going to make sure if Pete even touched me, if he did anything, I was going to shove that jagged edge at him.

"He came in and I started fixing dinner, acting like it was the same as always. He got a beer and then came over to stand next to me while I was paring potatoes, and said, 'No kiss for the old man tonight?'

"I said, 'No,' and went on paring. He didn't even see the broken Coke bottle on the counter.

"He grabbed my hair, I'm surprised I have any left, and turned my head around so my neck was like to snap and kissed me on the lips, real hard. Then he just walked into the living room and turned the TV on, loud. I went on fixing dinner but I knew something was coming. It was that terrible quiet before he lost it. I thought of running right out the back door, but I knew I had to make a stand. It had just come to be more than was bearable."

"Were you afraid for your life?" Cat asked.

"No. I had been many times, but last night, no. I felt calm as a cucumber. I was just waiting for him to make a move. I wanted him to. Do you understand? I had to have him make the first move. I couldn't just go in the living room and jab that bottle at him. He had to hurt me first."

Cat found herself breathing rapidly. She'd closed her eyes as though that would block out the horror.

"In about ten minutes, he called out from the living room, 'Dinner ready yet?' Of course it wasn't. The potatoes were still hard and I hadn't even started the hot dogs. I didn't answer. I guess I was trying to provoke him. A couple minutes passed and there he was standing in the doorway. 'Goddammit, answer when I talk to you.'

"I still didn't say anything, but my eye was on the Coke bottle, my hand ready to reach for it. But before I even knew it, quick as a flash, the back of his hand slashed across my cheek and I fell against the counter, my back to the bottle. He had a cigarette in his hand and I could tell what he was going to do, he'd done it a dozen or more times before.

" 'If I say jump, you jump, understand?' His face was close to mine, and the glow from the cigarette seemed to be getting bigger and bigger and my hand fumbled in back of me on the counter, trying to reach that bottle, and as my hand clasped it, I said to him, 'It's just one times too many, Pete. Once too many times,' and my hand shot that jagged edge right into his neck."

Lucy told this as calmly as though it had happened to someone else. There was no emotion in her voice, no life in her eyes.

"His eyes popped open, and the cigarette dropped out of his hand and he sort of slumped against me and I saw the row of knives in a holder and I grabbed one and just began stabbing him, over and over, until we was both covered with blood. I still couldn't stop. He cried, 'Hey, baby,' once, and that was all, but I still couldn't stop plunging a knife into him.

"He just lay on the floor, covered with blood, and I saw it all over me, and before I had time to think about it, I walked over to the phone and picked it up, getting blood all over it, and called the sheriff. He was out there so quick he must've flown.

"I loved him, you know. I did. For a long long time. I'll miss him, and I don't know what I'll do about money but I'm not sorry I did it, even if it means going to jail."

Cat sighed. She couldn't plead self-defense. That's what she'd feared. But her brain was already whirring. "You may have to go to jail for a night or two," she told Lucy, "but we'll take care of you."

Would she be able to?

She told Jason that Lucy had been at the end of her rope and that she had been afraid for her and her son's life over and over again. No more than that.

"Jason, this is as much as you're getting right now."

"Hey, you know perfectly well I don't want to send her to jail for this."

"I do know it, Jason. But knowing how you feel has nothing to do with the law right now, does it? You're going to arrest her."

"I have to, Cat. You know that."

"I'll pay bail," Red told Jason. "You know Lucy's not going to run away."

"I know that. But the judge who doesn't know her doesn't know that. Bail won't be cheap with murder."

Red walked down the hall and returned with checkbook in hand.

"I don't know what bail'll be. I don't set it. The judge does." Jason's look pleaded with Cat. "I have to, Cat."

"I know, Jason. But can you keep her in the jail here until I see about bail?"

He nodded, obviously not happy about what he was going to do.

Cat turned to Lucy. "I'm sorry, honey. Now, don't you say another word. Not to Jason, not to anybody. I mean not about what you did or about your marriage or anything. I'll get you out of jail . . ."

"What about Ricky?"

"I'll see he's taken care of," Thelma said. "You'll be okay, honey. Cat's not going to let anything happen to you."

"Who do I go see, Jason, about arranging bail?" Cat asked.

Jason told her. "I'll call him. He'll be expecting you. I'll vouch for Lucy, Cat." He wanted to show he was not the enemy.

"I'll go with you," Red said.

"I'd rather you took care of Matt," Cat said. "Since Thelma's going to Lucy's mother's and . . ."

Red nodded. "Sure. Let me make out a blank check, though . . ."

"Better let's see how much it'll be first."

"No matter what it is, I'll pay it."

"You'll get it back."

"I know that."

Sarah sailed into the room, looking surprised at all the guests.

"My goodness," she said, still in her robe. "What's everyone doing here at this hour of the morning?"

"Little problem," Red answered.

Sarah smiled and held out her hand to Jason, then she turned and asked Thelma, "Is breakfast ready?"

"No." Thelma shook her head. "You'll have to fend for yourself."

Sarah's face registered surprise. "Oh, my. Something must be really wrong."

Jason said to Lucy, "Sorry, but you'll have to come with me."

Lucy was silent, her eyes bloodshot. Thelma put an arm around her, and asked Jason, "Can she drive downtown with me? You could follow us?"

The sheriff nodded an okay.

"Two murders in two years," he muttered. He was remembering Darwin Clee.

Sarah stared at them all. "Will someone kindly explain what's wrong?"

Red put a hand on her shoulder. "I will, just a minute."

Cat told Lucy, "I'll be down to see you, just as soon as I arrange bail."

"Bail?" echoed Sarah.

As Thelma led Lucy through the door, with Jason following, Red said, "Lucy killed her husband."

Sarah's hand flew to her mouth.

"If I just could have figured what he wanted," Lucy's plaintive voice trailed into the house.

Red asked Cat, "What are her chances?"

"Depends on the jury," Cat allowed. "A woman cheats on her husband and he kills her, nine out of ten times he'll get off. A man repeatedly abuses a woman and she cracks, nine and a half times out of ten she'll get life or at least a really long sentence."

"Oh, Red." Sarah sat down, her eyes full of horror. "See she gets a good lawyer, can't you?"

"She has a good lawyer," he said, starting toward his office.

"Already? Who? Who do we know around here who can defend her against murder?"

"I'm going to," Cat told her mother-in-law.

"You? Oh, dear." Then Sarah reached a hand out in the air as though to touch Cat, who was across the room. "I didn't mean you're not good, dear. You know that. But murder?"

"I got a man off from murder one," Cat told her. She had her own doubts, but she didn't want anyone to sense that.

"Where's Miss Jenny?" Sarah asked.

"In Egypt," Cat answered, leaving the room to go upstairs and get some decent clothes on. If she was going to pay bail and convince the judge she'd be responsible for her client, she better look respectable.

She chose a light gray suit with a white blouse that was tailored but also conveyed femininity with its soft silkiness. The skirt was a bit tight, so she left it unbuttoned at the waist. She really needed some new clothes. Except in Davis's Western Clothing Store, she hadn't shopped for clothes since she'd bought maternity clothes. All she wore were jeans and slacks, even in her office. If she was going to appear in Baker as a lawyer, if she was going back into a courtroom, she'd better buy a couple of suits.

As Cat came down the stairs, Red, standing in the vast hallway, gave her an appreciative look.

"Forgot I was a woman, I bet." She smiled at him.

"I wouldn't think anyone could forget that." He returned her smile. "Are you nervous?"

"Well, the adrenaline is pumping. We lawyers must be an arrogant group. Here someone's life is in my hands, and I feel excitement. Maybe we're ghouls."

"Maybe you think you can do something to help."

She wanted to stretch up and kiss his cheek, but she suddenly realized she'd stopped doing that lately. She didn't even get close to him anymore.

"You'd have thought she was a seasoned murderer stalking the public for all it took to get her released on bail," Cat said at dinner that night.

"Like all women, she was a prisoner of her emotions," said Sarah.

Cat's mouth fell open, and Red acted as though he'd been slapped. His eyes hardened, and he gazed down at the lamb chop on his plate.

No one responded. They ate in silence, until finally Red asked, "When will the trial be?"

"The judge hasn't set a date, but probably three or four months."

"Why so long?" Thelma asked from the door to the kitchen.

"It takes that long to prepare a defense," Cat said, "and for the prosecutors to build a case, too."

"Seems to me they'd want to get it over with quickly," Red said.

"Well, since the criminal court isn't filled to overflowing in this county, it may be sooner," Cat responded. "There's other business I have to attend to, also. I may have to go to Eugene or Portland to the university law library to do some research. Can you handle Matt for a couple of days? Not until after Christmas, though."

"Miss Jenny will be back by then," Red said. "I'm sure we'll manage."

"From what Lucy's told me, this has been going on for years," Cat said.

"Why do women stay in abusive situations?" Red asked.

Cat shook her head. "No one seems to know. They're afraid they can't make it on their own. These men have destroyed any self-confidence they had. Some of them do leave and the husbands, or boyfriends, come after them and plead with them, promising never to hit them again, telling them how much they love them. Or they threaten them, telling them they'll kill them or their children if they don't come back. Even women who've managed to get divorced are often stalked by their abusers. If they date someone else or are independent in any way, they're beaten to a pulp even when they're not living with the man. Most women, it seems, go back because they're afraid of what will happen if they don't."

Red laid down his fork. "Is it always alcohol?"

"I think that often enters into it. And believe it or not, eight out of ten times the next man the abused woman gets involved with is also a wife beater."

"What makes men do it? Frustration? Joblessness? Feeling of inadequacy?"

Cat shrugged again. "I don't know, Red, I just don't know. Why do some men commit incest? It staggers the imagination. Or rape."

"It's always men, though, isn't it?" Sarah said. "Life's not fair. Men use their power over us to hold us hostage."

Cat's eyes flew to Red, who shook his head in bewilderment.

"Not all men, and you know it," Cat countered. "Look at the men we know. I don't know any woman who's ever been beaten."

"Maybe not physically," Sarah went on. "But psychologically."

Cat had lived at the Big Piney long enough to feel that Sarah couldn't possibly be referring to Red, who had to be the gentlest and most thoughtful man she'd ever known. She had so often wondered how he kept his equilibrium with a wife like Sarah, intoxicated two-thirds of the day, mentally absenting herself from the life around her.

Sarah poured herself another glass of wine. Some of it dribbled onto the white linen tablecloth.

Then she stood, arms outstretched, her wineglass in her left hand, and said, "I bid you good night," and swept out of the room like royalty.

Red pushed his chair back. "Let's have coffee in my office," he said. "I started a fire in there before dinner. First one of the year."

Cat folded her napkin. "I'll join you in a minute."

She went out to the kitchen to tell Thelma they'd have coffee and to ask how Lucy was.

"She didn't have enough money to pay the rent, so we moved her in with us."

"That's a tiny house."

"Tom suggested it."

"We have so much room. Would they like to move into one of the guest rooms? She could baby-sit in return."

Thelma shook her head hard. "She can baby-sit when Myrna has her baby, but I think it's good for her to have family around nights. We sit around talking about nothing in particular, and she sees how kind and nice a man can be. She's sort of confused some of the time still."

"We'll have coffee in the office," Cat told her.

"You're the best thing that ever happened to this family," Thelma said to Cat's back.

"And vice versa."

"Let me tell you, in case you're wondering."

Cat turned back to face Thelma.

"Tell me what?"

"Mr. Red's never been anything but a perfect gentlemen to Miss Sarah, not ever, and I've been here in this house longer than she has. He's never said an unkind word to her or laid a hand to her . . ."

"I know that," Cat reassured her.

"I just wanted to make it clear. She hasn't been a real wife to him for as long as I can remember. Not since before Torie was born even. Whatever bee's in her bonnet, it's wreaked havoc on him, though he never has showed a sign of it. He's been a husband she's never deserved, he's been a son that's about perfect, he's been a father any kids would want . . ."

"You don't have to tell me all this, Thelma. I know it."

"Well, yes, I guess I do have to tell you. I don't want you to think there's any dirty laundry in this house, not concerning Mr. Red. Maybe Miss Sarah has some, but Mr. Red and Miss Jenny, uh-uh. They maybe aren't perfect, but they're the two finest human beings I've ever known, and if Miss Jenny leaves here to go marry that Englishman, well, Mr. Red won't have no support."

"There's me."

"Not really. You're young. You're going to go off and marry Jason, or someone."

"Maybe Red will find love."

Thelma squinted her eyes. "He'll never divorce her. He's beholden to take care of her. I know it. He knows there's something not quite right, and she couldn't function in the world any better than she does here."

Cat turned and walked back through the dining room, across the hall to Red's office, where he was adding logs to the already glowing coals. "Feels good," she said, standing in front of it and rubbing her hands. "Though I hate to think it means winter's coming."

"I like the change of seasons," Red said. He was wearing a black-and-red check wool shirt and looked like he should be in a photograph for an outdoor magazine.

Thelma appeared with two mugs of coffee on a tray, which she set down on Red's desk.

"Soon's I put the dishes in the dishwasher, I'm off," Thelma said.

Cat and Red both nodded. He reached for the coffee cup.

Cat walked over to the French doors, to stare out into the darkness.

"Don't let your coffee get cold," Red murmured.

She knew he was watching her.

"Red"—she'd decided to take the bull by the horns—"what about having Sarah see a psychiatrist?"

He didn't answer for a few minutes.

Bree, who had been lying in front of the hearth, walked over to Cat. He was the perfect height to reach Cat's fingers and placed his head under Cat's hand, which automatically began to riffle the collie's fur.

"Cat, I've thought about it for years, but it's like her drinking. Unless she recognizes that something's wrong, she refuses to do anything about it. She doesn't think she's an alcoholic. We went over and over that years ago."

"She's more than an alcoholic."

"Where does one leave off and the other begin?"

"You can afford to fly a good shrink here and have him, or her, study Sarah without Sarah's knowing it's professional."

"You're thinking this because you can't believe I've abused her psychologically, aren't you. I haven't. You know me as well as most anyone does, my dear. I have tried for more than twenty years to figure what I could do to make her life easier, to make her happy, to . . ."

He sighed.

Cat turned to find him standing a few feet behind her. Impulsively, she threw her arms around him and put her head against his chest. For several seconds he stood there, and then his arms embraced her, holding her tight against him.

She closed her eyes. What had been meant as a gesture of sympathy suddenly turned into warmth. Tears glistened in her eyes, and she hugged him tighter. "Oh, Red," she said softly.

"Oh, Cat." His arms around her tightened. "My dear dear Cat." She could hear the beating of his heart through his flannel shirt.

"You have brought a happiness to me that is beyond words to express."

She unwound her arms from around him and stood back a step before looking up at him. The look in his eyes was indecipherable.

Thirty-nine

Miss Jenny returned from Egypt, filled with the wonders of the past but saying, "I think I'll stay home awhile."

Cat wondered if that meant she was tired of travel or wanted space between herself and Sir Geoffrey.

The older woman was horrified to hear of Lucy's predicament and fascinated that Cat would be defending her.

"I have another interesting case, too," Cat told her. "Some one is suing the school for teaching *Catcher in the Rye*."

Miss Jenny shook her head. "That was my favorite book when I was in my twenties. What in the world . . ."

"Oh, who can explain how minds work? That's about the purest book I know. These are the same people who pulled their daughter out of school last year because they claimed the teacher was advocating adultery because she was teaching *The Scarlet Letter*."

Miss Jenny sighed. "Isn't it amazing what closed minds some people have?"

"At least Bill O'Rourke," Cat referred to the principal, "says he will fight this to his last breath."

"Will it come to that?"

Cat cocked her head. "Who knows? But I'll help him fight. I recommended he not back down just because someone wanted to sue. Schools in general are too afraid of parents. Last year these same people home-schooled their daughter and now she's back and doing poorly in everything."

"What happens when these overprotected kids find out about the real world?" Miss Jenny commented, but Cat could tell she had lost interest in the conversation. She was mixing a batch of muffins. "My, it *is* good to get home to my own kitchen," she said. "Going away is fun, but coming home is the nicest part."

"So, you have no hankering to see what living in England would be like?"

Flour on her hands, Miss Jenny waved them in the hair. "Honey, I'm not going to get married if that's what you're asking. I enjoy things just as they are. I do think Geoffrey was a bit surprised when I turned down his proposal."

"Ah, so he did ask you."

Miss Jenny smiled as she worked. "Men are fundamentally unable to function for themselves. Now, that's a glaring generalization." Miss Jenny slid the muffins into the oven and walked over to the sink to wash her hands. "But I think men invented marriage for a couple of reasons."

"I always thought it was women who were supposed to have done that."

"Phooey." Miss Jenny grinned as she put the bowls in the sink and ran water over them. "Most men don't know how to have a social life without women around to set it up for them. Most men don't know how to iron their shirts and cook their meals. Of course, Geoff can afford not to do those things, and once you get past a certain age, it's just too much trouble to find a different woman to make love to each week, or month. Men like to be listened to and waited on. Men like to think someone thinks they're important."

"We all like that."

Miss Jenny went on as though she hadn't been interrupted. "Men like to have someone to tell what to do whether the woman does it or not. Men sort of ramble around at loose ends without a woman. You know, they just don't have the inner resources we do. When they stop work, for most of them, there's nothing left. We're used to little things making up the fabric of our lives, so we can knit and read and garden and bake. We find things to take up our days and keep our minds active, but once men no longer have their work, they don't know what to do. I don't want to provide that, fifty-two weeks a year.

"For the first time in my life I don't have to put others first. And much to my surprise, I like the feeling. I can do what I want when I want or not do anything but stare out at the birds in the trees or the quail along the path. Or the deer that pass by the back of the house. I can go to Portland and shop or take off for New York and see the plays. I can cook or settle for peanut butter crackers and soup if I want. I like it."

She sat down at the kitchen table, opposite Cat, and poured them each another cup of coffee. "Don't get me wrong. I like the attention I get from Geoff. I like the feeling that at nearly seventy I'm an attractive woman. I like sex. I missed that when my husband died, and thought never to have it again. But"—she laughed—"at my age, you do it in the dark and you never, not ever"—she smiled—"are the one on top."

Cat laughed so hard she felt a stitch in her side. "Miss Jenny, you are a sketch."

"I not only love men, but I like a lot of them, too. But I'm too old to want my life to center around one, to wait on him, and to do what he wants. So I prefer staying single and just enjoying with none of the responsibilities. Now at your age, I wouldn't choose that path. At your age I'd choose to have more children." She sipped her coffee. "Now, what about you?"

"I've been telling you about me. I have two cases, both of which may come to trial. Certainly Lucy's will, I'd guess in late February."

"You're not telling me about you, you're telling me about your lawyering. What about you and Jason?"

Cat inhaled. "I don't know," she said.

"You don't know what?"

Cat had deliberately not thought about herself and Jason. She'd let it flow. "I like him, Miss Jenny. I like him an awful lot. We have fun together, and we do go to bed and that's nice."

"Sounds lukewarm."

Cat shook her head. "I guess that's it. I've tried to figure out why someone as nice, even wonderful, as Jason isn't affecting me more. I wonder if it's because anyone after Scott would be a letdown."

"Scott's been dead near two years."

Cat shook her head as though bewildered. "I don't know. I usually see Jason about once a week. Sometimes I have supper over there during the week, but not as often as he and Cody would like. I take Matt with me most times, which is fine with both of them. During the summer I went to Cody's Little League games. I don't know what it is. I really enjoy Jason, and we're good friends. I have coffee with him every day at Rocky's, and he stops in to see me at least once a day. But something's . . . missing."

"Chemistry. He lights no fire within you," Miss Jenny said, getting up and walking over to peer in the oven. "Ah, another two minutes and we should be able to have a hot chocolate chip muffin."

"Chocolate chip! Oh, wow!"

Miss Jenny sat down and put her elbows on the table. "Tell me about Red and Sarah. You know, I'm gallivanting around the world having such fun and my son . . ."

"Miss Jenny, I think she's getting worse. I want her to see a counselor, for she's really spacing out."

"You know, when she first came here, when they'd come home here weekends from college, and when they were first married, we all thought she took to ranch life and Cougar like you do. We all thought here was the perfect girl for him, she learned to ride, like you have, she brought down deer and elk in hunting season, and she was the life of every party anyone had in town. She'd throw parties here at the ranch, too. Why I remember one costume party on Halloween. Cougar Valley had never seen anything like it. She made us all laugh, and Red was as happy as a man could be.

"And then it changed, and though Red and I've talked about it over and over neither of us can figure just what happened. She did have a mild postpartum depression after Scott was born, but that lasted just about six weeks."

The timer went off and Miss Jenny went to the oven and took the muffins out, placing them on a wooden breadboard. "Let 'em cool a couple minutes, and then we can have some."

She sat back down. "It was when she was pregnant with Torie that she got peculiar. The nearer to her time the more crazy-acting she became. She'd take off into the woods, just walking mind you, and come back, her long hair tangled, her eyes fierce.

"But she was still such a good mother to Scott, doting on him, hardly able to make herself leave him even for her walks. She'd do that when he napped. I asked Red if maybe she wanted a home of her own. God knows, we could have built a house anywhere on our land. We always tend to blame ourselves, and I wondered if it was something about not living alone with Red, but he said no, he didn't think so. When I mentioned it to Sarah she clutched my hand and I thought she was going to cry. She begged me not to send her away.

"Once Torie was born, she acted as though she didn't even want to see her. She refused to nurse her, and lay for days staring into space, refusing to get out of bed, scarcely looking at the baby. Red fed the little girl, and bathed her and diapered her and was mother and father to that girl for the first year of her life.

"Sarah was a different woman. You know, I've never asked him, but I've wondered all these years, did they ever sleep together again? I don't mean make love, but even get in the same bed. My son, as you know, is a man of enormous appetites, in all ways, and I've wondered what he's done about that particular one."

"Red's the finest man I've ever met."

"Hmpf," Miss Jenny muttered, going over to take the muffins out of the pan. "Got to eat at least one of these while the chocolate chips are still warm and runny."

Cat closed her eyes. "My mother used to bake chocolate chip cookies that were better than any I've ever tasted since."

"Do you ever hear from your father?" Miss Jenny asked.

"Sure. He calls me every month. But he's all wrapped up in his second family. He never paid that much attention to me, anyway. Now his wife just had a fourth child, younger even than Matt."

"That hurts, doesn't it?"

Cat raised her eyebrows. "Well, I guess I always thought it was second childhood. He is fifty-three. Isn't that rather late to have a new baby?"

"I guess not." Miss Jenny studied Cat. "You're just jealous, I imagine, feeling displaced. You thought he stopped paying attention to you."

"What do you call it? Sending me off to boarding school, seeing me only holidays. Sending me to summer camp while they had a baby each year?"

"And she's almost young enough to be your sister rather than your stepmother?"

Cat nodded, surprised to feel the sting of tears.

Miss Jenny leaned over and touched Cat's arm. "Even after all this time?"

Cat searched for a tissue and found it in her pocket and dabbed her eyes. "I guess I thought he had no right to happiness at his age."

Miss Jenny went and got two muffins, placed them on saucers and brought them back, shoving one in front of Cat. "Do you feel someone his age doesn't deserve to try to grab the brass ring?"

Cat was puzzled for a minute. "Oh. You mean Red, too?"

Miss Jenny nibbled at her muffin. "If I do say so myself, this is ambrosia. Yes, I mean my son. I want him to find happiness at no matter what age."

Cat bit into her muffin which melted in her mouth, leaving a chocolate coating that she wished she could keep forever.

"Oh, Miss Jenny."

Cat surprised them both by breaking into tears.

Forty

For her birthday Red had given Cat an Appaloosa, already bred. Cat was thrilled. There'd be a young colt for Matt. Now in December, with the days darkening at four-thirty, they could see the swelling in Felicia's belly.

"We'll have a March colt for sure," Red assured her.

They were out in the barn on a Saturday afternoon. Matt, bundled up in a snowsuit, ran around, poking his head in the horses' stalls, laughing as Bree and Brandy followed him, wagging their tails.

A litter of kittens mewed from one of the stalls where they were nestled in hay.

"You know what I'd love for Christmas? Cat asked.

Red looked down at her. "Tell me."

"I want a greenhouse."

"A greenhouse?"

"Yes, a greenhouse. We could have year-round vegetables, and I'll start seeds. I want to put a picket fence around the area south of the house, and plant roses and make a perennial garden there."

He turned to her. "You do, do you?"

"Well, I know you won't mind. It'll keep me out of trouble . . ."

"As though you haven't enough to do."

"I need something concrete to think about as a relief from this trial that's coming up. It's set for the end of February. Besides, you're like I am. You invent new things to do all the time. You're busier than any other two people I know. We're both people with restless minds and active bodies."

He broke out into loud laughter.

"Since I was twelve years old, I haven't really had a home until I moved here. I want an old-fashioned perennial garden, with annuals for spots of color, and I want an herb garden, which I can start in the greenhouse, and . . ."

"Knowing you, I imagine you already have catalogs."

"Well"—she smiled—"now that you mention it, I did send for some, but they haven't all arrived yet."

"After dinner, bring them down to my office and we'll pore over them and you tell me what you want."

She turned to hug him. "I knew you'd like the idea."

"Cat, I like all your ideas."

"That's because they concern the Big Piney."

"Not true. I like the library idea, and I like your setting up practice in town, and I like . . ."

"It's just because you love me."

He was tossing a last fork of hay into a stall, and his back was to her. He was very still.

From the other end of the barn, they could hear Matt's shouts and laughter.

She walked closer to him. "You do, don't you? I do make your life happier."

He hesitated. His back still to her, he said, "Yes, you do make my life happier."

Matt and Bree came barreling into sight.

She turned and caught her son up in her arms and began to skip toward the door at the opposite end, the dogs jumping around her as she ran.

"Why did I do that?" she asked her son, who had thrown his arms around her and was giggling. She kissed his cold red cheek, and said, "Let's get some hot cider," she said. "I bet Grandpa will like some, too."

But Grandpa didn't come in the house until dinnertime, when it had been dark for nearly two hours.

By then Matt had been bathed and fed and was playing in his pajamas in front of the fireplace in the living room. Sarah had floated into the room shortly after Cat and Matt settled in.

"You're not drinking yet?" were her first words.

Cat shook her head. "We just had cider."

Sarah went out to the kitchen and reappeared with a pitcher of ice. She put four ice cubes into a tall glass and filled it with whiskey.

Cat shook her head. It was enough to turn one away from drink, though when Red did enter about fifteen minutes later she accepted the glass of red wine he poured for her.

"There's the smell of snow in the air," Red announced.

Sarah's words were already slurred. "I hate dark and cold, that's what I hate."

"There's a letter from Torie," Red told his wife. "She's not coming home for Christmas."

"Christmas? Is it that time already?"

"I saw Joseph in town yesterday," Cat said. "He told me he's going down there for the holiday. He's taking the week between Christmas and New Year's off."

"I thought they were over," Sarah said.

"They'll never be over," Red ventured. "They're just trying it apart. They never said they'd broken up."

Cat stood up. "I'll put Matt to bed, then I'll get supper on the table."

She'd told Thelma to stop preparing Saturday night dinners. Thelma had her hands full with Lucy and her son. Cat said it was about time they learned how to do without her for at least one and a half days a week.

She'd prepared croquettes from the leftover chicken they'd had the night before, and boiled new little red potatoes, and baked spoon bread and tossed a salad. That should be enough. The croquettes had a mustard sauce she hoped Red would like.

She enjoyed her weekends puttering in the kitchen and had told Jason they'd have to get together another night than Saturday, which is why she'd spent last evening over at his house, though the previous Saturday he and Cody had come out for dinner. Afterward the three of them played hearts. Red had disappeared into his study, and Sarah, as always, had faded away upstairs. More often than not she fell asleep in front of the TV, and it was still on when Thelma arrived in the morning.

Cat made dinner-table conversation. "The most delightful woman came in to see me yesterday, right before I left. It was the middle of the afternoon and this elegant-looking woman, I'd guess in her middle thirties, came in. She was wearing a suit that was more like New York than Cougar, a houndstooth check with a stunning bag thrown over her shoulder and two young boys in tow. I learned they were eleven and thirteen. She said the sixteen-year-old was taking care of the dogs, wherever that would be.

"Anyhow, she just bought the Joslin place . . ."

"I was thinking of buying that myself," Red said, " 'cept he wanted too much."

"Well, this woman introduced herself as April Martin, isn't that a lovely name? She's been divorced about a year and decided it was time to make a move from New Jersey. Her sons begged her to move West and buy a ranch, since they're all into horses and hunting.

"Anyhow, she wanted me to draw up the legal documents and do a search on the title, and I think she's going to set the town on fire. She asked what there was to do, and when I told her we didn't have movies, she said, 'I don't mean that kind of stuff. We're moving here to get away from city life. I mean are there square-dances and 4-H clubs, and are there things I can do in town to meet people and become part of the community, and are there classes anyplace where I can learn about ranching?'"

Red laughed.

"I tried not to laugh, too. She was so enthusiastic and so full of excitement and so, well, just so nice. I liked her. I thought maybe next week I'd take her to have coffee with Dodie. They're staying at the Best Western in Baker. She was hoping they could be in by Christmas."

"Two weeks?"

"I thought I'd take her and we'd go see Mr. Joslin, and maybe he'll move out before the final papers are ready."

"Pete Joslin?" Red shook his head. "Well, I won't underestimate the power of two women, but it won't be easy."

"Would you mind . . . well, they don't know anyone, would you mind if I invite them here for Christmas? I thought we'd ask Jason and Cody as always. And Chazz and Dodie and the kids . . ."

"When's Dodie's baby due?"

"February."

Red sat back in his chair. "I like that mustard sauce. Of course, Cat. Talking of Christmas, I went up to Ma's after I saw you in the barn, and she says her boyfriend and his sister are coming for Christmas."

Cat clapped her hands. "Oh, what a time we're going to have! I used to dream of big family Christmases."

She stood and started to clear the table, and then said, thoughtfully, "What about Thelma and her husband and Lucy and her son, too? At least for Christmas dinner?"

Red stood up and gathered some dishes in his hands. "We'll have more people than we've had in this big house in twenty-some years."

"That's what a big house is for."

They put the dishes into the dishwasher and walked back to the living room.

"Want to go over those catalogs here or in my office? There are fires in both rooms."

"Yours is cozier." Though Cat loved the big living room, if she lived here long enough, she'd redecorate it. It was dark and, in the winter, depressing. She'd like light, airy colors, shades of aqua and mauve and cream. Floral prints, with green leaves. She could almost envision it.

"I've got to go out to the barn first," he said. "Meet you in my office in half an hour?"

She went up to her room to find the catalogs. When she came back downstairs, she saw he'd turned all but one light off in the living room, and the house was dark except for the glow emanating from his office.

She went outside to look at the stars and ended up walking as far as the barn.

There was only one bare lightbulb lit down at the far end, and it was so dark she couldn't see him. She walked the length of it, toward the dim light, listening to the horses munching their dinner, liking the smell of the hay, the horsy smell.

Red was at the far end, doing something with a machine, oil on his hands. He looked up when he saw her approaching. Her hands were jammed in her pockets. She leaned against a post and watched him, his broad shoulders hunched over whatever it was he was repairing.

"I told Ma about your greenhouse idea, and she's all for it, too, but she asks me to tell you to order snapdragons so she can have them all winter long."

She walked over and stood next to him, not saying anything.

She could feel him, though they were a couple of feet apart. She could feel the warmth of him, could smell his citrus aftershave mingling with the smell of hay and oil. She watched his big hands, graceful as a surgeon's, as he wiped the grease from them. He set down the pliers, wiped them off, too, and said, "That's enough for tonight."

He turned as if to leave, but suddenly his eyes were riveted on her staring ones.

Cat found herself breathing with great difficulty, swallowing hard. Her heart beat loudly and evenly, and she swore she could feel the blood pounding through her veins.

"Cat?" His voice was a question.

She didn't, couldn't, move. She was riveted to the spot.

His eyes bored into her as though looking for an answer to what he saw there.

He moved a step closer so that their bodies touched, and she heard a sound escape her that was either a moan or a cry, she couldn't tell which. His arms wound around her, he pulled her close, tilting her head back so that he could see into her eyes. And then his mouth was on hers, devouring her, parting her lips so that their tongues touched, hungrily, with a passion yet unleashed. He rained kisses over her cheeks, her eyes, her neck, and murmured, "Oh, God, Cat. Catherine." His lips sought hers again as her arms wound around his neck, pulling him closer, inhaling his breath, gasping to catch hers.

She pulled away, turning and running through the gently falling snow, through the kitchen, taking the stairs two at a time, closing her door once she reached her bedroom, standing against it as though to block out what had just happened, breathing so hard she doubled over.

"Oh, God," she whispered into the night. "What have we done?"

Forty-one

She sat down in the chair in front of the window and watched the flakes fall slowly. She hugged herself and bent over, shivering, closing her eyes.

Red was her father-in-law. Red was married. Red was old enough to be her father. Red was . . .

A sob escaped her. Red's kisses had lit a fire within her. The hunger and passion had been waiting to be unleashed. She had hoped it was something that could be cured by going to bed with Jason. It wasn't.

Red was a man of honor and integrity. He wouldn't let passion and desire rule him. Wouldn't hurt her for the world. She knew it. He had delivered her son, his grandson. He had cherished her, giving her anything that could make her happy, that would ensure her staying on at the Big Piney. He wouldn't do anything careless; he wouldn't allow himself to be controlled by momentary lust.

She got up and opened her door, glanced down the empty hall and walked next door to Matt's room, standing in the doorway to listen to his even breathing.

She wanted to go downstairs, see Red, tell him they had to forget what happened. Tell him she and Matt better move.

Pretend what happened tonight hadn't?

What she really wanted to do was tell him she loved him.

She sighed and walked down the hallway, away from the safety of her own room. She wondered if he'd even come in from the barn.

She heard a fire crackling in his office and headed toward it. His back was to her as he squatted before the fireplace, putting logs on the fire, whose flames sent shadows dancing on the opposite wall.

"Red?"

He turned so fast he nearly fell over, but he stood, graceful for such a big man. She could tell that probably for one of the few times in his life he was unsure of what to say, how to act. He stood there with a log in his hand, his eyes questioning.

"Would you like something hot to drink?"

Without waiting for an answer, Cat turned and walked down the hall to the kitchen, where she poured cider and a stick of cinnamon into a pan and put on the stove. She stood staring at it, not seeing it, until it began to boil.

She found mugs and poured the aromatic beverage into them, slowly walking back to his office. He was standing in front of the fireplace, hypnotized by the flames. She put his cup on the coffee table and sank into the leather chair opposite the sofa.

She sat, her mind a void. His back still to her, he said, "I'd like to tell you I'm sorry, but only if it's going to end our relationship."

Her breathing caught. She glanced up at him. He crossed the room and sat on the couch, reaching for the hot cup.

"I'm sorry if it is cause for alarm or unhappiness for you. I would do anything rather than be unfair or alienate you."

"Perhaps Matt and I should leave," she said, her voice a monotone.

"Oh, dear God," he said. "I would do anything to prevent that, Cat. I lost control. All my life, I have behaved as honorably as I know how. I don't know what happened to me. I would take that moment back if I could, Cat. I don't want anything to come between us."

"Oh, Red." Cat inhaled, a ragged sigh. "Perhaps it's just that since you and Sarah . . ."

"Sarah and I haven't made love in over twenty years," he said. "But I'm a normal man with normal needs and desires. So, Norah and I . . ."

"Norah?" Cat sat up straight, staring at him. "Norah Eddlington?"

He nodded. "I'm not ashamed of it, Cat. Norah and I have known each other all our lives. And after Stan's accident, that was over sixteen or seventeen years ago, well, Norah never has stopped loving him, but she couldn't stand a sterile life any more than I could, so . . ."

"Norah Eddlington?"

"Is it so shocking?"

Cat shook her head. "No, I think it's great." She managed to smile. "Great for both of you. How wonderful. Here I've worried about you . . ."

"There's never been romance involved, Cat. Warmth, friendship, respect, need. But it makes her marriage bearable and has made my life so."

"Does Stan know?"

"I think he suspects. For all I know, she's told him. If he does, he approves, because it gives him his marriage."

When she was quiet, Red continued, "So it's not that I haven't had a woman, Cat. It's not that."

Cat reached for the mug and wrapped both hands around it, trying to still the trembling that wracked her body. She couldn't look at him. She stood up and walked to the window, staring out into the darkness, seeing the tiny white flakes floating down.

"I guess I have some dragons to slay," Red said quietly.

"Can we pretend it never happened?"

He crossed the room to stand behind her. He didn't touch her, but she felt the heat from him. The hair on her neck stood on end.

They stared at each other, and finally she left, moving slowly and silently up the long staircase. She crawled into bed with her clothes on and lay, eyes wide-open, staring into the darkness for hours.

Sarah was still upstairs the next morning when Cat whipped up Miss Jenny's popover recipe while Red scrambled eggs, adding chopped onion and red peppers.

They hadn't said three words to each other, and nothing about the previous night.

"I have to call everyone this morning and invite them to Christmas dinner," she said. Her eyes were bloodshot from lack of sleep. "We'll have to put Miss Jenny's company up here," she went on, "at least the sister. I have so many things on my mind . . ."

Cat had always enjoyed the domesticity of Sunday mornings. She poured glasses of orange juice and set them on the colorful blue-and-yellow placemats and napkins she'd arranged on the oaken table.

Matt rolled back and forth on his rocking horse.

She bent over to take the popovers from the oven. They were golden and high. Cat sat down and waited for Red to bring the plates of eggs. She looked at him.

He looked like he hadn't slept much either. He sat down and bit into the popover. "These are as good as Miss Jenny's."

Just then, Sarah appeared in her robe. She'd brushed her hair but had foregone makeup. "Why are you eating in the kitchen?" she asked.

Cat stood up to set a place at the table for her mother-in-law. She poured juice and handed it to Sarah. Sarah sat at the end of the table. "Since when have we descended to eating here?" she asked.

"Sunday mornings," Red answered. "Cat and I like eating here on Sundays. We've been dining here Sundays for nearly a year, Sarah."

Sarah looked around. "Oh." She saw the popovers. "Has Miss Jenny been here already?"

"No," Cat said, sitting down. "But it's her recipe. Would you like some eggs?"

Sarah shook her head. "No. Since when did you start cooking?" She didn't wait for an answer. "Seems you can do just about anything."

Cat couldn't tell by the tone of her voice whether Sarah was complimenting her or was irritated.

"I try."

Red reached for the coffeepot and poured Sarah a cup of the steaming black liquid. His eyes met Cat's over his wife's head.

"There's snow," Sarah said. "Snow killed Scott."

"I'm going to get Matt's sled out of the barn and take him sledding," Cat said. She still hated snow, too.

"Let's move to Florida. Or Tahiti," Sarah said to Red, "where there's never any snow to remind me." She sipped her coffee and spread jam on her popover.

The three of them ate in silence, while Matt got off his rocking horse and ran upstairs.

Then Sarah said, "I hate winters. I feel imprisoned. I'll be a prisoner here all my life."

"You can do whatever you want, come and go ... You're no prisoner."

"You don't know. You just don't know."

Red stood up and went to the kitchen door, where his winter jacket hung on a peg. "I'll be out in the barn," he announced.

After he'd disappeared Cat sat and drank her coffee while Sarah declared that maybe this year she just wasn't up to Christmas.

"Well, we're having a big one. Miss Jenny's Brit and his sister are coming. They'll arrive on the twentieth. I thought maybe we could decorate the tree the following night. I'm going to invite Jason and Cody, Dodie, Chazz and the kids, and a woman who's new to town and her three kids, and Thelma and Tom and Lucy and ..."

Sarah raised her hands as though to ward off any more names. "Oh, Cat, I can't handle that many people."

"Of course you can, Sarah. Thelma and I'll fix the turkey and bake pies and ..."

"... and everyone will think you're wonderful and see that I'm not. Oh, Cat," she burst into tears. "I can't seem to do anything."

Cat found herself unmoved. She stood up and cleared the table. "Would you like me to buy something for you to send to Torie?"

Sarah shook her head and gazed out at the mountains. "I hate it here. Do you know that? You have nothing tying you here. Why don't you get away while you can?"

"I'm happy here," Cat answered, carrying dishes to the dishwasher. "This is where Matt and I belong."

"Happy." Sarah stood, cup in hand. "I wonder when was the last time I experienced happiness? Actually, I know when. I know when I was last happy. And this is the price God is extracting from me. I sold him my soul."

She carried her cup with her and left the room. Cat stood at the sink, looking out at the dark fir trees that dotted the snowy mountainside.

She called Matt and dressed him in his snowsuit and boots. She threw on her down parka and her boots, also, and headed to the barn to get his sled. The dogs would like the exercise, too.

Red wasn't in sight, to both her relief and disappointment. Matt danced around while she pulled the sled down from the nail where it had been hanging.

"What are you so excited about, big boy?" she smiled at him. "You can't possibly remember what a sled's all about," but as soon as she set it on the barn floor he hopped on it and sat, waiting expectantly. Cat leaned down to kiss his red face. "Do you have any idea how much I love you?" she asked, pulling the rope and, as it moved, the boy laughed and waved his arms.

"We'll walk down to the mailbox, how about that?" It was half a mile away. It would be good for her. Get her acting instead of thinking.

Bree wagged his tail and jumped in circles as the three of them took off over the lawn while Brandy disappeared into the barn.

Cat did not see Red standing in the doorway of the barn, one hand against the siding, the other shading his eyes from the sun's glare on the snow, watching them. He stood there all the time they came back, too. His throat felt tight. There were the two people who, aside from Torie, were the dearest in the world to him. Had he ruined it by his one impulsive action last night? He had fought the desire to kiss her for so long, somehow last night it seemed beyond his control, she stood so close to him in the barn, and the look in her eyes, the smell of her, her nearness . . .

And she had responded. She had thrown her arms around him and her tongue met his with the same eagerness, the same passion.

But that was for the moment. Had he shocked her? He couldn't read her feelings at all, she whom he thought he had known so well. This morning, she was aloof.

Was he being totally unfair to her, to the woman he loved with all his heart? Was their relationship destroyed? Why couldn't he have been satisfied to have life go on as it had, smoothly, the times spent together carefree and open, warm and loving, without awkwardness or discomfort. One moment where he had been unable to control himself, and now he was worried that what he and Cat shared was gone forever.

He had not done many impulsive things in his life, and certainly not ones that were destructive, at least to his knowledge. So, was the one time he had given in to his heart ruling his head going to ruin the one relationship that made his life worthwhile, that gave him untold happiness and contentment?

He wished he were a praying man. If so, he would pray and ask forgiveness.

When Cat noticed him standing in the doorway, she waved, and Matt jumped off the sled and ran toward his grandfather, who stooped to gather the few inches of snow into a ball and toss the lightweight stuff into the air.

It showered over Matt, who reached up, trying to catch it, giggling.

"You want me to take care of him while you make those phone calls?" Red asked. He'd be damned if he'd avert his eyes. He had to look right into hers.

She met his gaze levelly. "Red, what's done is done. We can't go backwards."

What did that mean?

She handed him the rope and said, "Will you put the sled up for me, please. I'll go invite everyone to Christmas dinner."

She didn't stop when he called "Cat," but continued to walk toward the house. He could not see her face or read her eyes.

What the hell did that mean, "We can't go backwards?"

Forty-two

Though Cat had had trouble sleeping for two nights, lying awake with desire and guilt, she leapt out of bed Monday morning while it was still dark.

Red had eaten and gone before it was light. Disappointment stabbed her.

Thelma placed apples fried in brown sugar in front of her and, coffee cup in hand, sat down opposite her.

"How many of us for Christmas dinner?" Cat had told her that the two of them would prepare dinner, but that Thelma was to consider herself a guest, or "at least a member of the family," and not spend her time waiting on others. Cat would share the work with her. But Thelma was too used to being boss in her kitchen.

Cat counted on her fingers, "The three of us, the three of you, the Whitleys, Jason and Cody, Miss Jenny and her English guests, the four Martins."

"Who're they?"

"She's a woman who's new to town, just bought the Joslin place, and she and her three teenage sons don't know anyone yet."

"What are you, Mother Earth?" asked a voice from the doorway.

"Miss Jenny, what are you doing here so early?" Cat stood and kissed the older woman's cheek.

"Thought I'd be in time for one of Thelma's breakfasts," she said.

"You sit right down, and I'll fix you something," Thelma said. "I just happen to have fried apples and banana bread."

"Your strange combinations always taste good." Miss Jenny had been eating Thelma's cooking for over thirty years.

"You're all dressed up."

"I'm going to drive over to Boise and Christmas shop. You don't have enough free time for us to drive to Portland this year, you said, so I have to use my own resources. Thought I'd stay overnight and take my time. What in the world am I going to get for Geoff and his sister?"

"I'm doing nearly all mine by catalogs this year."

"Shopping for men is so hard. What do you give men who have everything?"

"I'm getting Red a cappuccino maker."

Miss Jenny laughed as Thelma placed juice and coffee in front of her. "I remember one year Jock gave me a riding lawn mower for my birthday, because he was tired of mowing the lawns. That was before we had so much help of course."

Cat smiled. "I do think a cappuccino maker is something I'd like, you're right. I yearn for one every Sunday morning."

"I like your greenhouse idea. When do you have time for everything?"

"I think you make time for things you want," Cat said. "I'd love to have cut flowers all year, and some veggies, too. It'll relax me after dinner to go play under lights each night."

"Did Red tell you I have a penchant for snapdragons?"

Cat nodded. "I'll make sure you have as many as you want. That's what you can get me. All the greenhouse gardening books you can find."

"I don't imagine Boise is loaded with such." Miss Jenny frowned. "Well, maybe they can order them for me."

Cat told her their plans for Christmas. "I thought Geoff and his sister might appreciate a real American Christmas. No plum pudding but turkey and apple and pumpkin pies."

"I'll bake the pies."

"I was counting on that."

Cat had barely entered her office, her coat not even off, when Jason appeared. He walked over and kissed her cheek. "Hey, what's the cold shoulder?"

"Oh, Jason, I'm just so busy . . ."

"Too busy for a morning kiss? Too busy to see me once a week?"

She smiled at him and leaned forward, brushing her lips along his. "I just never seem to have time for anything."

"If this is what that Lucy case means . . ."

"Yes, it is. It does take all my time." Well, it soon would.

"Too much to go up to La Grande to the movies Saturday night?"

"Jason, I just have too much, you know getting ready for Christmas *and* the trial. Give me a rain check, will you?"

"Hey, is it something I said?"

She tried to smile reassuringly. "I will let you buy me lunch today, if you have time."

"I do, if nothing out of the ordinary happens, which it seldom does. You know what the hardest part of this job is? Telling people bad news. Fortunately, there hasn't been any of that lately."

"I'll meet you at Rocky's at twelve-thirty?"

"If that's the most you can spare me, I'll settle for that today. But not every day, Cat, my sweet."

As soon as he was gone Cat dialed April Martin, at the Best Western in Baker. She hadn't been able to reach her yesterday. April answered on the first ring.

"I'm hoping you and your sons will come out to the ranch for Christmas dinner," Cat said.

"How lovely. I never dreamed our first Christmas out here we'd be in someone's home. It doesn't look like we'll be in ours."

"I'm not too sure about that. If I can get hold of Mr. Joslin, and he'll see us, can you drive up here?"

"In less time than . . ."

"Okay, I'll call you right back."

As she dialed Mr. Joslin, Cat wondered what April's kids were doing about schooling until they settled into Cougar Valley.

Mr. Joslin said sure, he could see them.

April was there within the hour, in her dark green Dodge minivan.

"Where are your kids?" Cat asked.

"Davey drives them up here to school in the car," April said. She wasn't what Cat would call beautiful, but there was a quality about her that made her memorable. Her shoulder-length blond hair was cut straight yet managed to look sophisticated. She'd never find a haircut like that out here. "They think the school is 'quaint.'"

"Quaint?" Yet Cat understood.

"However, the kids wear boots and Donny's gone out for basketball and made the team, and Darrell has met a girl and what thrills me is that there are no drugs . . ."

"Don't bet on that!"

"Oh." April turned to look at Cat. "Shit! I'd taken for granted.

You know what I'm getting them for Christmas? Maybe I'm going to bribe them into being clean-cut."

"Tell me."

"I'm going to let each of them choose a horse."

"It was the first thing I learned to do out here, even though I don't seem to have much time to do it often nowadays."

"You ride? Well, maybe I'll get myself one, too, and in the spring you can teach me."

"I'm certainly not one to teach you."

They drove along, the stubbled frozen fields, ice reflecting on the dried stalks of corn and hay.

"At least it's not damp. The cold doesn't go right through you like it does in New Jersey."

They came to the turnoff to the Joslin place, hidden by willows, bare at this time of year. "I will be so glad to be through with motel living," April said.

"It needs a coat of paint," Cat murmured, as the house came into view.

"What do you think I have three strapping sons for?"

"How's their father going to take his first Christmas away from his boys?"

"Oh, probably he'll spend it in Barbados with his secretary. Or with his lawyer. Or with his accountant, all women."

"I see."

They pulled into the driveway of the two-story Victorian house. "Whoever built this must have had money at the time. Wait til you see it a year from now."

"The barn's in perfect shape."

"One of the deciding factors," April said as they got out of the car. "I'll put stalls in for our horses." She threw back her head and laughed. "All four of them."

Mr. Joslin didn't wait for them to knock. He opened the door and gestured them in. "Coffee's on," he said. He wore old-fashioned dungarees.

He led them through the high-ceilinged hallway to the kitchen. On the left was the living room, cartons piled high. "You can see I'm packing already. Hope to be out by the first."

Cat and April looked at each other. When they were seated at the kitchen table, Cat said, "What we came to discuss, Mr. Joslin, is the possibility of your moving before Christmas."

"Out of the question." The old man shook his head as he poured coffee into the white porcelain cups on the table. "I'm going to my daughter's in Montana for Christmas. I can't get things packed before then."

"My boys and I'll come help," April offered.

"Miz Martin, what're you going to do on a ranch without a man in charge, anyhow?"

"I'm going to run it," she said.

"You must have an awful lot of money to pour down the drain."

"It's not going down the drain," she countered. "I'll give you two thousand more if we can be here for Christmas Eve."

He sighed and studied the new owner. He turned to Cat. "You can have all the papers in order?"

"Sure. I can have them ready next week. Or even Friday if you want."

He sipped coffee, his mustache drooping into the cup, and said, "Two thousand, huh?"

"And our help, if you want it."

"If I can get out on the twenty-third, why, what'll you do for furniture?"

April smiled, "The movers promise that mine will be here by then."

"Any man can resist good-looking women, I haven't met, yet. Okay. You send those boys up."

"How about tomorrow after school? And every day you want them for the next ten days."

He shook his head. "My daughter won't believe it. She says I'll never get cleaned out of here. Forty years' worth of stuff."

"You want a sale in the spring?" Cat said. "I bet April would hold it for you."

April gave Cat a dirty look.

"No, no, no. What I can't take with me to Montana, I'll give away. Specially if I'm getting an extra two thousand. You can have all the tools in the barn." They'd already decided on that, but he didn't seem to remember.

When they'd finished their coffee, Cat stood up, and said, "Thanks, Mr. Joslin. All the Martins will appreciate it."

April offered him her hand. "The only thing I regret about buying your place is I won't get to know you better," she said.

A flush spread over Joslin's face. When they were back in the car Cat laughed. "Boy, you do know how to pour it on."

April just smiled.

"How about staying in town for lunch?" Cat said. "I'm meeting the sheriff at Rocky's at twelve-thirty. He's someone you ought to get to know."

"The sheriff?"

"Jason Fitzpatrick, most popular man in town. Your kids will like him, too. He's a real Westerner. He and my father-in-law are the big honchos around here."

"Sure," April said. "Tell me how to contact the phone company and see about transferring electricity and gas and that sort of stuff, and I'll use your phone."

"My phone is your phone."

Though Jason was polite, he didn't seem bowled over by April, but when the two women were back in Cat's office after lunch, April said, "He's some hunk. Married?"

"Not anymore. He and his eight-year-old son live on the street behind here, up the next block."

"Mm. I swore off men, but he is certainly attractive."

"He'll be with us for Christmas."

"You and him? Anything between you?"

"We're very good friends. He's been one of my best friends since I hit town."

"Good friends, hm? How nice."

Cat shook her head and turned her face away, so April could not see her smile.

Forty-three

At two, after April left, Cat prepared to go home. She made it a practice of leaving by two-thirty whenever she could. She accepted appointments only before one o'clock. There really wasn't that much legal business in a town of nineteen hundred people, though lately several people had stopped in to ask if she knew anything about tax law. She didn't, but maybe after Lucy's trial she'd take the time to learn about it.

A tightness clutched her chest. She always so looked forward to going back to the Big Piney, to home. Red, if he was not there when she arrived, would be there by five or five-thirty. They'd have drinks before the fire, share details of their day. Then there'd be TV, or sharing ideas, talking about something trivial or important in his study after dinner. Camaraderie. Companionship. Warmth. Love.

Funny how many relationships must be ruined because of sex. Because of a single kiss changing the whole dynamics. Because of male-female surfacing. One kiss and her whole world was turned topsy-turvy. Now there was tension where there had been warmth and companionship, where there had been something so rare and treasured.

Her father-in-law!

Just as she was ready to put the books she was studying for Lucy's case in her briefcase, Dodie marched into her office.

"I'm here on official business," she said.

Cat raised her eyebrows as she gestured Dodie into the chair across from her. Dodie, enormous with still two more months to go, held on to the arms of the chair and lowered herself gradually.

Cat folded her hands on her desk and waited.

"I want to make out a will and I trust your confidentiality."

"Of course." Cat reached for a yellow lined pad. "I swear I make out more wills than anything else."

"It's only in case Chazz dies before or with me. I mean I want to leave everything to him, since everything we have is ours, but if anything happens to us, like a car crash, or . . ."

Cat shivered.

"I want Jason to bring up these babies I'm carrying."

Cat looked up, surprised. "You're doing this even before they're born?"

Dodie nodded. "I just want to make sure. I don't want any loose ends."

"Have you talked this over with him? That's a big responsibility, bringing up two babies."

Dodie nodded and twisted her handkerchief, which she had crumpled up in her hands. "He and Chazz and I talked it over when . . ." she paused.

Cat looked up, pencil poised, waiting. "When . . . ?"

Dodie ignored that and said, "I want any monies we have to go to Jason, too, to help."

"What about the other children?"

"My mother will take care of them, and she has plenty of money."

Cat leaned forward. "Have you discussed all this with your mother, and with Jason?"

"Of course. I'm not about to just lay this on someone."

Cat began to write, and Dodie sat silently until she blurted out, "Cat, Jason's the father of these twins."

Cat dropped the pencil and stared at her friend.

Dodie was blinking fast. "Both he and Chazz would be real upset if they knew I'd told you. But you can't repeat it, can you?"

Cat shook her head, her mouth agape.

"Chazz has next to no sperm count. That's why we haven't had our own babies. And I love him to pieces, but God, I have wanted so much to have a baby. I mean grow one in my body, give birth, the whole thing. I have yearned for it so much it's pained me. Chazz has known that. He offered to give me a divorce when we found out, but I don't want that. I want to live my life out with him.

"So, a little over a year ago he asked if I wanted to have a baby by somebody else. We talked it over and thought the man we're closest to and admire most is Jason. He's a fine man. We approached him, and we all spent a couple of weeks talking about it. About could he stand not to bring up a child that was his, not even admit to it, not acknowledge it. Would he feel funny about him and me, you know . . ."

"You could have had artificial insemination," Cat protested, aghast at what she was hearing.

"I didn't want that even though I knew it would be hard for Chazz to think of my being with some other man. But he was willing. He loves me that much."

Cat thought back to last May. To April and March, when she'd asked Chazz for birth control pills when he knew she was sleeping with Jason. "You and Jason were doing that while Jason and I . . ."

"I knew about that," Dodie said. "Somehow, it made me feel closer to you."

"Oh, my God."

"Jason's one of the finest men I know, and I'm proud he'll be the biological father of my babies. Chazz is, too. It's bonded the three of us, like no friendship we've ever had before."

"And you don't want me to let Jason know I know?" Cat's eyes were wide.

"It took us three months of trying," Dodie said. "He hasn't been with me, that way, since May."

He might not have lied to Cat, but he was certainly hiding something. For a moment Cat felt anger, and then a sense of freedom came over her.

After Dodie left, Cat sat back in her chair and stared at the wall. Cougar Valley was a regular Peyton Place. Red had been bedding Norah Eddlington for years. The sheriff and the doctor's wife were sleeping together in the hopes of conceiving a child and had now conceived two.

What was that supposed to do to her if she married Jason? She wondered how she'd feel about all this if she were really in love with Jason.

Who else is doing what to whom around here?

As she drove home, Cat realized she and Red hadn't had a personal conversation since he'd kissed her. She wondered what was going on in *his* mind. Perhaps life could just go on as it had, she and Red living under the same roof. They'd have to get over this awkward period. It was just one moment. Nothing more. Couldn't they go on with their lives as they had been?

She was frightened. She didn't want to do anything to further fracture their relationship. Should she move? Well, she couldn't even think of that until after the trial. Christmas was coming and so much company and after that she just had to focus on the trial, not let any personal tribulations interrupt the energy she must put into that, the single-minded dedication. Lucy's life was in her hands.

She had to walk a tightrope. The Big Piney would one day belong to Matt, and any children Torie might have. The way it looked now, it would only be Matt's.

She wanted to be part of all that. To be forever entwined in Matt's and Red's lives. She hoped they could go on as they had been, not having to avert their eyes from embarrassment.

Yet on the other hand she wanted Red to kiss her again, hold her. She wanted to lie naked next to him, to feel his hands over her, his tongue touching the inside of her thighs, her breasts . . .

"Jesus Christ," she said as she almost missed the cutoff to the ranch.

As she entered the house, delicious aromas wafted down the hallway. Like magnets, they drew Cat to the kitchen.

"What's that divine smell?"

"I'm baking Christmas cookies," Thelma answered, her hands and apron covered with flour. "I figure we're going to need a ton of them with all the people coming."

"And three of them teenage boys," Cat said. "Will you slap me if I steal one?"

Thelma just grinned. Cat didn't take just one. She ended up nibbling three of them.

"Your cooking is one of the reasons I'm happy I live here."

"Go on," Thelma laughed, pleased.

"Well, I don't know what we'd ever do without you."

"Let's hope you don't find out for a long time."

Cat thought Thelma must be about Red's age, maybe a few years older. She'd been in charge of the Big Piney's kitchen for longer than Red and Sarah had been married, and it was more her home than the little house she lived in two miles down the road. She and Tom had three grown children, one in the army, one in Florida, and one in La Grande.

Cat decided to contact Mr. Claypool and ask where the Martin boys might find horses. Maybe she could talk him into teaching those boys. Saturday mornings, maybe. No one in the county knew horses better than he did.

Thinking of Claypools, she'd hardly seen anything of Joseph since Torie had gone. Perhaps she could arrange to have lunch with him someday, though she didn't even see him around town. Of course, his office was over outside Baker, but he used to be seen around town quite a bit.

Cat went upstairs, thinking of Lucy's case. The research she was doing didn't reassure her. She could find only three cases on record where a woman who had slain her abusive husband was not sent to jail, for a long term, too. Up until far too recently a man who murdered an unfaithful wife was sympathized with. A man who beat his wife did so legally, for a man could do anything he wanted to his wife. A man who insisted on his wife's having sexual relations with him was within his rights, legal and religiously. A man who forbade his wife to leave their house was within his rights, too.

A woman who cheated on her husband was ostracized, burned at the stake, kicked out of town. A man who cheated on his wife was just doing what men were expected to do. A woman who hit her husband could be punished in whatever way the husband inflicted punishment. A woman who killed her husband, her lord and master, was someone who threatened the very fabric of a patriarchal society.

What chance did they have?

At dinner, which was peach-glazed ham, sweet potatoes, Thelma's justly famous coleslaw, and Parkerhouse rolls, Cat said, "Everyone from here goes over to Baker or up to La Grande to have their taxes done, don't they?"

Red, fork in midair, said, "Uh-oh. The beginning of an idea from you is as good as having it done."

"Well, I don't know much about taxes, it's all I can do to fill out my own, but someone around here, maybe some housewife, must know something about accounting, maybe a CPA or at least a former accountant. Three people have come in lately wanting to know something about tax laws, and I thought I could start boning up on it after Lucy's trial. It wouldn't hurt to hire a part-time tax person, you know, to make out quarterly estimated taxes. Say, wasn't Lois an accountant?"

"Ed's wife, you mean?" The pharmacist.

"Uh-huh."

"Hey, I think she was. Seems to me she keeps his books."

Sarah glanced from Red to Cat, following the conversation as though it were a tennis ball.

"I wonder if she mightn't like to help with more than Ed's. I could buy another computer. She could do it while her kids are in school. Might not be enough business to completely make a living, but it certainly could provide vacations and some luxuries. I could pay the overhead and she could . . ."

"Why wouldn't she start her own business instead of just getting part of what they'd pay you?" It was the first time Sarah had entered the conversation.

"I don't have an answer to that," Cat answered, "so I wonder why no one's done it yet. I know the Davises have an accountant in Baker."

For the first time in days, Red's eyes met Cat's across the table.

Sarah gulped her wine. "Cat, I know you're my daughter-in-law, but get the hell out of here. Don't be drawn in deeper. That's what he does . . ." She nodded at Red. "That's what the men in Cougar Valley do. Tie you to them, rope you in so that there's no escape. Get out before you lose yourself."

"Oh, Sarah." Cat tried to keep impatience out of her voice. "I'm not losing myself. Maybe I'm finding me. In little ole Cougar Valley rather than a big city." But she and Red both knew she wasn't talking to Sarah.

"One of the things I like best about you," Red said as though Sarah were not present, "is your sense of self. You don't doubt that you can do something."

"I can do anything I set my mind to," Cat said. "And if I can't, at least I learn from it."

"Oh, rubbish," Sarah said, standing up. "All you two like to do is talk business. It's either the ranch, or Lucy or now new businesses. *She* should have been your wife!" She tossed this at Red as she swept past him. "I'm going upstairs."

Red and Cat sat, eyes locked. Finally Cat said, "You want coffee?"

He nodded. "I'll go light a fire in my office."

She almost told him he'd lit a fire in her.

In the kitchen she saw that Thelma had left an apple pie. She ground French vanilla coffee beans, and while the Braun machine made gurgling noises and dripped into the carafe, she cut wedges of pie, warmed them in the microwave, and found cheddar cheese to slice and place beside the pie.

She carried these into Red's office. "This will make your mouth melt," she said, placing the two plates on the coffee table. "I'll be right back with the coffee."

He was sitting in his favorite leather chair, the fire's flames dancing shadows across the room. Cat sat on the sofa on the other side of the coffee table.

They were silent as they ate. Cat liked the sound of the fire.

"Just another week until Christmas," she said as though this might be news to Red.

He licked his fingers and placed the plate on the table. Then he got up and walked over to the window, peering into the darkness.

Cat waited.

Finally, he turned toward the room, glancing into the fire, not at her. "If you need help setting up a tax business, let me know."

"I'm not ready," she said, disappointed that this was to be the conversation. "I can't focus on anything aside from the trial. I can't let anything interfere with my concentration."

"I understand."

She willed him to look at her, but he didn't. He walked over and picked up the coffee mug from the table, and asked, "Is there anything you want to watch on TV?"

She sighed. They were strangers. For the first time since they'd met two and a half years ago she did not find comfort in Red's company. "No," she said, "I guess I'll go upstairs and wrap Christmas presents."

"Good night," he said, not even waiting for her to get up.

Oh, damn. Damn damn.

Forty-four

Two days before Christmas Cat drove April Martin out to the Claypools'. She'd phoned Samuel, so he was prepared for them.

"I've never met a real Indian before," April said.

Cat laughed. "Mr. Claypool is a fascinating, though not terribly talkative, man. He's a world-renowned breeder of Appaloosas; people come from as far away as Texas and Virginia for his horses. And he's famous in these parts as a shaman . . ."

"Oh, I know. It's sort of New Age, isn't it?"

"New Age has adopted old age in many ways. Mr. Claypool can get into you, as can his son, Joseph. He can rid you of demons that make you ill or that cause you distress psychologically."

"My God, he should be a millionaire."

Cat shook her head. "He doesn't do it for money. And only if you truly believe. He doesn't go around broadcasting it. It's what's come between his son and my sister-in-law." She explained about Torie and Joseph and was barely finished when they came in sight of the little ranch house in the shadow of the mountains.

A dozen horses were in various paddocks, and Samuel was in one of them, a young horse on a lead, trotting around in a circle.

Cat pulled up outside the fence and sat watching him a few moments.

"His horses are pretty expensive for a novice," she told April, "but I thought he might give you some advice about where to look for horses that would be appropriate for your boys."

"How much are his?"

"They start at ten thousand."

"Oh, my. I don't think I'm up to that. I thought horses were a few hundred, maybe five or six."

"He can tell you where to find ones in that price range that'll be good for beginners," Cat said. "Come on."

Samuel stopped what he was doing and walked over to them. Cat introduced him to her new friend.

"I haven't seen Joseph in ages."

"He comes out to Sunday dinner usually," Samuel said. Cat admired his leathery face with its high cheekbones, his bottomless black eyes. One could never read them, never tell what he was thinking. He seldom smiled, though there was a warmth about him that made her feel comfortable. She imagined his patients trusted him. She'd like him better if he didn't stand in the way of Torie's happiness, though she thought that was mainly Torie's and Joseph's fault for not defying him. She'd have upped and married Joseph long ago, if it had been her.

"I wouldn't mind teaching three teenage boys to ride," Samuel said.

"That's more than I dared hope for," April allowed.

"It's winter. Things are slow. I can come to your place Saturday mornings or they can come over here if you've a horse trailer. They want to come out Saturdays and Sundays be fine with me," he offered. "I think I know where there's some fine horses that'd be right for them. Not all at the same place. But each should choose his own horse. Not get the first one they look at. I like teenage kids," he said. He was in charge of a 4-H horse group, Cat knew.

"I want to tell them they're getting horses for Christmas," April said. "They won't be able to stand it until they get them then."

Samuel nodded. "You at the Joslin place, did Cat say?"

"We'll be in as of tomorrow." The moving van was already in town, and April was paying for the drivers' motel while they waited for Mr. Joslin to vacate.

"You want, I'll come pick them up the morning after Christmas and take them around to look at horses."

April looked at Cat. "I'll be exhausted but they won't. Sure, Mr. Claypool, that'll be wonderful. I can't tell you how much I appreciate it."

"We may be gone a good part of the day," the Indian warned, scratching his ear.

"Later on, you can think of a nice gentle horse for me, but I don't have time to go looking now. I swear I'm never going to move again."

Samuel nodded. "Ten-thirty," he said.

When the women got back in the car, April said, "Hey, what is there about him that I'm ready to turn over my sons and my life to him. He's got some sort of quality . . ."

"You're not the first one to feel that."

"It's uncanny. Inexplicable. The boys will go out of their minds to think a full-blooded Indian is going to take them around to look at horses." She was smiling broadly. "Do you know what a thrill it is to know they're going to get such pleasure from this?"

"I'm surprised Mr. Claypool volunteered to teach them, though he does have a knack with young people. They act as though he's a Pied Piper. You know what he'll do? He'll psych out your boys and know exactly the right horse for each of them."

"He looks like he belongs in a John Wayne movie."

"He's one of the most respected people in these parts."

"I suspect the best thing that's happened to me, including buying the Joslin place, is meeting you, Cat."

"I'm glad. I like you, too."

Cat already knew what she wanted to give April for Christmas. Jason.

Sir Geoffrey and his sister had arrived by the time Cat reached home. She really had been too busy to take April out to the Claypools', but then everything about this season made one too busy. Red and Miss Jenny had flown to Portland the day before to pick up the British lord and his sister, Amelia, who was ensconced in a guest room by the time Cat reached home, in time for one o'clock lunch.

Amelia looked like her brother, tall, gray-haired, thin, with an elegance only the upper-class British conveyed. Her accent outdid the Queen's.

"I think it's simply mahvelous," she cooed, "to be in the American West for Christmas, even if my children will never forgive me."

She looked around the immense living room. "Really, it's rather grand. I hadn't expected this. And those mountains are rather a majestic backdrop.

"Sir Geoffrey and Jenny will be down for lunch as soon as he's unpacked," she told Cat.

Cat and Thelma had decided that a soufflé would be perfect for lunch. Thelma had called her cousin to help while the company was there.

"We're going to decorate the tree tonight," Cat told Amelia. "We waited, thinking you might enjoy that."

Red and his foreman, Glenn, had already set the ten-foot tree up in the living room. Invisible wires held it straight. Red had scouted the woods for at least six weeks before he found the perfect tree.

Cat had spent days wrapping the presents, which had been arriving daily from L. L. Bean, Eddie Bauer, Lands' End, and other catalog houses. She'd had a terrible time buying for Jason, trying to find something that wouldn't be a letdown after the last two Christmases but still would not be so personal. She hadn't been alone with him in over three weeks. He'd phoned every night and talked for over half an hour, but she'd been able to avoid him without hurting his feelings.

Sarah glided down the stairs, dressed as she hadn't been since Cat couldn't remember when. Since Scott died, perhaps. She wore burgundy gabardine slacks with a pale gray silk blouse that clung to her, showing what a wonderful figure she still had at nearly fifty. She had done wonders with her hair, which haloed her head with its dramatic gray streak accentuating its blackness. She looked as beautiful as when Cat had first met her.

Now, if she just wouldn't drink and be blotto by the end of lunch, Cat thought. But Cat had stopped being embarrassed by her, as Red and Miss Jenny had, long ago.

She could tell that Amelia was enchanted with Sarah. Sarah offered her wine and the two walked over to the long sofa in front of the fireplace. Cat heard Amelia invite Sarah to visit her in England. "May would be the perfect time to see the gardens," she said.

Sure, Sarah in England in May.

Cat went to find Matt and feed him in the kitchen.

"If Jenny's not here in fifteen minutes, the soufflé's going to fall flat."

Cat picked up the phone just as they heard the front door open and much laughter.

"She's here."

"It's a good thing," Thelma said.

Cat took Matt up to bed for his nap and came down to find the company seated in the dining room. Sir Geoffrey jumped up to pull out her chair, kissing her on the cheek. "So good to see you again."

He really was elegant. Certainly no one else in the whole valley would wear an ascot. Cat had the distinct feeling he felt at home wherever he was.

She looked up at the end of the table and was happy to notice that

Red was involved in conversation with Amelia, and that his eyes shone and his conversation was animated. He had been so subdued lately that she hardly knew him. Why had one kiss come between them, destroying the most satisfactory relationship she'd ever known?

Sir Geoffrey and Amelia were obviously enjoying themselves, tramping in the woods, drinking cider, and as Amelia said, she was "far more comfortable here than at home where we have no central heating. Maybe I'll just stay all winter."

Though with company present Sarah dressed with infinite care, applied makeup attentively, and took great care with her hair, it did not take Amelia long to figure out that talking with Sarah was a difficult chore. Fortunately there were so many people around and so much to do that Cat and Red had no time alone. Evenings, Cat deliberately went up to bed when Amelia did.

Christmas went without a hitch. Cat had to admit that part of her pleasure was being the hostess in what had become *her* home. She was so busy making sure that everyone was enjoying themselves, running in and out of the kitchen, that she could almost ignore the tension between her and Red.

His gift to her was a small box, tied with an enormous red ribbon that was at least six times the size of the box itself, which was filled with seed packets. All she could think of was whether or not she'd be here to enjoy seeing the results of any seeds she might now plant. "They promised that the greenhouse will arrive tomorrow and be up and ready for use by New Year's," he told her.

When he opened the cappuccino maker he paid more attention to the card than the gift itself, she could tell. He raised his eyes to meet hers across the room and nodded his head. The card read, "To many more Sunday breakfasts."

But they avoided each other. All day. They did not pass close to each other, took no chance of elbows touching; they stayed on opposite sides of rooms, they entered into conversations that excluded each other. Cat was surprised no one noticed. She wondered if Red was as aware of it every minute as she was.

The three teenage Martin boys had fine manners, and if they were bored, they never showed it. Red took them out to the barn, and told them when it really began to snow he'd be glad to load the snowmobiles on his truck and take them up in the forest where there were paths to ride on. Cat smiled. They might think Cougar was quaint but they must also feel they'd found the real West. April told her the boys could hardly wait to meet Mr. Claypool and find horses.

"You'll need hay," Red said, overhearing the conversation. "You'll also need that barn at Joslin's cleaned out. I'll send a couple of my hands over this week to help, if you'd like. Work's slow at this time of year, but I keep them on and try to find work year-round. I'll send some hay over, too. If I do say so, we have some of the finest you'll find anywhere."

"That's awfully nice of you. I'll be glad to buy hay from you." Her sons were all helping Cody with an Erector set.

"Nice boys," Red said.

"I know." Her smile dazzled.

Cat sat her next to Jason, and was pleased to see all their sons together, despite the age difference. April's blond hair hung loosely on her shoulders, and her robin's-egg blue sweater matched her eyes. The sweater was loose and long but couldn't hide her svelte figure. She was softer than Cat. Her voice was husky and her eyes focused only on you when you talked with her. Cat hoped this all wouldn't be lost on Jason.

The big shocker was a string of pearls with which Sir Geoffrey presented Miss Jenny.

"It was our mother's," Amelia said.

It was also his first wife's, and Cat wondered if this meant that he expected Jenny to be his second one.

She glanced to see Red's face reflecting pleasure at his mother's happiness.

"Geoffrey's going to stay here through January," Miss Jenny announced. "And we'd be most happy if you do, too, Amelia."

"I just might," Amelia responded, raising her wineglass to Jenny. "If they can put up with me here, I may stay longer than that."

Cat sent Thelma home without letting her do the dishes or even clear the table. She told Red, "I'll clean up while you feed the horses."

It was after eight by the time everyone had gone. Amelia said, "If you won't think it's rude, I'll go upstairs, too." As Sarah had. There was a TV in her bedroom and she loved American TV. "It's been quite an exhausting day."

"It has been that."

Cat cleared the table and filled the dishwasher and still had several loads piled up on the counter.

The moonlight spread over the frozen ground. She opened the kitchen door and walked down the back porch steps, trying to see the moon, hugging herself to keep warm. There it was, not quite full, behind the big spreading tree whose bare branches were framed against the white orb. She shivered with cold or with the beauty of the moment, she didn't know which.

"That you, Cat?" She saw Red silhouetted against the white background. He stamped his feet to kick the snow off his boots. "You'll catch a chill."

He leaned down to take off his boots.

"My father called," she said, "to wish me Merry Christmas."

"I'm glad."

"He said he and his family are coming west on a camping trip next July, and he wonders if we can put them up." She laughed. "He has no idea how many bedrooms we have. He said they can put up a tent and sleep on the lawn."

There was just a moment's hesitation. "Will that please you?"

"I don't know. I would like him to see this place. I haven't seen him in over three years. He has a baby younger than Matt, you know."

Red knew. "How old is he?"

"Fifty-three."

"Fifty-three. Your father is just three years older than I am."

He walked up the steps and stood looking down at her for a moment before he passed on into the kitchen. She felt her heart thumping in her chest, wondering if he had heard it as he passed by.

Come summer she might not even be here to show her father the Big Piney. She and Matt might be downtown in a little house. She might not even be in Cougar at all.

She wouldn't let herself take the time to think of all the complications one kiss had brought on. She'd have to wait until after the trial. One thing she was aware of. Ever since that night she lost patience more easily with Sarah, even if she hid the fact.

She hugged herself tightly as she turned to go in from the cold.

It was an enormous problem, one that was creating a chasm between her and the man she was afraid to admit she loved.

Forty-five

Amelia became Cat's security blanket. She was always there evenings so that Red and Cat had no time alone. When Amelia announced it was time for her to go to bed, Cat said, "Me too."

Cat found Amelia delightful company. She was a witty conversationalist, she was interested in everything, especially the new greenhouse. Gardening had been one of Amelia's lifelong hobbies.

"Would you mind terribly if I pot around in there a bit?" Evenings she and Cat spent an hour or so under the bright lights, planting seeds and discussing life in general. It was obvious that Amelia was thoroughly enjoying herself. "I hope I'm not a bother," she said one evening.

"You're no trouble, if that's what you mean, and it must be obvious we enjoy your company."

"Well, you know, I never have understood the lure of America, why half the world wants to emigrate here. I'd spent time, of course, in New York, and one winter in Florida, and I've been to Los Angeles and a week in San Francisco, but Gad, the idea of spending a lifetime in America has appalled me. Until now."

"You've charmed everyone, you must know that. You walk down the street of Cougar, and you know half the people already." To alleviate the awkwardness she felt inside, Cat had invited Amelia to join her and Jason and Red for their Thursday morning breakfasts. Amelia moved into Rocky's as though she'd been destined for it.

Not on Thursdays, but once or twice a week, she came into town with her brother and Miss Jenny, and they ate lunch at Rocky's with Cat. And with whoever else happened to be there. Jason sometimes. April a couple of times.

Thanks to never being alone, Cat and Red managed to act as they had in the days of their old camaraderie. Only the two of them knew there was an undercurrent, that something was different.

Cat would be in the middle of preparing for Lucy's trial, even going over and over details with Lucy, and that question she couldn't stop asking surfaced. Why would one kiss change the whole dynamics of their relationship? Why could they no longer even look directly at each other?

Though she could hardly wait for five-thirty, when Red would appear for drinks before dinner, she also dreaded that time. Her heart pounded in her chest as she walked down the stairs, hoping he might already be there, sure that she would see him, be in the same room with him, feel him even if he did not touch her. On the other hand, the wonderful feeling she used to have of belonging, of being part of the family, the comfort and coziness that she had so loved, was gone. She felt as though she were on stage, pretending. She knew she couldn't go on like this. But she also told herself that moving was out of the question until after the trial. In the spring, perhaps.

She did begin to look at "For Sale" signs on the little houses in town, but she asked herself over and over if it mightn't be smarter to move to someplace far away. Remove herself from the tension, the temptation.

She had no idea at all what Red felt. And she used to be able to tell from the look in his eyes what he might be thinking. She used to feel the warmth he emanated across a room, she used to be able to laugh a lot.

At the dinner table every night, though, Red asked about her day, interested in what was happening in her preparations for the trial. She could tell he sincerely cared, he really wanted to know what she was doing. In this way they could have personal conversation in public and be safe.

Cat knew why she wouldn't let herself think about the situation with Red: There was no possible solution. There was only escape. She sensed what she did not want to know: that she would have to give up this life, give up this family. She could never admit her love, even to Red.

"I'm going to have to plead insanity."

"She's not insane!" Red protested.

"I'm pleading temporary insanity because of his actions. I don't think it's an exaggeration. I can't plead self-defense. She wasn't afraid he was going to kill her, but she had been afraid of that other times.

You know, all the things he did to her and then finally to her son aren't justifiable reasons for killing him. Not according to the law."

Red studied Cat. "You're afraid you're going to lose and she's going to jail, aren't you?"

"The law is on the side of the husband and always has been. A man can do anything he wants to his wife and get away with it. Remember the movies from the thirties and forties when a man would spank a woman for not behaving!

"No, I have to show Lucy's action was the result of years of abuse until she was out of her mind, at least when she killed him."

Red studied her, drumming his fingers on his desk.

"Fortunately, the district attorney's office is sympathetic and will give me as much leeway as they possibly can."

"How do you know that?"

Cat smiled. "They've assigned a woman to prosecute. And I happen to know her. She won't charge into it like many men might. I suspect she'll go by the letter of the law and not a bit farther."

"So, you are hopeful."

"I'm indignant. The more Lucy tells me, and bits keep coming out, the angrier I get. The more research I do on battered women and the women who have killed the men who have abused them, the angrier I get." Her voice was icy.

"Why don't these women leave?"

"Red, they can't. Unless they uproot themselves and their children and move to some strange city and take on a different name, they're not safe. These abusive men consider them still their property, and are driven wild that the woman has left."

Red's voice was slow as he asked, "What about in the beginning? Don't these women sense the violence in their men?"

"Almost always, from reports, the relationships start out romantically, gently, even tenderly. The woman mistakes his obsessive desire for sex as affection. My research indicates Lucy's a classic example of an abused wife. A killer can be in denial, either telling himself he didn't commit the crime or justifying it in his own mind, saying she deserved it, that she was unfaithful, that she was a whore, that she didn't clean the house well enough, or whatever. So they can take lie detector tests and since they're lying to themselves can pass a test swimmingly. Their consciences don't bother them. Their repeated violence has dehumanized them. Perhaps at the first beating they're conscience- and grief-stricken, but their repeated bestial behavior removes compassion and humanity from them. Somehow they just want to justify it to themselves. There are many cases where the wives have been treated even worse than Lucy. I've come to think there's a victim personality."

Red smiled, and, for the first in a long time, their eyes met. "You don't have it."

Cat laughed. "I think that's pretty obvious."

She looked at him and thought about that. She might not be a victim, but she was a prisoner. A prisoner of her love for him. And she didn't know quite what to do about it. Maybe she should marry Jason. Call him tonight and tell him that as soon as the trial was over she and Matt would move in with him and Cody and they'd be a family. Certainly there were worse ways to live out her life.

But could she do that to Jason?

Perhaps loving him would come with time.

Before she went to bed she did phone him. "Just thought I'd call to say I miss you."

She could hear the pleasure in his voice.

"I was beginning to give up hope. You don't want to come to my house some afternoon for a quick roll in the hay, so to speak, do you? God, I miss you."

"Actually," she said, "tomorrow at two would be just fine." She hoped the hour she'd spend with Jason would erase the desire that was consuming her.

Forty-six

"Hey, you've never been like this!" Jason exclaimed. "You're a regular wildcat. This was worth waiting for."

She lay beside him, staring at the ceiling.

He rolled off her and lay beside her, but she sat up and reached down on the floor for her panties.

"Must you leave right away?"

"Your son'll be home from school any minute," she said, standing up.

"God, you don't even give a guy time to savor the moment."

She smiled at him. "I think you savored quite well."

He reached out for her, but she was pulling on her slacks and searching for her sweater, which was halfway under the bed.

"That was nice, Jason," Cat told him.

It really had been. The whole time they'd been in bed together she hadn't thought of Red. Jason's kisses were Jason's kisses, and she responded hungrily, with a frenzy she and Jason had not shared before.

Now, maybe she could look Red in the eyes.

"I feel good," she told Jason. "You work wonders on my mental health."

"To say nothing of the physical." He smiled, still lying in bed looking up at her. She gazed down at him, thinking he was making love with two women, and she idly wondered if there had been passion involved with Dodie, if he had felt the excitement she and he had shared.

Well, she had just had very satisfactory sex with him, and she didn't love him. She had enjoyed his kisses, his caresses, the passion that was now spent. She could manage to spend the rest of her life with a man who pleased her in bed this much. And he was one of the nicest people she'd ever known. For just a fleeting moment she almost told him she'd marry him. That would solve all sorts of dilemmas, wouldn't it? She could have a very nice life with Jason. He'd volunteered to be a father to Matt, and she loved Cody. They could have a couple of other children. She'd like more kids. They both loved Cougar Valley.

He held her close and kissed her good-bye. "I could get addicted to this."

"It was nice, wasn't it?" she said, slipping from his embrace and opening the door.

"Geoff's leaving next week," Amelia told them at dinner.

Cat looked down the table, and said, "From the tone of your voice I get the idea you wouldn't mind staying on here for a bit."

Amelia leaned forward, "Only if you wouldn't mind. It may be cold outside here, but it's warm inside, and I don't mean just the central heating."

Funny, Cat thought, it had been warmer every other year here.

"And I'd love to come see you at the trial," Amelia went on.

"That is, if it wouldn't embarrass you."

Cat made a face. "Trial lawyers have to have some of the ham in them. I won't mind an audience at all."

"I thought you hinted I'm not welcome," Red said.

"I think *you* might make me nervous."

She could sense they were embarking on a conversation that no one else at the table would understand, and one they daren't have in private.

"So, I make you nervous?"

"I—I guess at times you do." *Like when you kiss me.*

"See," Sarah chimed in. "I'm not the only one."

Amelia threw her hands in front of her. "Oh, dear, I didn't mean to start anything."

"You're not," Cat said, turning to Red again. "You can come if you want. I thought you might be bored."

"You think I'll be let down," he said. His eyes had not left her face. "You think I think you'll be better than you're afraid you'll be."

Was that it?

"It's a small courthouse," Cat said.

"I won't come if you'd rather I didn't," Red said. "But know that

I'd like to be there for any support you might need." Then he added, "I'd like to see you in action."

Cat turned back to Amelia and changed the topic back to Amelia's original question. "You're more than welcome to stay. We enjoy your company. And if your brother's leaving, I'm sure Miss Jenny will enjoy it, too."

"It will give me a chance to get to know her without my brother around," Amelia said. "I'd love to stay on if I'm no bother."

"Besides"—Cat smiled fondly at her—"I'm going to be too busy to transplant all those little seedlings that are beginning to poke their heads up."

"I thought of that," Amelia said. "I thought if I'm staying a bit longer that maybe they could use me in the library an afternoon a week or so."

"I'm sure we can," Cat said. "That's awfully nice of you."

"I love libraries," Amelia said, already having made good use of Cougar's pride and joy. "And, in case you can't tell, I love it here."

"You're a pleasure to have," Cat said. *And you make it so safe from Red.*

Forty-seven

"Now, tell us of the events leading up to your killing your husband. Take your time. Start with the first instance, if you can remember."

"It was five years ago," Lucy said.

The prosecution lawyer stood. "Your Honor, what happened five years ago has nothing to do with a death four months ago."

"We'll find out, shall we?" the judge asked. He was in his sixties, a small spare bald man who looked as though he were ready to fall asleep. Indeed, by afternoon, he always listened to cases with his eyes closed, and whether he was asleep or just resting his eyes was a moot question. But since he had a razor-sharp mind and a photographic memory, people assumed he was resting his eyes because he could repeat his trials almost verbatim.

The woman from the district attorney's office sat down, seemingly not at all dismayed.

"Go on," Cat urged.

"He was so sweet. He was nice to Ricky, too. When we was courtin' he told me Ricky would be like a son to him. He adopted him, too, soon's we were married. He used to bring me flowers, for no reason at all."

A vague smile crossed Lucy's face.

"I knew he drank, I knew that when we got married, but so did everyone else I know.

"I didn't think much about it, until we'd been married about six months. We'd been over to Copperton one night, at the bar there, where he was playing pool and I was dancing. They had a live band Friday nights. Pete didn't like to dance. Probably 'cause he never learned how, and he wouldn't let me teach him nothing. He had to be the one who was better at everything, which was okay with me. So, while he was playing pool I danced my fool head off. There was some guy there who had never been there before, and I haven't seen him since, and we danced near every dance. I had such a good time. All the way home, Pete was silent, which didn't bother me at all. I was sort of falling asleep I'd been exercising so, and we pulled up in front of our house, and as I got out of the car, Pete stood there in front of me, a funny look on his face, and his left arm drew back and before I knew it he'd hit me so hard I sprawled to the ground. I lay there wondering what had happened while he went on into the house. I picked myself up, my cheek hurting and followed, asking him, 'What was that all about?' but he didn't even answer. He walked right back to the kitchen and found a beer in the fridge, and took the cap off with his teeth, I remember. I stood in the doorway, thinking he must be drunk, though he didn't drive funny on the way home.

"Suddenly he looked up at me, with such anger in his eyes I was shocked.

" 'You ever throw yourself at a man like that again, I'll kill you.'

"I stood stock still, so surprised I couldn't believe he was thinking that way.

" 'I was just dancin',' I said, though I realize now I shouldn't have said anything.

"He was across the room in a second, grabbing my arm and twisting it so that I yelled.

" 'Yeah, sure.' His face was about an inch from mine. 'I know what your body close to him does to a man. I saw you rubbin' against each other. You just think 'cause you're so goddamn pretty you can have any man you want, don't you? Well, kiddo, I got news for you. I'm all the man you need or will ever have. You want a man, you got him!'

"And he ripped the top of my dress right to shreds. My pretty new dress. I'd only worn it once before, to Jean Louise's wedding. He pushed me across the room, up against the wall, his knee between my legs, and he said, 'You're going to see what it's like,' but I squirmed out of his arms and ran for the stairs, which got him really mad. He grabbed me from behind, so I sprawled on the floor and he wouldn't let me up. He put his boot in the middle of my back, and he said, 'You want a man to rub against you, babe, you got it,' and he pulled down his pants and ripped my panties off and entered me from the back with such a thrust that I screamed in pain. He kept pushing in and out so that it didn't feel like sex as I'd known it but like he was punishing me. I tried not to cry out but the more I kept silent, crying real quiet like, the more he rammed into me, and finally he said, 'God damn it, tell me it hurts.'

"I was sobbing so hard I could hardly talk. He kept saying, 'Come on, tell me you aren't ever gonna let another man do this to you.'

"I promised.

"When he got off me and I got up, there was blood over my skirt, and I could hardly stand up straight from the pain. He didn't say anything, he just went upstairs to bed. I sat on the bottom step crying so bad I thought I wouldn't stop. I cleaned myself up, but I didn't go into the bedroom. I slept on the couch.

"In the morning he acted like nothing had happened. When I didn't say anything all during breakfast, he grinned, and said, 'What you so glum about today?'

"When he left for work, he kissed me on the cheek, and said, 'I'd sure like your special meat loaf for dinner, baby.'

"I hurt so much I had trouble walking. I didn't do much except to take care of Ricky.

"We never mentioned that again. I thought it was a one-time thing and by the next week my feelings were back to normal, but you can bet I didn't dance with anyone again, ever.

"Then a couple months later, he was late coming home from work. I had dinner all fixed, flowers on the table, and by the time he came home everything was cold. I could tell the minute he came in he'd been drinking, so I didn't even ask where he'd been. I'd just put Ricky to bed, thank goodness. I didn't suspect anything awful was going to happen, though. I could tell by the way Pete was silent that he was angry at something, so instead of complaining about his not coming home to dinner, I just said, 'Wait'll I heat your dinner up.'

"He stood in the kitchen doorway not saying a thing while I took the cold food from the fridge, and I heated it up in pans, and I said, 'This could all be done in about two minutes with a microwave.'

"Maybe I should have heard the silence, it was so thick. But I was busy with the pilot light on the gas stove, which most often didn't light easy. I had three little pans in which I was heating the food, they was that glass kind you can see into, and before I knew it, he'd grabbed my arm and swung me around to face him and his face was so full of anger I gasped. He slammed me against the fridge, and kept slapping me and my head kept bouncing against the door until I couldn't see straight. I don't think I made a sound I was so shocked. He let go of me and I slid to the floor, wondering if my vision was always going to be that way or if things would stop moving so. My head hurt so hard I could hardly think.

"I did hear the water boiling on the stove, and I crawled over to it and pulled myself up to turn the gas off, but he grabbed me again, and he took me by the hair and jerked me so I thought my neck would break.

"And then I felt this awful pain in my neck and I realized he was biting me. I yelled this time. I could feel his teeth and I could feel blood oozing down my neck and I was so scared I like to die.

" 'You ain't ever going to learn, are you?' He whispered, but it sounded loud as thunder to me.

"I didn't know what it was I was supposed to learn, but I didn't ask. I began to whimper, and he still had me by the hair, and the pain in my head was so bad I couldn't see anything. I began to cry, 'Please, Pete, please let go.'

"He jerked me around to face him, and he said, 'On your knees!'

"And he pushed me down so I was kneeling in front of him.

" 'Okay,' he said, unzipping his pants, 'that'll be your dinner.'

"I was really crying now, because he knew I hated that. Hated it so much. But he made me do it until he came in my mouth and then he let go of my hair. I spit it out, and he said, 'You're too goddamn good to swallow me, aren't you?' He laughed.

" 'I don't need no supper,' he said. 'I ate already.'

"And he went in and turned the TV on. I went into the bathroom and threw up. I stayed in there a long time, cleaning myself up, taking some aspirin to get rid of my headache. Finally Pete called out and asked what was taking me so long. 'Come on out here, baby and watch TV with me.' Just like nothing had happened.

"I said no, I was going to bed. He come up a little later, I was still awake and he got in bed next to me and began touching me all over, real gentle like and made love to me like nothing had happened earlier, tender and nice, but I just lay there. I couldn't relax, and I didn't want him to touch me. The pain in my head was so bad I thought maybe I was dying.

"Nothing happened for a couple of months, then, not until he came home one day and said, 'I got you a job.'

" 'A job?' I was surprised. When we got married he made me quit my job, which I liked a lot, serving lunches in the school cafeteria.

" 'Yeah. Mr. Bollinger wants a cleaning lady to clean the bank and the offices above it nights. From eight to midnight.'

He was all the time telling me I didn't clean the house good enough, so I was surprised he wanted me to go clean the bank. I hated cleaning, and he knew it. I only kept our house neat because he'd beat me if I didn't. But I didn't want to be out of the house nights. I wanted to stay home with Ricky. But I said, sure, I'd go clean the bank.

"Pete drove me to the bank every night, even though it's just a dozen blocks away, and he was there at midnight every night waiting for me. I didn't like him leaving Ricky alone, but that didn't make a difference.

"One night I came out at midnight and he wasn't there, so I started walking home. I wasn't scared. I never heard of anyone being attacked in Cougar. I was about a block from home when he came roaring up, gunning the motor, and I could just tell from the sound of it he'd left Ricky all alone and had been out drinking. He leaned out the window and screamed so loud all the neighbors could have heard, 'And who brought you this far? Did he let you out a block ago so I wouldn't see?' I just kept walking and he followed, shouting dirty words at me all the next block. I turned up the path to the house and something inside tied me in knots. I just knew he was going to hit me. I wished I could go anyplace but into that house.

"He was behind me, jumping out of the car and leaving the door open. He pulled my hair until I thought my neck snapped. He turned me around and punched me in the belly so hard I doubled over and let out a cry. He took me by the shoulders and began shaking me, hitting my head against the wall until I was seeing double and triple. He leaned down and right through my dress he bit my breast so hard I screamed bloody murder and later I saw there was blood on my dress. I still got that scar.

"He kept hitting my face until I don't know what happened. I passed out.

"When I came to he wasn't in sight. I hoped he'd gone, but he was up in bed. I could hardly crawl to the bathroom. I looked in the mirror and my face was already turning purple and green, sort of. My breast was stuck to my bra 'cause of the dried blood. I just hung over the side of the tub and cried and cried and cried until I didn't have any more tears."

The judge called a ten-minute recess. One of the jurors had to go to the bathroom. Cat bet it was to be sick.

"Can we cut some of this out?" the prosecutor whispered to Cat. "I mean just have her hit the highlights. Or the low lights, rather. I gather she can go on and on?"

"Indeed she can."

When the recess ended, Cat asked, "Did you ever see a doctor?"

"Pete wouldn't let me. I couldn't get up and go to work so he told Mr. Bollinger I was sick and wouldn't be back to work, I mean I guess he didn't want people to see me looking like I did, but I think something about my insides went out of whack, because I could hardly walk for days and my periods stopped. After about a week, he railed at me about staying in bed and not cooking, and so I crawled out to the kitchen and made myself stand up and fix meals.

"But when Pete left for work one morning I called my aunt Thelma and she called Dr. Whitley and he came by and told me I belonged in a hospital. But Pete wouldn't even want me to have seen the doctor. I wouldn't let him bandage me because that would have shown Pete I'd seen him."

Chazz would be a witness later.

Cat could tell from the look on several jurors' faces that this testimony was making its mark.

She asked Lucy to describe the various things Pete had done to her over the years.

"It got so he had trouble getting an erection unless he was hurting me. He raped me, but not the normal way. He raped me with zucchini and with carrots, and he stuck things up my behind until I hollered bloody murder.

"I left him. I went home to mama, in Idaho, but he came for me. He told me he'd take Ricky, and he told me he'd hide him where I'd never see him again, and he told me he'd kill my son, the son that was the son of a whore, conceived out of wedlock. He burned him with a cigarette once. Pulled down his pants and burned his butt. I'm ashamed to say I just stood there with my baby screaming bloody murder. I don't know why I didn't do something then. I don't know why I took it, but once he started in on Ricky, I knew I couldn't take it for much longer.

"I wanted to kill myself. I couldn't conceive of any other way of getting out of it, but I couldn't leave Ricky alone with Pete. I even thought of killing him, the baby, before I killed myself. I dreamed of ways to do it. But when it came down to it, I just couldn't kill my son.

"After one of these beatings, I called the sheriff. I'd a walked downtown to his office, but I couldn't walk. Jason, the sheriff that is, put out a warrant for Pete, a restraining order, that if he got near me or Ricky he'd go to jail. And he did go to jail. He claimed I couldn't keep him from his own home. He swore he'd kill me if I didn't get him out of jail. Swore he'd cut Ricky's head off. So I dropped it.

"Ricky and I ran away, to a shelter up in Pendleton that I heard of. But after six weeks we had to leave and there was no place to go, and Pete found us and we all went home. He was real sweet for a while, but I knew it wouldn't last. I wanted to send Ricky to my mother's, and I put him on a bus, my mother waiting at the other end, but Pete beat the bus to Boise and got him off and brung him home and whipped him so he was bloody. He didn't touch me that time, but he knew that hurt me worse than anything he could do to me.

"I woke up one night feeling something cold at my neck and Pete was on top of me with a knife at my throat. 'I heard you dreaming,' he whispered so low I could hardly hear him. 'I heard you dreaming of running away.'

"And he pulled the knife across my throat, but he didn't bring no blood.

"When he wanted sex, it was never tender and nice anymore. He made me lie on my stomach all the time and did it from the rear and almost always I was bloody. He'd say dirty words to me and bite my shoulder and dig his nails into my buttocks and I don't know what hell may be, but it can't be any worse than what living was for me."

"Tell us," Cat said, her voice so low the jury had to strain to hear her, "of the day you killed him."

Forty-eight

Cat was walking a tightrope.

What Lucy had told her was that she knew before Pete came home that day that she was going to kill him. If Cat was clever, the prosecution wouldn't even have a clue of that. It would seem like a spontaneous act of passion. Of self-defense, even. Certainly not with malice aforethought.

Lucy looked directly at Cat as she answered.

"I saw his car coming down the street, weaving back and forth, and I was scared. I knew it was going to be one of those days."

She had initially told Cat she knew she was going to kill him that day when she saw the car. She could tell from the way the car wove what was in store for her.

"He wasn't so drunk he couldn't talk, but he was angry, like he'd get at nothing in particular. I knew there was going to be hell to pay."

"Were you alone?" Cat asked.

It was at that moment she'd told Cat she sent Ricky out the back door, over to the neighbors, with the admonition not to come home til she called for him.

"You mean when Pete came in? I was alone, paring potatoes for dinner."

Ah, good. Lucy's remembered. She'd also told Cat she looked around for something to defend herself with, and she saw two Coke bottles in the fridge. While he was still in the driveway she emptied one into the sink and broke the top off. She wanted it within reach so when he came at her . . . "If he even touched me," Lucy had told Cat, "I was going to poke that jagged edge right into his neck." Cat held her breath. She wanted not even a hint of that heard in the courtroom.

"Go on," she told her client.

"Pete came in the kitchen and I remember my hand was shaking so bad I could hardly peel the potatoes."

"Why were you shaking?"

"I could tell, I just knew it was one of those days. And I felt I couldn't take it one more time. I could feel it comin', feel the pain already, and I wondered what he'd do this time."

Cat nodded her head. "And then what?"

"He came on out to the kitchen and didn't say anything. He got a beer from the fridge and came over to stand next to me while I was paring potatoes, and said, 'No kiss for the old man tonight?'

"I said, 'No,' and went on paring.

"She'd told Cat she waited for him to observe the broken coke bottle on the counter, but he hadn't even seen it.

"He grabbed me by the hair, I'm surprised I have any left, and turned my head around so my neck was like to snap and kissed me on the lips, real hard. Then he walked into the living room and turned the TV on, real loud. For a second, I thought maybe that was going to be all there was to it.

"I went on fixing dinner, but I could sense something coming."

"What do you mean?"

"After all those years, I had like a radar that knew when he was going to start something with me. It was like the terrible quiet before a summer storm, a terrible silence just before he lost everything, before he sort of went out of his mind. I stood there thinking it was almost more than I could bear. I couldn't stand one more bit of pain, one more beating, one more something strange shoved up inside me, one more time he'd gouge at my eyes or slap my face or kick me in the stomach."

"Were you afraid for your life?"

"It was more like I was afraid of life."

Lucy had told Cat she knew for sure she was going to kill him right then, in that silence that surrounded her. Maybe she'd known it as long ago as the night he brought Ricky back home from Boise.

"I could almost hear him making up his mind to come out to the kitchen and do something to me. It was like I could hear his mind clicking. I looked up and there he was standing in the doorway, filling it up, that look on his face . . ."

"What look?"

Lucy was silent for a whole minute, staring off into some unseen place.

"I don't know how to describe it. But I recognized it, and I knew I was in for it. There was a Coke bottle on the counter . . ."

. . . ready, just waiting, though for heaven's sake don't let the jury know that, Cat had said.

"I knew then that if he even so much as touched me, I was going to hit him with that bottle.

"He started toward me, and I said, 'Don't, Pete. Don't hit me again.'

"But he reached out and grabbed my hair, which is what he almost always did, and he threw me up against the refrigerator so that I dropped the knife in my hand or I'd have used that. He kicked me in the belly, and he said something, but I was in too much pain, doubled over with it, to even hear what he said.

"I dragged myself up, and he had gone back to the living room. I grabbed that Coke bottle and broke the top off in the sink."

So, it's a little out of chronological time, Cat rationalized. She didn't even feel guilty about it.

"I stood there, waiting. I didn't even light a fire under the potatoes. I just stood waiting."

"Waiting for what?"

"For him to come back in. I knew he would."

"Were you at any time afraid he'd kill you?"

Lucy shook her head.

"I'd been afraid of that other times. Some times I'd even hoped for it. But no, not that night. I was waiting for him to come back and do something to me so I could turn and use that jagged bottle on him.

"And he did, quicker than it takes me to tell you. He started toward me, and I felt blood trickling from my mouth and my stomach still hurt so bad where he'd kicked me, and I remember saying, 'You son of a bitch, now it's your turn,' and I recall the look of surprise in his eyes when my arm shot out with that Coke bottle and plunged into his neck. He dropped to the floor, blood gushing everyplace, and I was so scared he wasn't dead, was scared he'd come to and be mad at me, I reached for the paring knife and just kept jabbing it into him, everyplace.

"Blood spurted everywhere. The more it spurted, the more I stabbed. My feet were sticking to the floor in the pool forming."

"Did you know you stabbed him twelve times?"

"I don't know what I did. All I know is I wanted to make sure he was dead. Dead, dead, dead."

"What happened then?"

Lucy looked dazed, as though she had just gone through this again.

"I don't know."

"Do you remember calling the sheriff?"

"I don't remember."

"Do you remember Sheriff Fitzpatrick arriving and bringing you into jail?"

Lucy shook her head.

"What do you remember next?"

Lucy looked squarely at Cat.

"I remember you. I remember hearing the sheriff tell you I'd killed Pete."

"So until then you didn't even know what had happened? How did you feel when you heard what you'd done?"

Lucy shook her head again.

"I didn't think I could have done it, because I loved him, and women who love their husbands don't kill them, do they?"

Cat looked at the jury. "Do they?" she asked them.

"There's one farmer," Cat said at breakfast the next day, "who might be a holdout. That one in the back left, who always keeps a toothpick in his mouth."

"How can you tell?" Red was enjoying Thelma's omelet with the salsa she'd put up last summer.

"Something about him. I have the feeling he either thinks women have no right to try cases . . ."

"Whoa, what has that to do with guilt or not?"

Cat shrugged, sipping tea. She had only eaten toast. "If Marcia Clark hadn't alienated the jury with her aggressive manner, who knows what might have happened there? All sorts of things enter into a juror's decision. I'm desperately trying not to be as aggressive as I feel. Aggressive men are often admired but never an aggressive woman, and I don't want to estrange the jurors. Not even one. I think actually Lucy's words are all we need. Anyhow, I bet you dollars to donuts he's beaten his wife or at least wanted to. He's at least hit a woman."

Red laid down his fork and stared. "How can you be so certain?"

"I just have that feeling. Either he'll hold out because he's scared shitless at the thought of what beating a wife can lead to, or he'll never beat her again."

"Come on, Cat!"

She shrugged again. "We'll see."

"When is your summation?"

"It depends on the prosecution's summation. I'd love to have a day to prepare a rebuttal, but I don't think that'll happen. Can you read the judge's face?"

"Nope," Red said, resuming eating. "Nor any of the jurors except that one that keeps looking ill at Lucy's descriptions. You know there's reporters from *The Portland Oregonian* and *The Seattle Intelligencer,* don't you?"

Cat smiled. "Ed's saving me copies at the pharmacy. I'll pick them up on the way to court. Usually stories like this are in the back of the front section."

"I'll bet stories like this usually aren't covered by reporters from Portland and Seattle. Not in a place the size of this."

"Hey," Thelma called. "Get this."

Cat and Red looked at each other and got up and went to the kitchen. Thelma was eating breakfast in front of her small TV and there, large as life, was Cat talking to a reporter. They were too late to hear what the reporter said, and Cat's picture was replaced by one of a flood in India.

"That's a Portland station," Thelma said. As soon as she'd done the dishes she'd pick up Lucy and head to court.

Miss Jenny, who was dying to be in court, had volunteered to take care of Matt. "Greater love hath no great grandmother," she'd said.

"You don't have to come every day," Cat told Red.

He just looked at her. "Do you think wild horses could keep me away? Do you think I'd miss a minute of your big case? Of seeing you in action? In fact, I was going to suggest driving over there together this morning."

"I may be late getting home. You'll be bored."

"Number one, I doubt it. Number two, it won't be the first time, and I imagine not the last that I'd be bored. Number three, any amount of boredom is worth driving back and forth with you."

Cat smiled at him. She knew he had no idea what his words meant to her. She stood up, and said, "I'll be ready in twenty minutes."

"The car'll be out front."

"I'll tell Amelia to be ready."

Amelia, dressed in a brown-and-tan check suit and British walking shoes, was coming down the stairs. "I'm ready," she said brightly.

Cat walked up stairs to check her makeup and get her briefcase.

Red couldn't know she was at war with herself, trying to concentrate totally on this trial, yet kept awake nights, lying in bed filled with desire, fighting the urge to go to him. Wanting to feel his fingers touching her, his kisses, to lie naked with him . . . wanting him as she'd never wanted another man, not even his son. And yet she couldn't do anything. She knew that. He was a married man. He was her honorable father-in-law. He loved her, she knew that, but not in the way she felt about him. She used iron will to keep herself from thinking of him every minute, of not searching him out wherever he was.

Did Red lie awake nights thinking of her? Did he ever want to reach out and touch her? She wondered if he ever asked himself if, under other circumstances, he'd have allowed himself to fall in love with her.

While her head told her no, of course not, her heart screamed yes, yes, yes.

Forty-nine

. The jury had been out for three days and ten hours.

Both Jason and Chazz had been terrific witnesses for Lucy, but Lucy had not feared for her life on that particular day. Would the jury believe that all the abuse of the previous five years had led her to being out of her mind for the moments when she'd killed her husband?

Cat had been right about the prosecution. They had performed to the letter of the law but had not made it unnecessarily difficult for her. Carol Matthews was good, though, and Cat decided that after the trial here was someone she'd like to become friends with. A woman with whom she had much in common.

That is, someone to become friends with *if* she stayed around here.

Cat had been astonished to learn that not only had the big Portland and Seattle newspapers sent reporters, but CNN and *Time* magazine also had reporters covering the trial. CNN claimed that "This might be the fourth case in the United States wherein a woman who murdered her abusive husband gets off without a jail sentence," and went on to comment on Cat's ability—combined with her good looks and ingratiating manner.

This had stunned Cat. Not that Lucy might get off, but their analysis of her own work.

"Ingratiating," Miss Jenny smiled. "That's the word I used for you when you first came out here."

"I'd never have generated this kind of publicity with such a case in Boston," Cat said.

Lucy's testimony about her abuse had revolted the American public, and mesmerized them. The swollen jaws, the black eyes, the blood, the bestial sexual acts. She knew that several members of the jury had been revolted, too, but would they buy the temporary insanity plea? Hundreds of juries in such cases throughout the land had not.

Jason called Cat at eight, before she'd finished breakfast. "The jury's coming back," he told her.

Cat felt her chest tighten.

"Come on," Red said, when she told them. The two of them and Amelia drove to the courthouse, churning up slush on the still snowy roads.

The bailiff led Lucy in and Cat grasped her hand.

The jury walked back in. Every juror, except the farmer whom Cat mistrusted anyhow, looked at Lucy. Promising. But one was never sure.

The foreman handed a slip of paper to the bailiff, who walked across the courtroom and handed it to the judge. He glanced at it, and glanced back at the jury. He nodded.

"Will the defendant please rise?" When Lucy did so, the judge continued, "Mr. Foreman, what is your verdict?" he asked, already knowing their answer.

"It is the unanimous verdict of this jury that the defendant is not guilty by reason of temporary insanity."

Applause broke out in the small courtroom.

The judge banged the gavel. "Counselor," he said to Cat, "it is the opinion of this court that your client would benefit from psychological counseling. We feel that justice has already been served."

That was it.

Lucy stood there, dazed, while Cat hugged her. Reporters rushed to telephones.

"What does he mean psychological counseling? A mental hospital?"

"Goodness, no." Cat couldn't help smiling. "He just means it will help you get over the trauma of it all if you see a therapist. There's a good one in Baker. And I hear there's a great one in Pendleton. We'll talk about it later. No, Lucy, you're free as a bird."

Carol Matthews walked across the aisle, reaching out to shake Cat's hand. "Congratulations," she said, and suggested, "How about lunch sometime soon?"

"I'd like that," Cat said. "I'd like that a lot."

"We may have much to talk about."

They smiled at each other before Carol gathered up her papers and shoved them in her briefcase.

Cat turned to see Thelma with her arms around Lucy, tears streaming down her face.

"This calls for a celebration," Red said. "I'll take you to lunch."

Amelia stood at his elbow.

"To that nice restaurant where we had hamburgers?" Cat asked.

"But this time it's steak. Or I'll take you to the Top of the Mark if you want."

"You'd fly me to San Francisco?" she laughed.

"Come on," he said. It was still early, not quite twelve, but the restaurant would be open. "However, if we don't phone Ma immediately, she'll have a fit."

He found a phone in the courthouse and phoned Miss Jenny. There was no answer at the ranch.

They found out why as soon as they came down the courthouse steps. Miss Jenny's car was across the street, and she, with Matt in the backseat, was waiting for them.

"You don't think I could stand the suspense, do you?"

"Come on," Red said, "we're going to lunch to celebrate."

"You won!" Miss Jenny threw her arms around Cat.

Once they'd ordered lunch, Amelia said, "Now that the excitement is over, it's time for me to go home. But I hope you'll invite me back for Christmas."

"With or without Geoff, you're welcome," Miss Jenny said. "Though I'll see you in May when I come over there."

Red flew Amelia to Portland the next day. He had business he could attend to, and wouldn't be back until late the following afternoon.

Cat spent the entire day thinking. Now that the trial was over she had to do something about her emotions. Face them at least.

In the middle of the afternoon she drove, with Matt, up to Miss Jenny's. The two of them hadn't been alone together since before Christmas. She opened the door to the smell of gingerbread.

"Yoo-hoo," she called. "Want company?"

Miss Jenny came out from the kitchen, a smile across her face. "How nice!"

"I thought Matt could nap here if you'll give me coffee and a bit of talk."

"That's an offer I can't turn down. Put Matt either in my bed or on the couch, and come on into the kitchen. I'll put coffee on and I'm just baking gingerbread cookies."

Matt fell asleep on the couch, a half-eaten cookie clasped in his fist. Cat walked out to the kitchen where cookies were on wax paper the whole length of the kitchen counter. "Do you do this just for yourself?" she asked, biting into one.

"I thought I'd bring some down to the house," Miss Jenny said. "Well, how are you? You must feel exhausted now that the trial's over."

"I imagine it's a bit like the way an actor feels after a play's closing. A letdown. Extreme satisfaction, but no adrenaline pumping, nothing I have to think about today. No life hanging in the balance. Or at least none in my hands."

Miss Jenny poured coffee and hugged Cat as she put a cup in front of her. "I'm so proud of you. We're all proud of you."

Cat sighed. She wanted to take Miss Jenny into her confidence, to tell her she was thinking of moving into town. To tell her she was in love with Miss Jenny's son. With her own father-in-law. But she didn't. Instead, she asked, "You're really not going to marry Sir Geoffrey?"

"Darling"—Miss Jenny brought a plate of cookies to the table, took her apron off, and sat down—"I love my freedom. I've lived on my own terms for so long I don't think I want to spend the rest of my life compromising. And that's a major part of marriage. Don't get me wrong. I like Geoff's company and his attention. We laugh a lot. We travel well together. We like each other's families . . ."

"I really like Amelia."

"Yes, she wears well, doesn't she? Well, she fell in love with you, too. I look forward to seeing them again in May, but right now I want time to myself. I *like* being alone. My own company doesn't bore me, ever. Aren't I lucky? I want breathing time. I had a wonderful time with Geoff and with Amelia, but now I don't want to have to think of anyone else first. Just for a while, but I need that while."

Cat wondered if that came with age. She had no desire at all to be alone. She'd been alone all those years since her mother died until she'd met Scott. Now, the very thought of moving even as far as downtown saddened her. The notion of leaving Cougar, of going off to find some other town in which to live and work, panicked her. She didn't want to leave.

If she had her way she'd spend the rest of her life on the Big Piney. When Matt married, after Red retired, she would come up here to live in Miss Jenny's lodge and leave the big house to Matt and his family.

"The only wisdom life has taught me," Miss Jenny said, "I mean the only truism that holds up, is that whatever we are experiencing now will pass. Happiness, pain, loneliness, joy, misery—they, too, will pass. Nothing stays the same. Nothing."

"So that's what you wish to pass on to me."

Miss Jenny laughed. "We are sounding terribly solemn. No, I don't know if that's what I want to pass on to you at all. I just said it's the only wisdom I have. The only thing I have truly learned."

When Cat didn't say anything, Miss Jenny waved a hand in front of her eyes and cooed, "Yoo-hoo?"

Cat blinked and shook her head and looked at Miss Jenny.

"You suddenly looked miles away." She rested her arms on the table and leaned towards Cat. "Has it been the trial, or have you been troubled for another reason these last couple of months?"

"I don't know what you mean."

"Don't give me that bullshit," Miss Jenny said. "Just an honest answer."

"I've been consumed with the trial, worried that Lucy would go to jail and that . . ."

Miss Jenny nodded her head abruptly. "I understand all that, but there's been a sadness in your eyes. Not worry, but sadness."

Cat unexpectedly burst into tears. "The pressure . . ." She sobbed.

"Cat, you may be trying to fool yourself, but you're not kidding me. The pressure of a trial isn't what has you in this state. Look, if you don't want to talk about it, you don't have to, but, look girl, I love you. And I want you to know that whatever you do and whatever you feel is all right with me."

Cat wiped her nose with a tissue.

Miss Jenny reached out a hand to put around Cat's wrist. "Do you hear what I'm saying?"

Cat nodded.

"No," Miss Jenny said. "I mean do you understand what I'm really saying?"

Cat's eyes blanked.

"You don't want to marry Jason, and I know it. Does he?"

Cat shook her head.

"Look." Miss Jenny lowered her voice though there was no one to hear them. "Sometimes you just have to say to hell with society. Sometimes it's far more important to follow your heart than to do what seems acceptable.

"I don't know what you mean."

Miss Jenny snorted. "Oh, Cat, Cat, Cat. Well, after all, I suppose the one I should be saying this to is my son."

"Oh, Miss Jenny . . ."

The older woman held up a hand as though to stop Cat. "I'm sorry I brought it up. All I really want you to know is that I know you're aching, and I love you, and whatever you do is fine with me."

She stood up and went over to take another batch of cookies from the oven.

"I'm thinking of moving."

Miss Jenny dropped the aluminum tray and cookies scattered over the floor. She sucked her thumb. "Damn, I burned it."

"Well," Cat felt guilty. "Just downtown, I think."

They got down on their hands and knees to pick up the cookies. "Damn hot," Miss Jenny said. "This whole tray ruined."

She didn't look at Cat until she'd cleaned up the mess and run her fingers under cold water. Then she turned around, hands on hips, and said, "You're a fool."

"I've been looking at a couple of little houses that're for sale."

"What's that going to solve?"

"If it doesn't solve anything, I'll move farther away."

"What, so you won't have to see him every day? Jesus God Almighty, girl, are you making a unilateral decision?"

"What do you mean?"

"I mean have you two talked about this?"

"Oh, no!"

"Cat, look at me. Catherine McCullough, does he know how you feel?"

"Oh, Miss Jenny!"

"Do you know how he feels?"

"He's honorable, he's . . ."

"He's about due for some happiness. Cat, before you do anything foolish, talk to him. Talk to each other."

"Oh, Miss Jenny . . ."

"What? You're afraid he doesn't feel the same about you?" She came over and stood before Cat, putting her hands on her shoulders. "Don't you feel you owe it to yourself to find out? He's probably scared, if you'll pardon the expression, shitless thinking you don't feel that way. So you both clam up and behave in what you consider honorable ways because what you're really afraid of, each of you, is rejection."

Cat stared up at her grandmother-in-law. "Even if we talk, there are no solutions."

Miss Jenny sat beside Cat, taking the younger woman's hands in hers. "What you mean is you can't see a solution. Perhaps together you can find one."

Cat threw her arms around Miss Jenny's neck, unable to talk. Hardly able to swallow. Miss Jenny held her close and patted her back. "There, there."

When Cat left, half an hour later, Miss Jenny said, "Just promise me you won't leave, won't make an irrevocable decision until the two of you have talked. Leaving may be what you have to do, but don't make the decision alone, Cat. I beg you."

Fifty

Cat and Sarah ate dinner in near silence, though Sarah sang a bit. Snatches from an old song, "A Pretty Girl Is Like a Melody," but she'd forget the words and hum, and then sing another few words. Actually, Cat thought, she had a rather pretty voice.

Months ago Cat had told Thelma that as soon as she served dinner, she could leave, so she could spend evenings with her husband. Cat was happy to serve the dessert, clear the table, load the dishwasher. Thelma would have stayed until midnight. She would do anything in the world for Cat, and she made that perfectly clear.

Sarah wafted up to her room after dinner, glass in hand, and closed the door. Cat tucked Matt in for the night, and then went out to the greenhouse. Its bright lights lifted her spirits. She'd hardly done any work out there in the last month.

She sifted dirt, mixing it according to directions, putting it into the trays Red had ordered for her. She planted seeds of beefsteak and Roma red tomatoes, of dill and basil, tarragon and rosemary; thunbergia, bachelor buttons, asters, snapdragons, petunias. She labeled each tray, and lost herself in watering and planting each at the recommended depth. Already seedlings were appearing in the trays Amelia had planted. Before long they would need transplanting.

Miss Jenny was right. She had to talk to Red. But if she told him the truth, said, "I can't stay here because I'm in love with you," wouldn't he spend the rest of his life feeling guilty about that one kiss, guilty about misleading her? Wouldn't he kick himself for sending his grandson away? For putting an end to the chess playing, the laughter, the shared plans, the pleasant cozy evenings they'd spent together the last two years? He'd never forgive himself, she knew.

She mustn't tell him how she felt. She should hide it, see more of Jason. Marrying him wouldn't be fair to him—he deserved more than another wife who didn't love him completely—but maybe she could learn to love him.

She wished someone could tell her what to do.

She spent the next day in her office until three. Somehow, in just the two weeks since the trial, the number of clients trying to hire her had increased tenfold, and they all weren't from Cougar.

A woman from the Baker Republican Club visited her and asked what her politics were. She was obviously disappointed when Cat made it clear that she tried to decide each different issue on its own merits but that she knew she could never declare herself a Republican. Cat never did find out what the woman wanted.

Dodie, who was expecting her twins any day, told Cat that she'd heard talk that it was about time to elect a mayor, and wouldn't Cat be a good one? Cat wondered how Jason was taking Dodie's imminent delivery.

Cat and Jason had managed to make love twice since the trial. Cat went to him when her desire for Red drove her mad. She was not being fair to any of them and she knew it. She lay in bed those nights after she and Jason had spent their afternoons together, and knew, with a certainty, that though making love with Jason was eminently satisfactory, with Red she would soar to the heights. She knew it from the way her stomach flipped over every morning, every single morning, when she saw Red already at the dining table, reading the paper and drinking coffee, finishing his breakfast, glancing up at her, his eyes meeting hers before he glanced back at the paper. He was almost always there, but he left soon after she sat down. Her heart turned over when she saw him, even if it was ten times a day.

Now, with Amelia gone, there was no longer a safety valve. How could they spend evenings together?

When she drove home at three-thirty, the sun was still high. In a week daylight-saving time would begin and with it the long lazy daylight evenings she loved so well.

As she pulled up the driveway she noticed the first tulips peeking through the ground in front of the long porch, Red Emperors that Miss Jenny had planted years ago. The first harbingers of spring. Next month, daffodils and the first green-gold of willows. Then the hillsides would be dotted with dogwood blossoms.

Up by the barn she spied Red's jeep, which meant he was home. He'd left it at the hangar yesterday morning when he'd flown Amelia to Portland. She realized that she'd been relieved by his absence. There had been no tension in the house. Her heart hadn't thudded against her rib cage when she came down for breakfast this morning. As it was doing now.

She walked into the house to be greeted by Matt, who rushed to her, reaching his arms up to her. She picked him up and kissed him, smiling at Thelma.

Thelma shifted her feet around. "Got a minute, Cat?"

"If you've got coffee, I've got a minute."

"Not only that," Thelma said, "but sour cream cookies, too."

"Let me change my clothes and I'll be right down," Cat said. She yearned to get in jeans and a sweatshirt, out of her suit and heels.

By the time she came back downstairs, she could smell the freshly brewed coffee. Thelma refused to learn to use the cappuccino maker, and that was okay with Cat.

The still-warm cookies were piled high on a plate on the kitchen table. Cat sat in the chair and put Matt on her lap. He delved into the cookies.

Thelma went to the refrigerator and poured a cup of milk for him. "It's about Lucy," she said, her voice holding a tone of apology.

"Mm."

"She doesn't mean to seem ungrateful, because for the rest of our lives our family can never thank you enough, but she's got to find a regular job. Working here four or five hours a day isn't enough, and Tom and I feel it's time for us to be alone again. It's time for Lucy to strike out on her own."

"You're telling me we need to find a new baby-sitter, right?"

"You're not upset?"

"I might be if you weren't around the house all day, but with you here to see whoever we get treats Matt like we want . . ."

"Oh, thanks." Thelma breathed a sigh of relief. "Lucy was afraid to tell you. She wants to move to Boise, where there're more jobs. Maybe get a job in the Hewlett-Packard plant there. She wants to go someplace where no one knows her."

Cat shook her head. "I think that's fine. Do you have any ideas who we might get?"

"Myrna might come back if she can bring her baby. Let me think on it. Lucy's going to take the bus over to Boise to see about housing and a job and leave Ricky here, and certainly I can take care of Matt til we get someone. She just doesn't want you to think she's not grateful."

"I want her to promise she'll go to a therapist."

"Therapists cost money."

"I know. But maybe after she gets a job."

"Maybe." Thelma didn't sound convinced. Most people around here thought they should be able to solve their own problems, except when they were out of work. Then Uncle Sam should do it. Seeing a shrink meant you were unbalanced, weren't normal.

Cat wondered if Lucy would ever come to terms with killing Pete. If Ricky would learn what his mother had done and judge her. If any man who might be interested in her, upon learning that Lucy had stabbed her husband, would worry that one day Lucy might do him in and take off. Was Lucy doomed to a life of isolation?

"Tell Lucy not to worry," Cat said. "We'll find someone to take care of Matt. How come there's not a preschool in Cougar?"

Thelma laughed. "Now, how much business would it get? How many working women are there around here who have small kids?"

The back door opened as Thelma said this. Cat turned to see Red walk in, and she thought she'd never seen anyone look so good to her. His temples had turned grayer in the years she'd been here, but his mustache was the same color as his rusty hair. His blue eyes were the color of the sky when there was no haze in it. His big frame filled the doorway. He'd obviously changed clothes since arriving home for he wore his black-and-red-checked wool shirt and his ubiquitous boots. Both dogs were at his side.

"Smells good," he said.

Thelma went to the cupboard and took down Red's favorite mug, pouring coffee into it and the amount of milk he liked. "Here." She plunked it on the table.

Red looked at Cat. Their eyes met and held for so long that even Thelma noticed, coughing to break the trance. He didn't say anything, but pulled out a chair and sat down, reaching for his favorite cookies.

He grinned at Cat, which somehow surprised her. "Up in Portland and in Pendleton, where I spent part of the afternoon, women's groups are clamoring for you to run for the House," Red said.

"Huh?"

"You're making a name for yourself, someone fresh and new, someone who'll fight for women, someone . . ."

"A Democrat wouldn't stand a chance in this neck of the woods."

"Al Ullman did, for years."

"Never heard of him."

"He was before your time, I guess, but was defeated after years and years, in the eighties, I think. Doesn't seem so long ago to me."

"Me neither," said Thelma.

Go to Washington? Not that she dreamed she'd have a chance, but maybe that would be an answer to the Red dilemma. Three thousand miles between them. "I used to dream of doing that, but only after years of proving myself," Cat said, almost in a whisper.

"This is bigger country, fewer people, easier to get known. Anyhow, I have returned to report enthusiasm in political circles for Catherine McCullough."

"How did they know what party I belonged to?"

"Come on," Red said. "It's been very clear. Your ideas about women mainly, and the whole world knows now how you feel about that issue. About being a woman."

"How does anyone know how I feel about being a woman?"

Red didn't answer that. Thelma opened the lid of the pot in which her pot roast was cooking, and said, "Don't you dare let those cookies spoil your dinner tonight."

Cat stood up. "I think I'll take Matt out to the barn to see the new kittens."

As she left the kitchen, Red got up from the table and left the kitchen, too, but not to follow Cat outdoors.

It was the first evening since early December that Cat and Red had been alone in the house, with Sarah absorbed by the TV in her room and Matt asleep.

When Cat came downstairs, Red stuck his head out of his office, and said, "May I talk with you?"

Cat inhaled, feeling her stomach knot. Now was the time. She should tell him what was in her mind.

She walked down the hallway to his office, where a fire was blazing.

He stood in the middle of the room, in front of his big desk.

Her breathing stopped. Her heart stood still.

"Cat," he said, an arm outstretched, gesturing to the wing chair in front of the fireplace. "Please sit down. I have some things I have to say."

She couldn't stay in the same house with him. She couldn't. She wanted him too much.

"Let me say something first," she said as she walked over to the chair and seated herself.

He cocked his head, in surprise, and sat on his desk, arms folded in front of him, waiting.

"Red, I think I should move."

She could see his Adam's apple bob. A frown furrowed his forehead. He stood up and crossed the room, sitting in the chair opposite her, their legs inches from each other. He reached out to take her hands in his.

"Cat, I wouldn't have alienated you for the world."

"Oh, Red," she closed her eyes, feeling his hands surrounding hers. "It's not that. Just the opposite."

"Look at me," his voice was low, his hands tight around hers.

She opened her eyes.

"Cat, I love you. I love you to distraction. I love you so much that sometimes that very fact physically hurts me. I am in love with you like I've never loved anyone in my life."

What was he saying?

"At first," he continued, "I thought I was perverted. My daughter-in-law. My son's wife. Young enough to be my daughter. Your son is my grandson. I fought it. God knows how I battled it. But every day you become more a part of me, of the Big Piney. Every day I am more a father to your son than a grandfather."

"I know." Her voice was but a whisper.

"Cat, I want you. I want you beside me every day the rest of my life. I think you love me. I think you've fought it just as I have. I think you went to Jason so that you wouldn't yearn for me. I am that vain.

"Sh, don't say anything until I finish. Please. I've looked for solutions. Cat, I am going to divorce Sarah." He held up his hand to ward off any objections she might offer. "She doesn't know what the hell's going on in life anyhow. The only time she comes out of her room is for dinner. I'll buy her a house, and hire a full-time companion and cook. She will lack for nothing. I'll buy her the biggest TV in the world. That's all the companionship she needs. Cat, I've come to the conclusion that won't be nearly as unfair to her as this last twenty years has been to me. As living the rest of my life without you would be. I want you, Cat, and I want you to be my wife."

Cat stared at him, trying to absorb the words he had just hurled at her.

"You're happy here, I know you are," he said as though trying to convince himself. "You love puttering in the greenhouse, you want to improve the gardens, you take care of all the finances, I'm already making more money thanks to your investments. The women of this family, you and Ma, are the smart ones financially. I not only want you, Cat, I need you. I need your intelligence, I need your warmth, I need your company, I need your love, and, God knows, I need your body."

"Oh, Red."

He stood up, pulling her with him. "Tell me you love me. Tell me you love me as I do you."

She threw her arms around him. "Red, I love you so much I thought I'd have to leave just so being in the same room with you wouldn't torture me. I love you, Red, I love you, I . . ."

His mouth crushed hers, his arms encircling her so that she could feel the beating of his heart, could taste the coffee on his tongue, could breathe his breath.

Fifty-one

"We'll talk about it tomorrow," he whispered into her hair, then smiled as she tossed her head back and looked up at him.

"I thought that one kiss was just a temporary lapse on your part. I thought I'd have to leave."

"It was a lapse. It may have been the first time in my life that I couldn't govern my actions. But I couldn't help it. Cat, I have loved you for so long. I have been unable to fall asleep for thinking of you. I see you in the shadows of the moon. I smell your perfume before you even enter a room. I use iron willpower not to reach out and touch you."

His mouth pressed hers again, their tongues touching, passion unleashing itself.

"Does that door lock?" she asked. "It better." She smiled at him as she began to unbutton her sweater. "It jolly well better."

In a few strides he reached the door, closed it, locked it and turned, watching her as she slid out of her sweater, as she unhooked her bra and tossed it on the floor, standing, facing him.

"Jesus," he said. He walked to her. "Cat, I want you like I've never wanted a woman. Like I've never wanted anything."

She began to unbutton his shirt. His hands reached out to cup her breasts.

He shrugged out of his shirt and leaned over to kiss her breasts, gathering her in his arms, picking her up, cradling her as he walked to the couch. He laid her down and said, "Let me," as he slid her jeans off. He knelt beside her, kissing her—his tongue running over her breasts, his hands touching the insides of her thighs, his fingers caressing her.

"Come here," she said, unbuckling his belt. "Oh, Red, come to me."

He stood up and slipped out of his trousers.

"Talk of beautiful people," she said.

"Men aren't beautiful."

She smiled at him. "I think you're the most beautiful human being I ever saw."

She reached up to touch him and heard him moan. "Jesus God, I feel I've waited all my life for you."

"I think you've got me for the rest of your life."

How they'd work that out, how they wouldn't scandalize the town she wouldn't think of now. As he lay down on her, all thought fled her mind.

"Oh, my beloved. My dear, darling Catherine."

And then he stopped talking.

It was three when Cat went to bed, trailing her clothes behind her up the long staircase, naked as a jaybird, while Red stood at the foot of the stairs, watching her, a grin on his face.

As she climbed into bed, sliding between the sheets, she could not help but smile. He loved her. He had become her lover, and what a lover he was. He had taken her to heights she had never known, he was a considerate, passionate man. Neither Jason nor Scott had affected her as he did, had ever touched the wells of ecstasy that Red brought her.

Tomorrow, together, they would face the future. She would not let the reality of life dilute what had happened to her tonight. She fell asleep swearing she could still feel him inside her, could still inhale his breath.

Four hours later she awakened, hearing Matt making his cooing morning noises. The few hours of sleep had revived her. She laughed aloud, before gathering her robe around her and going into her son's room.

Half an hour later, still in her robe but with Matt freshly bathed and dressed, she went downstairs. She heard Thelma in the kitchen and the familiar beating of her heart against the walls of her chest began. But this time it was not with tension, it was with joy.

Red sat, looking as though he'd had eight hours of sleep, his coffee cup in one hand, the paper in the other, but the moment she appeared he looked up, and an expression she'd never seen before filled his eyes. Oh, darling, she wanted to say, using willpower not to walk over and kiss him.

"Good morning," he said, his eyes locked to hers.

"You're up early."

"Work to do."

Matt ran over and climbed onto his grandfather's lap. Red gave him a piece of toast spread with jam and kissed the top of his head.

Cat slipped into her chair, her throat tight at the beauty of Red and Matt together.

"I thought if you could get home early, I could quit work early, too," he said. And for Thelma's benefit, he went on, "I have an idea to discuss with you."

"Sure," she said, smiling as Thelma brought her orange juice.

When Thelma disappeared into the kitchen, Red's lips formed *I love you.*

"Me you too," she said in a low voice. When Thelma returned with Cat's oatmeal, Cat said, "Lucy's leaving us as of next week," and explained what Lucy's plans were.

As she dressed for work, tying the bow at the neck of her green blouse, she saw Red standing in the doorway to her bedroom. He had never even come to her bedroom except to read to her the week after Matt was born. When their eyes met in the mirror, he walked into the room and gathered her in his arms, kissing her until she moaned softly.

"I'll be home by two. At the latest."

"Okay," he said, letting her go. "I do have plans to discuss with you."

She kissed his neck. "Oh, Red, I'm so happy. I don't care what we have to go through. Just knowing you love me . . ."

"You might also know I told Norah before Christmas that she and I couldn't go on. I haven't seen her—that way—since then."

"Does she know why?"

"She does."

"Does she hate me?"

"She's ready to be your friend. I want to tell Ma, too."

Cat nodded.

"I think Ma will most likely not even be surprised. If you mean do I think she'll disapprove, no. Now, the town that's another thing. But"—he grinned—"they could use a bit of scandal. I can stand it if you can. It's not as though Sarah were one of their favorite characters, as you're on your way to being."

"I'll have to pinch myself all morning to believe this."

He leaned down and pinched her bottom. "There. Let me help."

"You know what, Mr. McCullough? I think we're going to have fun together."

The first thing she did when she got to town was turn down Jason's invitation for Saturday night. And for this afternoon. She'd have to find a way to break that off without alienating Jason. She wanted, needed, his friendship.

Somehow she'd have to pull away so that he was yearning for a woman and voilà! There was April. She'd have to thrust them together in some more obvious way. And quickly.

Her phone was ringing as she entered her office. It was Chazz. "Dodie's had twins," he said. "I delivered them at home. Two little girls. She'd love it if you'd stop in."

"I'll get over there right now, before I get involved with anything. When did this happen?"

"Two hours ago." There was pride in his voice. As though he were the actual father. She wondered if Jason knew yet. How was he going to feel? Dodie claimed that Jason and Chazz had drawn closer together. Well, human nature was funny. Would Jason have told her if she'd married him? Before? After? At all?

Cat put her jacket back on and thought since it was a day so filled with spring, since there was a bounce in her step, since she couldn't sit still, that she'd walk over to the Whitleys. Even though she'd only had four hours of sleep, the energy that surged through her was amazing.

Dodie was asleep, but Chazz told Cat she'd want to be awakened. "For you I'll wake her. Not for anyone else."

Dodie's eyes looked drugged, though a beatific smile covered her face, even asleep. Cat leaned down and kissed Dodie's forehead. Dodie reached out to grab her hand. "They're both girls," she summoned her energy to whisper.

Cat went over to the bassinets to look at the red-splotched pointed-head little girls. Out at the ranch she'd discovered that baby animals were always so much cuter than human babies. It took at least three days for human babies to look adorable. "They're beautiful," she said.

Chazz stood next to her, looking down on them as proudly as possible. Cat pointed to one of them. "That one looks like you," she said, though she knew the impossibility of such.

"You think so?" he asked, leaning down to study the baby.

"Well, sort of."

She didn't at all.

There had been four different showers for Dodie, but Cat had a special present for the babies. "If I'd known before I left home, I'd have brought their presents. It'll have to wait til tomorrow."

She almost wanted to tell Dodie about herself. She really felt like climbing up on a rooftop and shouting it to the world.

"Dodie's mother is on her way from Everett," Chazz said.

"I would guess you'll need help. Where are the other kids?"

"Ilene Pascal's taking care of them. They stayed next door overnight."

"Let me know if I can help."

"I think we have everything under control. You know, this birth wasn't like any of my others," Chazz said. "It was—I don't even know how to explain it, seeing my own children being born, bringing them into the world."

Cat kissed Chazz. Dodie had already fallen back asleep. "I'll drop in tomorrow," she said, not knowing that it would be four harrowing days before she'd see them again.

She hummed to herself as she walked back to the office. Though there were no signs of buds on trees yet, spring certainly was in the air. Crocuses sprouted on a couple of lawns, and there seemed to be more birds.

She knew there were still hurdles ahead. She and Red could solve them. Sarah really was out of it. She might not even know what was happening. But how would Cougar react to one of its leading citizens divorcing his wife of nearly thirty years to marry his daughter-in-law? Cat hoped Red would tell Miss Jenny soon. She had a feeling she could use Miss Jenny's guidance.

How would Torie react?

And Jason?

She couldn't concern herself with those problems yet. She and Red would talk this afternoon. They would also kiss, and hold each other close. All she knew for the moment was that she was exquisitely happy. She thought she might even be able to go on living at the house with Sarah there, with the town not knowing of their love, with sleeping with him, with sharing meals and ideas and always being together. Sarah wouldn't interfere. She spent her nights and most of her days in her room.

But she knew that was impossible. Red wouldn't let her live like that.

She hardly knew what she did all morning. Her mind was not on her work. Jason bopped his head in, asking, "Lunch?" Showing no outward emotion at being a new father today.

Cat shook her head. "I'm having baby-sitter problems. Thelma's taking care of Matt, and I promised to be home by lunchtime." A lie. But she might just as well leave town. She wasn't getting any work done. Her mind was out at the Big Piney.

She did arrive home in time for lunch. Red wasn't around, though his jeep was up at the barn. Cat put Matt down for a nap and stared out the window from her room. There was Red, riding his favorite horse. He'd cool it down, spend about fifteen minutes with it, and then head to the house. She knew that routine.

She ran down the stairs and, instead of going through the kitchen, ran out the front door, down the porch steps and rounded the house, heading to the barn. She stretched her arms into the air, laughing, feeling like spring itself.

Red was just removing the saddle and blanket from his horse when Cat burst into the barn and ran down the length of it.

He looked up when he heard her. He just stood there until she was nearly upon him, then he spread his arms out to welcome her. She ran into them, out of breath, her eyes dancing.

"I couldn't wait," she gasped, and then opened her mouth to his.

He held her as though he would never let her go.

"I've relived last night all morning," he said, when he did let go of her and turned back to cooling down his horse.

"Tell me again," she said.

He looked at her. "I love you. I shall love you forever. I think I have loved you forever."

She watched him with his horse. "Are you going to make love to me again tonight?"

He reached out to pull her close to him. "I don't know if I can wait that long."

Cat looked around, then ran into the tack room, returning with a horse blanket, which she tossed on a mound of hay. "Are you going to put your money where your mouth is?" She unzipped her jacket and tossed it to the ground.

"I better get this horse outside in a hurry," he said, grinning. "I am going to put my mouth someplace, but it'll have nothing to do with money."

Cat practically ripped her sweater off, tossing her bra into the air, and sliding out of her jeans.

"My God." Red shook his head, but she could tell he was delighted.

"You said you couldn't wait." She lay down on the blanket, waiting for him to undress. "I'm only trying to please you."

"Oh is that it?" He looked down at her. "Cat McCullough, you are the most beautiful thing I've ever seen."

"Come on." She smiled up at him.

He lowered himself beside her. "This is so new I can hardly believe it. You, out here in the hay."

"I always wondered what they meant by a roll in the hay."

"The last time I was naked in a barn I was seventeen," he said, laughing.

"It's a first for me," she said as he kissed her, his hand feathering across her stomach. "Did you even think about us doing this?"

He kissed her breasts, first the left and then the right. "Think about it? God, I dreamed about it. But it didn't quite equal this."

"Oh, Red, that feels wonderful. Can we do this every day?"

In answer, he said, "My darling, it's the tip of the iceberg."

"Iceberg?" She laughed.

Fifty-two

Matt was awake from his nap by the time Cat and Red arrived back at the house. It was difficult to keep smiles off their faces.

"You chilly?" They had been outdoors in the nippy air, naked all this time.

"Want some coffee?"

"Meet you in the living room?" Matt enjoyed playing there. "I have some ideas I'd like to toss around," Red said. "I'll light a fire."

Matt beat his mother to the living room. She brought two mugs of coffee, Red's black and hers with Half & Half. Thelma provided a tray of freshly baked lemon squares.

Matt rocked back and forth in his rocking chair, the pastry clutched in his hand.

"Cat, I'd like to tell Ma about us tonight."

She nodded.

"And I think the thing to do is talk to a psychiatrist about the best way to move Sarah, so she has the least trauma. I'd move her to a house on the Big Piney but I don't want you to have to . . ."

When Cat started to say something, Red waved his hand. "This is my responsibility. Look, days go by when she and I don't exchange a word. We haven't shared the same bedroom in over twenty years. She's getting stranger and . . ."

"I know that, Red. And I appreciate your wanting to make it as untraumatic for her as possible. It won't bother me to have her in a house near here."

"It would look mighty damn strange to the town."

He'd lived here all his life. Of course it mattered to him what the town thought. "What I'm saying is I don't yet know *how* this is going to be accomplished but it's going to be. I'll be damned if I will allow myself to feel guilty about it, either."

Then, he glanced abruptly at Cat. "You're young enough to be my daughter."

"We both know that. It hasn't stopped love from developing."

"I'll be an old man while you're still . . ."

"Stop," Cat said. "We know all about that. What matters to each of us is the time we do have together. Look, you talked the other day of groups suggesting I run for Congress. That *was* my dream. My goal. Well, all those things I thought I wanted, I find are not what I now value. What I want is here, all of it."

"Are you . . ."

"I can run for the House years from now if I decide to."

"How confused is Matt going to be being brought up as the son of his grandfather?"

Cat stood up and went to glance out the window, at the herds of cattle grazing in the greening fields, at the mountains far across the valley. In the distance she noticed a car turning off the blacktop and up their dirt road.

"Someone's coming," she said. Red walked over to stand beside her. They both watched the approaching car.

"By God," Red said. "I'd swear that looks like Torie's Explorer."

Sunlight danced off the vehicle's roof as it approached the house. It *was* Torie's car.

"In the middle of the week?" Red wondered. She hadn't been home since she'd left at the end of August.

Usually Torie raced up that road, but she'd been taking her time, and she came to a halt farther away from the house than was usual, down by the big tree instead of directly in front of the porch.

Red walked through the living room and the entrance hallway. He opened the front door and stood as though undecided as he watched Torie slide out of the truck, shading her hand across her eyes to ward off the glare of the sun. He began to trot down the steps, walking toward his daughter in long strides.

Cat traced his path to the front door and stood there. How peculiar to have Torie come driving home on a weekday afternoon in early April. She watched Red and Torie greet each other. He kissed her and hugged her close. They started to walk up toward the house, arms wound around each other. Cat walked down the steps.

The two women greeted each other with kisses and an embrace.

"Where's Mom?" Torie asked.

Red shook his head. "In her room, as usual."

"Good, I wanted to be able to tell you before I approach her."

Cat sensed something amiss. "Come on in. You want something to drink?"

Torie shook her head. "Wait, I have someone I want you to meet." She walked back to the car.

"I didn't see anyone else there," Red commented, standing next to Cat, his eyes following his daughter's movements. They watched Torie open the back door and reach in, pull something out that she held in her arms and start walking toward the house. As she neared them, Cat said, "My God, it looks like she's carrying a baby!"

She was.

"Daddy, please oh please don't have a fit," Torie said before they could see inside the blanket. "We just didn't know any other way to do it."

She walked up the steps to the two frozen figures and looked into her father's eyes. "This is your grandson," she said.

Red didn't look at the baby for a minute but studied Torie. "Joseph knows, of course."

"Oh, Daddy, of course. We decided that it's just too bad if Joseph can't continue to be a shaman, if his gift isn't used, because we can't live without living together. We deliberately conceived this child, and I went away so no one could stop us. Joseph's been to visit any number of weekends. He was there for the baby's birth two weeks ago, and now we can go tell his father that it's too late, that we can get married because the bloodline is already diluted." She said this with a rush as though she was afraid her father would interrupt.

Instead, he gathered her and the baby in his arms. "Honey, I wish I'd known."

"I almost did tell you, and only you."

"I'd have helped you do it a long time ago."

Torie's eyes filled with tears. "Oh, Daddy, I knew you'd react this way. You are always so reliable. My rock." She offered him the baby, and he cradled his arms as she put his grandson in them. He smiled down at the tiny creature, whose dark eyes were unfocused.

"We're going together to tell Mr. Claypool. We hope that when he sees his own flesh and blood . . ."

"Does Joseph know you're in town?"

She shook her head. "He knows I plan to arrive today. We talked on the phone last night when I reached Klamath Falls."

Red said to Cat. "Look, my second grandchild."

"And my first nephew," Cat said.

"We'll make him legitimate as soon as we tell Mr. Claypool. When Mr. Claypool sees him, maybe he'll forgive us."

"Come on in, it's chilly for him out here."

"I'm not staying here overnight," Torie said. "I'm getting a room at the motel, and Joseph will meet me there. I stopped by his office, but he was out in the field."

Red led the way into the house, holding the child.

Cat was still in shock and was surprised Red wasn't more so.

Red said, "So, you didn't go to California to teach at all."

"I've been lying to you all year, Daddy, and I hated doing it. But we've been desperate. After all these years Joseph and I just decided we had to be allowed to spend the rest of our lives together."

They headed to the warmth of the living room. Matt didn't even look up from his toys. Red set the baby on the couch.

"Mom'll have a shit fit, won't she?"

"Yup. But you're not to let that upset you."

"It's created a wedge between us for years."

"No." Red's voice was stern. "Don't do that to yourself. The wedge began before you can even remember, my dear. Your mother cannot influence how you live your life."

"Easy to say," Torie murmured, "but I've been trying to win her approval all my life."

"I know. But I don't think your mother approves of anything. Or maybe disapproves either. Though if it's one or the other, it's the latter."

Torie sighed. "You know she never came to one single game when I was a cheerleader."

"And since Scott's death, she's been even more unreachable."

Torie sighed and turned to Cat. "I read about you even in California. You're a full-fledged heroine."

Cat grinned. "It's a nice feeling." She walked over and put her arms around her sister-in-law. "Torie, you should have done this ages ago. I think it's wonderful. But I wish you hadn't had to be alone all year."

"What I felt bad about was having to lie."

"You wouldn't have had to lie to me."

"I know that, Daddy. I really do, but we decided not to tell any-body."

"Stay here," Red urged. "It doesn't matter what your mother thinks."

"No, Daddy. I want to spend tonight and every night the rest of my life with Joseph. I want us to start being a family."

"You're going to live here?"

"Probably not, Daddy. Joseph's applied for a transfer. He's asked the Forest Service for the next vacancy over at Steen's or down at Grants Pass. We think it's best not to live here."

Red put his arms around her again. "Just know that you are my darling girl and if there is anything in the world I can do to help . . ."

Torie threw her arms around him. "I know, Daddy. And I love you so much I can't even put it into words."

Just then, Sarah's voice floated in from the hall. "Where is everybody? It's over the yardarm, isn't it?"

She stood in the doorway, in her royal blue velveteen robe with its flowing sleeves, her arms outstretched, an empty glass in one hand. "Isn't anyone going to join me?" And then she noticed Torie. She cocked her head as though perplexed.

"Hello, Mom."

"Well, look what the cat dragged in. When did you get back?"

"Just now."

The baby took this minute to gurgle, awakening from his nap.

Sarah came farther into the room, peering onto the couch. When she saw the baby wrapped in his blanket, her hand went to her mouth; terror filled her eyes. She stood as though paralyzed, her eyes flying to Torie's.

"It's mine," the girl said defiantly. "Mine and Joseph's, Mom."

Sarah grabbed the back of the couch and slowly sank to the floor. "Oh, dear God in heaven," she whispered, "it's an abomination."

Her wail slid across the floor like a snake, slithering in waves that sent chills down Cat's spine. Sarah beat her fists on the floor, her eyes closed tight.

Red put an arm around Torie as the baby began to cry. Matt looked up in surprise, clapping his hands over his ears. Thelma came running in from the kitchen.

Red walked over to Sarah and bent down, slipping his hands under her arms, pulling her up. He shook her so that Cat thought the woman's teeth would rattle. It did quiet her. Sarah looked into Red's eyes, but he didn't think she saw him.

"Stop it." He shook her again, and even brought his hand back to slap her across the face. That got her attention.

"Sarah, stop it. This is our grandchild, and you will stop this."

Sarah stood up, knocked his arm from her shoulder, and walked over to the couch, peering down at the now-crying baby. "It looks just like that Indian," she said.

She turned to Torie. "I hope you don't think you're going to sleep under this roof. I hope you don't think I am going to condone your sin. Or that God will either."

Torie looked at her father, who walked over and gathered the baby in his arms. "Come on, let's go out to the car. I think you're right to stay at Shumway's. Call me after you and Joseph have talked to Samuel, and I'll come downtown, honey."

"Never again step foot in this house," Sarah said, her voice a monotone.

Red put an arm around Torie, who now held the baby, and guided her to the front door. "I don't even know his name," Red said.

Cat didn't hear Torie's answer as they walked across the porch and down the steps. She stood in the doorway, not wanting to return to the living room and Sarah. Matt had run upstairs, but he stood on the landing, halfway up the stairs.

"Come on down, honey. Grandma isn't going to scream again."

When he came down, he sidled over to his mother and reached for her hand. They waited for Red to return. When he did the three of them stood on the porch, not saying anything as they watched the car distance itself from the ranch, becoming an indistinguishable speck.

"Is Mr. Claypool going to be as bad?" Cat asked.

"I don't know," Red answered. "Fortunately he's not driven by Sarah's God of wrath. Come on, let's take the bull by the horns," and he continued, and led the way back to the living room.

"You don't have to come," Cat told her son, who let go of her hand and went running to the kitchen.

Red sat down in the chair opposite Sarah. "Sarah, I want you to listen to me and listen carefully."

She looked at him. "This is God's punishment."

Red couldn't keep irritation out of his voice. "For the life of me I've never been able to understand why parents blame themselves when their kids become pregnant. Look, Torie and Joseph have loved each other most of their lives. We should have talked about this a long time ago."

Sarah got up from the couch and walked over to the table where the liquor was kept. Red was behind her, grabbing her wrist. "You will NOT drink until you've heard me out."

"You don't even know," she said, her eyes coveting the bottle there.

"Sarah, you will never again act toward Torie like that. You will not make her feel guilty."

"She will never step into this house again."

"Years ago you relinquished the right to decide about anything that goes on in this house. This is Torie's home and always will be. She is welcome here anytime, with Joseph and with our grandson."

Sarah stood mute.

Red had never talked this harshly to her. Cat stood in the doorway, realizing that she was not a participant in any of this.

Suddenly Sarah turned wild eyes upon Cat. "Get out! Get out before you're contaminated, too. Go far away!"

Sarah reached out and grabbed the bottle of whiskey and began running from the room with it. They heard her shoes clattering on the stairs.

She didn't come downstairs for dinner.

"I want to go over there, to Claypools," Red said. "I want to reason with Samuel if that's what it takes. But they didn't ask me. I can't. I want to help Torie, and Joseph, too, for that matter. I'd have helped them all these past months if I could have."

"I know," Cat said. "And Torie knows it, too."

"Just knowing isn't helping."

"Let's go up and tell Miss Jenny."

"I'd completely forgotten Ma."

"Don't tell her that! Let me get Matt." She certainly wasn't going to leave him alone with his drunken grandmother.

As they drove up the mountainside, Red wondered aloud. "Boy, is she going to have a lot to absorb. Torie's baby. You and me."

"You going to tell her about us tonight, too?"

"We'll see," he said, putting a hand over hers. "We'll play it by ear."

Fifty-three

"This is a surprise." Miss Jenny greeted them at the door with knitting in her hands.

"We've some news that it seems better to tell you in person."

Miss Jenny's hand flew to her chest.

"Everyone's alive and well," Red said.

"Thank goodness."

Cat asked, "Okay if I put him on your bed?" Matt was still half-asleep and bundled up in a blanket.

Miss Jenny nodded.

"You make better fires than I do, Ma," Red said, sitting on a chair before the fireplace.

Miss Jenny sat down on the edge of the couch, expectantly, still holding the ball of teal yarn in her hands.

"Wait'll Cat comes back."

When Cat did return she sat at the other end of the couch from Miss Jenny.

"First of all, Ma, Torie came home this afternoon."

"Home?"

He nodded. "With a two-week-old baby."

Miss Jenny's eyes were round as saucers as Red told her the story.

"Oh, dear me," Jenny said. "Aren't parents cruel." This in reaction to Red's describing Sarah's actions. "If we're not what they want us to be, they want to disown us."

"Torie's never been what Sarah wanted her to be. I don't think Sarah ever wanted her. Sarah's rejected her from the git-go."

His mother nodded agreement. "It's true. Well, what are we going to do to help Torie?"

"I'm going to wait until she phones after they've gone to see Samuel."

"Samuel's not as rigid as Sarah," Miss Jenny said. "But he's sure as hell fought this match." She turned to Cat. "It was fine when they were kids, but as soon as Samuel realized they were a boy and a girl he put his foot down. Though he was rather gracious about Joseph's taking Torie to her senior prom. I think he thought it wouldn't last. That they'd go away to different colleges and forget each other. Sarah nearly died when Torie said she wouldn't go with anyone but Joseph. Remember that?"

"I do, indeed." Now it was Red's turn to explain to Cat. "Torie went upstairs to get dressed for the prom and she screamed nearly as loud as Sarah did this afternoon. Sarah had cut Torie's prom dress to ribbons, leaving it in pieces all over the bed."

"Oh, my." Cat couldn't imagine a mother's doing such a thing.

"She thought that would mean Torie couldn't go. But Torie and I beat Sarah that time. Torie and I're pretty much the same size," Miss Jenny said, "and I had a black chiffon dress I'd worn to a number of occasions, and we had time to cut the hem off and make it shorter. I cut the sleeves out of it. Joseph had sent her a red-rose corsage and we cut the neck lower on that dress and just hemmed it, but we put the roses around that neckline and it was the smash of the prom. Or" —she smiled at Red—"so Torie said. At least Joseph thought she looked beautiful, and nothing else mattered. Sarah didn't speak to me for weeks after that. And Torie didn't speak to her mother. That was quite a time."

"Ma."

Miss Jenny turned to face her son.

"That's not all."

Red hesitated, looking across the room at Cat. Then he stood up and walked over to stand next to her, putting a hand on her shoulder. "Ma, Cat and I have fallen in love."

Miss Jenny looked at them, tears forming in the corners of her eyes. She reached into the pocket of her slacks and pulled out a tissue, sniffling into it. "You didn't have a choice," she said, smiling through her tears.

"What's that mean?"

"I willed it. Ever since Cat told me Jason didn't light a fire in her, I thought you two were made for each other. I've prayed, not that I'm ordinarily a praying woman. I've thought about buying a Sarah doll and practicing voodoo. Oh"—she really was crying—"I can't tell you how pleased I am. At last, my son, you'll be happy. After all these years, you'll have love."

Cat moved across the couch to put her arms around Miss Jenny.

"I knew when I first saw you, before Scott even knew he was in love with you, that you would be a McCullough, that we would share this name." Miss Jenny shook her head. "You and me," she said, "we might not have been born McCulloughs, but I think we've both been destined to be part of the McCullough history. Thank God you won't be lost to us."

"I was afraid you'd be shocked."

Miss Jenny smiled. "I was afraid the whole idea would so shock one or the other of you that it might never come to pass."

"So"—Red went back to the chair and sat down—"I have an idea about what to do about Sarah . . ."

"Just divorce her!"

"Ma, I can't do that. She can't even function. Maybe if we move her to some nice house . . ."

"All she cares about are her liquor and TV," Miss Jenny said. There was anger in her voice.

"Ma. I'm going to find a shrink to ask about how to do this so it's as untraumatic for her as possible. I'll see she wants for nothing . . . Maybe even design a room that looks like her bedroom so she doesn't feel dislodged. All I know is that I want to spend the rest of my life with Cat."

Miss Jenny turned to Cat. "I knew even before you did, I imagine, that you were in love with him." She nodded toward her son. "I could tell it by the way you looked at him. I could tell it in your voice."

"I fought it," Cat said. "I really did. But I've never loved anyone as much as I love him."

"Maybe you were meant for each other as much as Torie and Joseph are."

Cat laughed. "Well, I do feel that *you* and I were meant to be related."

"My dear, we were related the moment I met you, whether you know it or not. I may not be positive about Geoffrey, but I am sure about you." Miss Jenny reached out an arm to her son, even though he wasn't within reach. "Red, I have wanted your happiness all my life, and the last twenty years of your life have crushed me, even though they haven't done that to you. I know, I know, you've put your caring and your passion into your children and the land, but at last you're going to get what you really need. Cat, I am so happy.

And know, you two, whatever I can do to help, I will. It won't all be easy, will it?"

Mother and son looked at each other.

When it was time to leave, Miss Jenny said, "Don't wake Matt again. Leave him here with me. I'll bring him down in the morning, or maybe I'll just keep him up here all day. You're going to have more than enough to do, helping Torie in whatever way she needs help, deciding what to do about Sarah."

In the jeep, on the way down to the ranch house, Red reached out to put an arm around Cat and pulled her close.

"You know what? I want to sleep with you tonight. I want to feel your warm body next to mine as I fall asleep. I want to wake up to kiss you and hold you."

"There's a lock on my bedroom door." It sounded like an invitation.

"Torie has what she has always wanted and I have what I never dreamed I'd have. Maybe happiness is hitting the McCulloughs with force."

"You said you wanted to sleep with me. Well, I have ideas that include a bit more than that."

"Actually, my ideas include a *lot* more than that."

"Thank God the house is in sight or we might just have to stop right here and screw ourselves silly."

"My, my, the way you talk."

"Do you object?"

He pulled her even closer, his lips grazing her hair. "Object? Lady, you're the stuff of a lifetime of fantasies. No matter how long I live, I won't be able to get enough of you."

He parked the jeep in front of the house and, Cat's hand in his, took the porch steps two at a time.

The phone was ringing as they entered the house.

It was Jason. "Red, get down here to Shumway's on the double."

"What is it?"

"Just get here, as fast as you can." Jason hung up.

Red turned to Cat. "Jason wants me down to the motel now."

Cat felt a tightness in her chest.

"The motel? Torie?"

"Come on." He grabbed her hand again and walked back down the hallway, his strides forcing Cat to run.

It took them twenty minutes to get to Shumway's Hospitality Inn.

The sheriff's car was in front of unit number three. Jason was standing in the open doorway.

Red bounded out of the jeep, not waiting for Cat this time. She ran behind him, not hearing what Jason said to him. The two men disappeared into the motel room.

Cat was not far behind. She stopped in the doorway to observe the scene. Torie was hysterically crying in Joseph's arms. In the center of the bed lay their baby, stone-cold dead. Cat could tell that at a glance.

Fifty-Four

"Oh, Daddy." Torie left Joseph's arms and threw herself in her father's.

"I'll have to phone Chazz," Jason said. "But I thought the family should be together first."

Red stood stroking Torie's hair, his eyes meeting Joseph's.

Joseph said, "We went out to tell my parents."

They could hardly hear him for Torie's sobs.

"My father didn't react as badly as I'd thought he might. He just shook his head back and forth and sighed. Finally he said, 'I wish you happiness, my son and daughter.' He didn't say any more than that."

Cat wondered how Mrs. Claypool had reacted. Probably the way she thought Samuel would want her to. She was such a quiet woman. Cat couldn't remember ever hearing her speak.

"We came back into town. Torie nursed the baby, who fell back asleep. We decided to run down the street to Rocky's and get a couple of burgers. We surrounded the baby with pillows so he couldn't fall off the bed and planned to be back in fifteen or twenty minutes. But everyone seemed to be in town, and we didn't even get to Rocky's for ten minutes, everyone having to say hello to Torie. By the time we returned about thirty-five or forty minutes had passed. The door was ajar, and we knew we'd shut it.

"We came in and one of the pillows which we'd put next to him to keep him from falling off the bed was over his face. Torie reached him before I did and grabbed the pillow and screamed. He was dead, just like this. No way could that pillow have gotten on top of him if someone hadn't placed it there."

He spoke in a monotone the whole time, no life in his voice at all.

Jason picked up the phone and told Chazz to get over to Shumway's right away. He was the coroner, and they needed a report.

"Have you told your father?" Red asked Joseph.

Jason answered. "Phoned him right after you. He's on his way in."

Joseph said, "I told him. I told him the baby's dead."

Samuel couldn't have done such a thing, Cat told herself. *He just couldn't.*

Torie's tears were drying up, and she was back clutching Joseph's hand. He had an arm around her shoulder, too. They both looked as though they'd been battered.

"It's murder," Jason said, as though they all didn't understand that.

"But who?" Torie's voice sounded scratchy, as though little of it remained. "Who would kill a baby?"

Cat wondered if Red and Jason suspected Samuel. He was the first person who popped into her mind. Oh, not Samuel, please not Samuel.

Chazz and Samuel arrived within seconds of each other.

"God in heaven," Chazz said, walking over to stare at the dead baby. "What?"

"Smothered," Jason answered. "A pillow over his face." At that moment Samuel filled the doorway.

Jason explained what had happened.

Chazz bent over the baby, and Samuel, his hands on either side of the doorway, closed his eyes. He did not go over to his son, but his eyes did not leave Torie and Joseph.

Finally, he uttered, "It's my fault. All my fault."

They all stared at him.

He took a deep breath. "What time did this happen?"

"About two hours after we left you," Joseph said, his arm still around Torie, his face stone.

Chazz looked at Torie. "Do you want me to take him?"

Torie broke into tears again. Red walked over to put his arm around her, too.

Joseph nodded assent to Chazz.

Jason said, "Better keep this all under wraps for now, Chazz. No one else knows about it. Keep quiet at least til morning?"

"Of course." Chazz bent down and lifted the dead bundle in his arms. Tears gathered in the corners of his eyes.

Samuel inhaled and looked at Red. "We all better go out to the Big Piney."

Everyone looked at him. One didn't ask Samuel Claypool for reasons.

They formed a caravan, Red and Cat leading the way in his jeep, Joseph and Torie in her pickup, Jason in his sheriff's vehicle, Samuel pulling up behind in his battered pickup.

It was nearly eleven-thirty when they pulled up to the Big Piney and emerged from their cars as though already attending a funeral.

"Now what?" Red asked Samuel.

"May we gather in your living room?"

Strange. Odd, indeed.

It was as though Samuel were the host. Everyone sat while he stood in front of the unlit fireplace. Finally he turned to Red and said, "I think Sarah should be here too."

"Sarah?"

What good would she be? Would she even understand what had happened?

"Please," Samuel said, seating himself in Red's favorite wing chair.

No one said anything while they waited for Red to return. It was almost ten minutes before he reappeared, holding a wild-looking Sarah by the arm. Her blue velveteen robe had hastily been thrown on, her hair looked as though it had not been combed. Cat imagined she'd been drinking ever since she'd gone to her room after hearing Torie's news. She probably didn't even have a clue what was happening. Yet when she saw Samuel, one hand flew to her chest, as though clasping herself, and the other covered her mouth.

"Sit down, Sarah," Samuel said.

Red helped Sarah onto one end of the couch.

Samuel's glance went around the room, resting for a second on Red, then on Torie, Joseph, Sarah. He did not linger on either Jason or Cat.

"Do you know what happened tonight, Sarah?" Samuel asked, leaning forward, his elbows on his knees. He sounded as though he were talking to a child.

She didn't answer, but her eyes did not leave his face.

Silence permeated the room.

Samuel turned to Red who stood behind the couch. Finally he began to speak. It was as though his voice came from far away.

"You and I," he said to Red, "go way back. We've been friends since before either of us can ever remember. You taught me how to play baseball."

Red nodded. "You taught me the art of fishing and riding." He wondered where this was going.

"This is not going to be easy," Samuel said, looking directly at Red.

No one said anything.

"By the time you came home from college, married to the prettiest girl I ever saw, I already had one daughter." As Red knew, Joseph's older sister had married and moved to Lander, Wyoming, five years ago.

"Sarah wasn't like any other girl I'd ever seen." Now, he turned to look at Sarah, who seemed to be listening attentively. At least her eyes didn't stray. "Remember, we did things together, the three of us. She was fragile yet on the wild side. She was like a princess in the wilderness."

"You gave her one of your Appaloosas for a wedding present."

Samuel nodded. "I used to see her riding over those meadows and up the mountain trails on that pony. She never knew I was looking at her, following her, telling myself I was protecting her. After all, she was a city girl.

"And you"—his eyes went back to Red—"were my best friend.

"You had Scott, and I swear I loved that boy near as much as my Joseph, who was born three months later. We'd have picnics together, you and Sarah and your son, and me and Miriam and our children. We laughed a lot in those days."

Red shook his head, remembering.

No one understood where this story was leading.

"Then remember you took off for three months in Australia. And you asked me to look after Sarah.

"I'd ride across the valley midafternoons and up over that trail left by mountain goats and all I could think of was your wife. Of her pale skin and her hair the color of an Indian's. I wondered what she'd be wearing, those pastel dresses that flowed. I wouldn't even see her, and I could remember the pulse beat in the blue vein on her white neck.

"Nothing like this had ever happened to me. I became obsessed with your wife. I taught her, while you were halfway across the world, how to catch trout without a fishing line. We would lie for an hour in the tall grass by the rushing creek, watching the water, not saying a thing. Eventually she could reach out, ever so slowly, blending with the shadows from the leaves, and catch a fish with her hands, just as I'd taught her."

Red hadn't known Sarah could do that.

Samuel's eyes had a faraway look. "I taught her to shoot. We'd set up bottles behind the lodge, and I'd teach her how to shoot them. She learned to walk through fallen leaves as silently as I did. I made moccasins for her, sewed them with my own hands. When I first slipped them on her feet was the first time I touched her." His glance moved to Sarah, who sat staring at him as though hypnotized. "I knelt in front of her, her foot in my hand, and I saw in her eyes the same hunger that was gnawing away at me. We didn't speak of it. What was inside me was something I'd never felt for any other living being." Everyone could tell he remembered every minute of that time a quarter of a century ago.

His gaze bored into Sarah's. "And never have known again."

Her eyes were more alive than Cat had ever seen them. With fright, with remembrance, with what?

"It gnawed at me, Red. She was the wife of my best friend, and I couldn't think of anything else. I stayed away from her for three days after touching her, after slipping her foot into the moccasin. I rode off into the wilderness, fighting my dangerous war within.

"The fourth afternoon I rode back across the mountain pass to find her waiting for me. She said, 'I knew you'd come back today.'

"And we made love."

Red's face was impassive.

"Not in her soft four-poster bed, but on a high ridge under a pine tree, looking down on the valley with the creek a ribbon of blue, with mountains rippling across the horizon."

A low moan escaped Sarah.

"We met every afternoon for the next five weeks, making love with a wildness that seemed beyond our control.

"I loved her with the depth of all my soul."

Sarah's whisper could scarcely be heard. "You never told me!"

They stared across the room at each other.

Then Samuel continued, turning to Red. "We never mentioned your name. Until the day before you returned, and I told Sarah we could not meet again. It was not until then that my conscience bothered me. That I allowed reality to enter into this madness that enveloped us.

"But my conscience has tormented me every day of my life since then, Red. Not"—he gestured toward Sarah—"however, as much as Sarah has been tormented. Look at what has become of her."

They all looked at her.

"She never told me she was pregnant, but she must have been at least six weeks pregnant by the time you came home. Then one day you greeted me, telling me you were expecting again. And I knew that baby was mine."

A gasp went up from Torie.

"Seven months and three weeks after you returned from Australia, Sarah gave birth to Victoria. You thought it was early, but she weighed seven pounds. You thought she was the image of Sarah with her black eyes and dark hair. I thought she was the image of me."

"And a month after that your wife had a daughter, too. You slept with her at the same time you made love to me." Sarah's hollow voice accused.

Silence stunned the listening group.

Red and Torie looked at each other from across the room. In their eyes pain and lack of understanding were reflected.

"I betrayed a trust. I betrayed a friend whom I had loved my whole life, but I loved a woman in a way that I didn't know possible."

"You never told me," Sarah said as though no one else were in the room. "You left me to live in this house, to bring up a child who was an abomination in God's eyes, who . . ."

A keening wail swept the room, and everyone looked at Torie, whose eyes were wild. "Oh my God," she wailed, turning to Joseph.

"Yes," Samuel said. "You are brother and sister. It does not matter whether a shaman's blood is diluted or not. Man or woman, even some white people can become shamans. I used this as an excuse to keep you from committing incest."

"Incest. Oh, God!" Torie rubbed her fists into her eyes, hunched over as though in physical pain.

The palm of Red's hand hit his forehead. "Torie is not mine?"

Samuel didn't move from his chair. "Torie's ours. Her blood may be mine, but her heart is yours."

Joseph had backed into a corner, his eyes blinking very fast.

Cat thought she was in a horror film that would soon end. This was too much to comprehend.

"Why are you telling us this?" asked Jason, the only rational voice, the only uninvolved one.

"Because my grandson is dead, and I think Sarah killed her."

Everyone looked at Sarah, who only said, "You never told me you loved me. I thought you just wanted my body. You left me when he came home. Now, God is punishing us for those days of sin."

"Right after Torie and Joseph left tonight," Samuel said to Red,

"Sarah came to see me. She was wearing that same robe, her hair was tangled, her eyes looked like she'd ridden in the wind. She told me it was my duty to kill the child, that it must not live, that he was an evil upon this earth. It was our fault. Our sin had come back to haunt us.

"She said we would rot in hell, that she had been in hell for all these years. And now God was punishing us for those days of joy and lust. Our daughter had compounded our sin of adultery, and committed incest. We would all go to hell. The devil was within this new child. And it was our fault. Therefore, she said, we must kill it."

A stunned silence captured everyone in the room as they stared at Sarah, who was seemingly picking lint off her robe. She did not look up.

"When I told her what was done was done, and we should keep our secrets, that telling them would only harm people we love, she waved her arms in the air, and went out into the night crying, 'Lies, lies, lies.'"

No one moved a muscle.

Samuel, in the telling of the story, evidenced a world of sadness within. He looked at Red, and said, "I am sorry."

Cat closed her eyes, wondering how Red could stand to hear this story of betrayal and sin. She felt ill.

"In every fiber of my being, I know it was Sarah who killed our grandchild." It was a statement of fact.

Sarah began to hum, an off-key melody, as she picked at her robe.

Torie vomited, right on the living-room rug. No one moved to clean it up, but Red walked over and knelt beside her, gathering her in his arms. She burrowed her head into his shoulder, her body wracked with choking sobs.

Jason walked over to Sarah and put a hand on her shoulder. She didn't look up at him. "Is this true, Sarah?"

She didn't answer, but went on with her tuneless humming.

Jason glanced at Red. "I don't know quite what to do."

Fifty-five

"Daddy," Torie cried, throwing her arms around Red.

He held her tightly, close to his chest. They both looked dazed. He whispered into her hair. "Nothing could make me love you any less."

Samuel said, "I have carried shame with me for all these years."

Cat was surprised to hear herself say, "I would think so." No one paid any attention to her. She was not part of this scene, neither she nor Jason, and they knew it.

Suddenly Sarah looked up, across the room, at Samuel still sitting in Red's favorite chair. "You never told me," she said, once again. "You never said you loved me."

Jason asked, "Did you kill the baby, Sarah?"

Sarah didn't respond, her eyes still on Samuel.

Torie was crying. Joseph walked over to her, a sick expression on his face. They just stared at each other, unable, somehow, to touch.

"My son," Samuel said, standing and walking over to his son and daughter. "I have done you a disservice."

"A disservice?" Joseph's voice cracked. "You have ruined our lives."

"I should have told you long ago," Samuel admitted.

Torie backed away from him. "I don't know many people I've respected more than you. How could you have done this to us? How could you have kept silent? Why didn't you tell us years ago?" Her eyes were wild, her voice broken. The only one she let touch her was Red.

"Shame," Samuel admitted.

"You cared more for yourself than you cared for your children." Red's voice was a monotone.

"Do you not think that over the years when people have come to me for counsel and advice, when they have called me a wise man and put me in a position of honor and respect, that I have not punished myself, that I have not hated myself, that I have not recognized I'm a charlatan, a hypocrite, a liar?"

"You have ruined lives." Red voiced Torie's words.

"I have looked at Sarah disintegrate all these years and known that it was partly my fault."

"Partly?" Cat couldn't tell who'd asked that.

"I have looked at Torie all these years and loved her as my own, and lately I have asked myself, what would be the ultimate harm if she and Joseph were to live together the rest of their lives, if no one knew."

Joseph's gaze left Torie's face, and he turned to his father. "I have esteemed you as I have never respected anyone else. Only your opinion, caring what you thought, has kept me from marrying Torie. I have been proud to be your son."

The two men's eyes were locked.

"And now I wonder if I hate you. I certainly can never respect you again. Not ever." He almost spit out the words.

Torie crumpled up on the couch, bent over, her eyes closed, clutching her belly moaning. "My baby . . ." she wept.

"My love." Joseph's voice was but a whisper. "My sister."

A look of agony passed between them. They seemed unable to reach out to touch each other.

Red sat next to Torie, and put his arms around her. It was the only thing he could do. He stroked Torie's hair as she sobbed against his chest.

Sarah's voice faintly echoed, "You never told me. All these years and you never told me."

Cat wondered how Red could endure hearing all this. She wanted to comfort him, but nothing she could offer would be of solace. He and Torie needed each other. How must he feel to discover Torie was not really his. That she was the child of his wife's adultery.

Samuel picked up his hat. He looked at the mourning group of people, the ones whose lives he had sent into tailspins, and said, "I am sorry. Truly sorry."

Too late for that. Far too late.

Then he looked at Sarah. "You did kill the baby, didn't you?"

Sarah looked directly at him. "It was an abomination." Her eyes pleaded with him. "It came into the world with the sins of adultery and incest in its blood. It was the work of the devil."

Cat guessed that was an answer, a confession. Add murder to adultery, betrayal, and incest. Add to that psychological annihilation.

She knew that the baby's was not the only death being experienced in that room.

Samuel looked around, and, hat in hand, walked out of the room. They heard the front door close behind him.

"Jesus, Cat," Jason said in a low voice, walking over to her. "I don't know what to do."

"I don't think anyone does."

He put an arm around her shoulder. "I have to arrest Sarah."

"You don't have to do that tonight," she said. "Look at her."

Sarah was again picking invisible lint from her robe.

Jason shook his head. "Poor Torie and Joseph."

"Come back in the morning, Jason."

He glanced at his watch. "It's already after two."

"Sarah's not going anyplace. Leave the family alone, Jason. Please."

He nodded imperceptibly.

Cat thought of Miss Jenny, up in the lodge. She'd have to be told.

She wondered what was going to happen to everyone. It might not be on the scale of a Greek tragedy, but that's what it felt like. Worlds, lives ripped apart never to be the same.

After Jason left, Cat took Sarah by the arm and led her back upstairs to her room.

Around three-thirty Torie fell into a restless sleep, moaning as she thrashed around on the couch. Red and Joseph sat, empty-eyed, in chairs staring at her. Cat could tell that their minds hadn't yet comprehended the enormity of the destruction that had been wrought tonight. Joseph had lost as much as Torie.

And Red must feel that the last quarter century of his life had been a lie. He must hate Sarah and Samuel.

Cat fell asleep, finally, in Red's office, on the couch. Her last thought before sleep was being grateful that Matt was up at Miss Jenny's, and she didn't have to think of taking care of him when she awoke.

*   *   *

When she did awake, Red was standing over her and pale early-morning light was filtering through the curtains.

"Cat."

Cat jerked into wakefulness.

"Sarah's gone."

She sat up straight, her mind still muddled with sleep. "What do you mean, gone?"

"She's not in her room, and the back door's wide-open."

Cat shook her head, trying to rid herself of cobwebs. "Is a car gone?"

He shrugged. "I don't know."

"Where are Torie and Joseph?"

"Asleep."

Cat stood up, putting her arms around Red's waist, but he just stood there, numb. "I'll go look in the barn."

She swept through the kitchen, taking a jacket off a peg there, and ran on out to the barn. All the cars and trucks were there.

She dashed back to the house. "She can't be very far. All the vehicles are there." She looked at Red. "Do you hate her?"

His eyes were unfocused. "I don't know what I feel. Dreadfully sorry for her. Her guilt ruined her life. It surrounded her. I would have felt betrayed if I'd known about this years ago, but now it almost doesn't matter because I'd lost all feeling but pity for her."

"It's ruined your life."

"No," he said, in a positive tone. "It gave me Torie."

"But it's ruined Torie's life."

"That may very well be."

"What happens if we don't find Sarah?"

He shook his head vehemently. "We must."

"She'll go to prison."

"I doubt it. She'll go to a mental institution."

"Oh, Red." Cat threw her arms around him again, and this time he responded, clutching her close.

"What's going to happen to Torie and Joseph?"

"I don't know."

"Let's go look," Red said.

"Have some coffee first. It's warm. You need something."

"I don't know if I can swallow anything."

But he did drink a cup before putting on his boots and heavy jacket. "I suppose I should call Jason."

"I suppose so."

*   *   *

They searched all day for Sarah. Wherever she'd gone, she'd gone on foot. Red begged Jason not to call out the state police.

On snowmobiles, on snowshoes, in all ways possible they spent the daylight hours looking for her.

Red phoned Chazz and asked him to come out to the house to sedate Torie. He stayed to help search in the woods.

Red said to Cat. "Phone Ma. Tell her to keep Matt, and tell her nothing more than that Sarah's disappeared and we're searching. I'll face her later."

Cat wondered how he could think straight, how he was even functioning.

Joseph sat staring, trancelike, at the sedated Torie. Their world, the world they had built together over all their lives, was no longer.

"What if she's dead?" Cat asked, referring to Sarah.

Red looked at her as he went out the door and responded, "What if she is?"

Fifty-six

At five-thirty the next morning, while it was still dark, Samuel phoned.

Red, who had been asleep but two hours, picked up the phone from the sofa in his office where he'd fallen asleep.

"Red."

He immediately recognized the voice.

"I think I know where she may be. I'll be there by dawn." Samuel hung up without waiting for any reply by Red.

Red sighed, rubbing his eyes. He rolled off the couch and stretched, his mouth tasting like a bird's nest. He walked into the bathroom and brushed his teeth, stared in the mirror at his bloodshot eyes, and decided to forgo shaving.

In rumpled clothes he walked down the hall and through the dining room to the kitchen, where he busied himself preparing coffee. While he waited for it to be ready, and sat at the table, his head in his hands, his eyes closed.

He felt as though he'd been through a war. His nerves were stretched thin. He knew that his mind had absorbed all that had happened in the last two days, but his emotions hadn't handled it all yet. His mind was not on rescuing Sarah but wondering if there were anything he could do to rescue his daughter. His daughter? He really didn't give a damn that his blood didn't run through Torie's veins. She was his beloved daughter, the daughter of his soul if not of his flesh.

His greatest fear was that Torie might harm herself. *Please God, if you're there, give her the strength to go on.* He knew she felt there was no reason to go on living. That her life, indeed, had so far been lived in vain.

His heart bled for Joseph, too.

So far he had not felt resentment toward Samuel and Sarah for betraying him, only for the pain they had caused in their children. He was angry. And his heart had shattered into a thousand pieces, knowing what Torie must be going through.

She was upstairs now, asleep with something Chazz had given her that had knocked her out ten hours before. He had no idea where Joseph was.

He felt a hand on his shoulder and jumped.

"I couldn't sleep either."

He reached up to touch her hand on his shoulder. "Did you hear the phone?"

"No."

"Samuel's on his way over. He thinks he knows where she is."

"I do, too, in a way."

"Where?"

"On that ridge."

"What ridge?"

Cat shrugged. "I don't know exactly where. But wherever it was where they conceived Torie. You're going with him, of course."

"Of course."

"I'm coming along."

"No."

"Yes, I am. You're not going through this alone. Not alone with Samuel."

Red stood up and went to pour coffee. His raised eyebrows asked Cat if she wanted a cup. She nodded.

"You afraid I'll do something to Samuel?"

"Of course not."

"Then, why? It's dark. It's cold. We'll probably have to go on horseback."

"I'm coming, that's all."

He looked at her as he handed her a mug of coffee.

"Come here," he said.

She walked into his arms and closed her eyes as he held her close. "I love you, Cat. I love you more than anything in the world. I love Torie more than anything, too, but I love you in different ways."

"I won't leave you, Red."

He squeezed her. "Maybe I was wondering that. Wondering if all this is more than you can handle."

"Funny, I've been wondering the same thing about you."

"I'll go saddle up three horses. You get warm clothes on. I'll bring the horses around front so we can be waiting for Samuel."

She stretched up to kiss him.

Samuel arrived before the dawn. Red asked if he wanted coffee, and Samuel admitted that would be good before heading out into the cold. The three of them sat in the kitchen, drinking, waiting for the first glimmer of light, not talking.

When the first line of pearly gray appeared behind the mountains across the valley, Samuel stood up. "Let's go. It's an hour exactly on horseback."

Cat knew they'd find Sarah. She wondered if her mother-in-law would be alive.

They mounted their horses in silence and, single file, followed Samuel. Cat pulled up the rear. Red never turned to see if she was following.

They moved like shadows across the lawn and into the tall trees, onto a narrow trail that ran a different route than the road to Miss Jenny's. It went steadily up up up. They came upon a doe and her fawn, who stood and watched them with alert eyes, not moving. The dawn did not come quickly back among the towering trees, and Cat wondered how Samuel could follow the narrow path. It was cold. By late morning, or noon at the latest, the sun would be warm on their backs and it would be shirtsleeve weather, but as they climbed up into the mountains, it was frigid. Sarah would have hypothermia, at the least. Was that blue robe of hers warm enough to have protected her at night? How could she have walked so far in her condition?

The trees began to thin, and light filtered through the leafless limbs. After about three quarters of an hour, they came to a high meadow. Cat could see from the way Samuel moved his head that he was beginning to study the terrain, look on both sides of the now-open path. There were still large patches of snow and by now the sky was sapphire, and the sun blinding on the mounds of snow.

Samuel kept his horse at a slow walk while his eyes traversed every visible nook and cranny. Birdsong filled the air. Red's horse snorted.

Samuel turned around in his saddle and pointed ahead of them, to large boulders. "There's a bend around there, and though I haven't been up here in over twenty years, I think that's where we'll find her."

Cat knew what had happened there a quarter century ago. She wondered what memories it was bringing back to Samuel.

They passed through the meadow and rounded the curve into the big outcroppings of rocks, the path suddenly narrowing as it inched its way in front of the rocks, a steep drop off at the edge, so sudden and the view so fantastic that it literally took Cat's breath away.

Samuel rode another hundred feet until the drop-off was behind them and greening moss covered the earth under the pines that abruptly began again. He stopped and got off his horse, looking around. Red and Cat sat on theirs.

Samuel, saying nothing, explored the area on foot. "I could have sworn," he finally said, "that she would be here."

Red dismounted and came to help Cat down. "Let's look around."

"There's a creek back here," Samuel said, walking through the underbrush.

Did he expect to find her there? Sitting at the edge of it, ruminating about her past? Facedown in the icy water? Cat didn't follow. She tried to imagine what Sarah had been thinking. If she'd come all the way up here, she wouldn't have walked back in the underbrush to contemplate her sins. Cat suddenly knew, as much as though she were a shaman, where Sarah was.

Before she walked back to the path that ran along the precipice she waited for the two men to return. There was a puzzled look in Samuel's eyes.

"I know where she is," Cat said, starting to walk back to the rocky promontory.

The men followed.

"Down there." She pointed thousands of feet below.

There was no way to see anything but trees.

"You mean . . . ?" Red said.

"I think she came up here to throw herself off the cliff."

"Of course," Samuel said. "Of course."

It took two days of helicopters, of parachuting men into the wooded area, to find Sarah's broken body. Her blue robe was still intact, though she was unrecognizable in any other way.

The town never knew that Torie had returned home with a baby.

They knew only that Sarah, in a drunken stupor, had wandered away from the house in the middle of the night, her disappearance wasn't discovered until morning, and she must have stumbled over the edge and fallen to her death.

Neither Torie nor the Claypools attended Sarah's funeral, though nearly everyone in town did. There wasn't a person who mourned the loss of Sarah. They thought now Torie and Joseph could marry, and now Red was a free man. They almost breathed a collective sigh of relief. The last time most of them had seen Sarah was at Cat's wedding and Scott's funeral.

Red finally asked Samuel, "Did you love her all these years?"

Samuel shook his head. "I loved her with a wild ungovernable passion in those early years. But when I saw what she was doing to herself and to you, I stopped loving her. Years ago."

After a minute, he asked, "Did *you* love her all these years?"

"No," Red admitted. "I stopped loving her so long ago I forget when. I haven't loved Sarah in over twenty years. So what you two did together in the long-gone past gives me no pain. What does hurt is what you have done to Joseph and to Torie."

"I have done you irreparable harm, too," Samuel said. "Whether you know that or not, I know it. And it has kept me from happiness all these years. I know that no matter how long I live I shall never know peace of mind."

There was nothing Red could say to that.

Fifty-seven

Miss Jenny came down from the mountain with Matt, whom she'd kept up there for five days.

Torie had stayed out at the Big Piney. She slept in the room which had been hers as a child, slept for twelve and fourteen hours at a stretch.

Joseph came out only once, and he and Torie talked for hours. He left then, and they had not seen him since. Torie sat dry-eyed, staring into space, and Red hoped she was not going to follow in her mother's footsteps. All he could give her was his unconditional love.

When Miss Jenny marched in, at four o'clock one afternoon, she said, "We've got to do something about going ahead."

No one disagreed.

Matt was thrilled to be home with his mother and grandfather and followed Red around, not letting him out of sight.

"Anyone mind if I stay for dinner?" she asked, but it was really Thelma to whom she was talking.

"Having chicken fricassee with gravy and mashed potatoes," Thelma said.

Cat knew it would be useless to try to teach Thelma new ways of cooking.

"And something else, I smell it," Miss Jenny said.

"Lemon meringue pie." The only one who could smile around here was Thelma, who knew half of what had gone on but not the part about Torie and Joseph being brother and sister.

"Maybe I'll even stay overnight," Miss Jenny said. "It's time to have a family talk."

Cat agreed.

They didn't get around to it until after dinner, after Thelma had left and Matt was in bed. Then Miss Jenny said, "Come on," to Torie, "let's go sit in Red's study. I have some questions to ask and some suggestions to make."

Torie had lost weight in these few days. Her hair lay flat against her head, her dark eyes were blank.

When Red was in his favorite chair and Torie and Cat seated on the couch, Miss Jenny said, "Torie, I think you have something to learn." She looked at her son, and said, "Red, it's time to tell her."

Red looked at his mother, then his daughter. "You will always and ever be my daughter," he said.

She knew that.

"That's not what I mean," Miss Jenny said, her voice brusque. "Torie, your father and Cat have fallen in love."

This brought life to Torie's eyes. "Is this true?" she asked Cat. "I thought you and Jason . . ."

"It's true," Cat said. "I hope you're not shocked." Could anything shock after the recent turn of events?

"Daddy?" Torie turned her head so she could look squarely into her father's eyes.

"The three people I love most in the world just happen to be women, and they are here, with me, right now. Yes, it's true. I love all three of you more than I can ever express. I have fallen in love with Cat, and, if she'll have me, I want to marry her."

"Oh, Daddy." If Torie were able to evidence joy at this point in her life, it was at this moment.

"We were planning on this even before your mother died," Red told Torie. "I was going to divorce her."

Torie stood up and went over to Cat, leaning down to put her arms around her sister-in-law. "It's absolutely the only thing I could hear right now that gives me pleasure." She went over to Red and put her arms around his neck. "Oh, Daddy, at last. Happiness for you at last."

He held her close.

"Now you, Torie," Miss Jenny said. "It's going to take a long, long time. But you have to go on living even if you feel you don't want to."

"I have been thinking of that," Torie said. "I'm going to join the Peace Corps and get as far away from here as I can."

Red held her tighter. "Don't make a life-changing decision when you're in this condition," he told her.

"Daddy, I have to change my life if I'm going to go on. I have to leave here, at least for now. I don't know what the future will bring, but I have to lose myself in something. I have to do something where I have to put others first and not think about myself, about Joseph and me, about the baby, about all . . ." Her eyes filled with tears though she did not weep. "I don't know how I can live without Joseph."

No one said anything. Finally Torie stood up and walked over to the window to stare out into the twilight. "But I certainly can't live *with* him. I have to leave. You all know that, don't you?"

Red closed his eyes. He had known that. Perhaps he knew it even before Torie did.

"Everything that I believed in, except you, Daddy, and you, Miss J, has been ripped out from under me. I don't even know what or how to think. I'm so confused I feel like I'm going crazy." She turned to face them, her hands clasped in back of her. "But I'm not going crazy. I'm not going to become like Mom. I'm going on." She stuck her chin in the air. "I am not going to follow in Mother's footsteps. I am *not!*"

Miss Jenny shook her head. "It takes months or longer to get a response and accepted by the Peace Corps. How about you and I take a little trip someplace."

Torie gave her grandmother a grateful look.

"I don't think you should have to be alone to deal with all this," Miss Jenny went on. "And I think it might be nice for you and me to have sometime together. Where in the world would you like to go while you wait to hear about the Peace Corps?"

Torie's answer was amazingly immediate. "The Greek Isles. Turkey. Italy."

"Ah." Miss Jenny walked over and put an arm around Torie's waist. "All places I haven't been and which I'd also love to see."

Torie kissed Miss Jenny. "How soon can we get out of here?"

It was the first positive move Torie had made since her son was killed.

"Do you have a passport?" Miss Jenny asked.

"No."

"Well, first thing tomorrow we'll go to the post office and set that in motion. Apply for visas. And then how long does it take you to pack?"

"Could we get out of here before then? Wait someplace else for our passports and visas?"

"I've never seen the Grand Canyon, or Monument Valley . . ."

"Daddy, if Miss Jenny and I take off you could FedEx our passports and visas, couldn't you?" There was a rush in Torie's voice.

"I could do anything in the world you want me to do."

She walked over to him and leaned down to kiss the top of his head and throw her arms around him.

"You know I could never get through all this without you two," she said. "I know it'll take time, but somehow, though I don't know what the future holds, I know that I'm going to make it thanks to the greatest father and grandmother in the world." Relatives that were not hers by blood. She glanced across the room to Cat, and said, "And thanks to you my father is at last going to know happiness."

"*You* have always made me happy," he said.

"I tell myself I have not lost everything," Torie said, though Cat wondered if her eyes would ever lose their sadness.

"What's Joseph going to do?" Miss Jenny asked.

"He's already gone," Torie said, her voice evidencing no emotion. "He can't stay here either. He can't face his father, not after what he's done to us. He didn't know where he was going or what he's going to do. Nothing makes sense anymore."

Cat felt her heart would break for them.

"In the morning, after breakfast, let's go up to my place," Miss Jenny said to Torie, "and we'll get out maps and make some plans, not that we have to keep to any of them. I wouldn't mind junketing around the world, come to think of it, though that might take a year or more. Expand our horizons."

Torie managed a wan smile. "I love you, Miss Jenny. Nothing's more important than family."

Cat knew Miss Jenny had planned to visit Geoffrey and Amelia in England next month, but England would have to wait. Maybe a year or more. Until perhaps it would be too late to go to England again. But Cat had the distinct feeling that would be all right with Miss Jenny. Something more important had come up. Something that was more important than anything or anyone else in the world.

Miss Jenny made Cat proud to be a McCullough.

By ten both Torie and Miss Jenny had gone upstairs to bed.

Cat walked around the room gathering up the cups, but as she passed Red he reached out and grabbed her wrist. "I've been ignoring you."

She stopped, looking down at him. "You haven't had anything to give," she said. "I understand."

"I love you," he said, still holding on to her.

"And I love you."

"I want you."

She smiled. "Just let me take all this stuff out to the kitchen and you can have me."

"Hurry up."

She rinsed the dishes and put them in the dishwasher.

When she returned to his office, he was standing by his desk, but walked swiftly across the room and locked the door, gathering her in his arms, kissing her with a hunger that swept her away.

"You know what? I was thinking even if it shocks the town, let's get married when Ma and Torie return from the Grand Canyon to get ready to go to Europe. I'd like them at the wedding, just a small affair here at the ranch."

"I'll marry you tomorrow if you want. I was thinking along those same lines. What do you think of our honeymooning on Santorini?"

"Where's that?"

"It's one of the Greek Isles. We could meet Miss Jenny and Torie there. I've always had a yen to see the Greek Isles."

"Oh, yeah, now I remember. I hear they sunbathe in the altogether there."

"Just the place for a honeymoon, then."

He kissed her again. "I've been thinking," she said. "You seem to enjoy Matt . . ."

"Enjoy him? He brings me life."

"I once heard you say you'd have liked more children. It's not too late. I'd love more. Would you like to have children?"

He pulled her close.

"Three, anyhow," she said between kisses.

He lay down on the couch and pulled her to him. "I'd like that. I'd like McCulloughs, yours and mine, running around here." He kissed her again, and then said, "You wouldn't have time to practice law, then, would you?"

"You think not?" she laughed. "Watch me!"

He did more than that.